KATHRYN GUILD

Witches In Shadow

Contents

Content Warnings

Witches in Shadow is intended for adult readers. It includes strong language, sexual content, and explicit portrayals of mental illness and trauma, including emotional abuse, panic attacks, and self-harm.

Chapter 1

Standing in the middle of her tiny apartment and surrounded by boxes, Elena Hall clutched a bunch of old newspapers in her hands, trying to decide what to do with them . She'd been using them for packing, wrapping up her dishes and cups carefully so they wouldn't break in the move, but now had some left over. It wasn't exactly a crisis, but Elena's overwhelmed brain short-circuited on the simple decision.

The first witch hunt in nearly twenty years had rocked Elena's home of New Stirling City, resulting in the deaths of witches and humans alike. The death of one particular witch haunted Elena still, as did the event itself, as she'd been caught in the center of it all. Nothing was easy anymore— nothing was simple. The only thing Elena could do was leave and start over, even if it meant abandoning her home.

But no, she wouldn't think about that now. She had work to do, and giving into her grief wouldn't help anyone.

A knock on the door forced Elena's attention as Huey, her familiar, started barking madly. Elena shushed Huey, a large dog that looked like a bunch of brown cotton balls stuck together, before peeking out the peep hole.

It was Mila.

Elena threw open the door, and her sister strode past her

without a greeting.

"You're still packing?" Mila demanded, looking around the apartment. "The movers are coming tomorrow!"

"Oh, so you're perfectly packed?" Elena shut the door with a snap.

Mila straightened to her full height, which was rather impressive, looking smug. "Yes, two days ago. Like a responsible person."

Elena rolled her eyes, then shoved the stack of newspapers into her sister's hands. "Then figure out what to do with these, Miss Oh So Responsible."

"Oh, these are perfect! I can use them for the bedding in my new garden." Mila went to lean against the kitchen counter; all of Elena's chairs had been donated as she wouldn't be needing them in their new home.

Mila was the older of the two and she ran a gardening and plant shop for a living. Though she loved her tiny shop that was tucked between a bodega and an organic food store, the idea of actually having a real garden out in the country was enough to soothe the ache of starting over.

Elena, for her part, was looking forward to the quiet the countryside would provide and an actual yard for Huey to run around in. Her familiar was a lazy beast by nature, but he did need his exercise.

"Wow, just how old are these papers? Look at this headline." Mila held out one of the newspapers for Elena to see.

In bold letters it read, *KIERAN ANDRASTE CAUGHT DOING DRUGS, NUDES LEAKED ONLINE.*

Elena rolled her eyes. Kieran Andraste—youngest member of the infamous Andraste family and notorious powerful witch—had been out of the news for a few years now after seemingly cleaning up his act.

"That was like what, ten years ago? The neighbor who gave me these really is a hoarder." Elena shoved a box out of the way so she could more easily move through the living room.

"Or maybe she just had a huge crush on Kieran Andraste... like you did."

"I did not."

"Liar."

"Are you going to help me finish packing, or what?"

Mila grinned, flashing the newspaper once more before setting it down so they could get to work. Elena had *not* had a crush on Kieran Andraste when she was younger. It was more a passing fascination. As a witch in the city, the idea of one of her kind living so openly with their powers was appealing to her.

Even though witches and humans had been living side by side since spirits had granted humanity magic, most of their kind lived as regular humans in public to avoid drawing attention to themselves. The two groups had a long and bloody history with each other, trading power and subjugation in a twisted dance through time. The most recent wars resulted in a peace that lasted so far, but it remained far safer for witches to blend in rather than stand out.

But the Andrastes were one of those old magical families who in ancient times ruled over both their fellow witches and humans. They lived in full view of the world never having to hide what they were.

Elena always thought Kieran was hot as well, but that was besides the point.

The sisters started putting Elena's remaining possessions in boxes, neither speaking all that much. There wasn't much to say. This was the first time they would be living together since they'd been kids, and it would be a lie to say Elena wasn't a little nervous about how they would mesh under one roof again. But Mila refused to let Elena move without her, so there they were.

One thing was for sure, it would be an adjustment for Mila and Huey, who never really got along. Case in point, Huey was currently leaning against Mila's legs, begging for pats, and Mila was trying to brush him off.

"How do you turn off the begging?" Mila asked, trying to step back.

"Just ask nicely. He can understand you."

Mila glared at poor Huey. "Go away."

Huey whined, his tail drooping before he skulked off.

"You hurt his feelings!"

"Oh please, he's a dog."

"He's my familiar! He's smarter than other dogs, and you know that."

Mila rolled her eyes, and Huey whined. Elena took a deep breath, trying to calm herself down. Everything would be okay. It had to be.

* * *

Elena and Mila's new house was located in a town called Alberdeen. About two hours northwest of New Stirling City, it was very rural with thick forest everywhere one looked unless they stumbled upon one of the many farms in the area.

When they pulled up in the driveway, Elena's heart melted just as it had the first time she'd laid eyes on the house. The exterior was pure country elegance with pale blue siding and dark gray storm shutters on every window. A chimney stack from a fireplace that no longer existed jutted out from the roof, and birds perched on it, singing brightly into the summer sun. Surrounding the house was about an acre of open yard, with the rest of the four acres they owned covered in forested land with ferns and moss growing beneath towering trees.

As soon as Elena cut the engine, Huey used his magic to open the back door and bounded out, running madly back and forth over the grass.

"My baby is so happy," Elena said with a fake sniffle.

Mila snorted before she walked briskly into the house, giving orders to the movers who had pulled in behind them.

"Excuse me, miss," one of the men said to Elena, "where'd your wife say she wanted her gardening tools?"

"Sister, not wife," she quickly corrected, "and over on that side of the house. Thanks."

Blushing, the man quickly apologized before setting off to work. Elena sighed. It was a common mistake for people to think she and Mila were a couple.

Not that she could really blame them. At first glance, Mila and Elena didn't look like sisters—the result of having different fathers. Mila had dark brown skin, warm brown eyes, and towered over most people she met. At the moment, her thick curly hair was emerald green and kept in long, tight braids that hung down her back.

Elena, on the other hand, was pale with hazel eyes. Much to her irritation, she was also of perfectly average height. Though she'd been born with pure white hair, a fairly normal magical mutation, she could change it to whatever color she liked by using a simple spell. After the most recent witch hunt, she never wore it white, and it was currently a bright, sunflower yellow.

Still, if someone really looked, the resemblance between them became more obvious. They had the same chin and the same face shape. Their long, straight noses matched, as did their round cheeks.

They looked like their mother, the mother who passed on her magic to Elena, but not to Mila. The mother who'd long since died.

Pushing those depressing thoughts out of her mind, Elena walked briskly into the house.

The front door opened immediately into an open concept space that contained the living room to the right and a large kitchen with an island to the left. On the back wall was the entryway to the hall that led to the downstairs bedroom and a bathroom as well the stairs to the second floor.

Mila had already claimed the downstairs bedroom as she wanted to be "closer to her plants" and insisted it had nothing to do with the fact that the downstairs room was bigger. Elena relented because she didn't want to sleep on the ground floor and took the upstairs bedroom and bathroom for herself.

The movers started unpacking two apartments' worth of belongings into the house, as well as some antique furniture pieces inherited from their mother that had been sitting in storage. It took hours, but not nearly as long as it would have if they'd tried to do it all themselves.

Once the movers were gone, the sisters began sorting the boxes and moving them to their appropriate rooms. Elena immediately regretting taking a second floor room as she carried a very heavy box full of books up the stairs.

"You don't know a spell for that?" Mila called, watching from the bottom of the stairs as if she expected Elena to fall backward.

"Mind your own business," Elena snapped back. When she finally reached the landing, she let out a breath of relief before walking into her new bedroom. The truth was, she did know the spell for lifting heavy objects. While Mila was busy elsewhere, Elena had tried to use it, but like most of the spells she'd attempted in the last seven months, it failed.

Her therapist had assured her it was a result of trauma and that her magic would return in time, but surely she should be able to do *something* by now?

Brushing a droplet of sweat off her brow, Elena decided to try again.

Elena raised a hand and began, her goal to move the heavy box from one side of the room to another. It was a simple feat, one she could have done easily before the witch hunt. Now? Not so much.

The entirety of her body ached and strained as she focused her magic, the tingling in her limbs telling her that at the very least, it was responding. Magic, in theory, was simple. It required both physical and mental strength, control over one's emotions, and knowledge of spell work. Spells were either spoken aloud or a collection of thoughts, and the most powerful witches didn't need to use them at all. No, those individuals merely needed to think about what they wanted to make it so.

Sweat dripped from Elena's hairline and trickled down her cheek as her eyes welled with moisture. Something was blocking the magic from working. Even as she denied it, Elena knew it was fear.

A tear fell from her eye and mingled with the sweat. Elena let out a muffled curse. Was she really going to cry over this?

Yes, yes she was. After all, what was a witch without their magic?

A sitting duck.

A victim.

Elena didn't want to be a victim anymore. She wanted to feel strong, to move on. But how could she, if her own body was working against her?

A distant *bang* of a truck door slamming made Elena jump, the sound of men talking wrenching her out of the moment and back to that park in New Stirling City.

Blood.

Screams.

Smoke.

Elena clamped her eyes shut, trying to shake out the images as they consumed her mind.

"Breathe," she told herself. "Just breathe."

It wasn't working, and she collapsed to her knees, her breaths coming out in short, ragged bursts.

The voices downstairs continued, and distantly Elena realized it was just the movers having returned. They'd said they were coming back after grabbing some food. This was normal. Everything was fine.

An echo of the voice of her therapist broke through the chaos in her mind, reminding her to focus on the now, on what was real.

The floor beneath her feet was real. The walls around her protected her from unfriendly eyes. Huey was real. So was Mila. She wasn't in danger here.

Frustrated with herself, and desperate for a distraction from her thoughts, Elena knelt in front of the box she'd tried to move and ripped it open, coughing as dust flew into her face. At the top was a worn-out book she'd inherited from her mother. With some trepidation, Elena picked it up. *An Introduction to the World of Witches.*

Flipping through the pages, she landed on one with an image of a tapestry that was several hundred years old and depicted a witch fighting a human knight. The caption read, *Throughout history, humans and witches have been in conflict, resulting in war and subjugation on both sides. Although in modern times the two groups have found peace, there is still suspicion and mistrust between them.*

Elena's stomach churned, and she snapped the book shut. Sitting back on her heels, she tried to take a deep breath. She was safe, she was in her new home, and she wasn't alone. Over and over, she repeated the words in her head, trying to will her body to understand that it could calm down.

"Hey, El, did you see the box with all my seeds in it? I want to put them out in the shed." Mila appeared at the bedroom door. As soon as she saw Elena on the floor, however, her face fell. "Oh, El, what happened? Are you okay?"

Elena shook her head, unable to speak.

Mila dropped to her knees next to Elena and pulled her into her arms. For a few minutes, they simply sat like that, Elena finally feeling relief from her panic. Mila ran a soothing hand up and down Elena's back until Elena let out a long breath and pulled away.

"I was trying to move the box," Elena said, her voice sounding pathetic to her own ears. "Then the movers came back, and I just... lost it."

"Hey, it's okay. It was just the movers. No one is going to hurt you." Mila pulled Elena into her arms, holding her close and stroking her hair.

Huey emerged and shoved his head between them, his breath hot and moist as he panted.

It was enough to pull Elena back to herself again. Easing out of the embrace, she wiped at her eyes while Mila smoothed her hair down.

"There, all better?"

Elena nodded mutely.

Carefully, the two women got to their feet, Elena feeling shaken and a bit foolish. This was the third panic attack she'd had in the last two weeks. Her progress since the witch hunt seemed to be going away. All it took was a door shutting to set her off? How would she survive out here?

"You okay?" Mila asked.

"Yes." Elena wiped her eyes again, trying to regain her composure. "How's it going downstairs?"

Mila watched Elena for a moment, then shrugged, and Elena noticed the glint of sweat on her sister's forehead.

"You haven't unpacked a thing, have you? You've just been playing around outside," she accused.

"I don't need to unpack yet. What I need is to set up my garden. The movers did most of the work anyway." Mila examined Elena again. "Why don't you freshen up, then take it easy for a bit."

Elena didn't have the energy to argue. She left the room and went to the bathroom, where she was met by her own reflection. A terrified woman looked back, her eyes red and swollen and her skin flushed. Seeing herself like this made Elena want to run and hide. She felt weak and pathetic, like a child rather than a grown woman. Even though she knew better, Elena couldn't stop the disgust broiling in her gut.

Mila appeared behind her, looking worried. It was enough

to make Elena stop staring at herself and splash her face with cold water from the sink. Once she'd done that a few times and dried herself off with the bottom of her T-shirt, Mila grabbed her hand.

"Come on, keep me company outside!"

She dragged Elena down the wooden staircase and out the side door. Elena knew Mila didn't want to leave her alone after the panic attack, so she let herself be forced into the fresh air.

Elena was met with the shocking sight of the beginnings of ten neat garden boxes at the side of the yard. Mila certainly worked fast. Huey bounded past her, barking madly before shoving his face in the grass.

"Huey! What's in your mouth?" Elena cried, spotting that he was chomping away at some mysterious object near a tree. Upon hearing Elena's voice, he turned toward her, curly tail wagging.

"What is it?" Mila feigned interest.

"Oh, spirits, it's a dead squirrel," Elena said in disgust, as the smell of the corpse hit her nose, making her stomach churn.

"Ugh!" Mila gagged. "Did he kill it?"

Elena shook her head. The squirrel had obviously been dead for quite a while.

"Looks like he found it. Oh, Huey, why? So gross."

Her first instinct was to use magic to pick up the squirrel rather than actually touch it, but her stomach plummeted at the thought. Instead, she hunted down a sturdy stick and stabbed the carcass as best she could before she carefully lifted it into the air.

Despite Huey's protests, Elena managed to bring the squirrel to the trash cans at the front of the house and dispose of it. Tossing the stick away, that debilitating fear plagued her mind. She was a witch who was too afraid to cast spells. It was embarrassing, and more than anything, Elena wanted to just get back to normal. But what did normal even look like anymore?

Before the witch hunt, Elena hadn't exactly been a master at her craft, but she'd gotten by. City witches didn't need a huge catalog of spells at their disposal due to the modern conveniences their homes provided, and it wasn't uncommon for them to fall out of practice. But still, to not be able to cast any spells at all was practically unheard of. Or perhaps, those who it happened to were too ashamed to admit it publicly. Elena certainly was.

A prickling awareness tugged at Elena's senses, pulling her out of her thoughts.

As her eyes scanned the surrounding trees, she spotted a beautiful raven perched in a branch nearby. It seemed to be watching them. They were such intelligent creatures and she'd never seen one in the wild before. It fascinated her enough to draw her out of her own head, but before she could open her mouth to say anything to Mila about it, the enormous black bird opened its wings and took off.

"Hey, are you going to just stand there, or are you going to be useful? Grab that hammer for me, would you?" Mila called out.

Her shoulders sagging, Elena begrudgingly began to search for the hammer, all thoughts of the raven driven from her head in the face of physical labor.

It took so little to drive Elena to the edge, to fill her head with memories of the witch hunt and leave her panic-ridden and useless. But she had to keep going, to keep living her life.

To give up would be letting those humans win. At least, that was what the other witches in her old support group had said.

But how could she return to normal after what happened? Once these panic attacks were under control, once she was a little more whole again, Elena would tackle the issue of her poor magic. She would be a real witch again someday... she would be.

Chapter 2

Kieran Andraste was exhausted. That was his general state of being these days, but it was particularly bad after his parents dragged him out to a silly coven party the night before. There was absolutely no reason his presence was required, but they'd insisted the entire family make an appearance. All Kieran wanted to do was sleep. He'd only flown in from a work trip abroad that morning, then spent the rest of the day in mind-numbing meetings with other coven leaders, discussing everything from next year's inter-coven social calendars to the rising violence between witches and humans.

Then, of course, at the party, Kieran barely had a moment to think; so many people pestered him throughout the night. Not that they had actually wanted to hear anything he said. No, they simply wanted to force their existence upon his in the hope they would leave an impression strong enough to make him remember it.

"Mr. Andraste," a voice cut through his musings.

Kieran blinked, becoming aware of his surroundings once more. He was out with his sister-in-law, Therese, shopping at a luxury home goods store that felt more like a warehouse. Its aisles were so enormous and packed with nick-knacks and random wares, it was impossible to focus on any one item.

Worse, bright lighting illuminated the products while simultaneously giving Kieran a headache. Even more annoyingly, it wasn't even in New Stirling City. He'd been forced to go out into the suburbs. Kieran hated places like this—mostly because they were always packed with people who couldn't mind their own business.

It was frustrating that he needed to be here at all, playing bodyguard for his sister-in-law.

Therese was a perfectly capable witch, but since she was still relatively new to the family, she rarely went out unaccompanied for her safety. Usually this job was fulfilled by her husband, but Kieran somehow found the task assigned to him that day.

It seemed he wasn't doing a very good job, as Therese had wandered off while he was lost in thought, leaving him alone in the aisle filled with accent pillows. No, not alone.

"I hope I didn't scare you. Seemed a little far away there," the human woman who'd spoken before said, approaching slowly, like he was a wild animal. Middle-aged with dark skin and cropped short hair, she gave off the same sort of no-nonsense airs all federal agents seemed to have.

Kieran noticed a gun strapped to her hip under her blazer and he bit back a sneer. As if that horrible weapon would protect her from him.

"How can I help you, Agent Donaldson?" Kieran asked as calmly as he could, even while anger began to boil beneath the surface. These people had no shame. Approaching him in public? They must truly be desperate.

"Out doing a little shopping with your brother's wife? How nice." She ran a hand over a particularly impractical pillow covered in beads. "Though she seemed eager to ditch you."

"No," Kieran said flatly.

"No?" Donaldson repeated.

"Just saving you the trouble of asking. No, I'm not going to help you investigate my family. We're innocent of whatever bullshit you're claiming we did this time, so you can leave now, and take that disgusting weapon with you."

"This *disgusting weapon* is all humans have to protect ourselves from people like you," Donaldson shot back. "How are you all any better with your curses and killing spells?"

"Because magic requires effort, my dear Agent Donaldson. A killing spell takes tremendous strength and sacrifice. It harms the caster and darkens their soul for the rest of their lives. A curse can leave its caster permanently injured. A gun requires nothing more than the ability to squeeze a trigger. Any fool with ill intent can take a life with one of those. It is *easy.*"

Donaldson glared at him. "I didn't come here to debate the ethics of firearms."

"No, you didn't, but as I stated, I have no interest in working with you, so this conversation is over."

Kieran knew better than to turn his back on a fed, so he instead stared her down, daring her to keep pushing. Another shopper came into the aisle, but they seemed to sense the tension and quickly turned to leave.

A few years back, the feds had identified Kieran as a potential asset. Only the spirits knew why they thought he would work with them, but ever since, they'd been obnoxiously persistent. The fact that the government was investigating his family wasn't really a surprise, though. They were one of the true ancient and powerful magical families still left. Generations ago, they'd ruled kingdoms. Now, they owned international businesses and surrounded themselves with the world's leaders in economy and politics alike.

If that wasn't interesting enough, they had a certain reputation for getting what they wanted, no matter the cost—legality not really being an issue. But families like the Andrastes were above the law. They always had been. It was necessary in order to do what had to be done to protect their people.

"Kieran, darling!" a sweet voice called out from nearby, breaking the stalemate. "Where did you slink off to?"

It was Therese.

"Time for you to leave," Kieran hissed at Donaldson.

She glared at him in return. "This isn't over, Kieran. One day, you're going to wake up and be unable to live with yourself anymore. When that day comes, you better pray to the spirits I'll still be waiting and willing to save you from your family."

"Kieran!" Therese called again.

Thankfully, this time, Donaldson left, casting one last meaningful look over her shoulder as she did. Kieran gritted his teeth, his rage simmering. Save him? He didn't need saving.

Turning to track down his sister-in-law, he absentmindedly rubbed a hand over his ribs, trying to block out the interaction from his mind. The Department of Human and Magical Relations wouldn't give up, and he knew this wasn't the last time he'd see that obnoxious human stalking his shadow.

And just like every other time, Kieran had no intention of telling his father about it. No need to cause trouble or make Anthony Andraste angry. The feds had nothing. It was the reason they would be desperate enough to approach him like this. As long as they had nothing, there was no reason to sound the alarm.

Finding Therese a few aisles over, examining a set of sparkly pink bowls, he shoved the entire thing out of his mind.

"Aren't these wonderful?" Therese exclaimed.

"You should definitely get them. Declan would love it," Kieran encouraged, grinning at the image of his ultra-masculine brother eating out of the dainty little bowls.

Therese rolled her eyes. "You're assuming he gets a say about anything I buy," she said, putting them in her cart.

"Of course. How silly of me." Kieran laughed. He didn't always get along with Therese, but she wasn't so bad, he supposed, in small doses.

After a tumultuous courtship, Declan and Therese had married about a year ago. It was the event of the century—a uniting of two powerful magical families unheard of in the modern era. The entire wedding had been a circus, with Therese playing the ringmaster. As much as he found Therese to be, well, a bit much, Kieran was truly happy his brother had found someone to spend the rest of his very long life with.

"Come on, there's a gold and fuchsia coffee table that I think might make Declan cry."

Kieran chuckled as he followed her along.

Their parents had been delighted by the match. The idea of either of their sons marrying outside the elite magical community was out of the question. It wasn't just snobbery that drove that sentiment, though it certainly played a part, it was the fact that anyone who wasn't "one of them" would never be able to make it in their world.

It was impossible to really understand, unless you'd been

raised in a similar situation, just how intertwined these old families were. Modern sensibilities had permeated most magical communities when it came to what a family looked like and how they operated, but not the Andrastes. To be an Andraste meant you could never, ever walk away from who and what you were. You always had to live and breathe for the family every second of your life. Betraying them—betraying his father—in any sense wasn't something Kieran could ever fathom doing. It would mean the end of his life and everything he cherished.

Agent Donaldson did not realize what she was asking of him.

Eyes followed Kieran and Therese through the store. Though Donaldson may have left him alone, they were still under surveillance.

No one in the Andraste family could walk out in public and not be watched.

It wasn't as big a deal for his parents or his brother because they rarely went out to relatively normal places like this store, but Kieran often did for various jobs or errands he was always caught up in.

And right now, for his family, he had another task to perform. A witch and her human sister had moved into their coven's town and had finally passed the background check. Now it was his job to find this new witch and bring her into the fold. It wasn't something Kieran was particularly looking forward to, but he would do it all the same. The Andrastes, for whatever reason, had decided they wanted this Elena Hall, and his family always, always got what they wanted.

There was no obvious reason why the coven would be interested in Miss Hall. Kieran's research so far showed she wasn't particularly exceptional in any way. She had no previous connection to any covens, her magic skills were rudimentary—far below the coven's usual standards—and her career as a ghost writer was hardly prestigious enough to bring the coven any sort of esteem.

As far as Kieran could tell, the only reason the coven wanted Miss Hall was because of proximity. She was a witch. She now lived in the village their coven called home. Apparently, that was good enough.

This was a punishment. Recruiting a witch of such little value was beneath him. But a month ago, Kieran had failed to secure a deal with the Highland Coven to access their private collection of tomes. It had been a major blow. Those tomes contained secret histories pertaining to the Andraste bloodline itself that had been lost in some previous conflict centuries past. Getting those tomes back was a matter of honor. Still, Kieran had failed.

His father's anger had not been sated by a mere apology, and so now, Kieran was stalking some sad little witch and her human sister. Did anyone care that Kieran was deeply uncomfortable with it all? That he hated sending his beloved familiar to their land to spy on them and risk her safety? Of course not.

Nothing Kieran ever wanted mattered. Not when he was a boy, or a young man, and certainly not now.

Kieran pushed these thoughts away and focused back on the furniture Therese was now looking through. Resentment was a tool people like Agent Donaldson would use to try and push Kieran away from his family.

"What about these side tables, to go with the coffee table?" Therese pointed out two truly hideous side tables that screamed the designer had a breakdown while making them.

"They're perfect." Kieran grinned when he saw the price tag. "Yes, perfect for Declan."

Therese rolled her eyes. "I just don't understand the relationship between brothers. You two are always trying to get one over on the other."

"An only child can never understand. With siblings, you are either hiding their body or helping them hide a body."

Therese shot him an alarmed look. "Bodies? What are you talking about?"

Kieran resisted the urge to roll his eyes. "It's just an expression. The point is, I would die for Declan, but given the chance to fill his house with ugly furniture, then I absolutely will take it."

Shaking her head, Therese pushed her cart away from the furniture and toward the large hanging rugs against the back wall. Kieran didn't bother to contain his pained sigh as he followed.

While she sorted through the rugs, Kieran's mind drifted back to Miss Hall. At least recruiting her would be easy. Someone with her low status and unremarkable background would surely be thrilled to be offered to join a coven with such renown as the Greenwood Coven.

All he had to do was make her acquaintance, sweep her off her feet, and then put this entire unfortunate business behind him.

Chapter 3

It was a rare, rainy summer day, a week after the move, when Mila and Elena went into town for the first time to look over a store for lease. Mila's shop back in the city was now being run by her business partner, and Mila had plans to open a new store in Alberdeen. Though New Stirling City was only two hours away, the sisters' new environment could not be more different. No more would Mila be able to rely on the flow of foot traffic, and gaining a good reputation in the small community of Alberdeen was of utmost importance.

Elena was more of the creative type and didn't have much to add to the entire endeavor, so while Mila chatted with the building owner, Elena examined the outside. It was an adorable shop on an adorable street. Alberdeen was the type of small, mountain town that ended up on postcards or in tourism commercials, and this shop fit right in.

There wasn't a single chain business to be seen, and every establishment was named something cutesy like Sue's Corner or The Secret Garden. Large floral baskets hung from the lampposts. The buildings were either very old or very colorful, and everyone smiled and greeted each other as they met on the street. Even in the rain, the cheerfulness was palpable.

Elena shuddered. It was a bit much, and she was not

naturally the friendliest person. Back home, there were millions of people who minded their own business, and the predominant color was gray. Gray skyscrapers, gray sidewalks, gray buses, and gray subways. Spirits, she missed it.

Mila and the shop owner disappeared inside, pulling Elena from her thoughts. She waved to Mila before heading down the street, her laptop bag slung over her shoulder. Mila was in town to work, and so was she.

Elena was a writer and could work from pretty much anywhere. Though, homebody that she was, that was usually not too far from her bedroom. But now, she was trying something new and getting to know the town that was her new home.

Eyes followed Elena as she walked, and a few people smiled at her, almost looking like they wanted to stop and talk. She forced a smile back, but quickly hurried on her way. Her destination was a cafe on the corner of the main street where she hoped she could focus in peace.

Reaching the cafe doors, Elena stepped inside and shook the rain off her jacket as she looked around. It was larger than she'd expected and, for a town so small, there were a fair amount of people inside.

"Hello, beautiful," a man behind the counter called out. "What can I get you today?"

Elena blushed. The man had thick, black hair that was slightly curled and warm brown skin. There was a twinkle in his eye that spoke of friendliness, and Elena found herself giving him a tentative smile back.

"Hi," she greeted. "A large, spiced tea latte, please."

"Regular milk okay?" The man punched in the order without looking. "You a hiker? Never seen you before."

"Uh, no," Elena said, tucking a strand of hair behind her ear nervously, "I actually just moved to town."

The man lit up. "That's great! Always a treat when people are moving in rather than away. My name's Alex, very nice to meet you." As he spoke, Alex adjusted his stance, and a prickle of magic washed over Elena from his direction. It was just a nudge, something a human would never notice. It was a common way for witches to silently greet and identify each other.

Elena smiled, feeling a wave of relief. So it was true, witches were easy to find here. "I'm Elena, nice to meet you, too!"

After a short conversation about her move, Elena wandered off to find a place to sit.

She settled into a large, comfortable chair with an antique-looking table in front of it. The entire cafe oozed comfort, and Elena quickly discovered the WIFI connection was excellent. A few minutes later, Alex walked over with her drink. Elena thanked him before reading an email, the warm tea mug clutched in her hand. Time began to slip by, and Elena's tunnel vision blocked out everything around her.

An hour or so had passed when that focus was rudely shattered. The front doorbell jingled, and Elena's eyes darted toward the noise, her entire body on high alert. It was an unfortunate side effect of being a witch in public these days, but her alarm quickly turned to shock. At first, she didn't believe it. There was no way. What would someone like him be doing here? But as he moved closer, his powerful aura sweeping through the room, Elena knew her eyes weren't playing tricks.

Kieran Andraste was looking around the cafe. Elena blinked at him in awe. His face was familiar, since it was always featured in tabloids and on the news, but seeing him in person was a shock. Kieran looked foreboding yet effortless at the same time, dressed in a black button-up shirt rolled up to his elbows and dark slacks.

Onyx hair was swept back from his face where it curled around his ears and the back of his neck, and even from this distance, his emerald eyes were visible against his pale skin. And that fucking bone structure. It simply wasn't fair, Elena thought. In all her life, she had never seen a man so beautiful.

Elena quickly looked away before he caught her staring, but realized she was hardly the only one. Nearly every person in the shop openly watched him as he walked up to the counter. What the heck was someone like him doing in a place like this?

Alex greeted Kieran much more formally than he'd spoken to Elena, and Kieran ordered a black tea to go, offering Alex a polite but vague smile. Elena watched out of the corner of her eye, despite herself, while Kieran shot a look around the room. Was she imagining it or did his gaze linger for a split second on where she sat?

Approaching from the other side of the cafe, a human woman walked cautiously up to Kieran while he waited for his tea.

"Hello there," she said, flipping her hair over her shoulder and beaming at him.

"Hello," Kieran replied, his own tone neutral.

Undeterred, the woman continued. "Not very often we see you in town, Mr. Andraste. Here on business?"

Elena rolled her eyes and completely tuned them out. Seemed like the magical community wasn't the only one trying to land the last single Andraste. The eldest of the two sons had married another equally wealthy and famous heiress last year. There were few families with as much power and wealth that occupied both the magical and human worlds, and the Andrastes were at the top of that list.

Doing her best not to watch Kieran, Elena's attention was ripped away as a man's voice from right behind her let out a surprised yell.

"Watch out!"

Before she could react, boiling hot liquid poured over her shoulder and onto her arm. Elena jumped up in surprise, skin exploding in pain.

"Shit!" Alex cried from behind the counter.

"I'm so sorry! I tripped, it was an accident," the man exclaimed, holding his now-empty cup in one hand and staring at her swelling arm in shock.

"Are you all right?"

Elena looked up into the concerned face of Kieran, who was now standing over her.

"No," she gasped out, tears leaking out of her eyes from the pain, "I think I need help." Her skin was blistering where the liquid touched it, and Elena clenched her jaw. Why was Alex brewing the drinks so hot?

"Yes, I agree," Kieran said, staring at her arm.

"I'm so sorry," the drink-spiller repeated.

Alex appeared at the man's side, gently but firmly pushing him away from her.

"It's okay, accidents happen," Elena said through gritted teeth, although she meant it.

"Do you need me to call someone for you? Or I can drive you to urgent care. Someone in town can cover for me while I'm gone," Alex offered, gathering her things up.

"No need, I can drive her. It'll be faster that way," Kieran said.

Elena wanted to protest, but then thought better of it. Kieran Andraste was a world-famous witch. He could heal her himself, and if not, take her to a witch who could.

Kieran took Elena's packed-up belongings from Alex, who looked like he wanted to argue, then slung the laptop bag over his shoulder and guided Elena out of the cafe. Elena let him, cradling her burned arm as the tears continued to flow. Everyone watched them leave. It would have been deeply embarrassing if she wasn't in so much pain.

"My car's parked right around the corner," Kieran told her.

When they reached an expensive-looking black sports car, Kieran opened the passenger door for her, and Elena carefully sat down. Within moments, Kieran got in the driver's seat, started the car, and sped away.

Elena's breaths were shallow as she stared at her twitching hand. Darkness blurred the edge of her vision. The pain was keeping her present, but only just. Memories pushed and battered against her mind. The first time she'd gone out in public in her new home and she'd been attacked.

No, not an attack. It was an accident. An accident. No one was out to get her here. Two witches had come to her aid. One of them was taking care of her now. She was with another witch.

She was safe.

"That should be far enough," Kieran said after they drove a couple of minutes in tense silence. He pulled over to the side of the road, then turned to her. "Give me your arm."

Elena awkwardly twisted so he could access her right arm, wincing at the stabbing pain as her ruined flesh protested the movement. Kieran put his hand an inch above her skin at the bottom of the burn, then slowly moved it up to the top. As he did, a cold sensation spread under his palm, and instant relief rushed over her as the burn healed.

"There, did I get it all?" Kieran asked.

Elena made a few cautionary pokes at her arm.

"I think so," she said, trying to quell the queasy feeling in her stomach. She could never have healed a wound with such ease, or at all, really. Once again, she'd needed rescuing.

"Good." He smiled at her. "I'm Kieran, by the way. You must be the new witch in town I've heard about."

"I know who you are," Elena said, her shame at failing to take care of herself too close to the surface for manners. But he'd heard about her move? Word traveled that fast about her arrival?

"Of course you do," he said, giving her a devastatingly lovely smile.

Elena cleared her throat, her face heating. "I'm Elena Hall. You're right, I just moved here this week."

"Nice to meet you, though the circumstances are unfortunate," he conceded. "Now, I can take you home if you like? Or somewhere else if you prefer?"

"Oh." Elena blinked at him. "You would take me home?"

"Of course. Did you think I was going to dump you here on the side of the road?"

"Well, I guess not..." Elena said awkwardly. She was being ridiculous. Of course he would take her home or somewhere else safe.

Kieran smiled and started the car. He pulled out back onto the road, and they drove away.

"Thank you, you know, for my arm," Elena said to fill the silence.

"Don't mention it," he replied. "Although I suppose it was presumptuous of me to drag you away like that. There were just so many humans there, and you were vulnerable; my instinct was to get you away as soon as I could."

"You don't have to explain it to me," Elena mumbled. "And I can't heal a paper cut, let alone burns, so your instincts were right."

Elena wasn't sure why she was admitting such a thing to this man, but the words came spilling out anyway. If Kieran had any thoughts about it, he kept them to himself.

"I'll have a word with Robert. What happened was unacceptable."

"Robert?"

"The witch who spilled his coffee on you. I've heard him complaining around the coven that Alex doesn't brew the coffee hot enough, so he uses a spell to make it boiling."

Trees overtook the buildings as they drove down the back roads. Elena barely noticed as she blinked at him. The coven? Kieran Andraste was in the same coven as the locals of this small town? That didn't make sense. Rich and powerful people didn't join rural covens... did they?

"Do you know all the witches who live here?" she asked finally.

"Yes, and most of the humans as well, though they aren't aware of that." The car slowed as they pulled into Elena's driveway. "Will you be able to retrieve your car later?"

Elena didn't immediately answer. She was staring at the house, her thoughts suddenly frozen.

"I never gave you my address," she said, slowly, turning her eyes toward him.

Kieran gazed back, the corner of his mouth twitching.

"Yeah, sorry about that. I knew the residents who owned the house previously, so I knew they sold it to you and your sister. You seemed a bit out of it still, so I didn't want to pester you for directions when I already knew the way."

It was an uncomfortable explanation, but a logical one. Elena and Mila had, indeed, bought the house from an elderly witch couple who were moving to warmer climates. If Kieran really did know all the witches in the town like he claimed, he would have known the previous owners.

"Right..."

Well, this was awkward. Did she just thank him and be on her way?

Huey's anxiety pushed against their bond from inside the house. He knew she wasn't supposed to be home yet and that she had returned with someone who wasn't Mila.

"My familiar is about to have a heart attack," Elena said, taking advantage of the convenient excuse. "I should get going. Thanks for all your help."

Before Elena could make her escape, however, Kieran had gotten out of the car and came around to her side to open the door for her. It was an incredibly surreal moment as Elena's mind flashed to all the headlines she'd read about this man in the past. None of them had been particularly flattering or painted him as anything other than a bored, rich, entitled party boy.

But that was years ago now. He seemed perfectly...well not exactly normal, but responsible at the very least. As Elena got out of the car, she smiled tentatively at him. Kieran's eyes warmed as he looked at her before he turned back toward the house.

"It's a nice property. You're lucky you were able to get

it. The previous owners were here for ages. Not very social, though. I've never seen the inside."

Was he fishing for an invite?

"Uh, would you like to come in for a few minutes? I can show you around?" Elena felt her cheeks heating. What was she doing? Her natural inclination was always to avoid house guests whenever possible, but here she was, inviting a virtual stranger into her home because he was so gorgeous.

No, Elena admonished herself. She was doing this to be polite after he'd helped her. No other reason.

"I would love to." Kieran closed the car door and looked at her expectantly.

"Uh, right. Okay. This way." Elena led him toward the front door, but drew up short when she heard Huey whining on the other side. "Look, my dog," she turned to Kieran, "he's not comfortable with strangers, especially men."

"Ah, I see." Kieran took a step back.

"Why don't you hang back for a second, and I'll calm him down."

Kieran nodded, and Elena carefully opened the door to slip inside. Huey bounded into her arms, trying to lick her face. As soon as he got a whiff of her, however, his hackles immediately went up, and he dropped to the ground, growling.

"Now, none of that," Elena chastised. "It's just one guy, and you don't need to be nice to him, but you can't attack him either, understood?"

Huey barked defiantly.

"Huey," Elena admonished.

He finally looked at her and sneezed once before turning around and walking to the other side of the room, his tail high in the air. Elena sighed, turned back to the door, and opened it. Kieran looked inside with a little apprehension.

"Everything okay?" he asked.

"Yup!" Elena tried to sound confident.

Kieran walked in, his eyes immediately finding Huey, who was standing at the entrance to the hall on the other side of the room. Huey dropped his ears when he spotted Kieran, but did not growl or move.

"Hello there, boy," Kieran greeted softly.

Huey did not even blink.

Kieran sighed. "I usually have a special touch when it comes to animals. Was he a rescue?"

Elena nodded, placing her laptop bag on the couch. "Yes, he was on the streets before I adopted him, and he wasn't a bred familiar either. He's a Chow Chow mix, and my best guess is his previous owners didn't realize how much work that breed is."

"How old is he?"

"Fifteen. He took to the transformation extremely well; he's young yet." Elena picked up one of Huey's chew toys off the floor and tossed it toward him. It landed at his feet, but he did not react, still staring at Kieran. Elena sighed. "Stubborn mutt."

"Did you perform the spell to bind him to you?" Kieran asked.

"No, my mother did it for me."

"She must have been a skilled witch then. That's a fairly complicated spell," he remarked.

Elena felt her stomach twisting in knots at the harmless observation. She could never have performed that spell herself. Add that to the long list of her failures as a witch.

Seemingly unaware of her discomfort, Kieran began to look around the space, taking in the living room and the kitchen. There were still boxes littered everywhere, but it was starting to actually look like a home.

"Seems like someone has a green thumb," he commented.

"My sister. Plants are her life." Elena smiled mildly at the dozens of potted plants that decorated the walls and most of the flat surfaces. They were the first things Mila had unpacked and put in their proper places.

"Well, would it be too much to ask for a tour?" Kieran asked.

"I suppose not..." Elena became ultra-aware of every box, every piece of art leaning against the wall, and every speck of dust that had already gathered. The place was kind of a wreck. Great impression she was making. "So this is the living room and kitchen... obviously." She gestured lamely around the space. "Back there is my sister's room and the bathroom. Upstairs is my room, my office, and the balcony."

"Lead the way." Kieran's easy smile was still on his face, settling Elena's nerves a little.

Huey allowed them to pass into the hall, though his eyes never left Kieran. They walked up the stairs to the second floor. Elena's bedroom door was open, revealing the mess inside, and she quickly tried to cast a spell to shut it before Kieran could see. The door gave a little twitch but did not close.

Kieran didn't react. He either hadn't noticed or he was pretending not to. Most likely the latter. Trying to brush off her crushing embarrassment, Elena led him out onto the balcony.

"This is quite the space," Kieran said appreciatively as they walked outside.

"It was one of the major selling points of the house," Elena agreed.

Kieran gazed out over the back of the property. "Beautiful," he said. "Have you had any trouble with wild animals coming in from the woods?"

"No, Huey keeps a pretty tight ship," Elena replied, only half joking. The dog in question stood on the other side of the glass door, watching them intently like the menace he was.

"You might know this already, but there's a hiking trail that goes right through there, maybe fifty meters back. It's pretty popular." Kieran pointed in the general direction of the woods that bordered their yard.

"Huh." Elena pursed her lips. "The realtor mentioned something about a trail but didn't say how close it was."

"I wouldn't worry about it. People around here are pretty respectful of their neighbor's land."

If they weren't, they would be introduced to seventy pounds of angry fluff with teeth.

"That's my room over there, and this is my office." Elena led him back inside. The smaller room held a desk with a desktop computer on it, a squishy armchair, and a large bookcase.

"Cozy," Kieran observed. "What kind of work do you do?"

"Freelance writing, most of it ghostwriting for articles and books, stuff like that," Elena lied easily, hoping he didn't ask for more details.

"So, you don't get to put your name on your work?' Kieran looked at her curiously.

"I don't mind, I like my privacy."

"Fair enough." Kieran's eyes narrowed on the bookcase. He walked toward it and ran his fingers over the spines of a row of books. Elena noticed which ones and fought to control her reaction.

"You're familiar with Alys Sinclair's work?" she asked.

Kieran smiled widely. "Familiar? She's my favorite author," he said, pulling out one of the books and leafing through the pages. "I take it you're a fan? You seem to have every one of her novels."

"I am, sort of. My sister is a bigger supporter than I am." It was an inside joke Kieran wouldn't understand, but he didn't seem to notice. Elena felt very warm watching him leaf through the book, her mind spinning. Alys Sinclair was his favorite author. *She* was Kieran Andraste's favorite author. It was time to cut his perusal short before she gave anything away. "That's it for the house. Only thing left is Mila's garden."

Kieran looked up at her. "Right, lead the way!" he said enthusiastically, sliding the book back into place. "Which one is your favorite?"

"Favorite what?" Elena glanced back at him as they exited the room.

"Of Sinclair's books?"

"Oh, uh. I think *Winter Bird*. I know it wasn't her most popular." They reached the bottom of the stairs, and Elena turned to see Kieran looking at her with a surprised and excited expression.

"That's my favorite." He grinned.

Elena felt as if her stomach did a back flip in her gut.

"Huh, what a coincidence." She pushed the back door open.

Kieran smiled at her again. "After you."

Huey came running down the stairs, shoving past Kieran and bounding out the door. Elena walked out, shaking her head at her dog, leading Kieran into the garden.

"Wow." Kieran sounded genuinely impressed. Almost the entire acre that made up the side of the house was filled with the beginnings of Mila's garden.

"She's a busy bee," Elena said. "It's all arranged by sun exposure throughout the day. There are like ten different types of vegetables, and I don't even know how many flowers."

Kieran squatted down to examine the nearest plant, touching the leaves lightly. "No magical intervention on your part?" he asked.

"None," Elena confirmed. "Mila thinks it ruins the integrity of the plant. Or something like that."

Kieran stood. It seemed like he was about to speak, but there was a vibration from his pocket, and he reached in, pulling out his phone. He frowned, reading the notification.

"Everything all right?" Elena asked.

"Yes, just a family matter."

While he typed something on his phone, Elena's eyes were drawn to something in a nearby tree.

The raven.

The same raven she'd spotted on their first day in the house.

All her instincts told her it was the same bird. They were also shouting something she hadn't picked up the first time.

Familiar.

That raven was a witch's familiar. The magical energy radiating off it confirmed that. But it wasn't just any witch's familiar.

It was Kieran's.

The bond between them vibrated before it quieted. A silent exchange of information. Elena and Huey did it all the time.

Kieran Andraste's familiar had been at their house, watching them.

"Spirits," Elena breathed. " Your familiar has been spying on me." If she had been less shocked, she probably would have been smart enough to keep her mouth shut.

Kieran froze, then raised his gaze back to stare at her, slipping his phone into his pocket. "Don't be silly," he said. "She was spying on you *and* your sister."

Chapter 4

Elena didn't know any magical curses, but she wished she did right at that moment. The audacity, the *nerve* of this man. Spying on her and Mila since the very first day they'd moved to Alberdeen. He'd acted like he didn't know her. Acted like he was just being polite when the entire time it had been a lie.

"I understand you're angry," Kieran said, his tone calm, "but I want you to place yourself in my shoes, in my coven's shoes. After the witch hunt in New Stirling City this spring, things have been chaotic. Violence against our kind grows every day, and people are turning to the covens for protection. As much as we wish otherwise, not every witch can be trusted. There are plenty out there taking advantage of this horrible situation to infiltrate powerful covens and do them harm. I was tasked with making sure you and your sister were not amongst them."

"Mila isn't a witch," Elena said automatically, even as her mind processed what he was saying.

"I'm aware." Kieran took another step toward her, and behind him, the raven let out a warning cry that he ignored. "You know who I am but let me tell you something about me that isn't on the internet. The safety of my coven is my number one priority, and I'm more than willing to cross the line from time to time to protect the witches who've entrusted me with their lives."

Elena's heart gave a fluttering beat against her chest. Kieran's voice dropped while he spoke, his eyes alight with both power and passion, conviction dripping out of every word. It took her aback and diffused some of her anger.

"Fine," she relented. "But the surveillance stops now, understood?"

Kieran nodded, offering a small smile. "You have my word."

"And who is in your coven anyway? I thought your family was part of the Greenwood Coven."

"I am. Our headquarters are here in Alberdeen."

"Oh."

Kieran regarded Elena for a moment, his expression un-readable.

"I know you probably want me to leave, but I am afraid for all this interference to stop I need to say my piece."

Elena scowled, but nodded. "Go on."

"Through my observation of you and your sister, it has become obvious neither of you are a threat to the coven or this community," he began, "but what is also apparent is that you are a woefully unskilled witch."

Elena's eyes nearly bugged out of her head. She opened her mouth to say something, to tell him to fuck off, but he held up a hand to stop her.

"My familiar has observed you struggle with even the most basic spells. Things are changing, and not for the better. You need to know how to use your magic correctly, to its fullest potential, and not just for your own sake."

"What's that supposed to mean?" Elena asked.

Kieran gestured at the surrounding garden. "Your sister

may not be a witch herself, but she clearly inherited some magical genetics of her own. This green thumb of hers isn't entirely natural."

Panic shot through Elena at the accusation. "You have no proof—"

Kieran cut her off, taking a step closer. "If being related to you wasn't bad enough, she's in danger just by the nature of her existence. Humans with a witch parent are just as bad as a witch to some of the more bigoted humans," Kieran said quietly. "By refusing to learn how to use your magic, how to protect yourself, you are not only putting your own life in danger, but hers as well."

"Why are you saying this to me?" Elena asked, her voice wavering with embarrassed tears she was struggling to hold back. "What do you expect me to do?"

"Soon, the coven is going to reach out to you and invite you to join. I highly encourage you to accept."

Staring with wide eyes, Elena was speechless.

Kieran sighed, his expression softening. "I know I have no right to say any of this to you. You probably think I'm an asshole. And that's true." He smiled at his joke. "But I couldn't live with myself if I didn't say something. I don't want to see anyone else hurt."

Well then. Elena still didn't know how to respond. Kieran looked sincere, but he didn't know her. Didn't know her story. But there was no point arguing with him. She would just say whatever it took so he would leave.

"I appreciate the concern and..." Elena hesitated. "I'll think about what you said."

"That's all I ask."

They began to walk to his car, Elena feeling sick to her

stomach. Kieran looked out over the yard and spotted Huey standing there, glaring at him.

"Bye, Huey!" he called out.

Huey grunted in response.

With a final charming smile, Kieran got into his car, turned it on, and drove away. Elena let out a breath as soon as he was out of sight, his words ringing in her ears.

Huey appeared at her side, nudging her hand with his nose.

"It's all right," Elena assured him, though the words rang hollow with her own disbelief.

Being a witch was a dangerous thing. It made one a target of prejudice and violence from the human community, now more than ever before. For anyone, even other witches, to suspect Mila had hidden powers was a threat to her safety. If Kieran Andraste suspected this, who else would?

Mila had never shown any sign of magic in her life. Their mother had tested her repeatedly throughout Mila's childhood and adolescence. Mila was human through and through. But the truth didn't matter, only what people believed.

Elena sank to the ground, the grass damp under her jeans from the rain earlier in the day. The uncomfortable feeling of the cold moisture soaking through to her skin honestly helped. Fear for her sister was making her mind spiral as she imagined every worst-case scenario, but that cold kept her anchored to her surroundings.

Huey lay down and put his head in her lap. Comforting vibrations shimmered down their witch-familiar bond. Elena took a deep breath. Even if her head was conjuring up images of the townspeople arriving at their home with pitchforks and torches to burn it down and kill them both, it was extremely unlikely. There were at least dozens of actual witches residing in this town, and they seemingly lived without issue.

Come to think of it, if the Greenwood Coven was here, that meant the magical community in this area was likely much larger and much stronger than she'd realized.

They were going to be fine. Everything was going to be fine.

But no matter how many times she repeated that to herself, it just didn't feel true.

"Let's go inside."

Elena shakily got to her feet, her body feeling heavier than normal in the aftermath of her surge of adrenaline. Together, she and Huey went back into the house, and Elena changed her clothes in her bedroom to something dry and comfortable.

All the while, she could not stop thinking.

The presence of the Greenwood Coven was not something she could ignore. They were one of the largest and most powerful covens in not only the country but the entire world. Covens, traditionally, were an integral part of magical life. Witches were often born into membership and maintained that membership their entire lives. Their magic sustained the coven's influence and authority, and in return, the coven offered education, protection, and community.

But with modernization and the tentative peace between humans and witches, many had branched out to form smaller covens that were akin to social clubs rather than institutions. This was much more common in cities like New Stirling City and was fueled by a desire for freedom. Old covens like Greenwood had gone one step further over the centuries and controlled their members' lives to an oppressive degree. Some didn't allow their members to associate with humans in any capacity, or even witches from rival covens. They set rules that dictated when and how witches could use their magic and allowed the leaders of the covens to treat their witches as servants or soldiers. Elena's mother had experienced this firsthand when she'd fallen in love with Mila's human father, and her coven had ordered her to leave him...or else.

She'd chosen *or else*, thinking they were bluffing, and they placed a curse on him that resulted in his death.

And now, one of these covens was practically in their backyard. Elena let out a moan and flopped back on her bed. Huey flopped down next to her with a huff.

"What do I tell Mila?"

Huey didn't have an answer. On the one hand, if the local witches suspected Mila had magic, Mila should know. But really, what difference would it make? She didn't, and they would come to realize it with time. There was also the matter of what this could bring up for Mila. Being the human daughter of a witch and raised in the magical world came with its own emotional baggage. Elena knew her sister often felt like a mistrusted outsider in her own community growing up, and it had caused a great deal of pain. Kieran's insistence that Mila could have potentially had magic this entire time would not go over well. Was this really worth potentially ripping open those wounds?

No. It was not.

Mila deserved some peace, too.

Instead, Elena would explain that someone spilled coffee on her and one of the locals gave her a ride home to clean up. It was true enough to keep Mila unsuspecting.

After everything Mila had done to support Elena in the last few months since the witch hunt, she didn't want to burden her sister with her problems any more than necessary. Kieran's visit would have to be her own little secret.

* * *

Keeping the secret was harder than Elena hoped as not two days after the incident, a pair of witches showed up on their doorstep.

"Hello." A young woman beamed. "Alex brought me here on his apology tour for what happened in the cafe. I'm your peace offering!"

"Uh." Elena frowned at the woman's high energy. "Hi there."

Alex stood next to the woman, also smiling widely.

"Hello again, gorgeous! I felt so shitty after what happened the other day I wanted to stop by and make sure everything was cool, and my friend Maggie, here, wanted to meet you."

"Maggie Byrne," the woman introduced herself. Maggie was a touch shorter than Elena with deep red hair and large brown eyes that were full of mischief.

"Elena Hall, nice to meet you." Elena glanced over her shoulder. Mila wasn't within sight, so she was probably in her room. "My sister is around if you want to meet her too, but it would be a huge favor to me if you didn't mention anything about Kieran Andraste taking me home from your place." Mila finding out about Kieran's visit from a pair of strangers would not be the ideal way for her to hear about it.

"Sure." Alex smirked. "Totally follow. We won't say a peep."

"Thanks so much. Come in." Elena stood back and turned to the rest of the house. "Mila! We have visitors!"

There was a surprised squeaking noise from the direction of Mila's room. Huey emerged from upstairs and gave Alex a wide berth but immediately flopped on his belly for Maggie.

"Oh, aren't you such a good boy," Maggie cooed. "An excellent judge of character."

Alex rolled his eyes but didn't seem genuinely upset. Mila appeared a few seconds later, and introductions were once again exchanged. Alex and Maggie looked to be in their late twenties at most, which didn't mean much. Witches lived on average around one hundred and fifty years, and their aging slowed down significantly around twenty-five. These two could be close to Elena's age or much older.

Elena watched them all, a small smile on her face. She had a good feeling about these two. It was warm and fuzzy and felt... safe. Elena might not be the best witch, but she knew to trust her magical instincts when they spoke to her, and they were positively shouting right now that these two were all right.

Alex explained why they were there, and Mila enthusiastically welcomed them to their home. In a short time, the sisters learned that Maggie was a freelance photographer who lived only a few miles away and that she and Alex had been friends since childhood.

"Are you in the same coven?" Mila asked politely.

"Yup! The Greenwood Coven."

"Wait, not *the* Greenwood Coven, the one the Andraste family leads?" Mila's eyes were round with shock.

Maggie shot a glare at Alex, who looked a little sheepish, and Elena bit back a sigh.

"Yup, that's the one. Not too exciting though; they're kind of a grumpy family. I try to stay out of their way." Alex glanced at Elena as he spoke, still visibly nervous.

"Oh, they aren't all so bad," Maggie argued. "Kieran is a sweetheart if you catch him on a good day."

Elena's heart pounded uncomfortably. Was that last comment aimed at her? Had Kieran told Maggie about what happened?

Mila might have sensed Elena's discomfort as she quickly changed the subject. The perfect hostess, Mila invited the two witches to stay for dinner. Elena didn't mind, and it turned out to be a wonderful evening. Alex and Maggie were animated, funny, and just a touch awkward. Their enthusiasm for everything around them never seemed fake, and indeed, they came off like a pair of puppies.

"Your flowers are so lovely," Maggie gushed while they ate at the kitchen island. "I've never been able to get plant spells to work right, and there's no way I can keep them alive without magic."

"You couldn't keep a cactus alive without magic," Alex teased.

"Oh, shut up. Like you're one to talk. How many goldfish did you kill when you decided to put a fish tank in your cafe?"

"How dare you mention my babies to me."

Elena laughed at their antics, deciding that yes, she quite liked these two oddballs. Mila seemed to agree as she asked for phone numbers to be exchanged all around before Alex and Maggie left.

"I like this town," Mila declared. "I think everything is going to work out great."

"Why? Just because it happens you like two of its residents?" Elena asked while sitting on the couch, Huey trying to force his enormous body onto her lap.

"It's a good sign," Mila agreed, watching Elena hack as Huey's hair got in her mouth. "And I'm happy they're witches."

"Yea, me, too, as long as that coven leaves me alone." Elena accepted her fate, and Huey happily collapsed on top of her, knocking the air from her lungs. Because of what had happened with their mother and her coven, Elena had been raised and educated completely outside of one. After her coven left her husband to die just because he was human, Elena's mother swore to never let another coven hurt her family again. It was the last devastating straw in a long line of grievances she'd endured. Elena didn't mind not growing up in a coven. In fact, she firmly agreed with her mother on the subject, but that didn't mean Elena hadn't paid a price.

Being home educated wasn't necessarily a bad thing, but in Elena's case, it hadn't worked out that well. Despite her best intentions, Elena's mother was a horrible teacher, but after her coven's betrayal, her paranoia hadn't allowed her to trust anyone else to help.

It all muddled around in Elena's brain. Yes, covens were dangerous and could not be trusted, but that didn't mean other witches who were part of covens were all bad. Elena wished her mother had let go of her fear and allowed someone to help. Maybe then Elena wouldn't be such a failure now.

But that wasn't fair. Elena had long since become an adult and could have gotten additional training herself. She never had. Her magic was strong enough to get by in the city where life was so convenient for humans and witches alike, and she'd never felt the need to develop it further. That was until the witch hunt and now, she could barely cast spells at all.

Huey drew Elena from her thoughts by licking her face, letting him groom her.

"Oh that's so gross," Mila's disgusted voice came from behind them, and the evening dissolved into an argument over just how many germs were in a dog's mouth.

* * *

Mila signed on to lease the store on Main Street a few days later and immediately got to work. First off was meeting with a few contractors Maggie had been kind enough to recommend, along with an interior designer coming in from the city, who was an old friend of Mila's. Unfortunately, Elena wasn't much help. She didn't know much about renovating, so she lent her support by being a sounding board for Mila to talk through problems with.

"Out of these contractors Maggie sent over, two were normal and one was magical," Mila was telling her.

Mila sat at the kitchen island, a glass of white wine in hand while she looked through a book of paint colors.

"Oh? Are they from her coven?" Elena chopped up potatoes she was going to roast.

"Of course, but he does live in the area. He told me the Greenwood Coven hosts a lot of festivals and parties at their mansion, and having a flower shop in town as a vendor could be helpful."

"Really? They would make a human their primary source?" Elena asked skeptically, plopping the potatoes down on a pan and sprinkling them with salt. It seemed unlikely a coven like this one would ever employ humans for anything, even social events.

"Well." Mila shrugged, flipping the page of her book and not looking at Elena. "He did heavily imply that coven members support each other's businesses."

"I didn't realize you signed up," Elena said, finishing the

potatoes off with rosemary and placing them in the oven. As much as she liked Alex and Maggie, their coven was an entirely different issue. Elena couldn't just forget that they'd spied on her and Mila or sent Kieran to try and recruit her.

Mila cast an irritated glance at her sister. "You don't need to get an attitude with me. I know how you feel about covens." Mila was just as aware of their mother's past as Elena was.

"Exactly, so there's no point—"

"But don't you think things might have changed since then? Or maybe this coven is different?" Mila cut her off.

Elena turned, holding a raw chicken breast in her hand. "No, I don't."

"Would you put that chicken in the pan?" Mila said coldly.

Elena blinked once then, with a scowl, did as she was told. It immediately began to sizzle, and Elena went to the sink to wash her hands. Mila watched her quietly.

"This coven is famous, El, and you've met some of their members already. They're lovely."

Elena wiped her hands off on a dishrag. "I don't understand, Mila, do you want me to join this coven?"

Mila tilted her head. "I want you to be happy, El, and with things changing... I want you to be safe. I don't want you to dismiss this opportunity just because of what happened to Mom and my dad."

Elena walked back to the stove, checking on the chicken. Mila's words, her concerns, were aligning alarmingly close to Kieran's.

"I don't need a coven to do that," Elena said quietly. "Everyone is scared and running to covens they would never have joined until now. But are they really any safer? I don't think so."

Mila sighed. "Just promise me you'll think about it, okay? Really think about it," Mila urged her. "At least give them a chance."

Elena took a deep breath, then let it out. How could she deny her sister this simple request? "Fine, I promise."

"What was that? I can't hear you," Mila asked, leaning over the island and cupping a hand to her ear.

Elena rolled her eyes and turned around. "I said I promise!" she shouted.

Mila smiled and raised her hand, her fingers in a fist except for her pinky. Elena smirked and took a step forward, raising her hand and linking her pinky with Mila's.

"The pinky promise is sealed," Mila joked, and Elena let out a small laugh.

"Could you bring Huey in from outside? His food is ready." Elena turned back around to tend to the stove.

"That chicken better not be for the dog," Mila said as she stood up.

"Of course not, he prefers beef."

"You've got to be kidding me."

Chapter 5

Apparently, Maggie decided she and Elena were friends, proving Elena's instincts about her fellow witch were correct. Maggie seemed fun and kind, and her constant supply of energy fueled Elena rather than draining her. It started with grabbing drinks in town a few times and quickly escalated to movie nights and dinner outings to all of Maggie's favorite local restaurants. The two women just clicked in the way new friends sometimes do. Elena was very aware of just how lucky she was to have stumbled upon someone she and Mila both got along with so well.

The seasons were starting to change, and the oppressive heat of summer gave way to the pleasant warm days of early fall. One weekend, Maggie somehow convinced Elena and Mila to go hiking with her to engage in what Maggie called "leaf watching." That didn't make much sense to Elena, as all she had to do was look out any window in the house to look at the leaves, but still, it seemed a good idea at the time. Unfortunately, what Maggie classified as an easy hike turned out to be much more exercise than Elena had gotten in months.

"Hang in there, we're almost to the top, I promise," Maggie said, hanging back with Elena while she wheezed for breath.

Mila, who was much more athletic, walked ahead on the trail, snapping pictures with her phone.

Huey stayed by Elena's side, panting heavily, either out of loyalty or because he, too, was wildly out of shape. Huey slept nearly as much as a cat, and Elena's idea of exercise was the walk between her bedroom door and the kitchen.

"You said that a mile ago." Elena gasped, stopping and placing her hands on her hips. Her lungs were burning, and droplets of sweat ran down her face and the back of her neck. All this time, she'd been wrong. It wasn't bigoted humans who would be the death of her; it would be a massive cardiac event before the age of forty. That or the embarrassment that she was struggling this much.

"Drink water," Maggie reminded her.

Elena pulled her water bottle from her pack and took a swig. While Elena drank as if her life depended on it, Maggie took a deep breath before speaking again.

"So, I was thinking, and you don't have to say yes, but I have to go to the mansion next week for my check-in. Do you want to come and see what it's like?"

Elena lowered her bottle. She had several questions. "What's the mansion? And what is a check in?"

"Well, its official name is the Omron House, but no one calls it that. It's the headquarters for the Greenwood Coven. And a check-in is something members have to do every five years to monitor our magic levels and spell capabilities to make sure we aren't neglecting them or losing skill."

"What happens if you fail?" Elena asked, horrified at the thought of having to prove yourself so regularly.

"Oh, it's not that big of a deal. You just have to take some courses with a mentor until you improve. It's honestly a really helpful program. Keeps us in tip-top magical shape."

Elena had her reservations about that. It sounded like an invasion of privacy and a way to exert more control over the members' magic, but honestly, what did she expect from a major coven? Still, Maggie's offer hung in the air while Elena considered it.

Kieran had made it very clear that she was already on the coven's radar and that they were going to invite her to join. Perhaps it was a good idea to know what exactly she was up against before they made their offer.

"All right, just a visit."

Maggie smiled widely. "Awesome! I'll text you the details later. I think you'll really like it."

"Hey, you two! We climbing this mountain, or what?" Mila came trotting back.

Elena took a deep breath and willed her feet to keep moving.

"Only two more miles to go!" Maggie said, and Elena bit back a moan.

* * *

Getting to the Omron House was a bit more complicated than Elena had anticipated. Maggie explained in their living room that she had to open a portal, and only members knew the secret to summoning it.

"Once you know the secret, it's pretty easy," Maggie explained, "but we take security very seriously. Sorry, Mila, but you can't watch me open it."

Mila rolled her eyes. "I'm human, what am I going to do?"

"I know it's dumb, but those are the rules."

Sighing, Mila waved goodbye and went to her bedroom.

"You're going to open it here, in our living room?" Elena's voice came out like a squeak. Her nerves were starting to grow with every second that passed.

"Sure, it won't hurt anything. Now turn around and don't peek."

Elena obeyed. Whatever Maggie did behind her sent a rush of magical energy sweeping over the room and made Elena's spine shiver.

"Okay, let's go!"

When Elena turned, there was a very stately wooden door in the center of the room, carved with ornate images that she barely had any time to examine before Maggie led her and Huey through it. The portal tickled Elena's skin as she passed over the threshold. Was it a warning or a welcome?

On the other side was a garden enclosed with tall hedges. The flowers were in full bloom, even though Elena was quite sure they were out of season, and a little stone bench stood in the center.

"This is adorable," Elena said appreciatively. Mila would most certainly have much more to say about the plants, and Elena made a mental note to tell her sister all about them, which she forgot almost immediately as Maggie dragged her along.

"Just wait until you see the rest! The portals drop out to a dozen of these little reception gardens on the grounds. The mansion is this way."

Maggie led them down a gravel path that wound its way through the hedges. They emerged on an enormous, perfectly trimmed lawn, and up a slight hill to where the mansion stood.

It was clearly very old, built with deep gray stone that seemed to hum with magical energy. Large windows stood along the front, and a truly intimidating, ornately carved door stood at the entrance. Nothing stirred behind the windows, yet Elena couldn't shake the feeling that someone— or something—was watching her from behind the glass.

"Are you sure this is a mansion and not a castle?"

Maggie shrugged. "It used to be a castle, way back when. But not much of that building is left. This one was built on the ruins."

Maybe it was haunted. Wouldn't that just be a delight? Witches of the historic Greenwood Coven ranged from brutal conquerors to what today would be called mad scientists, and Elena didn't particularly want to encounter the departed spirits of either.

They approached the mansion, Elena's breath quickening and her mind growing foggier the closer they got. A voice that sounded a lot like her mother's was screaming in the back of her head to turn around and run. What if this place were a trap and once inside, Elena would not be allowed to leave until she'd agreed to submit herself and her magic to the coven's whims?

Signing up for a coven was a big deal. Part of your magic would always belong to the coven in order to fuel magic that served all of its members. But it was more than that. In times of crisis, the cumulative power of a coven could be controlled by their leader to defend or attack, although that hadn't occurred in centuries. On top of that, a coven member was expected to follow orders, even if it meant going against their own self-interest.

What if she'd been totally wrong about Maggie, and even now, coven members were descending on her home to capture Mila?

Logically, Elena knew that the scenarios her anxiety-ridden brain was throwing at her were ridiculous, but she couldn't stop them, much as she wanted to.

Maggie didn't seem to notice Elena's turmoil, and she opened the doors with a flick of her wrist, magic flowing with ease. On the other side was an expansive hall, and across it was a grand staircase up to the second floor.

"So if the coven has a party or social event, we host them in this room," Maggie explained, gesturing. "The library is over that way, and the kitchen is back there. There are a bunch of rooms we don't even use, but they're great for a private chat if you need one."

Elena looked around, feeling very small. All along the walls were massive statues of people, witches presumably, glaring down at them, and everything seemed to be either made of stone or marble. Massive paintings portraying presumably historical events from the coven's history hung throughout the hall, as well as portraits of famous members long departed. Elena recognized a few from her history classes in high school.

Huey was rubbing up against her legs, a low whine escaping his throat, and they huddled together as Maggie led them in the direction of the library. Down a hallway and through another very fancy door, they emerged in a truly enormous room where every wall was covered in books.

No, not a room. A labyrinth.

Elena gasped, her nerves temporarily forgotten, and darted to the nearest shelf to read the titles.

"Are these all books about magic?" She asked.

"Yeah, tomes, spell books, philosophy, that kind of thing. Come on, this way."

The library was much bigger than it ought to have been,

and Elena very quickly lost track of where they were going. Luckily, Maggie seemed to know the way, and soon, voices reached them. Maggie grabbed Elena's arm to stop her, silently placing her finger over her lips to indicate quiet.

"No one is arguing that we don't need to be concerned with the New Stirling City witch hunt, I'm merely saying it is likely an isolated incident. There's no need to take up arms, so to speak," a calm but cold voice spoke.

"I disagree. There was intense planning that went into that hunt. They'd been preparing for months. How do we know there aren't more humans out there doing the same thing? The coven needs to prepare for this to happen again," a woman said.

"Magnus, what do you think?"

The person, Magnus apparently, took a moment to respond. "I think it would be foolish to dismiss the hunt as a passing event. Their success will surely inspire others, but that being said, I don't want to encourage our members to see a threat behind every human. That will only increase tensions and make things worse."

"Always taking the middle road, eh?" the first man said with a laugh.

"That is usually where the truth lies, so yes. But never mind that, we have company."

"Dammit," Maggie muttered, "I never hear the good gossip."

They walked around a bookshelf to see the three speakers standing in a circle. One was a man who looked middle-aged, his graying hair matching his steely gaze. The second was a woman, short, but her magical aura sparkled with power. Both were dressed in business attire, like they'd just come from an office. The third was another man. He stood taller than anyone Elena had ever met and wore a dark green velvet jacket and thick boots. His skin was dark, even darker than Mila's, and his hair hung down his back in dreadlocks.

"Hello," he said, and Elena realized this was Mangus. His voice was incredibly deep, rumbling through her in a pleasant way. "It seems Maggie has brought us a guest."

"Yes." Maggie beamed. "This is Elena Hall. She just moved to Alberdeen! And of course, her familiar, Huey."

"Hi," Elena said, trying not to sound nervous but failing. Magnus offered her a kind smile.

"Elena, let me introduce Charles Landau and Lydia Banderas, they both sit on our board of directors. And Magnus Jelani is a professor of mathematics at New Stirling City College, but he's also one of the mentors here."

Everyone smiled politely at her. Elena smiled back, wondering if any of them were privy to the spying scheme on her and Mila.

"Very nice to meet you, Elena," Charles said, stepping forward. "We heard of your arrival and have been anxious for your visit."

"Oh, really?" Elena shifted, wishing more than anything she could vanish behind one of the bookshelves.

"Yes! Not every day we get a new resident witch in Alberdeen. Though I suppose your arrival is based on escaping New Stirling City?"

"Uh, yeah," Elena mumbled. "Just didn't want to stick around in case things got worse."

Charles cast a triumphant look at Lydia, who scoffed.

"You ready for your check-in, Maggie?" Magnus asked, changing the subject.

"Ready as ever!"

"Very well. Elena, you are welcome to use the library while you wait, or perhaps one of our board members could give you a tour?"

"I'm afraid I have to leave for a meeting, but Lydia, I don't suppose you're free?" Charles checked his watch with narrowed eyes.

"I have some time to spare. Come along, dear, and I'll show you around."

Despite Magnus's words, it seemed Elena wasn't really getting a choice in the matter, even though she would much rather stay and read. Maggie waved goodbye while Elena followed Lydia out of the library. Lydia kept up a constant stream of commentary, informing Elena and Huey about everything of note they passed. This included a stained-glass window that had been crafted nearly a thousand years ago, statues carved by some famous artist Elena had never heard of before, and artifacts from magical history. Of course, there was the building itself, which had come under attack many times during the Great Human and Witch Wars, hence the ruined castle upon which the mansion had been built .

"That was before we were able to secure it to be only accessible by portal," Lydia explained. "The town of Alberdeen has a rather bloody history if you look into it—not that you could tell by looking at it today!"

They popped into the kitchen, where several witches were working on potions, explored the greenhouse with multiple varieties of magical plants, and toured the meeting rooms and smaller libraries around the mansion. Around every corner was another room, another magical wonder, and it never seemed to stop.

Overwhelming. The place was overwhelming.

Everywhere Elena looked, there was magic being used so casually and out in the open. No one was afraid of being seen or attacked. Ancient power oozed from the very earth beneath the building, and every witch they encountered seemed to have an aura filled with the residue of it.

Never in Elena's life had she ever been in such a place.

The farther they went, and the more witches she met, Elena started to truly understand why many witches would find this appealing. They could be themselves here, without reservation.

Lydia finally led them back to the main library. "I'm sorry I couldn't show you more, but I have to run." She shook Elena's hand firmly.

"Thank you so much! It was very informative." And terrifying. And confusing.

Lydia nodded before heading back out the door, leaving Elena alone with Huey. Finally. There was no sign of Maggie or Magnus, so it seemed the perfect opportunity to read.

The first book Elena grabbed was a spell book on basic household spells. It was a bit dull, and she quickly put it back and picked up another. Engrossed in what she was doing, Elena didn't sense a presence behind her until the person cleared their throat.

Nearly jumping out of her skin, Elena whirled around, still clutching a book about defensive spells to her chest. Huey let out a low growl, hackles raised.

A woman stood there, unbothered by Huey, a smile curling on her lips.

"Hello, I didn't mean to startle you," she began, "but I must ask, just who are you and what are you doing here?"

Elena gaped like a fish for a moment. The woman was very beautiful, standing a few inches taller than Elena, with dark eyes that seemed to burn into Elena's skull. Everything about the woman shouted wealth, from her designer clothing and jewelry, to her perfect brown hair that cascaded in shiny waves over her shoulders.

"I'm Elena," she managed to say. "Maggie Byrne brought me as a guest."

The woman looked around them with an exaggerated expression. "And yet, Maggie does not seem to be here. Who gave you permission to go through our library unattended?"

Elena couldn't contain a scowl as her shock was quickly replaced with irritation. What was this woman's problem?

"Stand down, Jackie. Miss Hall is not doing anything wrong."

Elena let out a relieved breath as Charles materialized behind them.

Jackie didn't seem sated. "So this is how it is now? We let any witch with a wandering eye access our resources? Surely Anthony would never approve of this."

Charles frowned, and Elena looked between them.

"Uh, Anthony?"

Jackie scoffed. "Anthony Andraste? The leader of this coven? Honestly, what is she doing here, Charles?"

"Miss Hall is here on personal invitation from one of our members," Charles said coolly. "Her visit was indeed approved by Anthony Andraste. Now, if you don't mind, I wish to speak to our guest alone."

Jackie sent Elena one last withering glare before she turned and walked away. Elena watched her go, feeling a bit bewildered.

"You will have to excuse Miss Hammond," Charles said quietly. "She means well and is very protective of the coven."

"I see that." Elena carefully put the book back on the shelf. "You wanted to speak with me?"

"Yes, come this way."

Charles led her deeper into the library, where they reached a little sitting area. Charles gestured to one of the chairs, and Elena plopped down, Huey sitting at her knees. Anger was pounding down the bond between Elena and her familiar. Huey, for all his adorableness, could hold a grudge, and apparently, Jackie Hammond was now on his shit list.

Charles sat down across from them. "Well, Miss Hall, that is certainly not the introduction to our coven I was hoping for, but please understand this coven is a family. We look after our own. After the recent witch hunt, everyone is a bit on edge, and a mistrust of outsiders is only natural."

"I understand," Elena said, and truly she did, though she seriously doubted the "family" part of his statement.

"Admittedly, my meeting just now was to discuss you. On behalf of the entire board and the Andraste family, we want to formally invite you to join the Greenwood Coven."

Elena blinked. "Seriously? Just like that?"

"Well." Charles offered a lopsided smile. "Not quite just like that. We have done our research on you and your family, Miss Hall. We believe you are a perfect candidate for our coven."

"But I'm not a very good witch," Elena said bluntly. "I would fail one of your check-ins almost instantly."

"And that is what makes you ideal, Miss Hall. We want to help witches like you, witches who struggle with magic, find their way and develop their skills in a safe and nurturing environment where you are surrounded by your own people." It was the most animated Charles had been yet, but Elena wasn't moved.

"You know my sister is human, right?"

"Yes, of course. We are most accepting of our human relations. You would hardly be the only member with a human relative. Many of our member benefits would extend to her through you."

Elena pursed her lips. It would be so easy to accept; to enter this strange world and see where it took her, but Elena couldn't. Mila's father had died because of their mother's coven. When she refused to leave him, the coven had placed a curse on the man that prevented magical healing from working on him. The curse could have been broken but they didn't know it existed until too late...when he lay dying in the emergency room after getting in a car wreck and the last spell that could have saved him failed. Obviously, Elena had never known the man, but she knew how much her mother had loved him and how much he'd adored Mila.

"I really appreciate your offer, Charles, truly, but I'm afraid I cannot accept."

Charles gave her a blank stare before quickly recovering. "May I ask why?"

Elena fought to maintain eye contact, though her cheeks heated. "My family has a bad history with covens. I'd rather not get into it, but it resulted in a death."

"Well, now that is unfortunate. I'm so sorry your family experienced that, but I assure you, we take care of our own here. But if that is how you feel, we certainly won't push the issue. Just know, if you change your mind, you are always welcome."

Elena tried to smile. "I really am sorry."

Charles waved her apology away. "Not to worry. I will leave you to your reading."

Elena watched Charles go, her insides in knots.

* * *

It was late afternoon by the time Maggie dropped Elena and Huey back at home. Huey immediately ran off to greet Mila, who was outside in her garden. Elena waved at her sister before going inside and making herself a cup of tea. A few minutes later, Huey burst in through the doggie door Elena had installed, feet covered in mud and a look of absolute glee on his face.

"No! Look at the mess!" Elena cried, running to guide him away from any of the carpets.

Huey seemed totally unconcerned, licking her face as she held him down.

"I tried to stop him," Mila said, emerging from the back hallway, "but the mutt never listens to me."

"I'll take care of it," Elena muttered. She waved her hand in the air, quietly speaking the single word cleaning spell. The intent was to remove the mud, but it failed, merely moving the mud off Huey and onto the already-dirty floor.

"Woah!" Mila jumped slightly from the unexpected magic touching her.

"Crap," Elena looked helplessly around at the mess she'd made.

"Don't worry about it, I'll get the mop in a minute." Mila turned around to face Elena excitedly. "So, how was the mansion?"

"It was…" Elena started, struggling to find the words. "Interesting."

"Care to elaborate?"

"Well, it was very grand. The mansion was huge, and the gardens were spectacular. You would have gotten a kick out of them," Elena said, retrieving her favorite mug from the cabinet and adding a tea bag.

"Were the people friendly?" Mila leaned back against the counter top.

"For the most part. The man doing Maggie's check-in was nice, and so were two members of the board I met. But there was this one woman who got all nasty and defensive because I was there. It was weird." Elena poured water she'd already boiled into the mug and inhaled the earthy scent of the tea for a moment.

"They gave me a tour. People were using magic everywhere for everything! It was kind of disconcerting but also kind of nice? I don't know," Elena finished lamely, struggling to put into words how she was feeling about the entire experience.

"Sounds like you enjoyed yourself," Mila said cautiously. "Do you think they're going to invite you to join up?"

"Don't need to wonder, they already did."

"What?" Mila asked, surprised. She pushed off the counter and faced Elena directly. "And what did you say?"

"Well, I said no, of course."

Mila stared, her jaw clenched. "Of course," she repeated. "Of course! You promised me, Elena, that you would consider it!"

Elena took a step back, surprised by Mila's outburst. Mila rarely raised her voice in general, and never at her sister.

"I *did* consider it!" Elena defended herself. "I decided it wasn't a good idea!"

"Oh, come on, don't give me that bullshit," Mila seethed.

"What's your problem?" Elena demanded, her own anger growing.

Huey sat up from where he was lying on the ground, watching the sisters with sudden attention.

"My problem is that Mom has been dead for ten years, and you are still letting her control your life!" Mila said angrily. "When are you going to start thinking for yourself?"

"I am thinking for myself!" Elena shot back. "Just because you don't agree with it doesn't mean it's wrong! Mom knew what she was talking about, and I trust her judgment! Though I don't understand how you can possibly disagree, considering it was your father who—"

"Don't you dare." Mila cut her off, glaring viciously. "Leave my father out of this. I won't let you use his memory like this."

"What's that supposed to mean?"

"It means you're using him and Mom as an excuse. Yes, what happened to my father was a horrible tragedy, and Mom's coven certainly played a part, and it messed Mom up really badly. She was so determined to keep you away from covens, she even used to ground you if you asked to join any when you were a kid. You were literally conditioned to fear and hate them. If this was really about Mom and my dad, you wouldn't have gone in the first place."

"I went because you wanted me to."

"No, you went because some part of you knows you need a coven; you're just too scared to go through with it!" Mila gestured at the mud on the floor Elena accidentally created. "You're not good at magic, Elena! You have power, but you have no idea how to use that power properly. You need a coven to teach you, but you're too scared of your own abilities to ask for help."

"Scared?" Elena shoved Mila's hands out of the way. "Scared? I have every right to be scared after what happened! Magic is not a gift, Mila! It nearly got me killed! It got Saamira—" Elena's voice broke as she choked on the last word, tears blossoming in her eyes. She refused to let them spill, and instead, took a deep, shuddering breath. "You have no idea what that fear feels like."

Mila glared at her. "I don't know how that feels? Seriously? I have to live every day knowing that the person I love most in this world is being hunted because of what she is, and there is nothing I can do to protect her because I have no power. But you!" Mila pointed at Elena's face. "You can protect yourself, but you refuse to learn how, even after what happened."

"Don't," Elena said darkly. "Don't put what happened on me. It was not my fault!"

"That is not what I said."

"No, but it's what you meant." Elena backed away from Mila. "I'm done talking about this. I'm not going to join that coven or any other one, and you're just going to have to find a way to deal with it!"

Elena walked away before Mila could say anything and stomped up to her bedroom, Huey following behind. Mila was wrong. Joining the coven would be a mistake, why couldn't she see that? They were old-fashioned, controlling, and prejudiced against anyone different from them.

Flinging herself onto her bed, Elena buried her face in her pillow and silently wept.

Chapter 6

Kieran had promised himself he would put this whole business with Elena Hall behind him. He'd done what the coven had wanted and investigated her, but after talking to Charles and finding out why she was mistrustful of covens, the guilt over his harsh words had been eating him alive, and he had to make it right. It was hard not to feel like a stalker as he watched Elena walking through a local park with Maggie Byrne a few days after Elena's visit to the mansion. The park had a few different sports facilities and a playground, but as it was the middle of the school day, it was mostly deserted.

The two women ambled along the walking trails, Maggie dominating the conversation from what Kieran could tell. That formidable mutt of Elena's trailed behind, ears twitching in every direction as he constantly scanned around his witch, presumably looking for any threats. Elena's hair was a shade of dark pink today, standing out prettily against her skin. Kieran wondered how often she changed the color, as last time he'd seen her, it had been bright yellow.

Finally deciding to approach, Kieran emerged from his hiding spot behind a tree and quickly caught up with them.

"Magnus was impressed with me, even if he didn't say so. My fire work has really improved! Oh, Kieran, I didn't see you there!" The women paused, and Huey flattened his ears at Kieran, letting out a low growl.

"Hello, Maggie. Your check-in went well?"

"Very!" Maggie beamed. "What can we do for you?"

"I was rather hoping to talk to Elena for a moment, alone."

Maggie's eyes widened, then she glanced at Elena. Elena pursed her lips, then nodded.

"All right. Behave, Mr. Andraste." With a wink, Maggie walked off.

Kieran couldn't help his mouth twitching into a smile. He'd always liked Maggie, even if they'd never actually been friends.

"What do you want?" Elena asked bluntly, eyes narrowed on him.

"I heard you rejected Charles's offer."

"News travels fast. Let me guess, you're here to tell me I made a huge mistake, I'm just some shitty city witch who has no clue, and some other condescending bullshit I don't want to hear?"

Kieran flinched. "I deserve that," he said. "I came on too strong last time we met, and I realize now how cruel it was. I'm truly sorry. I didn't realize you had a traumatic history with covens. For what it's worth, I think your caution makes perfect sense. Maybe once you get to know us all a little better, you'll change your mind."

"Don't hold your breath." Elena crossed her arms over her chest, glaring up at him. "Is that all?"

It was a little unnerving how fast Kieran's heart was beating. There was absolutely nothing intimidating about this woman—from her lack of magical talent to her pretty but unremarkable looks—yet something in Kieran was on high alert around her.

"I suppose so," he managed to say. "It was nice seeing you again."

Elena actually laughed. "Yeah, sure. Nice to see you, too. Goodbye."

Kieran watched her walk off, her hand on Huey's back as they caught up to Maggie, who was waiting a good distance away.

There was something about her, something he was missing. To get to the bottom of it, he would have to follow up on his plans to check in on the sister. Based on the very brief time he'd spent in her house, there was no way this woman didn't have some latent magical ability, despite what her sister claimed. He could practically smell it wafting off her garden and touching everything within the area. Had the sisters really not noticed the way the wild plants in the forest around their house had started to grow faster since they'd moved in?

Kieran determined he would just have to see for himself.

* * *

Kieran had always liked the main street of Alberdeen. It was so quaint, with its storefronts and lamp posts decorated with flowers in spring and summer, and seasonal decorations in fall and winter. For the most part, the locals left him alone, used to seeing his face from time to time, which gave Kieran an escape from constantly feeling like he lived his life in a fishbowl.

On this particular day, Kieran was there for one reason

alone. Mila Hall opened her plant shop today. Beyond his curiosity about this family, Mila was a safety concern. A witch who didn't know they were a witch was dangerous, as their magic could explode out of them at any given moment.

And of course, meeting Mila could also shed light on his quest to understand Elena a bit better, understand her confusing motivations, and perhaps finally be able to put her out of his mind.

When he first stopped by, it was in the morning when Mila was opening the shop for the first time. Although Maggie had told him beforehand that Elena and Mila were half-sisters, and therefore looked very different, he was still slightly taken aback by the tall, dark-skinned woman hanging plants outside the shop. Her long, braided hair was pulled back behind her head, and she moved with confidence and grace that her sister lacked.

Kieran had decided it was the perfect moment to approach, but Maggie and Alex Moran showed up instead. Retreating, Kieran watched them *ooh* and *aah* over her for a few minutes and show her a large box of donuts they brought before she ushered them inside. Sighing, Kieran had decided to try again later. As much as he was willing to do almost anything for his coven, it didn't mean he wanted to spend his free time with them when he could help it.

Now, after lunch, Kieran could sense the shop was empty from the street, so he took a deep breath and strolled in. Immediately, Kieran was struck by the warm, humid air. It made his skin crawl, but he did his best to ignore it. Everywhere he looked, there were lush potted plants, both for indoor and outdoor gardens. Exotic plants from the tropics with their brightly colored blooms stood out first, with more subdued local options filling in the gaps. These plants did not have the same magical essence that Mila's garden at home did, but that could simply be because they hadn't been in her care for very long.

Mila was behind the counter, looking at him with a tentative smile, and up close, Kieran realized just how young she looked. Her records indicated she was in her forties, but no one would ever guess that.

"Hi there," he greeted, offering his most charming smile.

"Hello!" Mila almost shouted, then cleared her throat, looking embarrassed. "How can I help you today?"

Ah, there was the awkwardness he was expecting. Must be a family trait after all.

"Well, I thought I might buy some flowers for my mother. What do you have available?"

"Cut flowers are over here." Mila guided him to the back corner of the shop. "Are you celebrating anything in particular?"

"No, just felt like it." He looked over the flowers. Mila was only a foot or two away, and Kieran cast his magical senses out toward her. There was no response. A witch's natural magical aura—even a suppressed one—would have immediately flared at such prodding, but Mila's remained unmoved entirely. Human.

"If nothing here suits you, I can also custom-make an arrangement," she offered, snapping Kieran from his thoughts.

"Hm, I like this one." He pointed to the largest arrangement, which was very bright and cheerful-looking.

"Great!" Mila scooped up the flowers and headed to the counter. "Do you want them wrapped?"

"Yes, please," Kieran said. "So, I hear Alys Sinclair is your favorite author."

"What?" Mila asked, stopping in mid-motion and staring at him like he'd grown an extra head.

Kieran let out a low chuckle. "Sorry, I should've introduced myself first. My name is Kieran. I met your sister a while ago, and she mentioned you liked Sinclair's books."

Mila stared at him, clearly having no idea what he was talking about. Kieran's smile faltered; he felt a little uncomfortable now. Had Elena really not told her sister about him? For some reason, that was upsetting.

"My sister met Kieran Andraste?" she asked, shocked.

So, Mila knew who he was, but that didn't soothe his hurt ego.

Kieran frowned fully, not wanting to recount the unfortunate circumstances under which he and Elena had met. "Uh, yes, it was a weird moment. Someone spilled coffee on her, and she got burned. I healed her and took her home."

"I see," Mil said, tilting her head. "You told her Sinclair was your favorite author?"

"Yes, I did. Why? Is that funny?" He watched suspiciously while Mila very obviously tried to hold back laughter as she moved back behind the counter and wrapped up his flowers.

Mila straightened, the bouquet in her hands. "It's kind of hilarious, actually. Elena *is* Alys Sinclaire."

Kieran stood there, blinking at her. "What?"

Mila was full-on laughing now. "Alys Sinclaire is a pseudonym. She tells everyone she's a freelancer when in reality, she's a novelist," she explained.

Kieran's entire mind went blank for a second, then kick-started at a thousand miles a second, desperately combing over everything he'd said to Elena to try and remember just how badly he'd embarrassed himself.

Badly was the answer. Very badly.

"Well, now I feel like an idiot," he muttered.

"Oh, I'm sure it's fine." Mila grinned. "Also, your total is forty-five dollars with the twenty-five percent discount for cut flowers."

Kieran pulled out his wallet and began digging around for cash. "I can't believe I talked to Alys Sinclaire and didn't even realize it," he said to himself, handing her the money. Was he blushing? He felt like he was blushing. Kieran never blushed. But how else do you react to finding out you unknowingly met your favorite author and gushed to them about their own books like an idiot? Not to mention how he'd insulted her.

"I'm sure she was flattered. No one knows who she is, so she never gets to meet people who love her work." She handed him back his change and his receipt.

"Well, I'm going to have to process this for at least a day, perhaps two," Kieran said pensively, staring at the counter.

Mila watched him, eyes glinting. "You gonna be okay?"

Kieran looked up at her, snapping out of it, and smiled sheepishly. "I'll manage."

He paused, looking at the flowers in Mila's outstretched arms. Okay, it was all starting to make sense. Elena Hall was Alys Sinclaire. That was obviously why he couldn't stop thinking about her. No other reason. Now that he knew the truth, he would be a fool to let this opportunity slip through his fingers.

Kieran took the flowers then shifted them into one arm. "Do you have a piece of paper and pen?"

"Sure," Mila replied, producing a sticky note and pen from behind the counter.

Awkwardly with one hand, Kieran took them and scribbled something down. "This is my phone number, please give it to your sister, if it isn't too much trouble," he requested, sliding it back to her.

Mila raised her eyebrows. "Well, well. Mr. Andraste, is this a very roundabout way of hitting on Elena?"

"Not at all," Kieran said, most certainly blushing for real. "Tell her if she changes her mind about the coven or needs help, she can reach out to me."

"Or if she wants to spend some time with her number one fan?"

Kieran pulled the flowers tighter to his chest. "Well, if she wanted to use it for social reasons I wouldn't object," he said, entirely embarrassed now. This awkwardness was not normal for him, but to be fair, he'd never approached someone he had any sort of interest in through their older sister before— an older sister whose eyes glinted with mirth that was most certainly at his expense.

Mila smiled widely. "I'll make sure she gets it," she assured him.

"Thank you, and good luck with your shop, I hope you do well here."

Kieran left as quickly as possible, without letting it look like he was fleeing. As soon as the fresh air hit him, he relaxed, though he felt oddly shaky all over. All things considered, he thought he'd handled that well. Sure, he'd embarrassed himself in front of Elena horribly, and probably drove her off forever with his overbearing behavior, but at least she could reach out now... if she ever wanted to.

As Kieran walked down the street, a little pep in his step as he contemplated all the things he would say to Elena if she gave him the chance about how much he loved her books, he belatedly realized he completely forgot to finish checking Mila for magic. Nearly stumbling, Kieran groaned to himself.

Well, she had no magical aura, so the chances of her having hidden magic were extremely unlikely, Kieran rationalized. What he sensed at her house was probably nothing, maybe an extremely specific and dormant magical gene that gave her a connection to plant life. Satisfied with this conclusion, Kieran dipped down an alleyway and opened a portal, disappearing through it to go home.

Chapter 7

Elena stood outside in the yard, glaring at Mila's garden as if the plants within were the ones who'd hurt her feelings rather than the person who planted them. Elena loved Mila more than anything, but that woman could be so stubborn when she felt slighted. Of course, Elena was just as bad, so their fight was in a bit of a stalemate. It was two days since, and not a word had been spoken between them. Elena felt sick to her stomach over it, but neither sister was willing to let their side go. Luckily, or maybe unluckily, with preparing for the grand opening that had been this morning, Mila had rarely been in the house, so they didn't have too many opportunities to deliberately ignore each other.

Not speaking to Mila really put just how isolated she was in sharp relief. In the city, if Mila pissed her off, Elena would hide out in her apartment or go to a friend's place to vent. Here in Alberdeen, she was alone. Her last remaining childhood friend—Tora—was worried about her and Mila's move enough as it was. If she knew about the fight and everything going on with the Greenwood Coven, she'd freak out and drop everything to come try and fix it. As much as part of Elena longed for that, she couldn't stand the idea of being a burden to her.

She'd thought about opening up to Maggie when they hung out in the park the day before, but then Kieran had shown up again and thrown Elena off. His apology and overwhelming presence upset Elena in a way she couldn't quite put her finger on. Maybe it was because she hadn't expected him to apologize, or maybe because she wasn't sure if he meant it or not. Maybe this was just still part of his attempt to convince her to join the coven.

Mind muddled, the interaction made Elena feel mistrustful toward Maggie even though she'd done nothing to deserve it other than also be a member of the coven.

No, it seemed like if Elena wanted this situation to be fixed, she would have to put on her big girl pants and do it herself.

Mila's plants swayed in the light breeze, looking so cheerful and alive it made Elena feel irrationally angry. Enough was enough. She was going to fix this today.

Turning back to the house, Elena started to formulate a plan. Huey trotted behind her, his tongue lolling out of his mouth lazily. Perhaps a peace offering? After all, she'd been pretty horrible herself, bringing Mila's father into the fight like she had. Once inside the kitchen, Elena was delighted to find they owned all the ingredients she would need and got to work baking a cake. Cake was food for the soul, and also both sisters' favorite.

By the time she finished baking, night had fallen. Elena saw the headlights of Mila's car through the window just as she was adding the finishing touches to the cake. Huey bounded up to the door, tail wagging.

The door began to open, and Elena quickly arranged herself, holding the cake out in both hands and a big smile on her face. Mila backed into the room and kicked the door shut with her feet. As she turned around, Elena saw she was carrying a white bakery box in her arms. The sisters locked eyes, staring at each other for a second.

"Did you... buy a cake?" Elena asked, stunned.

"Did you bake a cake?"

There was a moment of silence where Huey glanced back and forth between them, his tail wagging uncertainly, then they both burst out laughing. Elena put the cake down and walked around the counter, and Mila put hers down next to it. They looked at each other for a moment before going in for a tight hug.

"I'm sorry for yelling at you," Mila said. "I made your trauma about me, which is so fucked up. And I never, *ever* should have used it against you. It was cruel and wrong."

"Thank you," Elena said, feeling a little teary. "And I'm sorry for not realizing that all this was affecting you, too. You've taken such good care of me these past months, and I've never stopped to think of how hard that must've been. And it was so fucked up to mention your dad. I'm so sorry."

Mile made a little sniffling noise, squeezing Elena extra tight. Elena hid her face in Mila's shoulder, trying to hold back tears. The two simply held each other for a moment, the weight of everything unsaid between them, the pain, the grief, and the unconditional love, settling deeply.

After a few moments, they broke apart, and Mila looked down at Elena, brushing a stray hair out of her face.

"I hate fighting with you."

"Me, too."

"Wanna eat cake until we are sick?"

"Yes, please."

The two of them did indeed eat cake until they were both

sick and nursed their stomach aches with large cups of mint tea while sitting on the couch in front of the TV.

"Oh! I almost forgot." Mila pulled something out of her pocket. "Care to explain this?"

"Uh? A piece of paper with a phone number on it?" Elena stared, not quite sure what she was missing.

"It's Kieran motherfucking Andraste's phone number," Mila explained.

Elena blanched. "He went to your shop?" She couldn't believe it. Was he *still* spying on them?

"So, you admit you knew about this then." It wasn't a question.

Elena blushed, rapidly trying to think of how to explain. "Okay, so. A few weeks ago I met Kieran at Alex's cafe. Some idiot spilled his coffee on me, and I got burned." Elena launched into an explanation of everything that happened, including what Kieran said about her magic and Mila's dubious abilities. By the end, Mila had a slightly horrified look on her face, and she got to her feet and began to pace in front of Elena.

"I'm not a witch," Mila said fiercely. "I don't care what he says. He thinks I wouldn't have noticed by now if I was using magic on my plants?"

"He wasn't saying you were a witch, just that you might have some magical traits, I think." Elena chewed on her bottom lip anxiously. The mere suggestion that someone was a witch could be enough for the more radical bigots to cause trouble, and Elena could see the fear behind Mila's anger. This was exactly why she hadn't said anything n the first place.

"And fuck him for saying all that shit to you about your magic!"

"You said almost the exact same thing, need I remind you."

"Okay, but you are my baby sister. I'm morally obliged to tell you things you don't want to hear. That man needs to mind his own business."

Elena shrugged.

"I think he likes you though," Mila added.

"What?" Kieran Andraste, like her? How ludicrous. He could be with models or foreign princesses if he wanted to. Why on Earth would he be interested in her?

"You really think he came to my shop to meet me? A lowly human?" Mila asked, stepping forward and putting her hands on Elena's shoulders. "He came there because he wants to get to know you."

Elena shook her head. "There's no way."

"Then explain the phone number."

Elena looked down at the paper clutched in her hand. For a moment, she allowed herself to imagine Mila was right, and he did have some sort of attraction to her. It seemed ridiculous to even entertain the idea, but it was intriguing. She pictured his dazzling smile, his beautiful green eyes staring into hers, wondering what those soft-looking lips of his would feel like pressing against her mouth...

"Oh, spirits, you like him, too," Mila said, snapping Elena out of it.

"I do not." Elena scowled. "And you're wrong. He probably just wants to keep an eye on me for the coven, since I turned them down—or something like that."

"Maybe. Just be careful, okay? He's hot, and rich, and probably used to getting what he wants."

It was a fair warning, and one Elena planned on taking seriously. She didn't know how she felt about Kieran Andraste or if she wanted to see him again. Elena couldn't deny part of her was drawn to him. After all, he'd been her celebrity crush throughout the majority of her twenties. That had ended though when lurid and awful stories about him started to flood the news on a weekly basis. He was a player with a wild past and far too much power. He'd invaded her privacy and insulted her magic.

But still, having his number on hand wouldn't be a bad thing. In case of emergencies, of course. And he had apologized for being rude and supported her decision not to join his coven...

While Mila wandered off to refresh her tea, Elena created a new contact in her phone, labeling it "K.A." After hitting *Save*, she stared at it for a moment. There was a tingling sensation in her chest, her magical intuition speaking to her. Whatever was going to happen, Kieran wasn't going away.

* * *

Winter came in with decided force and maliciousness, in Elena's opinion. The first snow fell well before the end of October, and by mid-November, there was a comfortable blanket of it covering the ground. Their first winter in the country was an adjustment for the sisters, who were used to the city where streets and sidewalks were plowed for them, and travel consisted only of brisk walks to the subway or a bus.

Mila tried shoveling the driveway once. Halfway through, she gave up and forced Elena to come out and help. This of course led to a great deal of complaining, and later that day they called a service to plow the driveway for them going

82

forward.

Elena stopped going to work at the cafe, not wanting to go through the trouble of leaving the house when she could help it. Most mornings, Mila scraped ice off her windshield, freezing all the while, and occasionally, Elena could hear Mila cursing her out through her bedroom window for getting to stay in bed. Even Huey, bundled up as he was with his thick fur, only wanted to go outside for very short periods of time.

The final draft of Elena's latest novel was complete, and she was up to her eyeballs in working on it with her editor to get it done by the deadline. Elena hardly had any time to think about Kieran Andraste and his offer to spend time together socially. Thankfully, in the two months since he'd shared his number, Elena hadn't run into him again.

Mila, thanks to the steady flow of customers at her shop, was meeting a ton of people and actually making friends. Elena wasn't jealous. Too many people bothering her all the time stressed her out. For now, she was content with occasionally hanging out with Maggie and Alex. Alex was a total sweetheart, Elena had learned, and matched well with Maggie's slightly manic energy. Time spent with them was never boring and, admittedly, left Elena needing time to recover afterward.

Mila had no such need to reboot her social battery, however, and was even going to parties—of all things—on a regular basis.

The horror.

"If you need me to come pick you up, just call me. If you even think of drinking and driving, I will kill you," Elena said on a cold and miserable night, curled up on the couch in a thick blanket, watching Mila wrapping a thick scarf around her neck.

"You sure you won't already be unconscious?" Mila pulled a fuzzy hat over her hair.

"Oh, I will, but for you, I'll take my phone off silent mode."

"The truest form of love." Mila grinned.

Elena looked at her sister suspiciously. "You're wearing makeup," she observed.

"It's a party, is that a crime?"

"Who did you say invited you again?"

"I told you a hundred times," Mila said, "the woman I found to do my braids introduced us, and her name is Ava. She's also been coming in to the shop pretty regularly to get help with her houseplants."

"Uh-huh, houseplants." Elena sank behind her fluffy blanket up to her eyes, watching Mila fix her hair in the mirror next to the door.

"I'll see you later." Mila stopped fussing over her appearance and made to leave.

"Make good choices!" Elena called after her, and the door closed with a snap.

Elena didn't hear from Mila that night, and when she awoke around nine in the morning, dreadfully early for her, she found a note from Mila scrawled on the kitchen counter.

I got home alive, FYI. Gone to take care of the plants.

–Mila

Satisfied, Elena brewed a cup of tea. A short while later, she and Huey braved the great outdoors to get some much-needed exercise. Even for her, the level of inactivity she'd reached lately was alarming. Elena was bundled up so that the only exposed skin was a slit on her face that revealed her eyes and nose, and Huey was wearing a doggie sweater and booties. The cold did not allow them to stay out long, and when they returned, Elena's cheeks were bright pink.

When they got back to the driveway, both Elena and Huey stopped in their tracks. There was a car she did not recognize parked in front of their house and a woman standing on their doorstep.

Despite the temperature, sweat broke out on Elena's forehead, and she swallowed back the rising unease in her chest.

"Hello there," Elena called out as they approached. Her voice cracked while she did so, and Elena winced.

The woman turned around, and Elena saw Mila's scarf from last night clutched in her hand.

"Oh, hi!" The woman sounded relieved. "Are you Elena?"

Relief flooded Elena's system. This surely was one of Mila's new friends.

"I am." Elena reached the woman.

Huey's ears pinned back on his head, and he let out a low growl.

"Hush, you," Elena reproached him. "Don't worry, he won't bite. He's just a grouch," Elena assured the woman.

The stranger did not seem so sure. She tucked a strand of her light brown hair behind her ear, keeping her hands out of reach, but did not look at Huey.

"Right, I'm returning Mila's scarf! She left it at my place last night. She said today was her day off, so I thought I would bring it back to her."

"Oh, you must be Ava!" Elena said, connecting the dots, and Ava smiled.

"That's me!"

"Well, come on in. Mila went to the shop to take care of her plants, but she should be back any minute," Elena told her, brushing past Ava and opening the door. The three of them quickly stepped inside.

"Are you sure? I could leave it for her. I don't want to intrude."

"Nah, I have no life, if my sister didn't mention that already, and I'm sure she wouldn't mind seeing you again." Elena watched out of the corner of her eye while she took Huey off the leash and pulled off his doggie boots. A blush rose on Ava's round cheeks.

Huey stalked off to the couch and jumped up on it so he was taller, staring intently at Ava, who did her best to ignore him.

"This is a nice place," Ava remarked awkwardly.

Elena smiled, also unsure what to say, and walked over to Huey to wrestle the sweater off of him so he wouldn't overheat.

"Do you want me to take your coat?" Elena asked when she succeeded.

"Oh, sure!" Ava slipped out of her coat and handed it to Elena, who hung it up on the coat rack. Ava was short and curvy, just Mila's type, and had light brown hair and large, round doe eyes to match. Her brown skin was flushed with the cold, and she still gripped Mila's scarf tightly in her hands.

"Tea, coffee, some leftover lasagna perhaps?" Elena of-fered, attempting to put her best hostess foot forward.

"Some tea would be lovely."

A tea girl. Elena approved. She made herself busy filling up the kettle and turning it on while Ava sat down at one of the kitchen island stools.

"What would you like? We have green, black, herbal... pretty much everything really."

"Some black tea would be fine."

"How about with rose petals? It's a *special* blend that Mila mixes herself," Elena said suggestively, and Ava's blush grew.

"Oh?" she asked.

Elena noted she clutched Mila's scarf a little tighter. It was adorable, and Elena couldn't help but smile even brighter at Ava. Mila, being utterly gorgeous, usually caught a lot of attention from potential romantic partners, but there was something about Ava that felt different—more genuine.

"Well, we buy the tea, and she adds the rose petals from her garden," Elena explained.

"That would be lovely." Ava sat down at the island. "Mila mentioned you were a writer?"

"Yes, though it's not terribly interesting. What about you? You live in Spring Glenn, right?"

"Yup, I'm a large animal vet at the clinic."

"Really?" Elena asked, genuinely surprised, due to Ava's short stature.

Ava smiled. "I know, a lot of people find that hard to believe, considering I'm pretty shrimpy."

"But tough as nails, I imagine. So you mostly work with the local farmers?"

"Yes! Cows, goats, sheep, horses, those sorts of things."

"One of my favorite shows is this vet show called *Dr. Nile.* Have you seen it?"

Before Ava could respond, Mila's car pulled into the driveway.

"Oh, she's back." Ava straightened up.

Elena poured her guest's tea and placed it in front of her, then took out an extra mug for Mila.

Mila burst through the door a few seconds later, and as soon as she spotted Ava, a dopey smile appeared on her face. "Hi!"

she said excitedly. "I wasn't expecting to see you again so soon!"

"You forgot your scarf last night." Ava held the scarf up, an equally dopey smile on her face.

Mila took it gingerly from Ava's hands, and Elena resisted the urge to roll her eyes.

"I made you both tea." Elena plopped the second mug for Mila down on the counter.

"Thanks, El." Mila peeled off her layers and slid onto the stool next to Ava.

"Ava was telling me about her exciting life as a vet," Elena informed her, leaning against the counter.

"Isn't that such a cool job?" Mila said, a tad too enthusiastic.

"Just the coolest," Elena replied mockingly, smirking.

Mila shot a glare at her.

"It's pretty cool." Ava smiled, not noticing the sisters' behavior. "I'm on call tonight though, so I can't stay long."

"Oh! I know about that. In case there's an emergency farm call right? Like a cow is having trouble giving birth or has gone down and can't get up," Elena said, trying to sound smart.

"Yup, just like that." Ava laughed.

"Well, I have some work to do. You two crazy kids have fun." Elena winked at Mila.

"It was great meeting you, Elena," Ava said. "Thanks for the tea!"

"Anytime!" Elena responded. "Come upstairs with me, Huey."

Ava left an hour or so later, and Elena's work was interrupted by Mila, who came into the office and flung herself into her sister's lap.

"Someone's in a good mood." Elena wheezed, shifting her weight so Mila wasn't crushing her legs. Considering how much taller Mila was than her, it was not a good fit.

"Isn't she the *cutest?*" Mila gushed.

Elena wrapped her arms around Mila's shoulders to hold her up. "Simply adorable. Are you going to ask her out?" she asked.

Mila sighed. "I don't know. Do you think she likes me?"

"Don't be silly. She came to your house less than twelve hours after spending the whole night with you to return your scarf. She obviously likes you!"

"Are you sure, because you thought Jill liked me that one time, and it turned out she wasn't into women."

"Okay, first of all, that was fifteen years ago; you need to let it go," Elena said, pushing the chair back and dumping Mila on the floor. "Second, you two were like dopey teenagers. Just suck it up and do it."

Mila stood, rubbing her butt where she'd hit the floor. "Fine. I will."

"Good. Now get out of here; I need to focus."

Chapter 8

Despite all the hopes of the magical community, another witch hunt broke out before the end of the year. A small town on the opposite side of the country saw a bunch of humans—local teenagers, it turned out—target the lone witch couple that lived there. At least there were no deaths this time, but the humans did burn the witches' house down and beat the couple pretty badly. There wasn't the media coverage that the New Stirling City witch hunt got, but coven leaders were meeting to discuss the concerning uptick in violence.

Although their country was hardly the only one experiencing this problem, they were experiencing it at much higher levels than anywhere else in the world. If things were not brought under control, it would surely spiral and spread across borders and continents. It was a fact they were all painfully aware of. This wasn't just about their own members and communities—the implications stretched to every witch in existence.

The tension in the air was accordingly thick. It always was when the coven leaders got together in general—they didn't trust or particularly like each other most of the time—but this was different.

Technically speaking, the High Witch's Council—an official

branch of the government—oversaw witches in a legal capacity. They were all that remained of an ancient organization that had once been the highest power in magical society. Kieran's ancestors had long held seats on the council, but that tradition was no more. Now, their members were elected by general election, and by law, could not be high-ranking coven officials. However, anyone who really understood the magical community knew that the large covens really controlled things.

Today, the Moonlit Covenant was playing host. Theirs was a coven that, in particular, followed the ancient ways of the so-called Moon Children—witches who worshiped the spirits of the night sky. At least, that was what they claimed. The decorations of their headquarters certainly played up the theme as everything was in shades of dark blue and silver, and moon imagery was everywhere.

It was a bit heavy handed in Kieran's opinion, and he seriously doubted these witches actually were as devoted to the spirits as they claimed, but who was he to judge?

Kieran and his brother Declan stood next to their father outside the meeting chambers door. Of course, it was decorated with an enormous, glittering, arcane symbol of a crescent moon. There was some mingling, and the brothers were currently wrapped up in an intense discussion with a few other witches.

Declan, a bear of man, who was even taller than Kieran and made of solid muscle, dominated the conversation with his booming voice and unshakable confidence. Kieran stood silently, listening and waiting.

"If the humans want a fight, we have to be ready for it," Declan argued.

"This was the action of bored teens out in the middle of nowhere. It doesn't represent humans in general," one of the witches they spoke to said.

Declan laughed bitterly. "Bored teens steal their parents' liquor or play pranks on their teachers. This was an act of extreme violence."

"I have to agree," an older woman from the host coven spoke up. "If their children felt free to behave this way, imagine how deep the hatred for witches runs in their community. This was just one town, but how many others are the same? We need to be able to identify the witches who are on the fringes, perhaps members of small covens or no covens at all, and make sure they are protected."

Kieran turned the words over in his mind, thinking of Elena and her refusal to join them.

"But some witches are inherently distrustful of covens. How do you suggest we convince them to join?" Kieran finally interjected.

"That is the question," a new voice spoke.

Everyone stopped to watch Anthony Andraste walk up to them. Anthony was an older man with gray hair and a carefully manicured beard, looking very distinguished in his tailored suit. He still stood nearly as tall as his sons, and an air of authority followed him wherever he went. Even the leaders from the other covens who were, in theory, just as high-ranking and powerful had trouble meeting Anthony's gaze.

"Come, let us continue this discussion inside. We are about to begin," Anthony said.

The doors opened to reveal a large room with tiered seating so everyone could see each other and be seen. Though officially covens were not required to sit with their own, that ended up happening anyway. Kieran and his family sat in the very front row next to covens they were closely allied with while others did the same throughout the room.

The meeting quickly started, and they dove right back into the topic of the witch hunts. Most of the coven representatives and leaders agreed that building a strong base within their numbers was a good start. They could offer witches protection, and together, all the major covens presenting a united front would be a force to be reckoned with.

Kieran had his doubts.

Elena flashed through his mind again as he contemplated her mistrust of covens and the mysterious death that haunted her. She could hardly be the only one. These days, witches who lived in major cities like New Stirling City rarely, if ever, joined covens. In many rural communities, witches usually kept to themselves, sticking with their small covens that their families had been part of for generations. It wouldn't be as easy as putting out a notice saying "now accepting new members" and waiting for witches to show up.

When Kieran voiced these concerns, many scoffed.

"If they cannot see the writing on the wall, they are fools," one coven leader said. "We are heading for a new witch and human war."

"Fools or not, they are our people. My son is right, many will not want to join us," Anthony said, not speaking loud, and yet, his voice carried throughout the room. "Our numbers have been dwindling over the decades of peace. This was a good sign, evidence that our society had truly put the past behind us, but now, we are facing the unforeseen consequence. Things are only going to get worse. Humans will take every victory and continue to escalate. How soon until they are implementing new laws against us? We only have one witch representative in congress. The High Witch's Council is little more than a figurehead at this point as their influence in the government has shrunk to almost nothing. More must be done to show these witches what a precarious situation we are truly in."

There were mumbles of agreement throughout the room. Kieran didn't like the fearmongering of his father's words. Everyone seemed so certain things would get worse, that conflict with humans was inevitable. Maybe they were right, but maybe there was another way than trying to scare witches into joining them. Fear was a powerful tool. It always had been. But using it against their own people made Kieran feel ill. He knew, however, as he watched the energy of the room escalate as the covens started to debate how best to influence the witches as large, that no one here would listen to him. Because that was the trouble with fear—it could not truly be controlled. It spread like a disease and infected those who wielded it just as much as those they sought to influence.

And there was little doubt that every witch in that room was deeply afraid.

* * *

After the meeting, Kieran decided to go into the office to take his mind off things. To his utter annoyance, Declan followed.

The Andraste family, in the eyes of the world, was mostly known for their real-estate empire. They owned hotels, resorts, and businesses around the world, which amassed them tremendous wealth. Anthony ran the company directly, and both Kieran and Declan held high positions within it. Declan's job was mostly for show as he hired people to do his work for him. Kieran, however, actually took his role seriously. As soon as the brothers entered the modern and luxurious office building in the historic district of New Stirling City, everyone went on high alert. People nodded their heads in respect or darted away altogether.

Declan beamed, greeting people as they passed, while Kieran faced straight ahead. His brother might revel in the attention, but it mostly made Kieran uncomfortable. Once he reached his office, he quickly shut the door and sat at his desk. Declan plopped down in the chair across from him, an irritated look on his face.

"I can't believe you actually came here to work. Doesn't father give us enough to do?"

"Someone needs to keep this company running, and we both know it won't be you."

Declan rolled his eyes, then leaned forward, a mischievous look in his eyes. "So, tell me about that new witch. I heard she turned Charles down."

Kieran shot Declan a withering glare that Declan completely ignored. "Yes, she did."

"Idiot," Declan huffed.

Kieran's temper flared. "She's not an idiot. Elena has perfectly valid reasons to be wary."

"Such as?"

"I didn't ask for details. All I know is she had a bad experience with a coven years ago."

Declan scoffed. "Well, then how do you know it's valid? Maybe she was at fault."

"A member of her family died, Dec. How could that have

been her fault?" Kieran said, not bothering to look at his brother while he focused on the computer screen in front of him.

"I thought you didn't know details," Declan grumbled, but Kieran ignored him.

"Maggie is keeping an eye on her. Elena may change her mind."

"Maggie?" Declan asked, face blank.

Kieran almost groaned. "Maggie Bryne? We've known her since we were kids, Declan."

Realization dawned on Declan's face. "Oh! Red hair? Really chatty?"

"That's the one. You should probably put more effort into getting to know our own coven members by name, if you're going to take over father's position one day."

"Mm." Declan shrugged. "That's what I have you for. We'll lead the coven together, just like we always planned."

Yes, that had been their plan, though their father didn't see it that way. In his mind, Declan was the oldest, and therefore, he would be the coven leader. Anthony was very old-school in that way, determined to continue the traditions of their ancestors. In reality, Kieran assumed it would end up being much how it was now—with Declan being the face of the coven while Kieran did the real work behind closed doors.

The two fell into silence, Declan checking his phone while Kieran read a report on a prospective new location that was for sale.

At least, he tried to.

Elena Hall never seemed to be far from his thoughts these days, and Declan bringing her up brought her front and center. It was deeply humiliating, but Kieran couldn't help himself.

Opening a new tab on his browser, he navigated to his official coven email. After considering for a few moments, he started drafting an email to Maggie.

Dear Maggie,

I hope you are well. One of our members recently acquired a phoenix for the mansion grounds, and I thought you might want to photograph the creature. My father would certainly pay a great amount of money for that portrait.

Kieran paused, trying to decide how not come off too desperate.

How is Elena doing? I hope she hasn't been completely turned off to the coven after her visit. Have you two kept in touch?

In his mind's eye, Kieran could see Maggie laughing at him. But did she know that Elena was really Alys Sinclaire? If she didn't, Kieran couldn't use that fact to defend his behavior. Although Mila had been the one who'd told him, he understood from that interaction that this was not information Elena handed out lightly, and he would not betray her confidence.

Feeling foolish, he hit send.

He barely was able to start reading the report again when a notification popped up, letting him know Maggie had already responded.

Dear Kieran,

Asking about Elena but not her sister was not subtle. They both are doing well, for the record. Honestly, I expect more from you. If you want to ask Elena out, suck it up and do it because this is just tragic.

But on the off chance I am reading your intentions incorrectly, I will say, yes, I speak to Elena fairly regularly, she hasn't mentioned the coven, and as her friend, I would respectfully ask you leave her alone. She said no, and the board needs to respect that.

Kieran didn't know what was more humiliating; the fact Maggie thought he wanted to ask Elena out but was too cowardly to do so, or that he was still keeping track of her on behalf of the coven even though she'd made her wishes clear.

"You all right? You've got that scrunchy look on your face," Declan noted as he looked up from his phone.

"Fine," Kieran mumbled. "These sellers have overpriced this property. They think they can squeeze more out of us than the building is worth."

The lie worked. As soon as Delcan realized it was about business, he stopped listening and went back to his phone.

This gave Kieran the opportunity to go back to his brooding. Thinking Elena would reach out after he gave her his number had been ridiculous. What had he expected? She would cast aside all he'd done to her and beg him to become her friend? In all his observances of the Hall sisters he'd learned they were not the sort of people to care about things like fame or power. They were ordinary people, who valued things like how a person treated others and general kindness. Someone like him was beneath them. Unworthy.

Declan let out a sigh and put his phone away, his gaze on Kieran suddenly intense. "Hey, you talk to that jeweler yet? The one who 'lost' the necklace I ordered for Therese?"

For all his faults, Declan enjoyed spoiling his wife and had truly outdone himself with his recent purchase. The necklace was a rare piece containing jewels that had never been mined, but rather, granted to humanity by the nature spirits directly, many centuries ago when the spirits still deigned to do such things. The powerful and mysterious beings that governed the natural order of their world and granted witches their power in the first place had stopped such direct contact with the magical community a long time ago. That only made Declan's necklace all the more valuable.

It cost a small fortune, but Declan hadn't cared. Only the best for his wife would do. Except, the necklace had never arrived. Suspiciously, the jeweler he'd bought it from claimed the necklace had gone missing in transit and was most likely stolen.

The Andraste family didn't believe him. The extra security that had been placed on this delivery should have easily ensured its safe arrival. As always, Kieran was expected to find out the truth. But with everything else going on, he honestly didn't care. What was a few gems in the face of their people's safety?

"Not yet, I'll get to it."

"Well get to it faster! You know that fucker is lying."

"Why don't you go down there yourself?" Kieran regretted the words the moment they left his mouth.

"Maybe I will. But you're coming with me."

There was a malicious glint in Declan's eyes that could only mean trouble. Kieran desperately hoped the jewelry store had managed to locate the missing necklace, for their own sakes.

"Give them a bit longer. At least until after New Years to find it. They may be telling the truth."

Declan scoffed and rolled his eyes, but the lack of a retort meant he would do as Kieran asked... for now. Seemingly done waiting for his brother to be interesting, Declan left the office. Kieran let out a breath of relief before being distracted by his phone vibrating on his desk.

Picking it up, he saw a new text message .

Hey, Kieran, this is Elena Hall. You gave your number to my sister to pass along? Just wanted to respond so you had my number, too.

Kieran's heart pounded. She'd actually reached out. He had her number now.

All thoughts of witch hunts and thieving jewelers slipped from his mind, and Kieran quickly began typing out a response.

Chapter 9

Elena hadn't attended a therapy session since she moved away from the city, and she was starting to think that was a mistake. Winters were always hard enough on Elena's mental wellbeing, but this year, she was really struggling. Living in the country was more isolating than expected. It was much harder to convince herself to leave the house and interact with the world when that meant getting in her car and driving into town compared with simply having to walk a couple blocks to one of her favorite local haunts.

It was so easy to simply stay in bed and watch the snow fall outside her window most days, her mind stuck on nothing and everything all at once.

Mila wasn't having this problem. Between work and her new girlfriend, she wasn't around as much. The lovely Ava had said yes when Mila finally worked up the courage to ask her out, just as Elena knew she would. Since then, they'd been spending more and more time together as their relationship blossomed.

Elena couldn't complain. She genuinely liked Ava. The woman was funny, smart, kind, and always had an animal story to share. It was easy to talk to her, and on one of the times Mila had brought Ava back to the house for dinner, Elena found herself spilling her heart out about her fraught relationship with her father while Ava listened gravely and commiserated with Elena at every turn.

"After she lost Mila's dad, Mom had a really hard time," Elena had explained. "Ended up getting pregnant on a one-night stand with a guy she met at a party. When she told him she was going to keep me, he informed her he had no desire to be a parent and would pay child support but nothing else. He's barely been part of my life."

"Oh, I'm so sorry," Ava said, gripping Elena's hand tightly. "That must have been so hard. But you know what, it's his loss, because you are an amazing person, and he should be honored that you're his daughter."

Yeah, Elena really liked Ava.

So she hadn't complained that she was the reason Mila wasn't around.

On top of that, Maggie was taking an extended vacation to the tropics for the winter, and Elena hadn't been able to pluck up the courage to ask Alex to hang out, just the two of them, yet. Elena knew she was making things harder for herself, knew she needed to make an effort to get out of this funk but she just... couldn't. Every action seemed utterly impossible, and it was so much easier to do nothing at all.

After another day of rotting away in bed, Elena was startled out of staring at the wall by her phone ringing. Looking at the caller ID, she saw it was her friend from the city, Tora.

She really should answer it.

But she didn't, and the call went to voicemail. Guilt pierced Elena's mental emptiness. Why hadn't she just picked up? She wanted to talk to Tora. Why was she so useless?

A text came through a moment later.

Girl, I know you're there. Pick. Up. The. Phone.

It started ringing again, and this time, Elena managed to answer.

"Hey, sorry about that." Elena's voice sounded croaky and dry to her own ears.

"When was the last time you drank something? Or ate? Or took a shower?" Tora's disapproving tone brought a perfect picture to Elena's mind of her friend's irritated face. Elena had met Tora in elementary school—human elementary school, that was—and they bonded as the only two witches in their class. Witches were still required to go to "normal" school to learn history, math, and all those types of things in addition to their magical training. Their friendship survived all the way to graduation, and Tora had been Elena's roommate in college. After all these years, Tora knew Elena inside and out.

"It's been a while, to answer all those questions." There was no point in lying. If Tora was asking about this, she already knew the answer.

"Babe, talk to me. What's going on? Do you need me to come visit?"

"No, spirits, no. I'm fine. It's just..." Elena's voice wavered, and before she could stop it, everything came pouring out. Her loneliness, the fear that haunted her every time she set foot outside the house, the nightmares...

And Sammi.

"I just miss her so much," Elena choked out through her tears. "And I'm so angry with myself because *I know* she wouldn't want me to live like this, but I can't help it."

"Listen to me." Tora's tone was firm. "You went through something super traumatic, El. That doesn't just go away after a few months, and Sammi would understand, okay? She loved you and would want you to be gentle with yourself. You are not failing. Every day you wake up and choose to keep living is a victory, and if the days aren't going like you hoped, that's okay, too. You can always try again tomorrow."

Huey had his head in Elena's lap and gave a low whine at her distress. Elena pet him—soothing both of them.

"Don't get mad at me, okay?" Elena took a deep breath. "I just feel like it should have been me. Why wasn't it me? Sammi had so much more to live for. She was beautiful, and powerful, and had so much to give the world. And I know that's my survivor's guilt talking, and I know Sammi wouldn't want me to think that way, but I can't stop no matter how hard I try."

Because more than anything, that was what kept Elena up at night. The witch hunt of New Stirling City had killed Saamira, Elena's best friend, when Elena managed to survive. Nothing could ever fix that. Not the government, not the covens, no one. Saamira was gone, and she was never coming back.

"Sammi never should have died," Tora agreed, "but that does not mean you should have taken her place. No one should have died. None of that should have happened. It wasn't a you or her situation. You dying would not have saved her, El. It only would have meant another amazing soul who was so loved was gone."

Elena could do nothing but sob, her grief overwhelming all else. Tora stayed with her on the phone, offering comfort or just letting Elena get it out while listening. When the worst of it passed, Elena felt... lighter. And thirsty. She managed to drag herself downstairs and drank a full glass of water.

"Good," Tora praised when Elena had finished. "Try to

take a shower, okay? And eat something, too. Are you sure you don't want me to come visit?"

"No, please. You can't leave work." Tora was a tattoo artist, and canceling her appointments would be costly. "I'll be okay. I just need to get out there more with my new friends, I think. That way I don't have so much time to be miserable."

"That's the spirit. But I'm still going to look at my schedule and plan to come soon. I miss you."

"I miss you, too."

With Tora's support, Elena did manage to take a shower and scarf down a peanut butter sandwich. After, she called Alex and chatted with him for a while. If he could sense anything was off, he didn't say so and enthusiastically agreed to hang out sometime soon.

After, sitting on the couch and watching TV, it still didn't feel like enough. With Maggie gone, having only Alex wasn't ideal. Though she was hardly an extrovert, Elena was used to having lots of friends in the area she could spend time with.

There was one person she could reach out to, if she was really desperate. Elena opened her phone and looked at the innocuous contact that had remained untouched.

K.A.

With her downward spiral lately, Elena hadn't had the energy to work on her novel at all. Kieran was a fan of her books. Maybe talking to him would help her get back into it. But was it worth willingly inviting him into her life?

Maybe she should start small and just text. That way he had her number, too. She sent him a message and waited with bated breath. Shockingly, it didn't take long for him to respond.

Hello, Elena. I'm so glad to hear from you. I hope you're

enjoying your first winter in Alberdeen. I've heard your sister's shop is doing very well. It always seems to be packed when I stop by to pick up flowers.

Kieran was going to Mila's shop regularly? Mila hadn't mentioned that.

Yes, she's really pleased with how everything is going so far. Elena paused, trying to think of something else to say. *Winter is much more intense than I was expecting, but I'll get used to it.*

Ugh. So lame.

Glad to hear it. If you ever need any help battling the elements, I know some spells that will keep you warm.

Elena gaped at her phone. Was he flirting with her?

For keeping your clothes dry and self-warming gloves, that sort of thing, Kieran quickly added. *Just let me know.*

A smile spread over Elena's lips. He was far less intimidating over text, and this seemed like an okay start.

Thanks. I'll keep that in mind.

* * *

The remaining week of the year was a bit easier. Tora called her every day to talk about everything and nothing. Elena suspected Tora had also told Mila what was going on as Mila started having her dates with Ava in the house so Elena wouldn't be alone so much. Elena hated being a burden, but having her sister around made life so much more bearable.

It was on one of those dates when Ava invited Mila to a party at her favorite bar in a nearby town for New Year's Eve. She'd asked Elena to come as well, but Elena declined, citing that she had her own plans. Mila gave Elena a suspicious look over

Ava's head, and when Ava left, Mila confronted Elena about it.

"What are you really doing for New Year's?" Mila asked as Elena was about to head upstairs for bed.

"Don't jump down my throat, but I'm just going to stay here," Elena said, preparing for her sister's disapproval.

"So, your plan is to sit alone in the dark, and what? Drink wine and stare out the window?" Mila asked sarcastically.

Elena sighed. "No! Alex is going to come over for a bit before going to the mansion party they are having, and I'm going to video chat Tora before she does go out, and then, yes, I'll watch movies until midnight."

"But why? Why not come out with us?"

Elena hesitated, then decided to be honest. "Because, and this is nothing against Ava, but large groups of drunk, loud humans make me nervous, and I don't want to spend my New Year's stressed out." Reminding Mila of her fear of humans always made Elena uncomfortable, but sometimes it was necessary.

"Oh," Mila said, visibly deflating. "That makes sense. We could always stay in with you?"

Elena shook her head. "No. Go out and have fun. I'll be fine." She offered Mila her best attempt at a reassuring smile, but Mila didn't look convinced. Not wanting to discuss it any further, Elena walked up the stairs, Huey on her heels.

New Year's Eve dawned, cold but clear, with good weather reported for the rest of the night. There'd been an ice storm the day before, but the roads had been cleaned up pretty quickly.

"Call me if you need a designated driver," Elena said to Mila as she made her final preparations to leave. Mila looked stunning in a tight, silver, sequined dress that hit her curves in all the right places.

"I will," Mila promised, throwing on a coat. "Try to have some fun, okay? I'll text you when I get to Ava's place."

Alex came over a few minutes after Mila left, and the two ate a short dinner. Thankfully, hanging out with him alone wasn't awkward at all, and Alex spent most of the time chatting about the party he was going to at the coven mansion.

"Will the Andrastes be there?" Elena asked, midway through one of his monologues about the various witches who he hoped to see.

"They usually make an appearance as a family early in the night, though the guys never stick around. They have their own parties to attend somewhere fabulous and surrounded by other rich people. Why?" Alex asked, eyeing her suspiciously.

Elena shrugged. "Just curious."

There hadn't been any further texts from Kieran since initial contact, and it was starting to make Elena think she'd completely misread him.

Alex left shortly after, wearing an outrageous green and gold tuxedo, the magical door to the mansion appearing in Elena's driveway like it had last fall. After a brief video chat with Tora, Elena settled on the couch in her softest sweatpants and a hoodie, ready to watch her favorite movie to usher in the new year. As the minutes went by, however, a feeling of unease began to grow in her stomach.

It was hard to tell what exactly the cause was at first. In the past, Elena had never had a problem discerning her intuition about bad things versus her anxiety, but ever since the witch hunt, the anxiety was so much worse that she struggled to tell the two apart.

As the minutes ticked by, Elena tried to meditate a bit on what could be upsetting her. Huey was fine. In fact, he was in a deep sleep on his bed in the corner of the room. Her mind drifted to Tora, then Maggie, then Alex, but none of that stirred any negative feelings.

Mila.

Just picturing her sister's face made Elena's heart start pounding. Mila wasn't an idiot, and would never drive drunk, and was perfectly safe as a human out with other humans. There was no reason to be worried about her. But still...

Elena took out her phone at eleven-thirty and texted her sister.

Hey, everything going all right?

She waited for a response nervously.

Yeah it is! Are you doing okay? Mila responded after a minute or two

Elena sighed in relief, although the bad feeling did not go away. *Yup! Just checking in.*

Elena put the phone down and tried to focus on the movie she was watching, but her mind would not settle. Midnight came and went, and still Elena could not stop the nagging feeling like a scratching at the back of her head.

Pulling herself off the couch, she began obsessively cleaning the kitchen. There was no way she would be able to sleep until she'd heard Mila was safely at Ava's place. When her phone vibrated while she was folding laundry, Elena nearly jumped out of her skin diving to see what the new text said.

One of Ava's friends needs her, so I'm coming home. Yes, I'm sober. Will be there soon.

Elena let out a breath. Okay, so she was coming home. That was a good thing, right? Elena could see Mila in person and know everything was fine.

OK. Be safe. I have a weird feeling.

Everything was fine. Soon, Mila would be home, and they would talk about her night. Elena would find out what the drama with Ava's friend was, and everything would be fine.

Huey had woken up a while ago and now sat near the front door, sensing Elena's fears over Mila. A few moments passed while Elena continued to fold laundry before Huey leapt to his feet in a panic, whirling around to look at Elena, who dropped the shirt she was holding, and stared blankly at the wall in sheer terror.

Mila was in trouble.

Every cell in her body, every bit of magic she had, was screaming that she needed to get to her sister *now*.

In a heartbeat, Elena was on her feet, throwing on her coat and boots and running out the door, Huey right behind her. There was no time to drive; she needed to get to Mila. Acting on pure instinct, she threw her hand out in front of her and a portal—a blinding blue light that ripped open in space—burst to life in front of them. The pair sprinted through, appearing in pitch blackness.

Elena looked around wildly, then spotted what she was looking for. They were on the side of a road in the middle of nowhere. A few feet away, Mila's car was crumpled against an ancient tree, smoke floating from the engine, and the headlights flickering.

"Mila!" Elena screamed, running toward the car.

Huey got there first and, with a burst of his own magical power, ripped the driver's door right off the car with his teeth. Elena rushed forward and reached into the dark, finding her sister. Mila's skin was cold, and Elena let out a sob.

"No, no. Please, don't be gone." She couldn't do this again. She couldn't lose Mila. Flashes of screams and the smell of gunfire swarmed Elena's mind, but taking a deep breath, she fought against them.

Mila let out a groan. She was still alive.

Elena hadn't been able to save Sammi. Back then, she'd been overpowered and bound, helpless against her attackers, but not now. Now, she was in control, and she would not lose her sister.

With a flick of Elena's wrist, a ball of light appeared above Mila's head.

She was unconscious, and blood was trickling down her face from a large gash in her forehead. The airbag had gone off on impact, but Elena realized a tree branch had broken through the windshield and struck Mila in the face. Adrenaline coursing through her veins, Elena ripped off the seat belt holding Mila with another spell and dragged her sister out of the wreck. Her hands flitted over Mila's body as she sank into the snow, Mila laying in her lap.

Panic surged again. Elena didn't know if Mila's bones were broken or if her insides were bleeding. The magical scan she was attempting on Mila's body wasn't working. She couldn't tell. She had no idea how to help.

Elena let out a strangled cry of frustration as her magic completely failed her once more. Now there was no one to blame but herself. This was her failing—*hers*—and Mila would pay the price, just like Sammi. Huey huddled closely to Mila's body to keep her warm, and nudged Elena's arm.

Right, right. She could call for help.

Elena shoved her hand into her sweatpants pocket and pulled out her phone. She was about to dial the emergency number when another thought came to her, and without any hesitation, she called a different number instead. She didn't need human paramedics who would take ages to get there; she needed a witch who could heal Mila right now.

Almost immediately, the person on the other end picked up.

"Hello?" Kieran Andraste's voice came through the phone.

"Please, help me!" Elena gasped. "I'm on Cavalier Road, I think, outside Spring Glenn. Mila was in a car accident. She's unconscious, and I can't do anything."

Just as she managed to get the words out, a portal appeared in front of her, and Kieran stepped through. There was no time to marvel at how he'd found them so easily as he shoved his phone into his pocket, assessing the situation, then dropped to his knees beside them as the portal closed.

"Let me see her," he commanded, though not harshly.

Elena leaned back so Kieran could get a better look, the light she summoned illuminating Mila's lifeless face. Kieran's hands moved over Mila's body, finally settling on a spot in her abdomen. The pounding of Elena's heart in her ears drowned out everything else, and her stomach churned and twisted while she waited for Kieran to speak.

"She's going to be okay," he muttered, then looked up at Elena's panicked face. "She is okay," he repeated more forcefully.

Elena didn't respond, not ready to believe him, and watched as Kieran began to heal Mila's body.

"There's a concussion, a broken bone, and some internal bleeding, but it's nothing I can't fix."

Elena felt sick at the words "internal bleeding," but held Mila still so Kieran could work. After a minute or two on her stomach, he moved to Mila's ankle, and Elena heard a sickening crack of a bone being forcefully mended, before he moved on to her head. After a few more agonizing moments, Kieran let out a breath and sat backward, his hand shaking as he raised it to wipe some sweaty hair out of his face.

Mila took a deep breath and opened her eyes. "What happened?" she asked, her voice hoarse.

Elena let out a little gasp and pulled Mila in closer.

"You were in an accident," Kieran explained, getting to his feet unsteadily.

Mila took in the sight of her ruined car, her eyes wide. "I remember," she gasped. "There was a deer. I swerved so I wouldn't hit it and—" Her voice broke, her hands grasping at Elena's arms. Mila turned to look at Elena, and Elena ran her hands over Mila's face, wiping away the blood that ran over Mila's eyes.

"How do you feel?" Elena asked, sniffling.

Mila stared at her, dazed. "I–I don't know."

"You're likely in shock," Kieran said, dialing a number on his phone. "Your body has been through a lot in the last few minutes. Be still for now."

He put the phone up to his ear and began to speak into it. Elena was vaguely aware that he was asking for a tow for the car, but she could barely pay attention over the storm of emotions she was feeling as she looked into Mila's face. Her sister, her best friend, the only family she had left—what would Elena have done without her?

The sisters sat in the snow, holding each other while Kieran wrapped up his call. Hanging up, Kieran watched them for a second before he cautiously approached.

"Let me get you home. Sitting out here in the cold won't be

good for either of you," he said softly, holding out a hand.

Hesitantly, Mila took it, and he guided the pair of them to their feet.

"My car..." Mila said, still sounding slightly dazed.

"A mechanic is coming to take care of it. One of us. He'll have it good as new by tomorrow," Kieran said, keeping a steadying hand on Mila's shoulder. With his other hand, he opened a portal leading right to Mila and Elena's front door. The sisters walked through, Kieran and Huey behind them. As the portal closed, Kieran led them into the house. Elena sat Mila down on the couch and looked at her in the full light.

Mila's face was splattered with blood, her coat soaked with melted snow, and her beautiful dress was ripped at the shoulder. Her skin was ashen and grayed, her eyes still wide in shock. Kieran put a hand on Elena's arm and led her away for a moment.

"Clean her up and get her warm. It will take a few hours for her body to adjust from the trauma. Just stay with her, and she'll be fine. Try to get her to drink and eat something in the morning," he told her.

Elena nodded, looking down at her hands, which had streaks of red on them from when she'd wiped Mila's face.

"Hey," Kieran said, squeezing her shoulder lightly.

She looked up at him, her eyes swimming in tears.

"Are you going to be okay?"

"Yeah, I just..." She didn't know what to say.

Kieran hesitated, then gently wiped a stray tear from Elena's cheek with his thumb. "I know, it's a lot. But it's over now. She's safe."

Elena looked up at him again. "Thank you so much," she said, her voice thick with emotion. "I don't know how I can ever repay you for this."

Kieran smiled softly at her. "Don't tell anyone at the coven, and we can call it even, okay?" He tucked a lock of hair behind Elena's ear then stood back.

Elena's entire body felt numb, but she still registered the loss of contact between them. With one more smile, Kieran left the house and vanished into the night. Forcing more air into her lungs, Elena hurried back to Mila and pulled her into her arms again.

The rest of the night passed in agonizing slowness. Mila remained silent and still as Elena cleaned her up and changed her into comfortable, dry clothes. Elena texted Ava from Mila's phone, telling her she was home safe, feeling guilty about the lie but knowing it was one they would have to keep for now.

Elena tried to get Mila to drink some water, but she refused, and so instead, she guided Mila to her bedroom and tucked her into bed. Huey jumped up on the bed in front of Mila and lay down while Elena crawled in behind her, holding Mila around her middle. Mila took a shuddering breath and began to cry, her soft sobs filling the dark room.

"It's okay," Elena said in her ear, her own tears returning. "It's okay."

Huey whined and snuggled up as close as he could to Mila, and to Elena's surprise, Mila wrapped an arm around the dog, burying her face into his thick fur. That was how they stayed for the rest of the night, until sleep finally took Mila, and her grip on Huey's fur relaxed.

Elena did not sleep, however. How could she? Her sister almost died. She could have lost her. She might have, if Kieran hadn't come to their aid so quickly. There was internal bleeding and brain damage. Who knew what would have happened without magical intervention, intervention Elena could not provide.

What if Kieran hadn't answered? He could have been asleep, he could have been drunk at a party. Most witches they knew probably were. Elena would have been on her own, and Mila might not have made it. Her own inadequacy could have killed her sister.

As the sun slowly peeked through the windows several hours later, Elena made a decision. She would never let her sister be in danger like that again.

Chapter 10

Elena waited as long as she could stand it before calling Kieran. At eight in the morning, she crept out of bed and into the kitchen. Nervous, she got herself a cup of water and sipped, hoping to give her exhausted mind some nourishment. Then, her phone gripped tightly in her hand, she called him.

Just like a few hours earlier, Kieran's response was almost immediate. "Elena? Is something wrong?" he asked, his voice raspy.

"No, no," Elena quickly assured him, "I'm sorry for calling so early, but I couldn't sleep. After what happened last night, I—" Her voice cracked. She cleared her throat and plowed on. "I realized you were right. I need to learn how to use my magic correctly so I can protect the people I care about. I want to join the coven."

There was a moment of silence before Kieran responded.

"I'm happy to hear that, Elena, truly I am, but I want to make sure you've thought this through."

Elena, in her exhausted state, could barely do anything other than gape at her empty kitchen. "What do you mean? I thought you wanted me to join."

"I do, but..." He hesitated. "You just went through something traumatic. I wouldn't want you to make a reactionary decision that you would end up regretting. Joining a coven is a commitment, one I'm sure you've been taught is not easily backed out of."

Elena chewed on her lip, digesting this. It was a valid point. After all, she was going against a lifetime of messaging drilled into her brain by her mother. Joining a coven wasn't like signing up for a social club. A part of your magic would belong to them, to be used however they saw fit in the name of protecting the coven. There were rules that needed to be followed, and if you were given an order by your coven leaders, you were expected to follow. The High Witch's Council had made it illegal in the last century for covens to forcefully stop their members from leaving, but that didn't mean they hadn't worked out loopholes since then.

But none of that mattered. Magic was more important than all of that. Magic could have broken Mila's father's curse. It could have saved Sammi if any of the witches at the witch hunt had been strong enough to wield it while being attacked. Magic was what saved Mila. Elena was done living life as a weak witch who lived at the mercy of others' power.

"I hear what you're saying," Elena said, "and I appreciate the concern, but I've made up my mind."

"All right. If you want, I can get in touch with Charles and set up the entry interview for Monday."

"Entry interview?" Elena asked, rubbing her eye with the back of her hand while suppressing a yawn.

"It's basically an informal background check, just to get to know you a little bit better. Don't worry, it's extremely confidential. Only two board members are present, and a strong protection spell binds your privacy. No other members, including myself and my family, are privy to the details of the interview," he explained.

"I don't love that, but I guess I'll have to deal with it," Elena conceded.

"Good. I'll reach out to Charles later today. I suspect he's passed out right now. The party at the mansion didn't end 'till four in the morning from what I heard."

"Right, and Kieran..." Elena hesitated again, not sure how she could ever communicate how grateful she was for his help in words.

"It's okay, Elena," Kieran said. "I'll text you with the details later. Try to get some sleep."

"Okay. And I'm sorry for waking you up."

"I was already awake," Kieran said.

Elena's eyebrows rose. "Really?"

"I don't sleep much. Usually only three or four hours a night," he told her.

Elena's brain almost imploded trying to grasp that idea, so instead, she moved on. "That sounds horrible. But I'm sorry for the early call, all the same. I'll talk to you soon."

She heard him chuckle. "Goodbye, Elena."

He hung up.

Elena took a deep, shaky breath. It was done. A lifetime of warnings drilled into her by her mother tossed down the drain.

But Elena's world was different from her mother's. Threats were all around, and Elena had failed yet another test of her power. She could not afford to fail again.

* * *

It felt like an eternity before Mila stirred. Elena forced herself to eat a banana and drink some water before she returned to Mila's room, keeping watch over her sister's sleeping form. When Mila did wake, she was still curled around Huey, who dutifully stayed with her all night long. Elena immediately darted to Mila's side as Mila coughed out a few dog hairs. Huey turned to lick her face, his tail wagging almost uncertainly.

"Are you okay?" Elena asked quietly.

Mila didn't respond, instead flipping onto her back and covering her face with her hands. Elena remained silent, letting Mila process.

"I think so? I just keep thinking about the accident. It happened so fast," Mila croaked. "One minute, everything was fine, the next, there was a deer, and I was spinning out."

Elena saw a tear slip down Mila's cheek, and her heart clenched painfully.

"How do you feel now?" Elena asked, wrapping an arm gently around Mila's waist.

Mila shifted. "I'm... not sure," she said, dropping her hands. "I don't feel real. Like my body isn't connected to my mind anymore." She looked at Elena. "Nothing hurts," she quickly assured her, "but I just feel weird."

Huey gave a low whine, nuzzling her shoulder with his fluffy head. Mila turned to him, then—Elena watched in amazement—her face screwed up as she began to cry. Mila pulled Huey close, burying her face in his fur.

"Thank you," she croaked, her voice so hoarse it was barely recognizable.

Huey's tail thumped happily against the mattress, and he let out a low grunt Elena could sense was full of affection.

After an apparently much-needed cuddle session, Mila

finally broke away from Huey and sat up. "What time is it?" she asked.

"Almost noon."

Mila squinted at Elena, and her lips twitched. "Did you sleep at all?" she asked.

"No?" Elena frowned. "Why?"

"You look a little bit unhinged."

Elena let the insult slide, reaching out to help Mila up. Mila took her arms and gingerly pulled herself out of bed, testing her own weight on her legs. Seemingly satisfied she wasn't going to collapse, Mila took a few hesitant steps toward the door.

"Kieran said you should eat something and get plenty of liquids," Elena began. "I can make you food?"

"Kieran?" Mila asked, confused.

"You remember Kieran being there last night... don't you?" Elena asked, suddenly terrified that Mila was suffering memory loss.

"Oh, right. No, of course I remember," Mila quickly said. "Sorry, I just need to clear my head, I think."

Elena nodded fervently. "I'll make you breakfast. Why don't you go to the bathroom."

After making sure Mila made it to the bathroom okay, Elena went to the kitchen and threw together a breakfast sandwich and a very large glass of water. When Mila returned, Elena examined her closely. Mila looked normal, for the most part. Her face was still a bit puffy, and there were dark circles under her eyes, but otherwise no trace of the accident.

"Eat," Elena commanded, steering Mila down onto a stool at the kitchen island.

Mila went for the water first. As she started her breakfast,

Elena picked dog hairs off Mila's face and arms.

Mila didn't react to Elena's poking and prodding at all, her mind clearly far away as she ate. When she was done, Elena dumped the dishes in the sink.

"I'm gonna shower," Mila said. "You should get some sleep, El. I promise, I'm fine."

Elena did not go to sleep. Taking up Mila's spot at the island, she waited, staring at the wall, for Mila to be done. Her mind completely revolted whenever she considered doing something else. Until she was completely sure Mila was okay, she couldn't rest or eat or manage any other task at all.

When Mila emerged almost an hour later, Elena nearly jumped out of the seat to run to her.

Mila was dressed in fresh clothes, her hair twirled into an old T-shirt on top of her head. Her skin was clean and glowing. "So, could you help with this?" Mila asked, holding up a bottle of hair oil. "I tried, but my arms wouldn't cooperate."

"Of course!" Elena gushed, taking the bottle and leading Mila to the couch.

Mila perched on the edge, and Elena settled in behind her. Carefully removing the T-shirt, Elena let Mila's braids down. Separating them out into sections, Elena dabbed a little bit of the oil onto her fingertips and began to massage it into the exposed areas of Mila's scalp. Moving section by section, Elena gently worked the oil into Mila's skin. They remained silent, soaking in each other's presence. Mila sighed, the tension slowly leaving her body. Elena thought back to all the times their mother had done this for Mila when she was a teenager. Elena would sit on the floor and watch, trying to distract Mila and make her laugh, until her mother would shoo her away.

When they got older, when both of them had moved out of their mom's house and were out on their own, they would meet up and do this for each other, ranting about the stress of being adults.

Mila's phone, which was sitting next to her, flashed with a notification, drawing both of their attention. Elena peered over Mila's shoulder as Mila opened the text message. Right after the text Elena had sent last night to assure Ava that Mila got home safe was a new one.

Glad you got home safe! You are missing a real shit-show here. Text me when you wake up! XO.

Mila let out a shuddering breath.

All her fingers still in Mila's hair, Elena angled her sister's head back and kissed her forehead. "It's gonna be okay. You can call her later."

"Yeah," Mila muttered.

Elena hesitated, leaning back and picking up the T-shirt to squeeze some spare water out of Mila's braids. Ava presented another problem. What were they going to tell her? She was nice enough, but she was human.

"Listen, when you do talk to her, you can't tell her about what happened."

Mila's entire body went rigid. "What?"

"I mean, you got in an accident and have no physical proof to show for it. I like Ava, but we can't trust her yet, about, you know..." She trailed off.

Mila nodded, wiping her eyes. "Of course. She can't know you're a witch yet. I won't say anything." Mila turned around all the way. "You should get some sleep, El."

"What? No! I want to stay with you," Elena complained.

Mila rolled her eyes. "I'll be fine. Please go to sleep, for me?"

"Let's watch TV!" Elena snatched the remote off the couch arm and turned on the TV. The news came on, and both sisters stared at all the bright red banners and horrific images flashing across the screen.

"In breaking news, a riot at our country's capital spoiled the New Year's Eve celebration as anti-witch protesters stormed the home of Senator Margaret Lorch, one of a small handful of public witch members of Congress. Although the protesters could not gain access to the property, they set fire to cars on the street, ripped down signposts, and caused other property damage to the neighborhood. Police were able to gain control of the situation shortly after three a.m., and reportedly ten arrests were made. The senator has yet to release a statement, and we have been told there were no injuries.

This event is another in a slew of anti-witchcraft hate crimes that have increased over the last few years. Tensions have been running high since the witch hunt in New Stirling City last spring, which left thirteen witches dead—"

Mila snatched the remote out of Elena's hand and turned off the TV, her entire body shaking. Elena could barely think, barely breathe. Her entire mind went blank. On the floor next to them, Elena was vaguely aware of Huey whining and trembling.

"Go to sleep, El," Mila whispered. "It's going to be okay. Just go to sleep."

Nodding, Elena got to her feet, feeling as if she was on autopilot. Moving slowly, she made her way upstairs. Huey followed behind, misery radiating out of him. When Elena made it to her room, she collapsed onto the mattress and wept. Before long, the utter exhaustion of the previous night caught up with her, and Elena fell into a fitful sleep.

* * *

Elena woke, completely oblivious to Mila standing over her and poking her gently.

"Wha—" Elena gasped out, blinking rapidly. "Where am I?"

Mila chuckled. "You're in your room, and it's past dinner time. I would have let you sleep longer, but I wanted to make sure you ate something."

Elena sat up and scrutinized her sister, noting that Mila looked much more like her normal self.

"I'll be down in a minute," Elena said, yawning. Her eyes were dry, and her head was fuzzy from sleeping all day long. A quick trip to the bathroom helped, but still, Elena didn't feel right as the grief and anxiety returned in full force. It was time to tell Mila what she'd decided about the coven. It was a decision that affected both of them, and Elena hoped her sister wasn't going to push back on it like Kieran had.

When she did arrive downstairs, she found a sandwich waiting for her and Mila sitting at the kitchen island, staring blankly at her phone. Mila smiled in greeting and patted the stool next to her. They sat in silence while Elena ate, the tension in the air thick. Once she was done, Mila whisked the plate away, and the two stood there, staring at each other.

"Look, um," Mila began, not sure what to say.

"We don't have to talk about it, if you don't want to," Elena assured her.

Mila shook her head. "You saved my life, El."

Bitterness practically choked Elena's throat. "No, Kieran

did," Elena said flatly. "If it weren't for him, I don't know what would have happened."

"You would've saved me anyway, I know you would have," Mila said, walking around the counter and taking one of Elena's hands.

Elena shook her head. "No, I wouldn't have. I got there, and you were injured, and I had *no idea* how to heal you on my own!" she said, her voice rising.

Mila gripped her hand tighter. "You got to me," she said simply. "You knew I was in danger, and you came. How did you even do that?"

"I summoned a portal," Elena admitted. She hadn't thought about it at all since it happened, but now, she turned that moment over in her mind when she'd summoned the portal out of pure instinct and fear. There was no skill or intention behind it. Just because she'd done it once didn't mean she could do it again in an emergency.

"You've never been able to do that before! Elena, that's a really big deal. You knew I needed you, and you found a way to get to me," Mila said, her eyes filling with tears again.

Elena shook her head. "It wasn't enough. I wasn't enough, and that is why..." She took a deep breath and looked up to meet Mila's eye. "I'm going to join the Greenwood Coven."

Mila eyes widened. "Really?" she gasped out.

Elena nodded. "You were right. This entire time, you were right. I need to know how to do these things. I get why Mom raised me like she did, but I can't be caught off guard again. I need help, and the coven can help me—can help both of us."

Mila pulled Elena into a hug. "I know this is hard, but you're doing the right thing," she assured her.

Elena hugged her back, breathing in her familiar scent. "I

hope so."

Chapter 11

Kieran scheduled Elena's entry interview as promised and made sure to throw in another comment saying she could change her mind if she wanted to. Elena did not change her mind, although the knowledge of what she would have to reveal haunted her. The witch hunt would come up. It had to. Elena never talked about it with anyone if she could help it, and the prospect of having to discuss it with strangers was making her feel ill.

The following Monday, the portal to the mansion opened in front of her house yet again, but this time, Maggie wasn't by her side to help.

Elena walked through it with Huey, who had also been invited. They emerged on the other side to see Charles waiting for them in the magical garden Elena had entered through on her first visit. He was joined by a woman Elena didn't recognize.

"Hello, Elena," Charles said, half smiling. "How are you today?"

"I'm good, and you?" she asked politely, returning the handshake. Hopefully, Charles didn't notice how clammy and cold her hands were or the way they trembled when he released her. Even though her mind was made up, something in her brain was screaming at her to turn around and run away. This was very clearly anxiety rather than intuition, as Elena felt the same way about going to the dentist or doing an interview, but the knowledge that, once again, her mind was overreacting didn't make this entire thing easier.

"Very well! And you must be the familiar, Huey." Charles smiled, seemingly unaware of Elena's inner turmoil, offering his hand for Huey to sniff. "This is my fellow board member, Sarah Lorch."

"Lorch?" Elena asked, the name ringing a bell.

The older woman smiled, nodding.

"Indeed! And yes, before you ask, my sister is the senator."

Right. The Senator whose home had been attacked on New Year's Eve by humans.

"I was so sorry to hear about what happened," Elena said genuinely. "I hope your sister and her family are all right."

"Well enough, given the circumstances," Sarah said stiffly. "It's a dark time for all of us."

"Yes, I do admit what happened is what finally changed my mind about joining," Elena lied. She'd promised Kieran she would keep the accident, and his role in helping them, a secret from the coven. Elena intended to keep that promise.

"I understand completely," Sarah said.

"Come, let's head inside." Charles gestured toward the mansion, and the four of them headed out of the garden, Huey staying close to Elena's side. The grounds were a winter wonderland, the snow perfect and sparkling, each tree and bush decorated with twinkling lights and colorful baubles.

"It's beautiful!" Elena gasped, despite herself.

Charles smiled, pleased. "Yes, we put quite a lot of work into the upkeep of the grounds. The decorating committee will be happy to hear of your approval."

They reached the magnificent front doors, which opened to let them in. The grand hall was similarly decorated and managed to have a warm and cheerful atmosphere.

"This way," Charles directed, leading Elena and Huey across the hall and up the grand staircase. Charles led them through the mansion to his office, and they stepped inside. As they did, Elena felt a slight buzzing over her skin that she recognized as passing through the barrier of a spell.

A tapestry depicting a famous legend of nature spirits gifting the first humans magic hung on the wall. Behind the desk was a large group photo of the coven that appeared fairly recent. Elena recognized Kieran standing near the back before Sarah bid her to sit down.

Sinking into a chair, Elena nervously pet Huey's head, who was still keeping close to her side. This was real. This was happening. Elena was going to sit there and spill her life story to these powerful witches so she could gain access to their coven, and more importantly, their resources. Part of Elena felt detached from the entire situation, like she was an observer watching from the sidelines. How could it have come to this?

But a flash of Mila's face steeled Elena's resolve. It was time to see this through.

Sarah and Charles positioned themselves in the chairs across from her, and Charles cleared his throat.

"So, Elena, I'm not sure how much Mr. Andraste told you about the onboarding process, so I'll give you an overview," he paused. "We are here to conduct the entry interview. We will cover your personal and familial history to ensure you are not a threat to the coven in any way. Anything you tell us will not leave this room. The magical spell we just entered through protects your privacy by making us unable to repeat the details outside of those present without your permission. Is this acceptable to you?" he asked.

Elena nodded, not trusting her voice. Huey patted his front paw in the air, trying to get Charles's attention.

"Ah, yes, Huey, I did not forget you," Charles said, smiling at the dog. "After the interview we will set you up with access to the familiar's portal, which will allow you to travel to the mansion even when Elena is not with you, should you wish."

Huey huffed then lay down in response to this news. At least he was satisfied. While Charles spoke, Sarah pulled out a pad of paper and a pen, which balanced perfectly on the paper without her touching it.

"Do we have your permission to begin, Elena?" Charles asked.

"Yes," Elena replied, managing to keep her voice even.

"To start, please identify the immediate members of your family, living and deceased."

Elena cleared her throat. "My half-sister is Mila Hall, she lives with me and is not magical," Elena began. As she spoke, the pen on the paper in Sarah's lap began to move across the page, taking notes. "Our mother was Laurel Hall, she passed ten years ago from witch's cancer."

"And your father?" Charles prompted.

"William Everett."

"The archaeologist?" Sarah asked, her eyebrows shooting up on her forehead. It was a common reaction whenever Elena was willing to speak her father's name out loud. Archaeologists in the magical world were much more household names than they were to humans due to their unique relationship with spirits, and her father was one of the most famous alive.

Elena nodded. "Yup. He's never been a part of my life though. My mother met him at a party and had no relationship outside that one night. He sent her money to help raise me, and I hear from him once or twice a year, but that's it."

Sarah tutted to herself, shaking her head. "And your sister's father, tell us about him."

"He was a human named Albert Hall. He and my mother were married. My mother gave me his last name so we would all match." An act of foresight Elena had always been grateful for. Legally, it made things easier for children and their mother to share a last name, but Elena never wanted to be an Everett after the way her father had treated her.

"And he is deceased, is that correct?" Charles asked.

"Yes. He—" Her voice failed her, and she cleared it again. "Unbeknownst to my mother, her coven had cursed Albert, so healing magic was useless on him. He was in a car accident while on a business trip. My mother was with Mila—she was only two at the time—at their home, and he was on the other side of the country. He died at the hospital before she could get there. A witch was on staff on the hospital, but by the time they figured out why their spells weren't working to save him it was too late."

Elena felt her body going numb but held herself together. Mila had nearly died the exact same way. Statistically, more humans died in car accidents than any other manner, but that didn't make the coincidence any less jarring.

"And then you were born three years later?"

"Correct."

"You mentioned, previously, you were home educated in the matters of magic by your mother, and she refused to let you join a coven. Could you expand on that?"

Where to start? The story of her mother's history with covens ended with her becoming a widow, but it stretched back farther than that.

"My mother had a difficult time with covens over the years. Her birth coven she left because they asked her to participate in a ritual that would involve hurting humans. That was over two hundred years ago now, when she was young," Elena clarified, involuntarily clenching the arm of her chair as she spoke. "The second coven she joined because her boyfriend at the time convinced her to, but they put a lot of pressure on her to get married and have children, so she left that one, too. Her final coven threatened her when she decided to marry Albert."

The dull pang of old anger and resentment tightened Elena's chest as she recounted all the injustices her mother had faced. Truly, how could anyone blame her for raising her daughter how she had?

"They didn't approve of her being involved with a human?" Sarah asked.

"They demanded she break up with him, and when she refused, they pretended to accept it. But when he got in that car accident, she sensed it, and begged her coven, who had members in the area of the crash, to go help him, but was refused. They left him to die."

Charles shook his head. "Terrible business. I can assure you we have zero tolerance for that sort of thing here," Charles said. "Please continue."

The tightness threatened to choke Elena's words. This coven was not her mother's coven, she reminded herself. She'd called Kieran, and he'd come. He'd saved Mila. Thinking of Kieran and the care he'd given Mila, Elena managed to take a deep breath and force herself to continue speaking.

"After Albert died, my mother struggled on her own, but as I got older, she decided she never wanted me to go through what she went through." And here Elena sat, feeding herself to the wolves. But this would be different. It had to be.

"So, she educated you at home," Charles commented. "How did that go?

Elena stared at a picture behind Charles's head so she wouldn't have to make eye contact, heat crawling up her neck. "It was... difficult, for both of us. My mother was many things, but a good teacher was not one of them, and I was admittedly not the best student when I was a kid. She refused to ask other witches for help. I think she didn't want to admit she couldn't do it all—raise me and teach me how to be a witch outside the support of a coven, on her own."

"Hm," Charles looked displeased but continued on, "And you were raised in New Stirling City?"

"Yes."

"Why did you decide to leave after all this time?"

Elena felt she might actually throw up and looked away from them, down at Huey, who sat up and put his head in her lap.

"Well, you are aware of the witch hunt that happened last year?"

"Of course, dear," Sarah said kindly.

Elena's hands shook, and she clasped them together to control herself. The urge to flee was overwhelming, but she had to do this—had to face it.

"I was there," she said without emotion, her blood pounding in her ears as she tried to keep her voice neutral. *Numb, stay numb*, she told herself. Elena felt like her chest was caving in. Every breath became a struggle.

Sarah lifted a hand to her mouth, and Charles sat back.

"Oh my. Elena, we had no idea," he said.

"The High Witch's Council did a lot of work to protect the identities of the victims who survived," she mumbled. "I lost my best friend that day and was nearly killed myself. Afterward, Mila and I decided it was time to leave the city."

Sarah nudged Charles with her foot, giving him a pointed look, and he nodded.

"We don't need to discuss it any further," he said quickly.

Elena pursed her lips, still not looking up. Maybe this was a mistake. Why was she ripping herself open for these people? It was none of their business. Huey licked her hand, love and adoration flowing down their bond to her.

"We can take a break, if you need, Elena," Sarah offered.

Elena took a deep breath, remembering Mila's bloodied face. She could face this. The worst was over, and they weren't making her go into detail. Mila needed her.

"No, it's fine. What else do you need to know?" she asked.

"Just some background about your career and how you acquired Huey."

* * *

The interview wrapped up quickly, and Charles and Sarah led them out of the room and to the kitchen for some refreshments. In the months since the witch hunt, Elena had only spoken about what happened to her therapist, and even then, it was hard. Now, after having to discuss it with two strangers, she was left shaken and feeling almost hungover in the aftermath of all that adrenaline coursing through her veins. After the break they had Elena review an extensive list of rules she had to agree to. They were mostly straight forward such as no stealing from the coven or revealing private information about the coven to non members, but others seemed a bit archaic. For example one included a clause about not using your fellow member's livestock for blood rituals without their permission.

Nothing seemed alarming to Elena so she agreed to it all and they moved on. All that was left was to get through Huey's part of the day and they would be able to go home.

A young man named Ned set Huey up to access the permanent portal built for familiars while Elena watched silently. Ned seemed very patient and kind, and he chatted mildly about his role as the coven's resident expert of horticulture while enchanting Huey. As he wrapped up, Elena felt a powerful—yet familiar—aura enter the room.

"Thank you, Ned, I can take it from here," a smooth voice said from behind them.

Elena whirled around to see Kieran standing there.

"Of course, Mr. Andraste," Ned stammered, his gaze running up and down Kieran's body for a moment. Elena caught his eye, and Ned flushed, embarrassed, before leaving without a word.

"What are you doing here?" Elena asked, feeling self-conscious.

"I wanted to be the one to escort you home after the test," he replied simply.

He held out his hand toward Huey, who sniffed it, then nudged it with his head, allowing Kieran to pet him.

"Wow, you won him over," Elena said, surprised.

Kieran grinned in triumph.

"Shall we?" He gestured toward the door, and Elena followed him out.

"So now what happens?" she asked.

"Oh, you're in," he said.

"That's it?"

"That's it." He raised an eyebrow at her. "Were you expecting a blood ritual or something?"

"Well, yes," Elena said sheepishly, and Kieran laughed.

"There will be a welcome packet sent to your house tomorrow, and you'll be invited back to the mansion for an official tour and to meet your mentor, but that's about it in terms of formalities," he explained.

"Huh," Elena said as they reached the front door. "After all I built this up in my head, it feels a little... anticlimactic."

"Understandable," Kieran said as the door opened to let them out. "It used to be a much bigger deal, back when my father was young, but now not so much."

They walked in silence across the grounds, back to the garden where Kieran opened the portal for her. Huey bounded through first, but Elena paused.

"Uh, would you like to stop by for a few minutes?" she asked awkwardly.

Kieran nodded. "That would be lovely," he said, and they walked through together.

As soon as they were through, and the door vanished, Elena let out a breath.

"How's Mila?" Kieran asked immediately.

"She's holding up, all things considered," Elena said, watching Huey run up to the front door, open it, then clamor inside. "She's very unhappy about having to lie to her girlfriend, and I'm pretty sure she's been having nightmares."

Kieran nodded solemnly. "Perhaps she would benefit from speaking to a therapist? We have one on staff who could be of service."

"I thought you wanted to keep this a secret from the coven," Elena said, surprised.

"Well, therapists are bound to confidentiality by law, so it wouldn't be an issue." Kieran shrugged.

"Oh, right..." Elena trailed off. "Out of curiosity, why do you want to keep it a secret?"

Kieran grimaced. "It's going to sound foolish."

Elena frowned. "Look, you saved my sister's life, I'm not going to judge you."

"All right. Well, I should start by explaining that hardly anyone in the coven has my direct phone number."

"Really?" Elena's eyes had gone wide, and she wrapped her arms around herself in a poor attempt to hide her discomfort. Why had he given her his number then, if his own coven members couldn't reach him?

Kieran looked out over their yard, not meeting her eye. "If people knew you were able to call me in the middle of the night for help, and I answered, it would open a can of worms for me and my family. People would want to know why you, who weren't even a member at the time, got such exclusive access to the Andrastes, while people who've been members their entire lives have not gotten such treatment."

Elena digested this slowly. "And," she began, "why did I get such treatment?"

Kieran glanced at her. Was that a blush on his cheeks, or was the cold starting to get to him? "I would like to think, despite how the coven might feel, I reserve the right to form friendships with people independently of their agendas."

Elena felt a little deflated, and yet, also pleased with that answer.

"Makes sense," she said, then glanced at him. "I gotta say, I'm impressed with how you handled everything. I mean—" She broke off, feeling awkward. "Not everyone could have stayed so calm in a crisis like that."

Kieran actually looked a little sheepish, the tips of his ears going pink. "Yes, well." He smiled at her crookedly. "I have a lot of experience with crisis situations."

"I see." Elena shifted. "Listen, Mila isn't here right now. I've got to go pick her up from work in a few minutes. She isn't ready to drive yet. I don't know if you're busy, but she really wants to thank you in person."

"I'm afraid I have to get going, but I'll stop by her shop to see her tomorrow," he promised. "Congratulations on joining up, and I'll talk to you soon?" he asked, his sparkling green eyes staring into her.

Elena nodded, swallowing hard. "Thank you, Kieran."

He briefly placed a hand on her arm in goodbye, and then, with a flash of light into a portal, he was gone. As he vanished, Elena's mental exhaustion hit her, and she dragged herself into the house to make herself a cup of coffee before she went to pick up Mila.

It was obvious the accident was still weighing heavily on Mila, and even as a passenger, she was on edge the entire drive home. Elena tried to distract her by talking about her day, but the only time Mila perked up was when Kieran was mentioned.

"He came by to take you home? That's so sweet."

Elena gripped the steering wheel tighter. "He's worried

about you and wanted an update, that's all."

Mila snorted but didn't argue the point. When they got home, she stumbled out of the car and quickly went inside, where Huey greeted her. Mila sat down on the ground and wrapped her arms around the dog, taking a few deep breaths. Huey nuzzled her back, his tail wagging wildly.

Elena watched, stuck between how adorable the moment was and how concerned she was for her sister. It was very obvious, however, that Mila didn't want to discuss how she was feeling. At least, not with Elena.

After taking a very long nap, Elena awoke that night to the sound of voices downstairs. She cautiously went down to find Ava and Mila curled up on the couch. Mila had her head in Ava's lap while Ava stroked her hair.

"I wish you'd called me sooner," Ava said. "I'm so sorry this happened."

Mila muttered something in response that Elena couldn't quite make out. Whatever it was made Ava lean down to kiss Mila's forehead.

The intimacy of the moment was too much, and Elena silently walked back to the stairs and up to her room.

Mila wouldn't have told Ava the full truth about the accident—about Kieran and Elena's role in getting her to safety—but the fact that Mila had gone to her new girlfriend for comfort was proof enough of how attached she'd grown.

The old familiar feeling of bitter loneliness crept up, constricting her chest, and Elena buried her face in her hands. She'd been alone for so long it was easy to forget the warmth and love being in a relationship could provide. Jealous—she was tremendously jealous of Mila and Ava. Not that Elena would ever begrudge her sister for her happiness, but by the spirits, it was hard being alone sometimes.

Elena never wanted to be that person who always needed to be in a relationship to get by. In adulthood, she'd been extremely independent and made her own way in the world. But after the witch hunt, she'd found herself feeling more alone than ever. Elena wanted her person. Her person. Someone by her side who really understood her pain without her having to explain it and could hold her at night when she was afraid.. Someone kind, and generous, who adored her—even her faults. Was that really too much to ask?

Laughter trickled up from downstairs. Elena took a deep breath and started to look for her headphones. She would not cry—not over this. She had so much to be grateful for, and she refused to let her loneliness get the better of her.

Chapter 12

Kieran would have loved to be anywhere else than where he was at two in the morning the following Friday night after Elena's entry interview, standing on a dark street corner in the jewelry quarter of New Stirling City, waiting in silence.

You should have stepped in. When will you learn to take responsibility? Your unwillingness to intervene caused this mess! His father's voice rang through his head. Kieran shook it, his dark hair slipping from behind his ears and falling against his cheeks.

Fix this, Kieran. Fix it now. I don't care what it takes, just make this go away.

He took a deep breath and shifted his weight, his gloved hands clenched tightly into fists. Dressed head to toe in black, he almost blended into the shadows of the dark street. A car turned the corner and stopped, dropping off a man down the block. Kieran waited for the car to drive away, then swiftly, but quietly, approached the man as he fumbled with his keys at the door to one of the buildings.

"Harrison," he said the man's name harshly just as he reached him.

Harrison turned and opened his mouth to shout as he spotted Kieran, but it was too late. Kieran opened a portal right behind the man and shoved him roughly through before he could make a sound. The man was thrown back into a room and landed on a perfectly placed chair. With a snap of Kieran's fingers, ropes jumped to life and wrapped themselves around Harrison's arms and shoulders, binding him to the chair.

"What the hell, Andraste?" Harrison shrieked, "I could have you thrown in prison for this! Using magic against a human is against the law! You know what that is don't you, the law? Or do you not have those in your freak world?"

Kieran looked down at the man, his expression blank. "Where is the video, Harrison?" he said coolly.

Harrison raised his chin, defiant. "What video?" he asked, his city accent thick.

Kieran tutted. "Now, let's not play dumb. You know how that annoys me, and I don't think you want to annoy me right now."

Kieran's tone was casual, but a knife appeared in his hand as he spoke, and Harrison's eyes locked on it. Kieran raised the knife and began to examine it closely, not looking at Harrison.

"Look, I don't want any trouble," Harrison began, his bravado fading, "but business is business, you know, and your brother—" He cut off, letting out a shaky breath. "You were there, you saw what he did to my shop. He was out of control! I can't work with someone like that. And frankly, it's not good for one of you lot with such a loose temper to be on the streets. Think of the greater good here, kid."

Kieran regarded him coldly, the aura of power radiating from him.

"What happened at your shop was a regrettable incident, but one that does not need to involve the authorities. You crossed a line, trying to send that recording to the cops.

Luckily, one of our own intercepted it before it could reach its destination.”

“I’m out of line?” Harrison yelled, his voice high-pitched. “Your brother walks into my shop, demanding delivery on that fucking necklace. When I try to explain to him it hasn’t arrived yet, he goes ballistic and starts shooting his magic off everywhere, claiming I’m a liar and a thief. What else am I supposed to do?”

“But you are a liar and a thief,” Kieran said calmly, pulling a chair up in front of Harrison and sitting down in it, facing him, his arms crossed over his chest, the knife still gripped tightly in one hand. “We received word that the necklace arrived three days ago and that you were planning on telling us it got lost in shipment so that you could resell it for a higher price. You can understand how that would be upsetting to hear.”

Harrison was pale now, sweat dripping down his face. “Not true! If you guys had let me explain, I would’ve told you what happened, but your brother, he blew it all up! He scared my employees half to death!”

Kieran felt sick to his stomach remembering the rage in his brother’s eyes as he’d destroyed that jewelry store, and the fear in the eyes of the humans as they’d fled for what they thought could be their lives. He did not betray any of this on his face, however, remaining calm and collected.

“Your employees have been appropriately compensated and their memories wiped,” he said, “but you, Harrison, you need to tell me where the original copy of that video is, or I’m afraid things are going to have to get ugly here. You see,” He leaned forward so his elbows were resting on his knees, “my brother may have lost his temper that night, but do you know why no one was hurt? Because he did not lose control.

Declan chose to destroy your shop, just as he chose not to hurt anyone. Do you know what that means?"

Harrison did not respond, his eyes darting around the room, looking for an escape. Kieran lunged forward and grabbed Harrison by the hair with one hand, wrenching his neck backward and pressing the knife to his neck with the other. Kieran slowly dragged the knife across Harrison's neck so that a thin line of red sliced through the skin. It was a small cut, but Harrison let out a strangled cry.

"It means we choose who and when we hurt. Right now, I don't want to hurt you, Harrison, but I will, and afterward, you won't remember who did it, but the pain will remain. Crippling, agonizing pain. And only when I come for you the second time will you realize what happened, and we will go through this again and again until I get what I want," he snarled, his voice low and dripping with venom.

"Stop!" Harrison cried, his entire body trembling. "I'll tell you."

Kieran let him go, and Harrison collapsed forward, breathing hard. Looking down at him, Kieran felt his stomach churn with contempt.

"Well?"

"It's in my safe at my apartment. Combination is... is..." Harrison faltered, trying to remember. His eyes were locked on the knife still in Kieran's hand. "455689," he finally gasped out.

"And is that the only copy?"

"Yes."

"Are you lying to me, Harrison?"

"No!" Harrison squealed, and then he started to sob, a pathetic, animalistic sound that made Kieran recoil. "Please, just don't hurt me."

"I'll be right back."

Kieran opened a portal directly into Harrison's apartment and vanished through it. He quickly located the safe and opened it, finding the copy of the video inside just as Harrison said. Slipping it into his inside coat pocket, Kieran didn't bother with anything else in the safe and stepped back through the portal to face Harrison.

"Well then, that wasn't so hard, was it?" he asked in a mock cheery tone.

"Fucking scum," Harrison spat through gritted teeth.

Kieran raised an eyebrow at him. "Come again?"

"You heard me," Harrison said, although his entire body shook with the effort it took to muster this act of bravery. "You, your brother, your father, the whole lot of you! Animals! Someday, someone is going to stand up to you. I just hope I'm there to see it."

Kieran tried to block the words out. He hoped that day would never come, because whoever did stand up to them would surely be destroyed.

"Perhaps, but if that does happen, you won't remember why you wanted it in the first place."

With a flick of Kieran's hand, Harrison slumped over, unconscious. Waving away the bindings, Kieran lifted Harrison's body into the air, using magic, and carefully guided him through the portal into the man's apartment. Kieran laid him down on the couch in the living room.

The anguished expression remained on Harrison's face. Kieran knelt and gently placed his hand over the man's forehead. He muttered a few words, and a flash of light absorbed into Harrison's head. Harrison's face went slack, and Kieran stood up.

"I'm truly sorry for all this," he said quietly, before turning and leaving through a new portal that had opened into the hallway outside his father's study. Walking inside, he saw Anthony Andraste sitting behind his desk, reading a book. He didn't look up as Kieran approached.

"Is it done?" he asked, still not looking at his son.

Kieran pulled out the disk containing the video recording and dropped it on his father's desk in response.

"Good," Anthony said. "And Harrison?"

"Memory wiped, along with all his employees. It's like it never happened," Kieran confirmed.

Mr. Andraste nodded. "You may go," he said simply.

Kieran's jaw clenched, but he did not respond, instead, he turned on his heel and left the study. As soon as the door snapped shut behind him, Kieran walked as quickly as he could to the nearest bathroom and locked the door. Bracing his hands on the edges of the sink, Kieran's entire body shook as he breathed hard. He turned on the sink and splashed cold water on his face, trying to calm down as his heart pounded. The water dripped away, and Kieran looked at his reflection, his eyes dark as he met his own gaze.

Monster.

Recoiling, he collapsed backward against the wall, slipping down it, putting his head in his hands. Nausea bubbled in his stomach and his fingers dug painfully into his own scalp. Kieran's phone buzzed inside his jacket, and taking a deep breath, he let himself go so he could shakily pull it out. It was a text from his brother.

Everything good?

Kieran glared at the message and flipped it away, then

opened one of his social media apps instead to distract himself. After scrolling through pictures and status updates from his various acquaintances, he paused on one in particular.

It was a photo posted by Maggie Byrne. The caption read "Back in town and freezing to death, but glad to be with my friends!" The picture, he recognized, was taken inside the mansion, and in it was Maggie, Alex Moran, and Elena. He realized with a jolt that it must have been Elena's welcome party tonight and that Maggie came back early from her winter trip for it. Elena sat on a couch between the two witches, smiling brightly, her hair a beautiful deep maroon, and her hazel eyes sparkling with glee as her friends laughed around her.

He felt a pang in his chest as he looked at the photo, and he put the phone down, leaning back against the wall. His mind drifted to that night a week ago now, when he'd rushed to her side, tracking her magical aura blindly through the darkness of the world. She deserved a better hero than him. Mila, too. Someone who didn't abduct and blackmail others, who didn't have the government stalking their every move, and who could protect them without the stain of pain and fear on their hands.

The way Elena had looked at him that night after they'd gotten Mila home safely, and again when she'd joined the coven—it was with such adoration and awe. Mila had looked at him much the same when he'd gone to her shop a few days ago to see how she was doing. The way she'd clutched his hands and thanked him for saving her life... it made Kieran want to be sick.

The Hall sisters were good people. They were genuine in their emotions and motivations. Why shouldn't they be? They had nothing to hide except a lifetime of being law-abiding citizens and overall just good people.

If they knew what he was really like, who he really was, they would despise him.

Kieran forced himself back to his feet. Taking a deep breath, he left that small bathroom and headed for the exit. He needed to be anywhere but in his family home right now. The oppressive tension in the air, the weight of knowing his father was in the building and no doubt plotting their next scheme was too much for Kieran to handle.

Once outside, he took a deep breath.

Perhaps he was not the hero the Hall sisters deserved, but he'd been the only one they had that horrible night. There was no doubt in Kieran's mind that if they were in need again, he would be there, because no one looked at him like they did... like Elena did. Like he was someone who was actually worth something more than his family name.

Chapter 13

The welcome party was a pleasant surprise. Maggie was very upset Elena hadn't told her she was joining the coven, but that lasted all of a few minutes before she was planning the party. She kept it small, and it ended up being quite fun with a select group of friendly witches invited. It made Elena feel a lot more confident about her choice to join the coven, and hopeful that maybe she could make some new connections here. Now that the shock of Mila's accident was fading a little, Elena was starting to hope that perhaps she might gain a true community out of all this as well. A community she could rely on and face down her loneliness with.

One of the witches in attendance was Magnus, the man who'd conducted Maggie's check in. After re-introducing himself, he announced that he had been assigned to be her mentor. It was a welcome development as Magnus seemed like a kind and highly capable witch.

That didn't make going to her first lesson with Magnus any less nerve-racking, however. A few days after the welcome party, Elena stood in her living room trying to summon the portal to the mansion. Magnus stood by her side, offering gentle encouragement.

"Picturing the mansion in your mind is a good start," he

said after Elena's first attempt utterly failed, "but it is more important to focus on the aura of the place. Reach out with your magic to connect to the mansion's."

Huey, who was standing next to her in his finest doggie sweater, barked once in encouragement. Her familiar believed in her. She'd summoned a portal to Mila without even knowing where her sister was. She could do this. Elena took a deep breath and raised her hand, her eyebrows scrunched together as she concentrated.

It still didn't work.

After a dozen more attempts, she was ready to give up, feeling utterly defeated.

Magnus placed a hand on her shoulder. "It's alright. Take a deep breath. There's no rush, and no shame."

There was something about Magnus' steady and calm energy that kept Elena from getting upset. She was safe with him. There were no humans around. In her home with Magnus no one was going to hurt her.

A wavering blue light ripped through the air, growing wider as the now-familiar door began to emerge from within it. Huey barked again, his tail wagging, and Elena let out a small grunt from the effort. A heartbeat later, the fully materialized door stood before her. Elena lowered her hand, grinning widely.

"I did it!" she proclaimed triumphantly.

Huey jumped up on his hind legs in excitement, and Magnus let out a low chuckle.

"Well done, now place your hand on the knob for a moment before opening. It will recognize your unique magical signature and let you in."

Elena followed his instructions. A strange tingling filled her hand, and a moment later, the door sprang open. Huey ran through ahead of her, tail wagging, Elena right behind him. When they emerged on the other side in the small garden once more, Huey frolicked out to the main grounds.

"He seems happy to be here," Magnus noted.

"I think he's hoping to make some new friends. I don't suppose there are any other familiars here today?"

Magnus considered. "I'm not sure, but there are usually one or two hanging around. Let's head inside, and we'll be able to find out." He gestured forward, and together, they walked up to the mansion, Huey bounding through the snow gleefully around them.

"I wanted to start out by going over the basics with you today," Magnus told her. "And it is not because I don't think you are capable of more, but a strong base is important to mastering any form of magic. Plus, it will give me a chance to learn more about your particular magic and help identify any weak points."

Elena nodded, her heart pounding, unsure of what his idea of basics were.

They reached the front doors and quickly went inside, warmth overtaking the chill of winter. Huey shook the snow from his fur, splattering it everywhere, before looking around excitedly.

"Why don't you see if there is anyone here, boy?" Magnus suggested.

Huey didn't need to be told twice. He let out a tremendous bark, laden with magic, that reverberated throughout the mansion. There was a pause, then another bark sounded back to them from deep within the building. Huey was shaking all over with glee and took off running toward the other dog.

"Oh, okay, I see how it is!" Elena called out after him, but she was smiling.

"That will be Filly. She's the familiar of one of our board members. Very friendly—they should get along well." Magnus ushered Elena out of the main hall toward a side corridor.

He led her through the hallways to a large room on the west side of the mansion. It had a large, glass, domed ceiling over a raised stone platform. Elaborate designs were carved into the stone, and Elena recognized it as a dueling circle.

"Wow," she said appreciatively.

"Are you familiar with dueling circles?" Magnus asked.

"Yes, but I've never seen one like this before. Growing up, we just used chalk on the pavement."

Magnus chuckled. "Yes, life is a little different for a witch in the city, but we won't be dueling today. This way." He directed her attention to the edge of the room.

It felt a little silly, looking on this magnificent structure now, to remember the dueling circles she and other neighborhood witches had made growing up. They'd thought they were so grand, carrying on the grand traditions of their ancestors. Looking over this room, Elena realized they'd might as well have been playing hopscotch.

Other than the circle, every wall was covered in enormous bookshelves, and all along those bookshelves were reading chairs, tables, and various knickknacks that looked like they had been experimented with and warped by magic. On the wall was a framed poster that read:

RULES OF MAGIC:

1. Everything must be created from something else. Matter cannot be created from nothing.

2. Magic requires physical and mental energy. Attempting a spell you are not ready for can kill you.

3. Magic comes from nature spirits, and respecting nature is of chief importance for magical wellness.

4. Magic can be used to perform most tasks, but it has limits. It cannot bring back the dead, it cannot create new life, and there are certain rare diseases it cannot cure.

Pursing her lips at that last line, Elena turned away. Her mother had succumbed to one of those rare diseases. They were a curse, so the legend went, that spirits had created to punish the hubris of witches in ancient times, when they'd enslaved humanity with their power, and now, a reminder of that dark past.

Magnus and Elena settled down at a table near the poster, and Magnus collected three items: a glass cup, a piece of paper, and a large book. He placed them on the table in front of her, and Elena looked at the objects with trepidation. One of them she recognized as a talisman that enhanced and stabilize witch's power. They were usually used to help children when they were first learning.

"Now, we are going to attempt to complete simple tasks. They may seem childish at first, but I assure you this is necessary for the process."

Elena swallowed. "All right, what am I doing first?"

"Make the book levitate," Magnus commanded.

Elena nodded, feeling a little relieved. Very simple indeed. Magic was mostly wrapped up in a person's strength of will, focus, and energy reserves in order to manipulate natural law. More complicated spells required an enchantment, but something like this was straightforward and didn't require it.

Elena lifted a finger, and she felt the talisman's influence wrap around and reach into her body. After a moment, the book rose off the table, hovering in the air.

"Good, now hold it for me for a moment." Magnus leaned forward, his eyes narrowing.

Elena obliged, wondering what he was doing. After a few seconds, he nodded, and Elena let the book fall. Even though the talisman helped, using magic so easily after so long was like a relief so all her senses.

"See anything interesting?" Elena asked Magnus as he continued to stare.

He smiled. "I was examining your magical energy. Through years of training and practice, some witches can develop the skill and awareness to actually be able to see another's magic and dissect its attributes."

"Wow," Elena said, wondering what her magic looked like.

"Next, I want you to fill this cup with snow from outside."

Elena inhaled slightly through her nose, pursing her lips, then blinked hard. The little physical actions most witches did to conduct their magic weren't strictly necessary, but they often helped with helping the witch feel control. The cup filled with snow, and out of the corner of her eye, Elena saw a little clump of snow that was on the windowsill next to them disappear. She wondered if Magnus saw that as well and cursed herself for not using snow that was out of eyesight.

"Wonderful," Magnus said encouragingly. "Finally, I want you to light this paper on fire without burning it."

"Great," Elena muttered, picking up the piece of paper and staring at it.

The top edge of the paper burst into flame, but the paper did not burn. It remained intact and perfect as the fire danced merrily above it.

"Excellent, now hold it for a few moments," Magnus

instructed.

Elena continued to fuel the flame, only sensing the slightest of energy drains from her magic as the flame was so small. Her mind began to wander, wondering if Huey was having a good time.

"Oh, shit," Elena said angrily, noticing the corner of the paper beginning to singe and burn.

"That's all right, you can put it out now."

Elena lowered the paper, feeling embarrassed.

"Do you know what went wrong there?"

"I lost focus," Elena said, glaring at the paper. This was a task a child could perform, and yet, Elena had failed. Obviously, she was here because she needed help, but not even being able to pass this basic test shamed her to her core.

"Yes." Magnus peered at her. "As your mind wandered, you slipped from conjuring magic to elemental magic. Conjuring magic requires more focus and calm, whereas elemental is based on strength and emotion. But do not feel bad, it's a common mistake even the best witches make from time to time, as it is an easy line to cross."

Elena fidgeted uncomfortably. "Any other observations?"

"A few," Magnus smiled. He sat back and regarded her. "Your magic is what those of us with the sight call 'cold' magic. This has nothing to do with its temperature, as it has none, but traits. It is complicated, methodical, and multifaceted. Cold magic is usually associated with witches who have active minds and rely more on mental strength than physical in their everyday lives."

"Makes sense," Elena said. "I can't remember the last time I worked out."

Magnus laughed. "That will change when we delve deeper

into elemental magic," he promised her. "Now, as to the tasks you performed..." He paused, thinking. "The book levitation was easily done, but I could sense more magical energy flowing from you than necessary for the task. This could just be because you are in an unfamiliar environment and were overcompensating, but properly being able to ration one's magical energy, no matter what the situation, is an important skill."

Elena felt extremely self-conscious, having her abilities picked apart like this, but there was no judgment in Magnus's tone, and she kept reminding herself he was just trying to help.

"The snow was adequately done, but I couldn't help but notice you instinctively used snow that was in your line of sight. Do you struggle to summon objects that you can't see under regular circumstances?"

Elena's pride rushed forward, demanding she tell him she was perfectly capable of doing such a thing, but it quickly faded. Lying would only hurt herself and her purpose here.

"Well, sometimes," she admitted, blushing a little.

"There's no need to be embarrassed, Elena," Magnus said. "I cannot tell you how many adult witches I have taught who struggle with the same things. It is why I always start with this test, no matter what level my student is at."

Elena managed a small smile. "So, what next?"

"Just a few more tests." Magnus summoned new objects for Elena to mess with. She bit back a sigh, resigned to finding out what all her flaws were for the rest of the day.

The next few tasks were a bit more difficult. They included boiling a cup of water, breaking a stick without touching it, and making a book move in a circle in the air above their heads.

With each one, Elena's anxiety grew, which meant she steadily was losing control of her magic. Her hands shook with the effort to summon her magic, and she knew, without a doubt, she was expending massive amounts of energy for the simple tasks. Sweat dripped down the back of her neck, and she couldn't stop herself from glancing nervously at Magnus's face every few seconds.

Magnus offered gentle encouragement and eventually offered her a break.

"How long have you suffered from this anxiety?" The question was harmless enough, and there was no judgment in his tone, but Elena flinched, regardless.

"I got diagnosed with an anxiety disorder when I was a teenager, but since I was so young, I was able to get professional help and learn how to manage it. But it's been way worse lately."

Elena's face burned with shame, and she didn't meet Magnus's eye.

"There's nothing to be embarrassed about," Magnus assured her, his deep voice rumbling. "Your brain works how it works. I'm not a mental health professional by any means, but I have worked with other witches with your condition. It is extremely difficult to overcome the messages from your brain that you are in danger, even when you know you're not. There are certain exercises you may already be familiar with that can be a huge help. With your permission, I would like to try to incorporate those into your training."

"Yes," Elena said, without hesitation. "Whatever you think will help."

"Good. Let's start with helping you calm down. Let's start with some guided meditation."

Elena took a deep breath and closed her eyes, allowing Magnus's steady voice to lead her into a meditative state. Or, at least that was the idea. Elena had never been very good at meditation. Magnus asked her to imagine herself in a place she felt the most safe and comfortable, then walk through it and imagine every detail she could.

For Elena, this was, of course, her bedroom.

A presence entered the room where they sat, and Elena's body immediately relaxed. Huey had arrived with his new friend. In the presence of her familiar, Elena felt her power replenishing a little, and a sense of calmness radiated down their bond, which Magnus noted with interest after they'd finished the mediation.

"You have a healthy bond," he commented. "Magic flows between you two freely."

Huey sat up a little straighter, oozing pride, and Elena laughed while petting Filly, an elderly-looking chocolate lab with a kind face and very happy tail.

"That's my good boy," she cooed at Huey.

Their lesson was cut short when a group of witches entered the room and began to set up on the dueling circle.

"Would you like to watch?"

"Yes." Elena couldn't deny she was curious. In all honestly, she'd never witnessed a proper magical duel before.

The two duelists entered the circles on the platform and faced each other. The idea was that the witches could not leave their respective circles. If they did so or were knocked out, the duel was over, and they lost.

The other onlookers set themselves around the platform and clapped their hands together. A large burst of shimmering air erupted and encased the platform in an enormous dome.

"The shield will protect those outside the duel and the room itself," Magnus explained quietly. "Most spells cannot pass through it."

"Most?"

"The type of spells that could are not allowed in the mansion. To use one would result in immediate expulsion from the coven."

That was all the explanation Elena needed. Whatever those spells were, they were likely very powerful and extremely dangerous.

The duelists bowed to each other before taking their defensive positions. Elena waited with bated breath. The lines and carvings of runes of the circles burst into light, and both witches moved at once. One fired a column of fire straight at the other, but it was blocked by a wall of water. Steam filled the air, but that didn't deter them. One of the witches even took control of the steam—warping it into a dense cloud and using it to obscure their opponent's vision before blasting them with a wave of pure magical energy. The witch on the receiving end stumbled back but managed to stay in the circle by literally making the stone beneath their feet rise up and clamp around their shins to keep them steady.

"They're mostly using elemental magic," Elena noted, eyes wide as she watched explosion after explosion of raw magical power unleashed before her.

"Yes. Is it favored for duels. Curses are forbidden in any legitimate duel, and conjuration can be a useful tool, but is difficult to pull off in the heat of battle."

The witches on the platform seemed to manage it as one summoned a large mattress from who knew where to squash the other. Before the pinned witch could recover, the mattress wrapped around them and trapped them before rolling off the platform and out of the circle.

Laughter erupted from the crowd at the ludicrous victory, and Elena couldn't bite back a giggle. The losing witch seemed irritated, to say the least, but cracked a smile when the other clapped them on the back.

"They're siblings," Magnus whispered. "They've been dueling since they were children. That often requires more creative methods of winning when you know your opponent so well."

Elena couldn't ever imagine dueling with Mila if she had been born a witch, but the age gap between them would have likely prevented it when they were growing up anyway.

Magnus introduced Elena to the others, and she rained compliments on the duelists for their skill. Everyone was polite and friendly, and Elena received an invitation to join their dueling club when she felt ready.

"I'll decide when that day comes," Magnus informed them. "Stop trying to poach my students."

The witch who'd made the offer laughed. After a few minutes of socializing, Magnus led Elena away to grab a quick snack from the kitchen before she headed home.

"Remind me, Elena, how old are you?" Magnus asked he pulled out some oranges from a large fruit bowl in the kitchen and handed one to her.

"I'm turning thirty-six in April," she told him, digging her nails into the skin and beginning to peel. It did not escape her notice that Magnus used magic to accomplish the same task.

"Ah, a few more years before your next birthday celebration then," he said, "And your sister, does she celebrate every year since she is human, or every five years like a witch?"

"When she was a kid, my mom made sure we celebrated every year for her, but when she hit twenty, she decided she wanted to do it the witch way. I think she felt weird, having us do the birthday thing for her all the time but not for us," she explained. "Which turned out fine anyway; she isn't exactly aging like a normal human."

"Not uncommon for humans with a witch parent," Magnus noted. "My mother was human, and my brother was human as well. When he was nearly one hundred years old, he didn't look a day over sixty."

"Your mother was human?"

Magnus nodded, his eyes twinkling. "Indeed. Some witches turn their nose at such a thing, but I am quite proud to have been her son."

Elena smiled at him warmly. Another witch in the coven had human relatives. A high-ranking witch by the looks of it, one who was respected—one who could understand Elena's situation better than anyone.

"Is this coven really okay with human family members then?" Elena asked quietly. "I know they said they were, but that doesn't always mean everyone is."

"In general, yes, no one will bother you about having a human sister, and many of the privileges you are entitled to as a member extend to her as well."

"But?" Elena pressed.

"Well, there are always going to be witches who have issues with humans, no matter who they are related to. It isn't anything you should worry yourself over. No members of our coven are openly hostile toward humans, but don't expect everyone to be fully accepting of her, either."

"I understand," Elena said, her shoulders drooping. It

wasn't the answer she was hoping for, but it wasn't as bad as it could have been.

After they finished their oranges, Magnus escorted Elena and the two dogs back outside and to the garden they'd entered through. Huey and Filly sniffed each other frantically in goodbye while Elena, once more, struggled to open the portal.

"I'll see you the day after tomorrow," he said as she finally opened the door, Huey trotting through ahead of her.

"Yes, see you then!" Elena waved before stepping through and returning home.

Chapter 14

Later that week, Elena was lounging on the couch watching TV while Mila made herself a snack in the kitchen. Elena's phone was sitting on the kitchen island and lit up with a notification while Mila was waiting for her popcorn to finish popping in the microwave.

"Hey, you got a text," Mila called out to her sister.

"Who from?" Elena asked lazily.

"K.A.," Mila read off, picking up the phone. "Is that Kieran?"

Elena bolted upright, her eyes wide, and quickly flung herself over the back of the couch before trotting over to the kitchen and snatching her phone out of Mila's hands.

"I'll take that as a yes!" Mila laughed.

Elena ignored her and opened up her phone.

Hey, just wanted to check in and see how you were doing. I spoke with Magnus earlier today, and he sounded pleased with your first few lessons together. He's a good man and an even better mentor.

Elena digested this slowly while Mila read over her shoulder.

"Hm, just checking in," Mila muttered. The timer on the microwave went off, and Mila went to collect the popcorn "What are you going to say back?"

Elena thought for a moment, then started typing.

I'm excited, too! I can tell Magnus is going to be a great teacher.

Mila watched with amusement as Elena nervously sent her reply. She emptied her popcorn into a bowl then gently put a hand on Elena's shoulder, guiding her back toward the couch. Elena plopped down and reached her hand toward Mila's bowl to grab some popcorn while she watched her phone. There was a bubble at the bottom of the chat indicating he was typing. Mila swatted Elena's hand away territoriality.

"I asked if you wanted some, and you said no," she grumbled. "Now you have to make your own."

Elena glared at her, but her attention was drawn back to her phone as Kieran's text came through.

I hope this isn't too forward, but I was wondering if you would be interested in getting together soon to maybe talk about your books? I understand if you don't want to, but I couldn't live with myself if I at least didn't ask.

Elena's heart did a little backflip, and Mila leaned over to see what he'd said.

"Oh, it's happening!" she squealed. "He wants you."

"That is not what he said," Elena said grumpily. "He wants to talk about my books; he isn't interested in me."

It was an unthinkable thought. True, Kieran hadn't turned out to be anything like what she had expected, but that didn't mean he would pursue a nobody like her. After all, what did she have to offer him? A witch who barely left her own house, with a pathetic amount of magic, and middle of the night panic attacks. No, this was about her books, nothing more.

"Uh huh." Mila sat back with a wicked smile on her face. "So, are you going to say yes?"

Elena thought about it for a moment. There were so many

things to consider. She'd never talked with one of her fans about her work before, and the idea was both nerve-wracking and exciting. But he'd just saved her sister's life. Indulging him a little was the least she could do.

"Okay, I'll do it," Elena said, feeling a little queasy. She quickly typed out a response and sent it.

Sure, that would be great! My schedule is pretty flexible, except for my lessons with Magnus. When would work best for you?

Elena let out a breath and let her head fall against the back of the couch. What was she getting herself into? Mila laughed and tossed some popcorn to Huey, who was sitting at her feet. Elena's head snapped up.

"Oh, I see, you'll share with him but not me?"

"He asked nicely."

"You can't understand him!"

"Don't need to!"

* * *

Elena and Kieran settled on that Sunday to hang out, and much to Elena's displeasure, they decided on her own house as the location for their friendly get together, as she was calling it.

"So convenient! Your bedroom is right there," Mila teased her.

"Stop, this is not a date," Elena snapped. The flare of irritation she felt at Mila's teasing was, in itself, very annoying. Elena didn't want to examine the cause of her ire too closely, afraid of what she might find.

Despite that fact, Elena made sure that Mila promised not to return to the house that day until Kieran was gone. Not because she wanted to spend time with Kieran alone—that was not it at all—she just didn't want Mila around, making suggestive comments.

Sunday morning, Elena was more awake than she felt in months. After going on a walk with Huey, she took a shower and stressed out for a few hours over what to wear. She wanted to look nice, after all, but not like she was trying too hard. After driving herself mad, she settled on jeans and a dark blue knit sweater. Appraising herself in the mirror, she decided that she looked very author-y. Elena threw her hair—which was, at the moment, a deep maroon—into a bun and went downstairs to wait.

At precisely one in the afternoon, Huey let out a low bark as he sensed Kieran's presence outside.

"What did we talk about?" Elena chastised him.

Huey huffed at her and sat down dutifully a few feet in front of the door, ready to greet their guest. There was a knock, and Elena took a deep breath before opening the door. Kieran stood there, smiling, his dark hair more unkempt than usual, and on his shoulder was perched a large black raven.

"Hello, Elena," he greeted.

"Hi." Elena stepped back to let him in, her eyes on the bird.

Kieran walked by and immediately made eye contact with Huey.

"Hello, Huey."

Keiran held out his hand, and Huey once again allowed the witch to pet him. The raven on his shoulder let out a little squawk in Elena's direction, and Kieran turned his attention back to her.

"Elena, I wanted to introduce you to my familiar, Briar. She's excited to be here."

The raven, Briar, bowed her head toward Elena respectfully.

"Ah, the little spy," Elena said, although *little* was the wrong word. The bird was huge, the size of a small dog, and Elena wondered how Briar's talons were not ripping through the fabric of Kieran's coat.

"Briar sorry," the bird croaked out in a deep, human-like voice that made Elena jump.

"She can talk?" Elena asked, stunned.

Kieran laughed, which Briar mimicked perfectly. "Yes, she can. Most ravens, even non-magical ones, can be trained to mimic human speech."

Elena tried to compose herself from this unsettling information.

"Well, Briar, it's nice to meet you, and you're forgiven for spying on me. You were just following your companion's orders," she said, shooting a look at Kieran, who grinned in response.

"Happy!" Briar croaked, flapping her wings.

Elena shook her head and turned to Kieran. "Well, can I get you anything? Tea, water?" she asked, trying to sound casual despite the fact there was a famous witch and his giant bird in her house.

"Tea would be lovely."

Elena nodded. "You can hang your coat up there." She gestured to the hooks hanging on the wall. "I'm not sure where Briar will be able to hang out though; we don't have any bird-ready furniture."

"It's all right. I have a stand for her if that's okay?"

"Go for it," Elena said, filling up the kettle and placing it on its base.

She watched out of the corner of her eye as Kieran summoned a perch for Briar, who hopped on and immediately turned to Huey, squawking lowly at him. Huey began to whine and make strange yipping noises in response, which Elena knew was how he spoke to other familiars outside his species.

"They seem to be getting along," Kieran noted, hanging up his coat.

"Huey has been a little lonely without his friends from the city. I think he's excited to make new ones." Elena retrieved two mugs. "What type of tea would you like?"

"Green is fine, if you have it." Kieran sat down at the kitchen island.

Elena tried to make herself busy and not stare at him. Even though this was his third time in the house, it was still unbelievably strange to have a famous person sitting in her kitchen. He was wearing an expensive-looking, dark green sweater that matched his eyes, and Elena couldn't help but notice he filled it out quite nicely. It was more than a little distracting.

Kieran was watching Elena flutter around the kitchen, a smile tugging at the corner of his mouth. "Do I make you uncomfortable, Elena?"

Elena froze for a second and then blushed furiously. "Not at all."

The words didn't even sound convincing to her own ears. Of course she was uncomfortable. Putting aside all their interactions so far, Kieran was one of the most famous and influential witches in the world. Even while he just sat there, there was an intensity about him that made Elena's heart race and set her entire body on attention. Perhaps it was the way he watched her without shame, or his aura of magical power, which was unlike any Elena had ever encountered.

Kieran tilted his head, and Elena stood up straighter, placing a mug with a tea bag down in front of him.

"Are you sure?" he pressed.

Elena managed to return his stare. "I don't know how to act around you, I guess," she admitted.

"Well, if you were Maggie, you would tease me relentlessly," he said with a smile.

Elena grinned. "I could try, but Maggie has a gift for it that I just lack." She placed her own mug down and turned to get the kettle, which was now steaming. "So, I cleared the snow off the balcony and even managed a temperature control spell to make it warm up there. Would you like to sit outside for a bit?"

If he said no, she was going to be very upset. It had taken a lot of time and effort to clear the snow and six tries to get that damn spell right.

"That sounds great."

"Wonderful." Elena poured the hot water into both mugs before they headed for the hall door.

"Briar, come," Kieran ordered Briar, who, with a flutter of her wings, launched from her perch and landed gracefully on Kieran's shoulder again.

Elena led them upstairs, Huey following behind, and onto the balcony. Kieran looked out over the scenery, breathing in deeply. As he did, the perch appeared once again, and Briar flew to it.

"This is lovely." The balcony was completely cleared of snow and, thanks to Elena's spell, the air was warm enough they could look out over the snow-covered trees comfortably.

"Thanks." Elena sat down at the small table against the railing.

Kieran joined her, his gaze dropping to his mug. He took a cautious sip, and for the first time, Elena thought he looked a little nervous.

"So," he began, "what can you tell me about your next book?" The words rushed out of his mouth one after the other.

Elena laughed. "I was wondering if you were going to ask about that." She sipped her tea. "What do you want to know?"

"Ah, where to begin. How much longer does it take place after the last one? Are you going to resolve the question of Hagar's birth? Why did you end it on *that* cliffhanger?" Kieran asked, rapid fire.

"Woah now, slow down." Elena clutched her mug as she thought over the conversations she'd had with herself in preparation for this meeting. It wasn't anything she'd meant to do, but in the days leading up to this, she hadn't been able to stop herself from imagining every possible scenario. "I'm not telling you any spoilers, and as for why I ended on a cliffhanger..." Elena sighed dramatically. "I enjoy making my readers suffer."

Kieran shook his head. "You absolute sadist."

"Of course."

Kieran looked out over the still forest, his face pensive. "How do you do it?" he asked her finally.

"Could you be a little more specific?"

"How do you come up with these stories? They feel so, I don't know, so real." Kieran leaned forward, looking at her intensely. "I remember the first time I read one of your books. I was wandering through some random bookstore outside of New Stirling City and picked it up by chance. I read it in one sitting and was practically in tears by the end. It spoke to me."

Elena leaned forward, too, as if drawn to him like a magnet, searching his face to try to determine if he was being genuine. He gazed back, his expression guarded, but there was an eagerness in his eyes that seemed true.

"Really?" Elena wanted to hear more. Needed it. The idea that she'd had such profound effect on Kieran's life before they'd ever met was intoxicating.

"I just..." Kieran hesitated. "You and I have led such different lives, and your life is nothing like that of your characters', but the emotion they feel, their thoughts, their pain, it is so *familiar* to me. Sometimes I read a passage and have to put the book down because it hits me so hard—like looking in a mirror and seeing myself for the first time."

Elena had never had an out-of-body experience before, but she thought she could be having one right now with how elated she felt.

"I don't really know how I do it," Elena told him. "No, it's true," she added when Kieran raised his eyebrows skeptically. "Writing has always been my thing, my way to express myself. I just, I don't know, I see people, I guess, and I take what I see in others and use it in what I write. I might have never been in most of the situations I write about, but I can feel what my characters are feeling, and that helps me write honestly."

Kieran looked away again, almost guiltily. "I can see people, too," he said. "But I always see the worst in them and use that to my advantage."

Elena dropped her hands, sitting back, not sure what to make of that statement. She decided not to press him about it.

"Well, sometimes people are truly awful," Elena conceded, "and it's certainly harder to see the good in the world now than it used to be, but I can't live like that, only seeing the bad, and it's not accurate anyway. There's tremendous good in this world. There is love, there is beauty and struggle and victory, and those are the things we live and strive for. The minute we lose sight of that, we lose ourselves."

Kieran smiled, recognizing the quote she was making. "That's from *Winter Bird*, your third novel, I believe."

"Yup!"

"That one is my favorite, you know."

"I do know. You mentioned it before," Elena reminded him, petting Huey, who'd come over to check on her.

"Oh right." He paused, then continued, "I re-read it once a year," he admitted. "It's by far the one I relate to the most."

"Oh?" Elena asked, her heart pounding so hard she was sure he could hear it. "How so?"

"The main character, Jessie, I get him."

Kieran waved his hand over the table. A copy of the very book they were discussing appeared in front of them. Elena stared at it, seeing the worn spine and crinkled pages, the signs of a book much loved.

Kieran opened it reverently and turned the pages, one by one. "When I first read this book, I was in a dark place, and I saw myself in Jessie so perfectly. He helped me see my pain clearly for the first time, and because of that, I was able to ask for the help I needed. The loneliness, the anger, the grief—it all felt so bitterly and beautifully real."

Kieran ran his fingers over the pages as he spoke, and Elena swore it was as if he was running his fingers delicately over her skin.

Stop it! She chastised herself.

Kieran looked up at her, smiling sheepishly. "I just really

love this book."

"I can see that," Elena said, her heart in her throat. "I-I actually wrote it right after my mother died. It was my way of processing my grief without self-destructing. I was really angry because she was taken by a disease. It didn't make sense that a witch like her could get cancer. She never hurt anyone, revered the spirits, and always tried her best. I didn't know how to deal with that anger, and it manifested in a lot of ugly ways. Writing it all down helped."

"Really," Kieran breathed. "I'm sorry you went through that."

"We all do, at some point. At least I got to say goodbye. Not everyone is so lucky."

Kieran didn't say anything to that, though Elena noticed his breathing had gone rather shallow. Things had gotten rather serious very quickly, so she decided to change the subject.

The sun was starting to set, casting a beautiful golden light over the glistening white trees. "You know..." Elena sat back and looked out over the scenery. "I was worried when I moved out here that I would hate it."

"Why's that?"

"I lived in the city my entire life. The noise, the people, it was all I'd ever known. I thought the quiet and the isolation out here might drive me crazy."

"I love it for precisely those reasons," Kieran said. "When I'm out here, I feel so much lighter, freer than when I'm in any city."

"I feel that way now, too," Elena agreed. She glanced over at him. "Why don't you move out here full time? You mostly live in New Stirling City, right?"

Kieran sighed and ran a hand through his hair.

"If I had it my way I would, but my father needs me in the city to help run the family business, and it would be too exhausting to portal back and forth every day over that distance. Plus, with the family home being here, it wouldn't be deemed acceptable by the old crowd to get my own place. I would be expected to stay there, and who wants to live with your parents when you're almost forty years old?"

"Being rich and powerful always sounds like a good idea in theory, but the way your family does it seems exhausting." The words came out before Elena could stop them. They were true, but were they close enough for her to be so frank with him?

Kieran looked at her in surprise, then started to laugh.

"An accurate assessment," Kieran said, still chuckling. "There's so many archaic rules and traditions that we have to keep to maintain face in upper magical society, which is bad enough as it is, but to have one foot in the past and one in the present is a balancing act I get sick of. What is the point of a hierarchy created a thousand years ago when most of the population was illiterate and never traveled away from within ten miles of where they were born? But I don't get to make the rules, so here we are."

Elena thought she knew what he meant. These old, magical families had a reputation for being very traditional, and there were surely parts Elena wasn't aware of that Kieran had to deal with every day of his life. Though, back then, a witch like Kieran never could have engaged socially with someone like her. The Andrastes were all that remained of an ancient dynasty that had ruled a kingdom that no longer existed. As far as Elena knew, she was born of a very long line of farmers and other people who worked for a living. She would have been part of the illiterate rabble Kieran's family ruled over but never engaged with.

There were still witches, Elena knew, that still believed things should stay that way.

Kieran shifted the conversation back to the current series Elena was writing, asking her about different plot lines and characters, and trying to trick her into revealing something about the new book. All the while, she kept trying to not appear as if she was staring too hard at him while he talked. As the sun continued to set, the light was hitting him right in his eyes, illuminating the green brightly and somehow making him even more beautiful.

The nerves at being in his presence had faded and were replaced with something else. A fluttering in her chest every time he spoke or looked at her, and a heat in her body, accompanied by a yearning to be even closer to him.

Oh, spirits, she was in trouble.

"Well," Elena said after they'd been outside for about two hours. She cleared her throat. "I have to take Huey for his walk before it gets dark."

Huey, who was laying at the foot of the perch with Briar, picked his head up and started to wag his tail.

"Ah," Kieran said with a small smile, "you're kicking me out."

"I would characterize it as a gentle nudge more than a kick, but essentially, yes."

She needed him to leave before she did or said something stupid. He wasn't here for her, just her books. He didn't want her like that.

They both stood up, Kieran taking his copy of *Winter Bird* off the table and vanishing it into thin air. Briar took off, landing on a nearby tree branch rather than Kieran's shoulder again.

Kieran frowned at the bird. "Where are you going, little lady?" he asked sternly.

"Fly home, hunt dinner," Briar said in her unnatural voice.

Kieran rolled his eyes. "All right, fine," he conceded, vanishing the perch as well.

"Goodbye, Briar!" Elena called out to the bird, and behind her, Huey barked.

"Bye!" Briar shouted before taking off and vanishing into the sky.

The three of them walked back inside and down the stairs. Elena walked down first, and her foot slipped on a step, causing her to stumble.

"Careful." Kieran placed his hand on her arm to steady her, leaving a tingling sensation in his wake. As they reached the front door, Kieran took his coat off the hook and slipped it back on.

"Thank you, Elena, for talking with me, I really enjoyed it. It's not every day someone gets to spend time with their favorite artist."

"I'm glad I lived up to the hype," Elena teased. "See you around?"

"Yes, definitely," he promised.

A beat of silence fell where they simply looked at each other, before Kieran reached up one hand to cup Elena's cheek. Her lungs stopped working as she gazed up at him. Almost in slow motion, Kieran leaned down and pressed a soft kiss to her other cheek.

"I'm very glad to have met you, Elena."

His deep voice rumbled down to Elena's bones. Nothing in her body was working as she watched him step back and give her one more lingering look before leaving.

Leaving. He'd just kissed her, and he was leaving.

Elena rushed to the front door and threw it open in time to see Kieran drive away.

Did a kiss on the cheek mean something different to him? Was this a traditional witch thing she didn't know about?

Or... had it meant something.

Either way, it meant something to her—something she couldn't ignore anymore.

"Fuck," Elena muttered to herself, and closed the door.

Chapter 15

There was no word from Kieran in the following days, which was a big issue for Elena as she could not get him out of her head. Whenever her mind drifted, which was often, she saw him sitting across from her, his eyes sparkling. When she closed her eyes at night, his perfect face swam before her, the imagined feeling of his fingers dancing over her skin, and his lips on her cheek tormenting her and leaving her writhing beneath the sheets.

But in the two weeks after their afternoon together, Kieran went silent. Elena texted to say she'd enjoyed spending time with him, and he responded he felt the same but then… nothing. It was extremely upsetting, especially since Mila told her he was still coming into her shop every week to buy flowers for his mother. Elena tried to not let Mila know how much it bothered her, as she knew her sister would want to get involved if she realized how Elena felt. No, best to let the entire thing go.

It turned out, however, that Elena could not keep her mouth shut entirely. It was the first week of February, and Elena was hanging out with Maggie at her cozy cabin home. Now that Maggie was back from her winter trip, their friendship had picked up right where it left off. It was a huge help to disperse some of the loneliness that had settled over Elena like a weighted blanket in the last few months.

They were watching a movie about a famous legend of a witch who fell in love with a human, back when it was illegal to do so. Maggie was curled up against Elena's side like a happy cat, a glass of wine in her hand.

"I love this story." Elena sighed, sipping her own wine. "It reminds me of my mom."

Maggie glanced up at Elena. "Because of her and Mila's dad?" she asked, as the witch and her human lover embraced on the screen.

"Yes. Obviously, I never met him, but I know they were the loves of each other's lives. I asked her a few times why she married him, even though he was human, and she would outlive him by centuries if he hadn't died in an accident."

Elena paused, and Maggie sat silently, waiting for her to continue.

"She told me she never regretted a single moment of it, because being with him made every day of her life better, even after he was gone. She could look back at their time together and remember she experienced the love of a lifetime, and many people never get that, so she would never take it for granted."

"She was right," Maggie said miserably. "You know, I'm starting to wonder... I mean, I'm only thirty-four, I'm not old, but sometimes I feel like, why haven't I found that person yet? Is there something wrong with me?"

"There's nothing wrong with you," Elena told her, patting Maggie's head with her free hand. "You're very particular. It's a side effect of knowing yourself. You know what you want and won't waste your time with anything that isn't good for you."

Maggie mulled this over. "Doesn't make it any easier though," she muttered, dropping her head against Elena's shoulder.

"Seriously," Elena said with a sigh. "My last relationship was two years ago now, and it lasted three months before I got bored and dumped them. That's how all my relationships have always gone. We get together, it's fun at first, and then a little while later, I lose interest, or they lose interest, and it falls apart."

Maggie sighed. "Well, if we are both single two hundred years from now, we can move in together and become crazy old ladies."

"That sounds fun," Elena said, amused at the idea of her and Maggie sitting on some front lawn, yelling at people who walked by.

Elena's smile faded as she remembered how many times she and Sammi had made a similar bargain—usually after a bad date or a breakup. Grief, as it so often did, reared its multifaceted head and sank its fangs into Elena's heart.

It was still difficult to believe that Sammi was gone, that she wasn't having this conversation with her. But there was no doubt in Elena's mind that Sammi would have adored Maggie. Her vibrancy and honesty radiated out of every pore, and somehow... drove the grief away just enough that Elena could keep talking.

No one could ever replace Sammi, but Maggie was helping Elena's broken heart find its way again, in a way she hadn't realize she'd needed.

"Mags, can I tell you something?"

Maggie sat up and turned to look at Elena curiously. "You

tell me everything already. What don't I already know?"

If only that were true. Maggie had no idea the secrets Elena kept, but she could start here, with this.

"Well, this is fairly new…"

"Who do you have a crush on?" Maggie asked, taking a sip from her wine and raising an eyebrow. Of course, she suspected already. Was Elena really that obvious?

"Ugh, don't say crush. It sounds so childish," Elena muttered.

Maggie grinned. "All right, who do you have very adult, mature, romantic feelings for?"

Elena rolled her eyes.

"Kieran," she admitted, after a moment.

"Ha! I knew it!" Maggie practically shouted.

Elena quickly shushed her, even though it was just the two of them. "What do you mean you knew it?".

"Well, you always seemed weird when he was brought up, and a little more curious about him than someone who wasn't interested in him should be." She tilted her head "What made *you* realize this though?"

Elena looked into her glass. "A few weeks ago, he came over to my house, just to hang out and talk about my books and…" Elena took a deep breath, casting her eyes to the ceiling. "This is going to sound so strange."

"Now, you know I am a judgment-free audience; you can tell me anything," Maggie assured.

Elena looked at her friend's kind face and spilled her guts. "He was talking about his favorite book, and well, that book means so much more to me than any of the others I wrote. I wrote it right after my mother died," Elena began.

"Oh," Maggie said, inching closer, "go on."

"I've never been more vulnerable than when I wrote that story. That is also the first time I really started to struggle with depression. The book was my coping mechanism, my way of dealing with her loss. My mother and I had a complicated relationship, to put it lightly, but then suddenly she was gone. I poured myself onto those pages, every ounce of pain, every insecurity, every flaw went into the main character and..." She took a steadying breath. "Kieran loves it. He loves that book. I mean..." She ran a hand through her hair nervously, unable to stop herself from rambling, "You should have seen the look on his face when he talked about it. He related to Jessie, the main character, who I basically made as a reflection of myself at that time, and he felt so connected to them. It made me feel like, I don't know, like he could see me, really see me. The real me, not the publicly happy, somewhat stable person I pretend to be."

Maggie nodded slowly. "That doesn't sound strange at all," she said.

"And the way he ran his fingers over the pages, like they were something precious, like my words, my essence, was something precious..." Elena closed her eyes, picturing the memory in her mind. "It made me feel like he was running his fingers over me."

She opened them again to find Maggie smirking at her.

"Are you laughing at me?" Elena demanded, feeling self-conscious.

"No! Not at all," Maggie said quickly. "I've just never seen you like this."

Elena shook her head. "It's idiotic, is what it is."

"Why do you say that? I don't think your reaction is unreasonable."

"Come on, Maggie, you're an artist. You know that once you put a piece of art out there, it takes on a life of its own, one completely removed from your original intent. Kieran doesn't read that book and see me. He sees a piece of fiction he personally connects to. He has his own relationship with the work that predates ever meeting me and has nothing to do with me. His understanding of our conversation, and my experience with it, are two totally different things."

"Ah, I see your point," Maggie conceded. "But just because that's probably true doesn't mean he doesn't have feelings for you. Mila has been telling you he does for months."

"Mila is full of it," Elena muttered. "You've known Kieran for a long time. Do you think he could feel the same way I do?"

Maggie hesitated. "I don't know, Elena, honestly. It's a little weird he sought out time with you. He's never done that with any of the other coven members that I know of. He does seem to have taken a special interest in you beyond the norm, but that could mean a lot of different things. I've never seen you two together, so I can't judge how he treats you when other people aren't watching."

Elena sighed, looking back at the TV. "Even if he did, what would be the point?" Elena asked rhetorically. "He's an Andraste. They're just so old-fashioned, you know? They're practically magic royalty, and I'm no one. Just a pathetic excuse of a witch with anxiety and a pen name."

"Hey, don't talk about my friend like that," Maggie admonished. "You're amazing, and if they didn't accept you, that's their loss. I wish I knew the answer to this, Elena. I wish I could tell you that love conquers all and you should chase after it like your mother did, but your concerns are valid. If you're looking for something real, something you can build a life off of, then getting involved with that family would put you front and center of not only this coven's spotlight but global politics and controversy. As much as it might not be fair to Kieran, whoever he ends up with will carry his family's baggage with them the rest of their lives."

"I keep telling myself all of that," Elena said. "But I still can't stop myself from thinking about him, like all the time. These last few weeks have been a nightmare."

"I bet," Maggie said sympathetically. "I think the only thing that can help is time. If you don't want to pursue this, then pull back from him a bit."

"Shouldn't be hard," Elena mumbled, "I haven't heard from him since we hung out."

"Well, that's just Kieran. He always vanishes then reappears," Maggie told her dismissively. "Hey." She smiled, poking Elena in the ribs. "If you change your mind, and you decide he could be worth it, I will support you with that, too."

"Thanks."

They fell into a comfortable silence, their attention going back to the movie once more.

* * *

In order to take her mind off Kieran, Elena threw herself into her work. Instead of staying home and writing, she started going to Alex's cafe every day. It was a convenient way to stay close to Mila and check on her if need be while getting out and getting a change of scenery.

Alex gave her permission to bring Huey along as long as he behaved himself around the other customers. Elena had honestly been worried about it and had a long conversation with Magnus about Huey's distrust of men and how they could handle it.

"Has he ever bitten anyone?" Magnus asked, examining Huey at one of their training sessions.

"No one who didn't deserve it," Elena muttered. When Magnus raised an eyebrow at her, she explained, "I was walking him at night one time, and this guy started following me. Run of the mill creep type. Huey went after him and got his arm pretty bad."

"Hm." Magnus's lips twitched at Huey's unrepentant expression. "It is very possible he was mistreated in the past before he became your familiar, but based on what I know about witch and familiar relationships, it is likely your own anxiety around strange men fuels his aggression. You may be practiced at controlling yourself in those situations, but he is reacting to your unspoken feelings."

Huey's tongue lolled out of his mouth as he looked at her happily, radiating that canine smugness that usually came from being told he was a good boy.

"Well, who isn't stressed out by strange men?" Elena couldn't help herself from petting Huey between the ears. "Especially growing up in the city as a woman. You have to be careful." And especially when a group of strange men attack you and murder your best friend before your eyes.

Not that Magnus knew that.

"I don't disagree," Magnus assured her. "But if you want to take Huey out in public more, he will have to learn to contain his urge to protect you. It is certainly possible. When I first met him, he didn't show any signs of aggression. I'd like to believe it was because I didn't make you nervous."

He smiled at her, and Elena blushed.

"Well, maybe. Do you have any advice?"

Of course, Magnus did. It basically amounted to talk therapy for Huey, conducted by a witch at the coven who specialized in helping familiars navigate the transition from normal animal to a magical familiar. Huey was quite a few years removed from that by now, but it couldn't hurt.

So far, it seemed to be working, as he hadn't growled at anyone at the cafe yet. Elena did buy him a "not friendly" vest to wear though, just in case. Taking a break, Elena absent-mindedly watched Alex make drinks behind the counter while she contemplated what the familiar expert had told her the last time they spoke.

"He seems to be hanging on to quite a lot of guilt," they'd informed her. "Was there an incident recently where you were in danger and he failed to protect you? It's none of my business of course, but that guilt is making his protectiveness worse."

That night, Elena had wept into Huey's fur, overwhelmed with her own feelings of regret for not realizing Huey felt this way.

"You're the best boy," she'd told him through her choked sobs. "None of it was your fault."

Huey whined and cried along with her, and eventually, Mila had to intervene to comfort them both.

"One large tea for my favorite customer," Alex said cheerfully, pulling Elena out of her thoughts and back to the present as he placed a steaming mug on the table before her. "And a dog safe foamy drink for good behavior." He put down a paper cup before Huey, who eagerly began to lap it up.

"Aw, thanks, we both know I'm not your favorite though."

Alex laughed. "Don't sell yourself so short! You're by far the best tipper out of all my regulars."

Fair enough.

Alex slid into the chair across from her, a wicked look on his face. "Have you heard what happened this weekend?"

Elena perked up. One thing she'd learned about Alex was that the only thing he loved more than collecting coven gossip was sharing it with her and Maggie.

"No, what?"

"The coven was hosting some high-class party at the mansion. Us regular peasants weren't invited. Only the old families," Alex explained, leaning in as he spoke. "Afterward, one of our rarest tomes was *missing*."

Elena's gasp was not at all put on. "Someone stole it? How is that even possible? Shouldn't the mansion wards have stopped something like that?"

"You would think." Alex glanced around then lowered his voice even lower. "But the tome wasn't at the mansion. Declan Andraste invited a bunch of the younger attendees back to his home for cocktails. The tome was there."

That was interesting. There were a collection of books that were never meant to leave the mansion for any reason, they were so rare. Elena could only assume, by the way they spoke about it, that this tome was one of them. Why did Declan have it?

"Are there any suspects?"

Alex shook his head. "None that have made it through the grapevine. It's difficult because these are other coven leaders we are talking about and the most powerful magical families in the world. It's dangerous to just go pointing fingers."

"Right. Wow."

The entire thing was way above their heads and wouldn't affect them either way, so it didn't worry Elena at all. Really, it was just baffling. If someone wanted the book that badly, why didn't they just ask to borrow it? Perhaps in return for one of their own tomes.

Rich people would never make sense to Elena.

Her phone buzzed in her pocket, and she pulled it out to check the notification.

"Is that the love of my life?" Alex tried to see the screen, and Elena pulled it back.

"Maybe, mind your business."

Alex chuckled. A few days ago, he'd caught her looking through her old friend Tora's social media posts and claimed to have fallen instantly in love with her. Elena knew he was just teasing, but she wasn't about to encourage him either.

"When is she going to come visit? I want to meet her."

"Soon," Elena muttered, already typing out a response to the text. "Probably when it starts to get warmer."

Alex grumbled before darting back to the counter to serve a customer who'd just walked in. Elena put her phone down and pet Huey a bit while looking out the window toward the street.

Elena felt a twinge of contentment as she watched people and cars go by. Life really was turning out to be not so bad here. One might even say things were good. Sure, she wasn't exactly the picture of mental stability, still hadn't made an appointment with her therapist, and she missed her friends in the city terribly, but overall, the move to Alberdeen was going as well as they could have hoped. Mila had a girlfriend she adored, and Elena was working on her magic and actually making progress.

Who cared that Kieran had ghosted her?
Certainly not Elena.
Not one bit.

Chapter 16

"Good, Elena! That was a good effort. Now try again, but this time, shift your stance so your knees are shoulder-width apart," Magnus instructed her.

Elena wiped a stray hair out of her face and adjusted her legs, staring at the boulder materializing in the air.

"Ready?" Magnus asked from where he was standing on the other side of the courtyard.

"Ready!" Elena confirmed.

Magnus made a large sweeping motion with his arm, and the boulder went flying straight for Elena's body. She stood firm and summoned her magic, feeling heat rush through her body and her muscles strain to summon the power she needed, as she thrust her left wrist forward. A bolt of sizzling light shot out and struck the boulder as it came hurtling toward her. It hit and, with a crackling sound, reduced the boulder to dust. Elena smiled, panting hard, her entire body drenched in sweat underneath her hoodie.

"Very good!" Magnus shouted from across the yard.

It was near the end of the month and still unbearably cold, but in the courtyard with magical temperature control, they were having few difficulties with the intensive self-defense training Magnus was putting Elena through.

"This is why, in case you were wondering, I told you to work on your core strength," Magnus said, walking toward her.

Elena laughed. "No kidding! I'm going to be so sore tomorrow."

"Let's take a break and get some water. After that, we can work on a smaller target."

Elena and Magnus walked back toward the mansion, chatting about her progress from the day as they went. Over the weeks, they'd developed an easy partnership. Magnus was steady and patient, but a powerful witch who demanded excellence from her, although he never pushed too hard. With his guidance, Elena was quickly advancing through her lessons. Learning from him, compared to learning from her mother, was like night and day.

Her mother had tried her best but had little patience and found it difficult to explain things in a way Elena had understood. It led to more than one tearful shouting match in her youth. Elena had never imagined she would be able to destroy boulders with such ease.

Huey accompanied her most training days, making friends with the familiars and witches that hung around the mansion, or helping Elena with her spell work by lending his own magical energy to her.

Meanwhile, Mila's shop became a raging success after Elena's coven membership became official. Coven members came from all over the country to buy their plants from her. Mila's Menagerie was now so successful she was able to hire staff so she could have more free time—and to be with Ava, of course.

Their winter romance had blossomed into a true love match since New Year's Eve, and they were hardly ever apart. Thanks to weekly therapy sessions, Mila was back driving herself again, although she refused to drive at night. A new normal settled in for the sisters, and they were more than happy to welcome it.

Elena felt a little guilty encouraging Mila to keep up with the therapy when she was actively choosing not to engage in it herself, but every time she seriously though about making an appointment, a deep weariness settled over her. She didn't want to talk about her problems or her feelings. It was exhausting and wouldn't change anything. More than anything, it was easier just to move on.

As she and Magnus reached the mansion, a witch Elena had met a few times, named Chelsea, approached them.

"Hi, you two!" she said excitedly. "I thought you might need something to drink." In her arms, she carried a tray with two glasses of ice water.

"Thank you!" Elena exclaimed, taking one and downing it.

"How's it coming along?" Chelsea asked. "Looked like you were making quite the mess out there!"

"Elena is progressing nicely. After our break, I think I'm going to try throwing smaller rocks at her from different angles to see how that goes," Magnus replied.

"Ugh, those rocks. I remember when I was learning to disintegrate oncoming objects. I ended up getting hit in the face so many times!" Chelsea said with a twinkling laugh.

"Ah, something to look forward to." Elena grimaced.

Chelsea held the empty tray up against her chest and rocked back on her heels excitedly. "Before you head off, I wanted to invite you to our winter social this weekend! Singles only!"

Magnus sighed heavily and walked away. "I'll meet you back in the courtyard in fifteen minutes, Elena," he said over his shoulder before going inside.

Chelsea rolled her eyes. "He's just bummed he isn't invited."

"He isn't? I thought Magnus was single," Elena asked curiously.

"Yes, but this party isn't going to really be his scene. Think trendy city nightclub meets witch's festival."

"Oh," Elena said, her eyes going wide.

"Exactly! Everyone will be young and sexy and ready to party. Can I count you in?"

"Uh..." Elena began hesitantly. "Yeah, maybe. Send me the details, and I will see if I'm free. I'm sure Maggie will drag me along anyway."

"Great, see you there!" Chelsea said happily before vanishing in a puff of purple smoke.

Elena waved the smoke away with her hand, coughing. Maybe she could convince Tora to come out for it. After casually mentioning Alex to her friend, Tora was undeniably interested, so perhaps getting them in the same room wasn't such a terrible idea.

Playing matchmaker wasn't exactly Elena's strong suit, but the idea of making two of her favorite people happy put a little extra pep in her step.

Part of her wondered if Kieran would show up, but she quickly silenced that voice. She'd learned that Kieran rarely attended coven gatherings that didn't hold some official purpose, and a party to help singles meet and mingle was never something he'd attended in the past.

Besides, she was supposed to be putting him out of her mind. This party was the perfect way to do that. And who knew, perhaps she'd meet someone herself. Someone not like Kieran at all, who was present and attentive and didn't leave her guessing about how they felt.

* * *

The nonsense with the stolen book from Declan's house did not resolve itself, which meant Kieran was the one tasked with finding and retrieving the damned thing. While everyone else in the coven chattered about the party coming up at the mansion, Kieran had been planning a heist to steal back their tome and prove that the eldest son of the Orozco family was guilty of the original crime. Well, that was debatable. Kieran suspected the whole reason the Orozco boy had stolen the book was because a few weeks prior, Declan had used a banned spell against him in what was meant to be a friendly duel. Anthony Andraste had quickly covered the entire thing up, but the Orozco family hadn't forgotten.

Which led Kieran to where he currently stood—in the Orozco family home, flanked by two officers from the High Witch's Council, watching his mother go toe to toe with Gordon Orozco, the patriarch of the family.

Even though he was still, Kieran's heartbeat wildly at the close call he'd just suffered. It was not the first time Kieran had found himself on the receiving end of a killing spell, and he doubted it would be the last.

Thankfully, his wards were strong enough to lessen the blow and spare his life, but the bruise it left behind on his chest still hurt like hell.

In the aftermath of the battle, he hadn't yet had the time to heal himself. The two officers' iron grips on his arms cut off circulation to his hands, preventing him from tending to his wound. He didn't complain and simply stood silent as he watched his mother arguing with Gordon, who also happened to be the leader of the Northern Mountains Coven, and the same man who'd just tried to kill him.

Not that Kieran blamed him. After all, Kieran had broken into his home and was sneaking around in the dark when he was discovered. It was only after the coven leader attacked that the man realized exactly who he was up against.

"First," the coven leader snarled in Josephine Andraste's face, "your oldest son nearly kills my boy in a duel with illegal magic, then your wretch of a second-born breaks into my home? And you have the nerve to show up here and try to have me arrested?"

"You shot a killing spell at my son!" Josephine glared at him, drawing herself up to her full height. "You tried to murder him."

"A witch has the right to protect their home and property," the coven leader shot back, pointing a finger in Josephine's face.

Kieran shifted, his eyes narrowing at the man, and the officers on either side of him tightened their hold.

"Would you let go of him? He isn't resisting," Josephine snapped at the officers, who exchanged glances.

Josephine leveled them with an icy glare, and the two officers let Kieran go. Blood returned to his arms, but Kieran did not move.

Josephine turned back to the coven leader with a sigh. "Things have gotten out of hand here," she said quietly. "We both nearly suffered devastating losses. Surely, there's no need to make the situation worse. How can we fix this?"

The coven leader sneered at her, and Kieran clenched his

fists in barely contained anger.

"You cannot be serious."

"I'm perfectly serious," Josephine replied. "Talk to me, Gordon. What can be done?"

Gordon considered her for a moment, weighing the implications of her words. "Very well," he said after a moment. "I'll drop charges against Kieran in return for a few promises from you, and maybe a favor."

Josephine smiled lightly and turned to the council officers. "You hear that? He isn't pressing charges. You can go now."

The officers looked to Gordon, concern on their faces. He nodded to them, and they quickly left the room.

"First, Declan will appear before the High Witch's Council for his actions, no trying to get out of it," Gordon said immediately.

Josephine's jaw clenched, but she nodded.

"Secondly, you have to tell me what Kieran was looking for."

"The spell book your son stole from Declan," Kieran said smoothly.

Gordon fixed him with a glare. "My son stole nothing."

Kieran tilted his head, his eyes glinting in the half dark of the room. "So he says."

Gordon bristled and turned back to Josephine. "Send your boy away. You and I will discuss what else I require in private."

"Absolutely not," Kieran said, his voice in a low growl as he made to step forward, but Josephine held up a hand to stop him.

"Go home, Kieran." Her voice was hard with command.

"Mother, please," Kieran pleaded with her, but Josephine was not looking at him.

"Go home," she repeated.

Gordon was staring at Josephine with a greedy look on his face, and Kieran could practically see him calculating in his head what he would get from her. Would it stop at money, or would he demand more? Kieran wasn't sure, but he knew they'd lost this particular round, and now, it was time to face the consequences. Taking a deep breath, he turned away, opening a portal as he did, and stepped through.

Emerging in his father's study, Kieran was immediately met with the outraged face of his brother, who grabbed his shoulders roughly with both hands as the portal closed.

"What happened?" Declan demanded. Although they were roughly the same height, Kieran always felt like his brother towered over him, especially when he was angry, with his muscular bulk and broad frame.

Kieran brushed Declan off and instead turned his attention to their father, who was looking at him with an all-too-familiar expression of disgust and disappointment.

"You failed," Anthony Andraste said simply.

Kieran felt a numbness begin to creep over his limbs, but he held his head high.

"The wards protecting the manor were trickier than I anticipated and took longer to unravel than I planned for. When the coven leader arrived home early, I was caught off guard," Kieran tried to explain, though he knew it would do no good. It never did.

"You failed!" Anthony roared, stepping forward. The older man's magical aura surged, sending both of his sons stumbling backward. "Once again, you have failed to protect this family, and now your mother is out there cleaning up your mess. Tell me, Kieran, when will the day come that your inadequacies stop bringing the rest of us down? Now your brother will have to stand trial, and spirits know what your mother is being forced to promise that man to keep you out of prison. You are weak!"

Kieran blinked, his fists clenched so tightly at his sides his fingernails were cutting into his skin and drawing blood. He barely dared to breathe as his father's words sliced through his chest and straight to his heart.

Anthony stared at him for a moment longer. "Get out of my sight," he barked, then turned his back.

Stumbling, Kieran made for the door and left as quickly as possible. Barely registering his surroundings, he walked briskly to his bedroom on auto pilot, his mind racing.

He should have told his father no. Kieran had known what he'd been doing was wrong, knew that stealing the book back was a reckless and petty plan, but his father had ordered him to do it. No one could say no to Anthony Andraste, least of all his youngest son. Numb, he felt numb. All he knew was an unbearable sound in his head, like the wind roaring through a tunnel.

Kieran collapsed onto his bed, pain shooting up his chest from the large bruise there. A shudder ran through his body as his shattered mind registered it, breaking through the unbearable nothingness that consumed him. Taking a deep breath, Kieran slid his hand up under his shirt, settling it against the bare bruise, then pressed down with his fingertips.

Pain radiated through him again, and Kieran closed his eyes almost blissfully. He needed a release, an escape, anything to get away from this.

For some horrible, cruel reason, Elena Hall's face flashed to his mind. Of her soft body underneath him, what she would sound like as she moaned his name, what she tasted like... Kieran shoved the thoughts away instantly, disgusted with himself for even thinking about it. He could never use Elena like that—to distract himself from his pain—ever. He'd cut her out of his life to protect her from this, all the drama and corruption that consumed every aspect of his existence. As soon as he realized that it was her smile, the sound of her voice that made his heart start pounding, and not her books, Kieran knew he needed to end their friendship. Especially after he'd kissed her cheek and she'd looked at him with such gentle adoration. So he'd ceased all contact, for her own good.

No, he would find someone else to distract him. Maybe even multiple someones. Whatever it took to silence his mind screaming at him.

Weak.

Chapter 17

Tora readily agreed to come to the party, and thankfully, since the event was open to members outside the coven, Elena was able to get her added to the guest list without any trouble. When she saw said guest list, however, and realized how many witches would be in attendance, Elena's nerves started to take root. For some reason, she'd been imagining something smaller and more intimate, like her welcome party, but it turned out there would be nearly one hundred witches in attendance. To make matters worse, she learned Kieran would most definitely not be attending. Word of his altercation with the Northern Mountains Coven spread quickly, and no one expected him to make an appearance.

The day of the party dawned much faster than Elena was ready for. Tora arrived in Alberdeen the day before so she could meet Ava—a dinner Elena was told went very well— and then spent the rest of the next day getting ready.

Elena, Tora, and Mila were all crammed into Elena's bedroom, working on their looks for the night. Mila was in the process of braiding Tora's hair into a sleek updo while Elena carefully applied a deep red lipstick to her lips.

Tora was a few inches taller than Elena, with straight jet-black hair and angular dark eyes. Tattoos ran up one side of her neck and covered both of her arms and part of her chest. A septum piecing brought the entire look together, and she always looked awesome without trying.

Though Tora would probably argue that having to sit through hours of tattoo sessions over the years definitely counted as trying.

"What do you guys think for hair? Purple or red?" Elena asked, flicking her hair color between the two options.

"I have a wild idea, why don't you go all natural, just for tonight?" Tora suggested.

"Yes! It's all witches there, so it's not like anyone will think it's weird," Mila agreed.

Elena considered for a moment. When was the last time she'd had her natural hair unaltered in public? She honestly couldn't remember.

"All right, all white it is!" With a flutter of her eyes, all the bright color drained from Elena's hair, leaving it completely white. For a moment, she couldn't recognize herself. It was like a mirror into the past gazing at her reflection—back to a version of her existence that hadn't been so afraid of the world around her. It made Elena's heart race with nerves... and perhaps a bit of excitement.

Mila nodded approvingly. "Looks good! Let me finish with Tora, and I will do your hair next."

When it was time to go, the witches filed outside, Tora and Elena wearing aggressively high heels and tight clothing that made breathing just the tiniest bit difficult. Elena's hair was flowing freely around her shoulders, shimmering softly in the moonlight.

"Have fun, be safe, try not to get pregnant!" Mila called from the front door.

Huey barked once next to her.

"Get pregnant with a bunch of babies, you got it!" Tora called back.

Mila rolled her eyes and shut the door.

"All right, let's go!" Tora said excitedly.

Elena sighed and threw up her hand while Tora looked away, the door to the mansion appearing in front of them. Tora nearly stumbled over herself in her rush to go through, leaving Elena laughing behind her. When she arrived outside the mansion, Tora could barely contain herself, commenting on every tiny detail. As they reached the doors, Elena saw Maggie and Alex waiting.

"Woah, look at you out of sweatpants! You look hot," Alex teased as they approached.

"Hardy har," Elena responded sarcastically, rolling her eyes. "You guys, this is my old friend Tora, and this is Maggie and Alex."

Elena watched with a touch of anxiety as the three witches observed each other.

"I am absolutely delighted to finally meet you," Alex stepped forward, taking Tora's hand and bringing it to his mouth for a soft kiss. "Your pictures hardly do you justice."

Tora threw back her head and laughed. "Oh no, I'm in trouble with you, aren't I?"

"If he gets too annoying, Tora, swat him on the nose and send him to bed with no treats." Maggie smirked.

"You wound me, Mags. Isn't tonight all about getting treats?"

Maggie ignored him and focused on the other two women. "Just wait till you see the inside! The decorating committee went all out."

They walked through the doors into a room that was totally unrecognizable. The lights were low, and dark red and golden velvet curtains were draped from the ceiling. There was a dance floor in the center of the hall, and all around it were couches, chairs, and standing tables. No less than six bars were scattered along the walls, and tiny glowing balls of light floated through the air.

"Damn," Tora said, taking it all in.

"Can I buy you a drink?" Alex offered her.

"It's an open bar, you idiot." Maggie rolled her eyes.

Alex shrugged, and Tora laughed.

"Sure you can, but you should know that Elena has told me all about you."

"I promise they are all true." He gave her a sultry look before leading Tora away toward the nearest bar.

Elena shook her head. "Well, that was quick. Should I be worried?"

Maggie laughed. "Nah. He talks a big game, but it's Alex. The bravado will wear off after one cocktail, and he'll be putty in her hands."

"Oh dear, Tora is going to eat him alive."

Two hours and several shots later, the entire group was out on the dance floor, surrounded by over a hundred single witches. But even in that crowd, the expanse of the room and the way it was set up made the number feel far less, and Elena was able to relax. Alex quickly found himself in competition for Tora's attention from a member of their own coven and a few witches Elena didn't recognize. Tora basked in the attention, though she slipped away more than a few times to check on Elena.

Maggie and Elena were keeping to themselves so far, dancing with each other and throwing the drinks back. The pair was having a ton of fun, reminding Elena of her party days where she'd dance like this with Sammi and her other friends at nightclubs all around New Stirling City. Everything was so different from then, but at least Elena's surprisingly good alcohol tolerance hadn't changed. Maggie was an enthusiastic dancer, and so far, Elena was managing not to trip over her own feet.

Maggie grabbed Elena by the arm and swung her around, laughing gleefully when they were interrupted.

"Hey, beautiful," a man whispered in Maggie's ear when the pair stopped spinning.

She whirled around, looking pissed, but froze when she saw his face.

"Well, hey there yourself," she purred.

"Wanna dance with me for a bit?" he asked.

Maggie nodded, and he whisked her away from Elena, who was suddenly alone. Pouting, Elena left the dance floor and headed for the nearest bar. On her way, she tripped over her own ankles and stumbled, colliding with someone's back.

"Oh, I'm so sorry!" she said, righting herself and mentally blaming the shoes rather than the alcohol.

The person she'd collided with turned around to see who ran into them, and Elena did a double take. It was Kieran.

Shock took over her system as she stared up at him. He was here? After everything? Part of her wanted to poke him to see if he was a real and not one of her fantasies come to life, but she managed to resist the temptation

"Hello, Elena, it's been a while." Kieran smiled at her, his eyes slightly unfocused.

"Uh, yes it has!" she said, shouting maybe a little too loudly over the music. "How are you?" she asked, taking in his appearance as her heart pounded in her ears.

He looked, if Elena could nail it down to one phrase, obscenely fuckable. He wore tight, dark wash jeans and a black V-neck that clung to his lean, muscular frame. His dark hair was tousled and messy in a way that was so utterly perfect, Elena had to stop herself from reaching up and running her hands through it.

Spirits, her impulses were all over the place tonight.

"I'm fine," Kieran said in a tone that made it sound like he was anything but, forcing Elena to focus on his face. Completely perfect there as well at first glance. Elena couldn't quite put her finger on what was wrong with him, but there was something definitely out of place.

"Kieran! You made it!" Chelsea, the witch who'd invited Elena to the party, came flying in out of nowhere, shoving herself between Elena and Kieran.

Elena stumbled backward then scoffed as she watched Chelsea drag Kieran away without another word. Elena's heart clenched, and she felt a prickling at the corner of her eyes that she quickly blinked away.

"Holy shit, was that Kieran Andraste?" Tora asked, appearing at Elena's shoulder.

"It was," Elena confirmed bitterly.

Maggie also appeared and eyed Elena suspiciously. "You okay, babe?"

"Nope, don't think so. I'm gonna get another drink."

News of Kieran's arrival at the party totally changed the vibe of the entire event. His name was on everyone's lips, although it seemed no one knew where he went off to. He would appear for a few moments here or there before vanishing again. It was all driving Elena a bit mad as she was doing her best to ignore it all, so she threw herself into the theme of the night and tried chatting up a very good-looking man from the south.

It went well, and Elena was just drunk enough to be feeling a little frisky, so she dragged the guy off down a hallway to make out with him in some dark corner. The pair were stumbling and laughing as they looked for a spot, and as they rounded a corner, they found they were not alone.

"Whoops, looks like this is taken," the guy, she thought his name might be Jeff, muttered in her ear.

Elena blinked a few times at the couple in front of them. The man was unmistakably Kieran, even if he was facing away from them, and in his arms was Jackie Hammond—that awful woman who'd been so rude to Elena her first day in the mansion. Jackie had one of her hands up his back underneath his shirt, the other clamped tightly on his ass, while Kieran kissed her neck. Jackie was moaning loudly and, when she opened her eyes and spotted them, smirked in their direction. She looked directly at Elena as she moaned again, then turned to lightly nibble Kieran's ear.

Anger and disgust pounded in Elena's head. What the hell? A few weeks ago, he was kissing her so sweetly on the cheek, and now this?

Shit, she was *jealous*. Now angry at herself for her reaction, she turned away.

"Come on, I know another spot."

Elena wished, by the spirits she wished, that would be the only incident she witnessed with Kieran that night. After finding out Jeff—or maybe it was Kyle— was a terrible kisser, she ditched him and went back to the main party. After another forty minutes or so, she spotted Kieran being dragged away up the grand staircase by a woman Elena didn't recognize.

Then, a little before one in the morning with her second attempt of the night, a guy she was sure was named Allan, she slipped into a study room with him only to discover Kieran kissing a man Elena recognized as the witch that had performed Huey's portal enchantment, Ned, whose hand was down the front of Kieran's pants. Ned, for his part, didn't even notice the intrusion; he was so focused on Keiran. Elena was able to back out of the room without being spotted.

It was common knowledge that Kieran had a reputation in the past for his romantic trysts, but seeing it in action was something else, and Elena would be lying if she said every new person he brought into his embrace wasn't hurting her feelings more and more as the night went on.

After having a successful interlude with Allan herself, Elena made her way back to the dance floor, no longer really able to tell who was who, and not caring that much at that point, anyway. A little while later, she found herself on a couch with Alex, who held his arm protectively around her and was forcing her to drink water.

"Having fuuun?" she asked, slurring her words.

"Of course." He grinned down at her. "Oh, you will never guess who I saw?" He ignored a woman sitting next to them, who was clearly trying to get his attention.

"Maggie and that blond guy? I knew it!" Elena shouted.

"No, no. It was Kieran! He was up there, somewhere." Alex gestured wildly, almost smacking the woman next to him in the face. "And some woman, I think from the southern coven, was going down on him!"

"Ugh, I saw them going off together earlier," Elena said,

trying to block that image from her head. What was wrong with him?

Putting her own jealousy and wounded pride aside, Elena started to feel herself get genuinely worried. Elena didn't judge people for their sex lives as long as no one was getting hurt but this... something seemed very wrong. Kieran's past was well known and well documented in tabloids and the news—it was true—but all that had ceased years ago. Was something going on with him?

By the early hours of the morning, the party started to wind down, and a large group of coven witches gathered on some couches away from the dance floor. Elena and Tora were sitting on the floor, leaning on each other for support, while Alex was on the couch behind them, the woman from before happily in his lap. It seemed he and Tora hadn't worked out, and she was nowhere to be seen.

"Can you believe he showed up tonight?" one woman, Natalie, was saying. "He never comes to these sorts of things."

Elena groaned when she realized they were once again talking about Kieran.

"He seems a bit funny though, doesn't he? Not like himself," someone chimed in.

"Maybe he's just loosening up a bit, about time, too. Been a bit too responsible lately, in my opinion. I've missed the old Kieran."

"It's a hell of a time to let loose, with what happened with the northern coven."

"Oh please, you all don't know what you're talking about," another voice cut through the conversation.

They all looked to see Jackie sauntering her way over to the group. She held a cocktail clutched in one hand, the other perched on her hip.

"Oh, and you do?" someone shot back.

"You bet your ass I do!" Jackie shouted, swaying. She was clearly very drunk. "He's here because I personally asked him to come, and we've been together all night. We have a truly special bond, I mean"—she threw her hair over her shoulder—"out of all the witches here tonight, he chose to spend it with me. "

Elena burst out laughing.

Everyone turned to look at her, and Jackie's eyes narrowed into a deadly glare. "You think that's funny?" she asked haughtily.

Under normal circumstances, Elena would have kept her mouth shut and stayed a thousand feet away from this situation, but she was extremely drunk and upset, so she couldn't seem to help herself.

"That you think you two have some sort of connection because you made out at a party? I do!" Elena laughed. "You didn't even get as far with him as Ned did," she added nastily.

"Don't be stupid," Jackie said, her voice low with anger. "He's been with me the entire time."

Elena did not back down. "No, he has not," she shot back

"Actually, I saw him with Ned, too," Natalie chimed in. "Which like *woah*, who saw that coming? Ned is usually so quiet."

Jackie turned her glare on Natalie, who shrank away.

"He told me things, important things about the coven that no one else knows about!" Jackie shrieked, swaying as she did, the drink in her hand spilling all over the floor. "I'm important to him!"

Elena snorted. "You're just another number," she said harshly, "and last I checked, spilling coven secrets is against the rules. Are you trying to get Kieran in trouble, Jackie?"

Jackie's pretty face contorted in rage at the accusation. "What do you know about this coven?" Jackie shouted back, throwing her glass to the floor in anger, shattered pieces flying everywhere.

"Woah, Jackie! Calm down!" someone said, but she ignored them.

"You didn't even want to join! But you were such a weak and pathetic witch, you signed on to steal our knowledge from us. You're just jealous of me! Jealous of my power, jealous that Kieran pays attention to me and you are nothing to him!"

Elena jumped to her feet with surprising grace for someone as drunk as she was. "You think I'm jealous? I don't give a shit! You could be marrying him, and I wouldn't care! Just because you're obsessed with becoming the next Andraste doesn't mean the rest of us are!" Elena shouted back.

Sparks flew out of Jackie's hands, and she took a menacing step toward Elena. It was at this point, the surrounding coven members intervened. Alex leapt to his feet and jumped between Elena and Jackie, blocking Elena with his body. A few others grabbed Jackie by the arms and pulled her back.

"You're all fucking idiots! Let go of me!" Jackie said viciously, yanking herself free and storming away.

Elena peeked her head around Alex's shoulder. "Oops," she said, glaring at Jackie's retreating form.

Chapter 18

Kieran did not know why he was being summoned to the mansion the Monday after the disastrous singles party, but he had a feeling it wasn't for anything good. When he arrived in the great hall, his eyes scanned the room, remembering how it had looked that night. Most of it was a haze, but one particular face stood out in his memory. The image of Elena blinking up at him in surprise near the bar—her eyes sparkling under sultry makeup, her hair a glistening pure white, and the tight dress she was wearing teasing him ruthlessly—was burned into his brain.

Kieran had needed to get away from her, or he would have ended up doing something he regretted. She'd found someone else to occupy her night, anyway, judging by the fact Kieran spotted her a while later in a dark corner with some man Kieran hadn't recognized. The man reminded Kieran of his brother, handsome and exceedingly masculine. It figured she would move on from him with someone his complete opposite.

Shaking his head, Kieran walked briskly across the hall and up the grand staircase to the second floor, before heading to Charles's office. Reaching the large ornate wooden door, Kieran raised his hand to knock. As he did, a jolt of intuition shot through him. Whatever was about to happen in there, it was going to be disastrous. Taking a deep breath to steel himself, Kieran knocked.

"Come in," a deep voice said from inside.

Kieran recognized it as his father's voice. He entered the office, barely breathing.

Charles sat behind his desk, looking grim. Three other board members were in the room, along with Kieran's father. Kieran kept his external demeanor calm, but internally, he was starting to panic. What was going on?

"Father," he greeted, "I didn't realize you would be here."

Anthony Andraste regarded his youngest son but said nothing.

"Have a seat, Kieran," Charles said wearily.

Kieran obeyed, his eyes slipping to each of the board member's faces, trying to get a read on what they were thinking.

"Is something wrong, Charles?" Kieran asked.

Charles sighed. "I'll get right to it, Kieran. After the social event held here two nights ago, a formal complaint was filed against you," he began.

Kieran's heart started to pound hard. He clasped his hands in front of him, his elbows resting on the arms of the chair. He held Charles's gaze, not giving anything away.

"Jackie Hammond, according to the report," Charles continued, "got into a minor altercation with Elena Hall late in the evening,"

Kieran's eyes widened slightly at the mention of Elena.

"During that altercation, Jackie claimed you told her coven secrets."

Charles paused again, but Kieran did not say anything, so

he continued.

"At first, we believed Miss Hammond to have been simply drunkenly boasting, however, after speaking with her and making it clear she would face severe consequences for her claims, she revealed to us what it was you told her. It was indeed a coven secret, information she could have only gotten from you," Charles concluded.

Heart pounding in his ears, it was only years of practice that allowed Kieran to keep his expression neutral. Spirits, what had he done?

The board members were all openly scowling at him, and his father looked absolutely livid.

"You told her about the ongoing negotiations between our coven and the Coastal Coven!" one of the board members, a man named Nao, seethed. "Do you have any idea what could happen if word of those plans got out to the other covens? Or were you too interested in getting your dick wet to care?"

Kieran's mind was racing, desperately trying to think of a way to defend himself. He remembered being with Jackie, of course, and they'd spent quite a bit of time together, but he'd told her that? What would have possessed him to do such a thing? Slowly, horrifyingly the memory dawned on him.

"Yes, I did tell her," Kieran admitted.

"That's all you have to say for yourself?" Charles asked disbelievingly.

"Is there anything else to say?" Kieran asked. "I'm guilty of what you have accused me of. There is no excuse I can offer for what I did. I was drunk, I was not in my right mind, and I made a mistake."

"Ah, well then, all is forgiven," Nao said sarcastically.

Kieran glared at him. "I'm not expecting to be forgiven. I

will accept whatever punishment the board sees fit.”

Kieran saw his father nod out of the corner of his eye.

“It's important the coven sees that even we are not above the rules,” Anthony said.

Kieran felt his stomach twist uncomfortably.

“May I speak to Kieran alone for a moment?” Charles asked.

The board members all looked to Anthony, who paused to consider, then nodded. Feeding Kieran to the wolves, as usual. The bitterness tasted like acid on Kieran's tongue.

Anthony started for the door, shooting Kieran a stern look as he went, the three board members following him. Once the door closed behind them, Charles sat back in his chair, a concerned look on his face.

“Kieran, I know this is an uncomfortable situation, but I need to know why this happened. You've always been someone we trusted more than most. Accidentally spilling out a secret isn't like you.”

“It's been a difficult week for me, Charles, I suppose I just lost it,” Kieran said, wishing more than anything to leave this room as quickly as possible.

Charles frowned. “We spoke to several attendees from the party. You more than lost it Kieran, you were out of control.”

“It won't happen again,” Kieran said tightly, looking down at his feet.

“Is Miss Hammond special? Are you pursuing a relationship with her?” Charles probed.

Irritation shot through Kieran. It was none of Charles's fucking business.

“Not at all,” Kieran said, barely containing his anger, “she means nothing to me.”

“And yet you decided to tell her something she had no

business knowing," Charles said flatly.

"What do you want me to say, Charles?" Kieran calm demeanor cracked. "I was drunk, I was angry, I wasn't thinking clearly. She's a clever woman, and she knew exactly which buttons to push to get me to give her what she wanted. I was weak and stupid."

Charles' eyebrows raised. "Are you saying she was deliberately trying to get information out of you?"

"Does it matter? We've always known what type of woman Jackie is. She's ambitious, she wants power, and I let her get to me. She didn't break any rules by asking. I'm the one who screwed up. Just give me my punishment, and we can move on."

Charles regarded him for a moment. "Very well, I'll need to discuss this with the entire board and then we will let you know what we've decided. You may go," Charles dismissed him.

Kieran shot to his feet and walked out the door. His father had the other board members deep in discussion outside, and Kieran didn't spare them a glance as he made his escape.

"We'll discuss this more at home," Anthony called out after him.

Kieran winced. How could he have let this happen? Ever since his brother got married, Jackie had made her intentions toward Kieran quite clear. What was he thinking, giving in to her?

Though, to be used as a steppingstone to power was probably all he deserved, Kieran reasoned. He was a pathetic fool who only ever broke anything good he touched. He didn't deserve someone who genuinely cared about him, even though right now he ached for that more than anything else in the world.

* * *

Elena was hanging out at Alex's coffee shop after hours, helping him set up some new furniture and listening to him wax poetic about Tora's rejection when Maggie came bursting in.

"You guys!" she practically shrieked. "Look what I got in the mail!"

She flung a piece of paper down on the nearest table and Alex leaned down to read it.

"Shit," Alex whispered. "Elena, you need to see this."

Elena frowned and picked up the paper to read.

Valued Coven Member,

It has come to the attention of the board that over this past weekend a member of our founding family, Kieran Andraste, leaked confidential coven information to one of our members. This was a breach of trust and protocol that we take very seriously. Mr. Andraste has been immediately relieved of his official position of coven ambassador and will remain on probation until he has earned our trust back. He has also paid a fine of ten thousand dollars. Finally, it has been deemed, as part of his punishment for breaking such an important coven rule, that Mr. Andraste must publicly apologize to the coven for his behavior. You are henceforth invited to this public apology, and we strongly encourage attendance, as uncomfortable as it may be.

Kieran Andraste is a valued member of our coven, but no one is above the rules we all agreed to follow in order to keep the coven safe. We hope that after this, we can all move forward from this incident together.

Signed,

Your Board of Directors

The Greenwood Coven

Elena gaped at the document, then re-read it. "I can't believe it," she muttered. "I thought Jackie was lying."

"We all did," Maggie said. "I mean, why would Kieran do that?"

"Do you think they're actually together?" Alex asked.

Elena's stomach dropped.

"No, there's no way. He may have told her something he shouldn't, but he was also off hooking up with other people that night. He must have let it slip or something," Maggie reasoned, looking at Elena worriedly.

Elena set the paper down. "So, are you two going to go?" she asked.

"Of course I am! This kind of thing never happens. I wouldn't miss it," Alex said enthusiastically.

"I think a lot of people will go for that reason. I mean..." Maggie shook her head. "Everyone pays lip service to the Andrastes but secretly loves it when they screw up. They're going to eat this up."

Elena looked out the window into the dark, pursing her lips. She didn't know how she felt about that. Part of her was angry at Kieran for what he'd done, for screwing up in such a stupid way, but another part couldn't help but feel bad for him. She shoved those feelings away. He didn't need her pity. He didn't need anything from her, it seemed.

"All right, I'll go, too," she said.

Maggie frowned, but Elena ignored the look. If Kieran was going to apologize, she wanted to be there, even if it had nothing to do with how he'd treated her. Perhaps this was the closure she needed to move on.

* * *

Kieran forced himself to be numb. It was all he could do to make it through this. He just needed to go out there, state his piece, then leave. As long as he remained cold to it all, he could make it through.

His mother stood next to him silently, holding his arm tight in her hands. She was aggressively against this entire spectacle, but her husband had refused to stand up against the board's decision. Kieran knew, deep in his gut, that if Declan was in this position, he never would have been forced to go through this punishment. It all would be handled behind closed doors, and Declan would never need to face the entire coven. Kieran shoved the thought away. It did nothing to help him, so there was no point dwelling on it.

Speaking of his brother, Declan and Therese appeared in the hallway where Kieran and his mother were waiting.

"How is it out there?" Their mother asked, nervously.

"A lot of people showed up," Therese said sadly. "Nearly the entire coven, by the looks of it."

Kieran felt sick but fought to push it down. Numb, he had to be numb.

His mother scowled next to him. "Of course, they all showed up to watch our family be humiliated, after everything we do for them," she said bitterly.

Declan put a bracing hand on Kieran's shoulder. "It'll be over quick. Just be as boring as possible, and they'll forget all about it in a few weeks," he said.

Kieran nodded as Anthony appeared, looking grim. In truth,

none of them really cared about the other details of Kieran's punishment. The money was nothing, and they all knew Kieran's title of coven ambassador had always been a smoke screen for what he really did for the coven anyway, and that work would continue.

But this? Public humiliation. Offering him up as a sacrifice to the public's fickle opinions and contempt? For the upper class of magical society, there were few things worse. It was an attack on their reputations, their authority, and threw into question their ability to care for their own covens. Kieran was usually a predator among these halls, but now he was little more than a scrap of meat about to be fed to the hyenas.

"It's time to start, everyone follow me. Kieran, when it's your turn to speak, Charles will call you forward. Stick to the script we agreed on." Anthony's tone was vaguely threatening, the anger he'd unleashed on Kieran in private still evident there.

"Yes, Father," Kieran said, his voice empty of emotion.

* * *

Elena waited in the crowded main hall with Maggie and Alex for nearly an hour, and during that time, Elena's anxiety grew worse. While being in large crowds had been hard for her over the last year, at the mansion she'd never had a problem because everyone was spread out, and the atmosphere was always friendly and fun.

This was entirely different. It seemed the entire coven was crammed into the hall, and as time went on, the crowd was becoming more and more restless with a dangerous energy that made Elena's entire being squirm.

"What's taking so long?" a witch behind Elena said irritably. "I want to see him already!"

"Who knew it was so easy to get confidential information out of Kieran? All anyone has to do is get him drunk and give him a blow job," someone else said, laughing.

"Are you surprised? He's always been such a whore. I'm more shocked this didn't happen sooner."

"I wish it had been me! Jackie is so lucky," a witch crooned.

"You do not," another replied sternly. "I heard she was told she wasn't welcome today, and to stay away from Kieran for the foreseeable future."

"Ha! And I bet Kieran didn't do anything to stick up for her. Typical. An Andraste does something wrong, and someone else gets punished for it."

"He *is* being punished for it, that's why we are here," the speaker was reminded.

"If you gave me an hour alone with Kieran Andraste, I could punish him enough for the entire coven," someone said crudely, eliciting more laughter.

"This is horrible," Maggie muttered to Elena.

Elena nodded mutely, her arms trembling. She crossed them over her chest, holding herself. Any resentment she felt toward Kieran was long gone after listening to the vile things his own coven was saying about him. Now, she just wanted to get out of this place as soon as possible.

The Andrastes appeared at the top of the stairs, and a hush fell over the room. Elena craned her neck to see Kieran, who was standing at the back. He looked paler than usual, but his expression was blank. She couldn't imagine what it looked like from up there for him, gazing out over a sea of hostile faces

It was hard to tell, but it seemed like he wasn't really looking at them, but rather over the crowd's head toward the exit. The board was waiting, standing in a single row on a makeshift stage at the bottom of the stairs. Charles stepped forward and began to speak, his voice reverberating around the room. Elena barely heard a word. Heart pounding, her hands gripped onto Maggie's arm as she started to feel a bit dizzy. There were so many people pressing in.

Focus, she had to focus. No one was going to hurt her here.

Charles finished speaking, and Kieran stepped forward.

Elena forced herself to watch him. His back was straight, and his head held high, but his face was empty of any emotion. Now that he was closer, Elena could see the slightest shadow of circles under his eyes.

"How does he still manage to look so arrogant right now?" someone whispered, displeased.

Arrogant? Elena thought he looked like hell.

Kieran reached the platform and carefully made his way to the front. He glanced at Charles, who nodded, then cleared his throat.

"My dear friends," he began, his voice strong and smooth, "I come before you today humbled and apologetic. I have behaved in a way unsuitable for a leader of this noble and honorable coven. I have broken the trust of not only my family and the board, but of all of you. It's inexcusable, and I am deeply sorry for betraying that trust. I will be taking a step back from my position of leadership to reflect on my behavior and to work on bettering myself so an incident like this never happens again. I hope, in time, I can be forgiven for my lapse in judgment. There is nothing I value more than the safety and prosperity of this coven and its members, and I will do everything I can to make it right," he finished.

Elena watched him miserably. A few witches loudly jeered, though Kieran continued like he hadn't heard them. Every word that left his mouth sounded like nails on a chalkboard in Elena's ears. Her fists were clenched tightly, and she struggled to control her breathing. The energy of the crowd was still buzzing around her. She begged Kieran to wrap it up in her mind. While he was still speaking, Elena heard the witch in front of her whisper.

"Look at him beg, so pathetic."

Elena lost focus on the room, her head spinning.

"That's right, you disgusting little bitch, beg for your life!" a cruel voice said in her mind.

"Please, let us go! We've never hurt anyone!" she sobbed.

"Beg!"

Elena let out a small gasp and felt her knees buckle. Alex and Maggie quickly grabbed her and held her up.

No, no, no. Not here. Not in front of everyone.

"Are you all right?" Alex whispered worriedly.

Elena looked up, her face full of anguish as her panic attack began to take hold. Her wild gaze darted toward the stage, and her eyes, for one brief moment, met with Kieran's.

He was looking straight at her, an agonized expression on his face.

Elena couldn't breathe, and Alex and Maggie pulled her away, through the crowd toward a side door.

"Is she all right?" someone asked.

"She's claustrophobic, it's a bit too crowded in here for her," Maggie lied smoothly.

At these words, the crowd parted so Elena could move more freely. The three of them escaped the hall and through the door. As soon as it closed, Elena collapsed, her legs completely giving out as she hyperventilated.

"Elena!" Maggie cried, horrified.

"Let's get her to the garden, let her get some air," Alex said, lifting her up in his arms.

He walked down the hall and through a door that led to a small courtyard that was open to the sky, where Alex carefully sat Elena down on a bench.

"It's okay, just try to breathe slowly, everything's all right," Alex said, his eyes wide.

"What's going on?" A deep voice boomed through the courtyard, and Magnus burst through the door.

"I don't know! She started freaking out; I think she's having a panic attack," Maggie squeaked.

Magnus rushed forward and knelt in front of Elena, who was now sobbing gently between gasps for air.

"Elena, listen to the sound of my voice," Magnus said calmly, placing a hand on the side of her face. "It's okay if you can't talk yet, but I want you to think of five things you can hear right now. Nod when you've done it."

Elena's entire body trembled, but she tried to do what he asked. She could hear Maggie breathing near her, a bird singing in the distance, her own haggard breath, Alex scratching at his hand nervously, and a bush rustling nearby. She nodded.

"Good, now think of five things you can see," he said.

She could see Magnus's kind face looking at her, her hands twisted around each other in her lap. There was a pebble on the ground, Maggie's shoes and ankles were visible, and a pen poked itself out of Magnus's jacket pocket. She nodded.

"Wonderful, take a deep breath if you can. Now what are

five things you can feel?"

Elena's breath started to slow, and she spoke out loud.

"My feet are cold," she mumbled, her voice crackling. "I can feel the inside of my coat on my skin, and the cold from the bench and…" She looked away toward the ground. "The cold breeze on my face, and my nails pinching my skin," she finished.

She felt much calmer now and took a few steadying breaths, wiping away the tears on her face.

"I think you're just cold," Magnus said, smiling. "Let's go inside, okay?"

Elena nodded and shakily got to her feet. They all went inside, and Magnus led them to a room nearby with a roaring fire and comfy armchairs, gently guiding Elena into one of them. Now that the panic was gone, shame began to replace it, and she couldn't look her friends in the eye.

"I'm sorry," she said. "That was stupid."

"No, don't apologize!" Maggie said fiercely. "I'm just glad you're okay."

"It's all right, Elena, you don't have to be embarrassed," Alex agreed.

Being told not to be embarrassed only made her feel more so, and Elena looked away toward the fire. Magnus frowned, then turned to Alex and Maggie.

"I need you two to give us a moment alone. Go back to the hall, and if anyone asks, it was a moment of claustrophobia, and she's fine," he said in a tone that made it clear this was not up for discussion.

Maggie and Alex glanced at each other, then nodded, leaving the room.

Magnus sighed and sat down across from Elena. "You know

you're safe here, Elena, no one is going to hurt you. You don't have to be afraid in these walls," he said comfortingly.

"I know that," Elena said quietly, looking at Magnus's face and considering. She needed to talk to someone, and after all these weeks, she found that she trusted Magnus. "There's something I haven't told you."

Magnus raised an eyebrow and sat down across from her. "Go on," he said encouragingly.

Elena shook her head, looking down again. "The witch hunt in New Stirling City last spring—I was one of the witches attacked," she mumbled, her heart thundering in her chest.

Magnus was silent for a moment, then he let out a breath. "Elena, I'm so sorry," he said, his voice somehow getting deeper with what Elena suspected was emotion.

She couldn't stand to look at his face, so she studied her hands in her lap.

"The High Witch's Council made great efforts to protect the identities of the victims who survived. I've suspected a few times that you may have been involved but didn't want to push," Magnus said, his voice full of sorrow. "I'm glad you told me now."

He leaned forward and placed a comforting hand on Elena's shoulder. She finally tore her gaze off the ground to look at him again and managed a small smile. For maybe the first time ever, talking about this wasn't so scary. Magnus was her mentor, her guide. He understood.

"I know I'm safe here," she said, a strange sort of relief helping the words flow, "it's just that crowd. I felt so cramped, and then everything people were saying about Kieran, it was awful. I felt like I was trapped in a mob, and it was too much. It reminded me of that day."

Magnus nodded, withdrawing his hand. "I understand, and I know it's not helpful, but you really do not have anything to be ashamed of."

Elena let out a strangled sound. "What am I going to tell Maggie and Alex?" she asked miserably.

"Only what you want to. If they are really your friends, they won't press you to tell them anything you're not ready for them to hear," Magnus assured her. "Let me take you home. There's an exit portal used by board members inside the mansion that I know about. I don't think they'll mind if we use it this once."

Magnus managed to get Elena out of the mansion and back home without running into anyone else, and Elena was relieved to find that Mila was not there yet. She thanked Magnus for his help before he left, then curled up on her bed, Huey cuddling up against her, and fell asleep. Her dreams were troubled and full of violence, and when she awoke a few hours later, she did not feel like she'd rested at all.

* * *

In his own bed, Kieran stared at the ceiling, replaying one moment from the day over and over in his head. All through his speech he'd done his best to ignore the crowd, though their rabid hostility rolled off them in waves. But then a tugging sensation had drawn his attention, and he'd seen Elena. Their eyes connected, and his heart plummeted. She was looking at him with complete and utter disgust. A tremor ran through Kieran, but he quickly tried to hide it, looking away. Whatever Elena felt for him was over; she hated him now, and he did not blame her.

He'd led her on. He'd made her feel special and given her affection even against his better judgment, then tossed her aside like she was nothing.

There wasn't any energy left in Kieran's body to lie to himself anymore.

He cared about Elena. She sparked something in him he couldn't remember ever feeling for anyone else before, and he desperately wanted to explore what that was.

But he'd ruined it, and now, any chance for them was done.

Chapter 19

Elena decided to tell Maggie the truth about the panic attack. It was an extremely difficult conversation, and her voice trembled the entire time, but in the end, she was glad she did it. Maggie was loving and supportive and assured her she wouldn't tell a soul, even Alex. Elena felt guilty over excluding her friend, but as much as she cared for Alex, she didn't feel close enough to him to trust him with this. For his part, he didn't pressure her at all to tell him what was going on.

Kieran was not seen publicly for weeks. No word of him in the news, no whispers on the internet, even the tabloids couldn't track him down. If his family was in contact or knew where he was, they were keeping it to themselves. Rumors flew around the coven faster than lightning on where he could have possibly gone, but they all seemed to be based on speculation.

Elena would be lying if she said she wasn't worried about him, but it appeared he'd made his choice concerning their relationship, and if he didn't want to speak to her, she wouldn't try to force it. Instead, she channeled all her focus into two areas—working with her publisher on the upcoming release of her book and her continuing training with Magnus. They were about to start healing magic, and

Elena was particularly excited about it, as this was the main reason she'd signed up with the coven in the first place. Healing magic was tricky, but with all the progress she'd made over the last few months, Elena was feeling cautiously optimistic.

The first week of April, Mila and Ava surprised Elena with the news they were taking a week-long vacation to the islands to visit Mila's family on her father's side.

"This is a big step." Elena watched her sister pack. "I'm not second-guessing your decision, you guys are clearly grossly in love, but have you prepared her for this? Your family is a little…"

Mila raised her eyebrows. "A little what?"

"Judgmental?" Elena suggested.

Mila sighed. "I know they don't like you, but that doesn't mean they won't like Ava."

"The *little accident* is what your grandmother calls me," Elena reminded her.

"I know. But look, I've already told them all about Ava, and they're really excited to meet her. I don't know how much longer my grandparents are going to be around, so I would rather this happen sooner than later." Mila tossed some sandals into her bag.

"Well, I hope it goes well, for Ava's sake." Elena moved aside from the door so Huey could come in to inspect Mila's bag.

"And you'll pick us up from the airport, right?" Mila asked.

"Fine, I will pick you up after watching over your shop all week," Elena moaned, flopping onto Mila's bed dramatically. "So much work."

"My employees are running the shop, you're just closing

each day," Mila reminded her. "And at least I'm not asking you to also get us there."

"Think of me while you're sipping cocktails on the beach and I'm still here in the cold."

"No one is stopping you from going on vacation, you know."

"Don't distract me with your logic."

* * *

Healing magic was just as complicated as advertised. It involved a decent understanding of human anatomy, which required a great deal of study and an absolutely clear head. The first lesson went well enough, although Elena struggled when faced with healing a broken toe. It wasn't really the spell that tripped her up, it was the fake but disconcertingly real-looking human foot Magnus brought for her to practice on.

After the lesson, Magnus had to teach a class at his university, leaving Elena to her own devices. Normally, she would head straight home, but Maggie had tipped her off about a secret garden on the grounds with a rare breed of marigold growing in it that Mila had tried to track down for years, and Elena was determined to get one for her.

The snow was finally melted on the grounds, but the air still held a chill, and there was a perpetual dampness that hung over everything. The trees and plants were bare, and every step through the grass squished under Elena's feet.

Holding the piece of paper with Maggie's instructions in her hand, Elena followed them through a hidden gap in the hedges and down a passageway surrounded by a crumbling stone wall. The path sloped down a hill and emerged in a small clearing.

Elena's eyes widened as she took it all in. It was a circular space surrounded by a hedge wall with a small pond in the center, the water crystal clear. Large, golden fish were swimming around inside, and a small fountain bubbled merrily in the center. All around the edge of the clearing, the marigolds Elena was looking for grew in abundance. It was a pale blue flower, with shimmering silver veins shooting through the delicate, ruffled petals and leaves. They were truly stunning.

Summoning the pot and small hand shovel she'd brought with her, Elena began looking around for the perfect specimen. She spotted one a few feet away and made her way over. As she did, a presence tickled at the corner of her mind, and Elena froze.

She was not alone.

Quickly whirling around to face whoever it was who was sitting in the corner of the clearing, the pot and the shovel discarded on the ground, both of Elena's hands exploded into flames.

"Easy, Elena, it's just me!" Kieran stood hastily, his hands up in front of him in surrender.

Elena blinked and dropped her arms, the fires going out.

"My apologies," Kieran said, not moving toward her. "I didn't mean to scare you, but in my defense, I was just sitting here minding my own business when you came in to, what looks like, steal a flower."

Elena frowned, ignoring the jab, and tried to see his face more clearly. Kieran looked drawn and tired, his eyes un-usually dark. Weeks had passed since she'd seen him, and to Elena's annoyance, she found she was excited to see him, though that was mostly overshadowed by worry at his haggard appearance.

"What are you doing here?" she asked bluntly.

Kieran raised an eyebrow. "I have the right to wander the mansion grounds as I wish, do I not? Or has that privilege also been taken away and they haven't yet informed me?"

Elena swallowed hard, feeling uncomfortable. "Kieran, listen..." She began, unsure what she was going to say.

Kieran cut her off. "Briar was injured," he said curtly, gesturing to the ground near where he was sitting. "Her body is healed, but she's been depressed ever since. I thought a change of scenery might help her feel better."

Elena peered at the ground and saw, her heart dropping, the magnificent raven nestled up in a blanket on the grass. She looked as rough as her companion, her dark head drooping.

"Hello, Briar," Elena said as kindly as possible, taking a hesitant step toward the bird. "I'm glad to see you again."

Briar turned her head toward Elena and blinked once in recognition but otherwise did not respond.

Kieran pursed his lips.

"Is she going to be okay?" Elena asked, concerned.

"Yes." Kieran's voice was hard. He paused for a moment, then said, "She was attacked."

Elena gaped at him. "What? By who?"

"Another familiar—an eagle," Kieran told her, his jaw clenched. "She was out hunting when she was ambushed, less than a mile from our fucking house."

Rage radiated from him, and Elena resisted the urge to wrap her arms around herself. "Surely you know the witch behind it. I mean, how many people have eagles for familiars?"

"Not many," Kieran agreed. "Whoever it was, they didn't

intend for Briar to survive, but she's much cleverer than they gave her credit for." He threw a loving look at his familiar, and she managed a small caw in response. "I'll find out who did it and make them pay soon enough."

His words held the promise of violence—the air charged with the inferno of his power—and Elena glanced between him and Briar nervously. Kieran apparently caught this, and he let out a breath.

"I'm sorry, Elena, I'm making you nervous, aren't I?"

"A little," she admitted, "but I'm not afraid of you. I'm just worried you're going to get into trouble with the High Witch's Council. Seems like the last thing you need right now."

Too much, she said too much. She could practically see the defensive walls building behind Kieran's eyes as he leveled her with a stare.

"So, you think I should sit back and do nothing, after my familiar was attacked?" he asked, his voice low. "Would you do nothing, if someone did that to Huey?"

"That's not—" Elena began, frustrated. "Of course, you want to get justice for Briar. I'm just saying be careful and try not to do anything illegal."

"What do you care?" Kieran asked bitterly.

Elena blinked at him. "Why wouldn't I care?" Elena could feel her temper rising at his insinuation. "I never stopped caring. You're the one who vanished on me." Elena was unable to keep the accusation and hurt out of her voice.

Kieran scoffed, apparently not believing her. "I saw you, Elena, at my... apology. I saw how you looked at me. You don't have to pretend you don't hate me."

Elena opened her mouth to respond, but nothing came out as she tried to think of what the hell he was talking about.

"I..." She started, realizing dawning on her. "Kieran, that wasn't what you thought." Elena swallowed, looking away as a blush crept up her neck, her previous anger vanishing to be replaced by shame. "I think you saw me having a panic attack," she admitted.

Kieran stared at her, his defensiveness melting away. "What?"

Elena took a shuddering breath. Spirits, how many more times would she have to explain herself?

"I have, uh, an issue with crowds. Most of the time, it's under control, but it was so packed, and the energy was so hostile, it sent me over the edge. Maggie and Alex practically carried me out of the room."

"I had no idea," Kieran muttered. "All these weeks, I thought..."

"Well, you were wrong," Elena said harshly, more harshly than she intended. She closed her eyes and took a deep breath. When she opened them, Kieran was looking straight at her.

"I'm sorry that happened to you, Elena. I didn't know you struggled with that sort of thing."

Elena sighed. "Sit down with me for a minute," she instructed him.

Kieran obeyed, and the pair moved to a stone bench nearby. Elena watched the pond for a moment, trying to decide how much to tell him.

"This isn't something I like to talk about," she began, watching the fish in the pond. "So if you're going to keep being an asshole, tell me now."

"I'm sorry," Kieran said quickly. "I didn't mean to be rude. I'm just... not having a good day. But I would never judge you or anything about this."

Elena looked at him, trying to determine his sincerity. All she saw was concern shining back at her. Biting her lip, Elena nodded. He'd admitted some very personal things to her, way back when they'd sat in the sun and talked about her books, about his own struggles with mental health. Perhaps he would understand.

"I've had anxiety my entire life," she said, "but more recently, it's become worse. I've gotten help for it, but I should've known that I shouldn't have gone to that... event," she chose her words carefully.

"Then why did you?" Kieran asked, looking toward the pond. "I would've much preferred you hadn't."

"Because I was angry with you," she admitted, and Kieran flinched at her direct honesty. "I was angry at you for ghosting me, Kieran. I thought, I don't know, that we'd bonded, and then you stopped talking to me. I wasn't angry at you for anything else. It was really none of my business. I just thought I'd made a friend," she told him. "And I certainly wasn't angry at you for what happened that day. It was out of line, how people were acting."

Kieran was silent for a moment, then looked back at her. Elena was watching him with wide, earnest eyes, silently pleading with him to say something.

"Elena, I—" Kieran began. He licked his lips nervously and started again. "I wish I had a good reason for how I've been acting, but I don't. It was nothing to do with you, I just... have trouble trusting people and trusting myself. And after spending time with you... I don't know, it scared me I guess, because I wanted to trust you... I want to trust you, but I still don't know how to do any of this."

Elena frowned, then against her better judgment, placed a

comforting hand on Kieran's. It wasn't in her nature to be so forward, but how could she not comfort him when he was in so much pain? Even in the cold, his hand was warm, though Kieran's skin was much rougher than she'd imagined. His eyes darted down to where their hands touching, his breath hitching.

"I get that, I really do," Elena said, ignoring his response. "Doesn't make you any less of a jerk, though."

Kieran actually snorted at that and managed a small smile. He snuck his thumb upward to curl around Elena's little finger, stroking it gently. Elena's heart gave a wild thump in response, but she did not dare move.

"Life has been shit lately," Kieran admitted, still looking at their hands. "I don't want to drag anyone down with me, especially you." His emerald eyes slid up to hers, and Elena found breathing a little difficult.

"That's not what friendship is about," she managed to say. "It's about being there for someone when things are good and when things are shitty."

"I wish I could've been there for you, when you were having your panic attack." Kieran's eyes bored into hers. "I was there. I should have realized something was wrong. I'm so sorry I didn't."

"I was in good hands," Elena assured him, "and you weren't having the best day yourself."

Kieran smiled grimly. "One way to put it," he muttered.

Elena hesitated, then leaned against his shoulder, relishing her little victory when he didn't pull away. "So, you want to be there for me on my bad days, and I want to be there for you on yours. Does that mean we're going to be friends, after all?"

Kieran looked down at her, almost reluctantly, and Elena could practically see the war raging behind his eyes.

Perhaps she was being naive, throwing herself headfirst into this again, but it was so hard not to when they sat side by side like this—when her senses were clouded with his scent and all she could see was him.

"Okay, friends," he agreed, making his decision.

Elena smiled widely. "Good, then as your friend, please promise me you'll go about getting revenge for Briar the right way, the legal way," she amended.

Kieran let out a dramatic sigh, looking toward the sky. "Fine, if you insist," he said, then looked sideways at her.

"And if Briar wants some company while she recovers, I'm sure Huey would like to see her. He's warmed up to you and would enjoy having another familiar around. Drop by the house whenever," Elena added, glancing at the raven watching them.

A genuine smile finally graced Kieran's face. "I appreciate that," he said, then paused, his smile fading. "And, Elena, about everything that happened at the party... I feel like I should apologize for that as well."

"Why?" Elena asked, confused. "You didn't do anything to me, Kieran."

Kieran stared down at her intensely, making Elena's heart pound so loudly she was sure he could hear it.

"That's not true... at least it doesn't feel that way." Kieran broke eye contact, staring at the fish in the pond instead.

Elena waited, immensely curious but a bit scared of what he was thinking.

"Did you hear about the incident with the Northern Coastal Coven?"

When Elena nodded, he continued, "It was a lot worse than the rumors. I can't say exactly what happened, but I got blamed for all of it. That night at the party I was angry, so angry I could barely breathe, and looking for a distraction. I didn't want to feel anything anymore. When I saw you..."

Under Elena's hand, Kieran's clenched.

"It's okay, Kieran," Elena soothed, even though she was having trouble processing what he was trying to tell her.

"No, it's not," his voice growled. "I was so angry and disgusted at myself for wanting to use you in such a cheap way. I lost control. You're worth so much more than that to me, Elena. I'm so sorry."

The only reaction Elena could conjure up was stunned silence. He'd wanted her? Wanted to spend his night with *her*? Not the others? But he hadn't. She was worth something to him. Something more.

"It's okay," Elena heard herself saying. "Spirits know I've been there myself with people I respected. You aren't a monster, Kieran."

The expression on his face still seemed anguished, but he nodded. "Thank you."

An alert went off on Elena's phone, and she pulled it out of her pocket, muttering a curse. "I have to get going. Mila's gone on vacation, and I have to close up her shop while she's away."

"Oh, good for her." Kieran looked downcast at that.

"Text me later, okay? So I know you haven't changed your mind again," she said sternly.

"Promise," he assured her.

Elena let go of his hand and stood, immediately missing the warmth of his skin against hers. Elena hesitated, then reached out and gently brushed a stray lock of hair behind his ear.

"You're going to get through all this, Kieran, you know that, right?"

"Right," Kieran agreed, though he didn't sound convinced. "See you around."

It was terrible seeing him look so dejected, like sad puppy. In another burst of bravery, Elena leaned down to give him a quick hug before straightening.

She quickly said goodbye, face burning, and started to walk away, giving Briar an encouraging wave as she did. When she reached the passageway, she paused, looking back at Kieran. He sat at the bench, watching her. She smiled softly before turning and disappearing.

When Elena arrived home about an hour later, having stopped at Alex's cafe to soothe herself with a tea, she discovered a potted plant waiting for her on the front step. It was the marigold she'd gone to the garden to retrieve and attached was a note.

Dear Elena,

After you left, I realized you did not have the chance to steal your flower. I hope I removed it correctly. I'm very glad we ran into each other today, and I hope to talk to you soon.

–K.A.

Chapter 20

Keeping promises was something Kieran had thought he was good at, but keeping his promise to Elena was turning into a nightmare. The mental wounds left on his beloved companion were not so easily healed. Always so bold and brave, Briar now kept to Kieran's side like glue. She wouldn't hunt, and she wouldn't fly around the property like she used to. If Kieran wasn't able to have her constantly on his shoulder, she clung to one of his family members—particularly his mother. Every time the raven cuddled into his shoulder, her little body trembling in fear, or cried out in relief when he returned from leaving her, Kieran felt an overwhelming fury towards the one who hurt her consuming his mind.

The witch who'd done this must pay, and every part of Kieran's being was screaming out to deliver that justice himself. But he'd promised Elena, and this time, he didn't want to mess things up. The hope in her eyes, the gentleness with which she spoke to him, touched him, made Kieran feel *more* than he felt in a long time. It didn't matter what the coven thought of him- as long as that lovely, generous, devoted witch liked him, he could endure everything else.

But that meant controlling his anger, controlling his need for revenge.

"Out of everything your girl could ask me for, why did it have to be this?" Kieran asked Huey a few days later. Elena wasn't home, at another lesson with Magnus, but he was taking advantage of her open invitation to bring Briar around to spend time with Huey. They were taking a walk together through the trails behind the Hall's house, Briar riding on Huey's back as they went along. It made Kieran feel all warm inside to see her bouncing along in Huey's thick fur, the large dog moving with decided care and sticking close to Kieran's side. The trees were in full bloom, their bright green leaves freshly born into the spring air. The forest around them buzzed with life, and Kieran silently marveled at Huey's self-control not to go chasing after every squirrel or chipmunk they saw.

Huey snorted in response to his question, a gesture Elena would have understood the meaning of, but Kieran could only guess.

"You know when my father was young, trying to kill a witch's familiar was a crime punishable by death," he continued. "And in his grandfather's day, if a fellow witch attacked your familiar, you were *obligated* to hunt them down and kill them yourself."

Huey made a chuffing noise that almost sounded like a laugh.

"But she's also not wrong," Kieran conceded as they rounded a corner, the damp air clinging to his skin. "I can't afford to get in trouble with the law right now." They reached a fork in the trail. "What do you think, Huey? Head for the right trail if you think I should do what Elena says, the left if I should avenge Briar myself."

Huey grunted again, giving him an indecipherable look,

before trotting over to the trail on the right. Briar gave a little squawk, flapping her wings once before settling deeper in Huey's fur.

"That's what I thought you'd say," Kieran sighed. "Don't worry. I'm going to, I was always going to."

A wave of approval came from Briar, and Kieran chuckled. Even she was smitten with Elena. Taking a deep breath, Kieran reached down to pat Huey's head. He knew exactly what he must do.

A few hours later, Kieran stood in the lobby of the High Witch's Council Headquarters. Not just in service of the council, it was the center of the entire magical branch of the government. The lobby was made almost entirely of white marble, with large pillars going up to the vaulted ceiling made of glass. Sunlight flowed in through the glass onto the frazzled-looking employees scurrying around.

Shifting, Kieran looked toward the front desk. Three grumpy-looking witches sat behind it, pointedly ignoring him. Briar, once again on his shoulder, gave an angry caw. One of the witches flinched at the sound, and Kieran smirked.

"How much longer is this going to take?" he drawled. "I would hate to have to come back here again." As he said this, Kieran allowed a ripple of his power to release. Not enough to actually cause harm, but just enough to set the witches' instincts on high alert.

"I'll call again to see what is delaying them," one hurriedly said, picking up their desk phone.

"Kieran Andraste," a voice called out, and Kieran turned. "Terrorizing the receptionists. Why am I not surprised?"

Grimacing, Kieran put his hands behind his back. "Agent Donaldson, what a pleasant surprise," he said, even as his tone and posture said the opposite.

The human woman approached, eyeing him. "I heard you were here causing a fuss. Why don't we speak in my office? I can assist you."

"No, I don't think so," Kieran quickly said. "This is a matter for witches, not humans. Your assistance is not required."

"Well." Donaldson rolled her shoulders, looking around the lobby dramatically. "It seems like I may be the only person in this building willing to help you, so you don't really have a choice."

Kieran bit back a retort. He'd already waited for nearly an hour, which was extremely unusual. He also knew that Donaldson's department, while it did have a satellite office in the High Witch's Council Headquarters, was not based here. It didn't take a genius to realize he was being set up. Under normal circumstances, he would walk away and deal with this himself, but he'd promised Elena...

"Fine," Kieran bit out.

Donaldson did not do a very good job of hiding her surprise, but quickly covered it up. With a jerk of the head, Donaldson led him out of the lobby and to the elevator. As they got in, a handful of witches who were already inside took one look at Kieran and quickly scampered out.

"That can't feel good," Donaldson remarked as the elevator doors shut, leaning against the wall.

"You get used to it," Kieran muttered, stroking Briar's head comfortingly.

"Your familiar okay?"

"She hates elevators."

"So do I, to be honest."

Kieran glanced at the human, an eyebrow arched. She

certainly did seem uncomfortable, almost as if she was holding her breath, her eyes staring fixedly at the elevator doors. Perhaps it was the truth.

"These elevators are enchanted. They're far safer than any human-made elevator could ever be."

"Yes, well, knowing that and feeling it are two different things," Donaldson said through gritted teeth.

Kieran actually chuckled. "True enough."

Thankfully for both Briar and Donaldson, they quickly reached their floor and walked out into the hallway. It looked the same as every other government hallway. The walls were painted a muted yellow, and cheesy pictures of scenery hung every few feet. They walked a short way down the hallway until they reached an office door with the number 845 on the front. Donaldson led him inside.

"So," she said, "this is the Department of Human and Magical Relations office here at the witchy headquarters."

It wasn't much. A few individual offices, and in the center, a single long table that looked like it had seen better days. Everything had the appearance of being out of date and shabby. There was still a physical filing cabinet, for goodness' sake. Hadn't they gone digital by now?

"Not the most well-funded department, I take it?" Kieran remarked. "I mean, how old is that water cooler? It should really be in a museum."

Donaldson glared at him but let his jab go, directing him to one of the small offices. A few curious faces poked out from open doors, then just as quickly disappeared again. Agent Donaldson's office was just as threadbare as the rest of the place. A small desk, filing cabinet, and stacks of papers covering every available space.

"So." Kieran flopped down into the chair facing the desk. "What can the D.H.M.R do for me? Or is this the part where you say if I want anyone in the government to help me, then I have to agree to work with you to take my family down?"

Donaldson sighed, rubbing the bridge between her eyes. "Look, let's just start over, okay? We aren't going to hold hostage justice for your familiar to get you to do what we want. The fact that you believe we would ever do something like that tells me we screwed up. A crime has been committed against you, a serious one. We just want to help. I just want to help."

Kieran didn't believe a word of it. "Oh, really? Then do tell why you, a human, would be tapped to get involved in this at all. Witch on witch crime is not your territory."

"Normally, no, but since you lodged your complaint, we've discovered that was not the case."

Well, that was surprising. A human was involved?

"Oh?"

Donaldson pulled out a folder from the stack. She was about to hand it to him when she hesitated. "I'm sharing this information with you as an act of good faith, Kieran. There's no doubt in my mind that if you wanted to deal with this yourself, that you could and would have done so. But for whatever reason, you've decided to do the right thing, so I trust that you won't have a change of heart and decide to take matters into your own hands when I show you this."

"You're right. If I was going to go after the shit myself, I would've done so by now. But..." He hesitated. "I made a promise, and I intend to keep it."

Briar made an affirmative-sounding caw, and Donaldson raised an eyebrow. "Fine." She slid the folder forward. Kieran snatched it and flipped it open, his eyes scanning the page.

"We identified the witch who ordered their familiar to attack yours. You can see from his profile that he's held a grudge against your family for decades, due to an offense your father committed against him before you or your brother were even born," Donaldson explained. "Unfortunately, you're currently the only member of your family that has a familiar, which made poor Briar there an easy target."

Briar nuzzled into Kieran's neck, her body giving a little tremble.

"And how does a human come into this?" Kieran asked.

"Flip the page," Donaldson commanded.

Kieran obeyed. A second profile stared up at him, a human he only vaguely recognized splattered on the page.

"That is a human by the name of Gregory Phillipson. The former owner of eight-hundred acres of land out west that was in his family for five generations. Three years ago, you and your father somehow strong-armed him into selling it to your development company. At the time, blackmail was heavily suspected, but as usual, we couldn't prove anything."

Kieran glanced up at her, his eyes narrowing. Kieran had indeed used blackmail to get the man to sell, but he wasn't going to confirm that to Donaldson.

"So, this Gregory Phillips enticed the witch to send his familiar after Briar?"

"Yes and no." Donaldson crossed her arms over her chest. "It was not an arrangement between them. He manipulated the witch, provoked his anger to the point that the witch acted of his own accord. Mr. Phillips was very closely monitoring them. Upon searching his house, we discovered surveillance equipment."

Kieran's eyes widened. "It was a trap," he muttered. "He was hoping to catch me killing the witch, or whatever he thought I would do."

"And ruin you and your family's life for manipulating him out of his family's land," Donaldson agreed.

Kieran let out a breath, sinking back into his chair. "So, what happens now?"

"We have Mr. Phillips on illegal surveillance and conspiracy to commit a violent crime. That is a done deal. And obviously, we have the witch for attacking Briar. We'll just need to swing by the Magical Justice Department and allow one of their specialists to extract her memory of the event for the trial."

Briar cawed, ruffling her feathers.

"Don't worry, Briar," Donaldson said, her voice tilted in a way that suggested she was not used to speaking directly to a familiar. "The process is entirely painless."

"No one touches my familiar," Kieran growled.

"You'll be there with her, of course," Donaldson assured him, shifting in her seat.

"And monitoring your specialists," Kieran added, "making sure you aren't poking around in Briar's mind where you shouldn't be."

"Mr. Andraste." Donaldson sat up straighter. "We would never take advantage of the situation by violating your familiar's mind."

"Oh, right." Kieran laughed. "Because governments are always honest and never break their own rules to get what they want."

Donaldson shook her head. "If you have no other questions," she said, "we can head over to the Magical Justice Department now."

"That's it?" Kieran asked, disbelieving. "No bargaining? No laying out your terms?"

Donaldson stood, grabbing the file out of his hands. "I told you, Mr. Andraste, this isn't about you helping us. This is about justice. We expect nothing from you in return."

A smile spread across Kieran's face, and Donaldson flinched. They really thought him a fool. Sure, they might not expect anything from him now, but this was all about getting him to work with them. They took a calculated risk. If he'd murdered that witch, like they'd clearly expected, and gotten caught, there wouldn't be a deal they could offer him enticing enough to get him to turn on his family, and they would lose the chance to work with him forever.

That is if he got caught at all. Which he wouldn't have. Kieran was confident of that. Not that he would have murdered the witch. No, he would have done something far more impactful. First, he would have severed the bond between the witch and his familiar in the most brutal way possible. It would create a wound on the soul that would never heal and possibly drive the witch mad with enough time. Then, with the help of his family, he would set to work slowly destroying the witch's life from the ground up. Dismantling his connections, his livelihood, until there was nothing left.

But he'd promised Elena. So now the witch would go to prison, his familiar humanely rehomed with a new witch, and the D.H.M.R garnered good-will with Kieran for being so accommodating and transparent.

As Donaldson led him and Briar away, Kieran hid his smugness. They were fools, complete fools, for believing that he would remember this as anything other than what it was: a trick. But let them think they got one over on him. Let them think that he could still be swayed. And in the end, he kept his word to Elena while making sure the fuckers responsible paid for what they had done. That was all that mattered.

Kirean was in a much better mood as they strolled through the halls. He wondered if Elena would be proud of him, if she would give him a real smile. Not one of the fake ones she wore like a mask to hide her true feelings, but rather that beautiful, shocking smile that lit up her entire face he'd only witnessed a few times. That image in his mind Kieran didn't even notice the glares of the government workers they passed in the halls, or the angry whispers that followed him as they went. What did they matter anyway? For the first time in his life, Kieran had a real friend, and as long as she cared about him, what the rest of these people thought didn't matter.

Chapter 21

Mila and Ava returned from their vacation on the wings of victory. Ava handily won over Mila's family, and the two regaled Elena with tales of their trip on the way home. Elena was only slightly bitter that Mila's family was so accepting of Ava when they'd rejected her since she was a child, but she did her best to let it go.

True to his word, Kieran stayed in touch. Over the next few weeks, he sent Elena text messages occasionally, asking how her day was going or telling her about something that happened to him. It was all shallow conversation, but Elena appreciated that he was making an effort.

In truth though, it wasn't enough. Not for Elena. She wanted to see him, spend time with him.

"Just ask him to hang out, for all our sakes," Mila finally snapped after Elena spent the better part of one of their movie nights stressing about it. "You're driving me nuts."

Metaphorical tail between her legs, Elena finally worked up the courage to ask Kieran to spend the afternoon with her in New Stirling City. She had to go visit her editor at the publishing house's headquarters, and it would be easier if she had a witch along who could summon a long-distance portal to bring her straight to the building and back.

When she pitched the idea to Kieran, he immediately said yes.

"Good morning," she said, when he arrived at her house.

"Morning?" Kieran arched an eyebrow at her. "It's one in the afternoon. Are you feeling all right?"

"Time means nothing to me." Elena did her best not to stare too openly at him. How was it possible for someone to look so good? It didn't even look like he was particularly trying. Kieran was wearing a hoodie and a cap but he still looked fantastic.

Elena had tried really hard to look good but she wasn't sure her knit dress and jacket were doing the job. If Kieran thought she looked nice he didn't say so, greeting Huey as he entered the house. Huey would be accompanying them and was wearing a leash for once.

"Have you traveled through a long-distance portal before?"

"Once, and it was a long time ago. I don't remember loving the sensation."

"Hang on to my arm, and you'll be fine."

Kieran smiled as he extended his arm out to her, and Elena flushed.

Long-distance portals were tricky business, and dangerous if attempted without proper training. Elena held her breath and clutched his arm as they walked through the bright blue portal Kieran had summoned in the kitchen.

There was a brief dizzy spell as they emerged on the other side, but it quickly passed.

"Oh, Huey." Elena leaned down to comfort Huey, who had immediately sunk to the ground and was panting heavily with distress. Thankfully, he recovered quickly, and they were able to press on. Kieran had brought them to a private portal room in his apartment building that was conveniently only a few blocks away from their destination.

"Wow, fancy," Elena commented as he led her into a marble lobby overflowing with statues, gold accents, and lush exotic plants. Everything dripped with wealth, and every staff member bowed their heads respectfully to Kieran as he walked by.

"I like it," Kieran shrugged. "They value privacy here."

Stepping out onto the city street was like a punch in the gut.

Elena blinked rapidly and swayed for a moment, eyes wide as she took in the once-familiar environment. People were everywhere. The buzz of activity that she'd once found so comforting and normal now drilled against Elena's brain like a jackhammer. No one was looking at her, but she still felt like a million eyes were watching, waiting, ready to strike.

"Hey, are you okay?" Kieran placed a hand on her shoulder.

"Yeah, yeah. Let's go."

Sweat dripped down the back of Elena's neck under her hair, and her own shallow breathing filled her ears. Her grip on Huey's leash was like iron, and instinctually she walked closer to Kieran.

A powerful witch like him would protect her. There was nothing to fear. No one would try to hurt her with him at her side.

A warm touch yanked Elena out of her spiral. To her surprise, Kieran had taken her other hand in his own and was holding it securely.

"It's all right," he murmured. "We'll be there soon."

Elena took a deep breath and nodded. Having Kieran hold her hand was like an anchor. Instead of obsessing about her surroundings, she was now obsessing about that. What was he doing? Friends didn't hold hands, not with their fingers intertwined like this. Especially friends who had admitted attraction for each other fairly recently. Wait, had she ever told him she was attracted to him? Surely, he knew from the look on her face whenever she saw him. Subtle, Elena was not.

Before she knew it, they were at the office building.

"Do you want me to go up with you?" Kieran asked. "I was planning on running an errand during your meeting, but I can do that after, if you need."

Gosh, he must think she was so fragile. Technically she was, but still, it was embarrassing.

"No, it's fine. I'll text you when I'm done."

* * *

That five-minute walk between his building and Elena's publisher was disconcerting, to say the least. Kieran immediately realized she was experiencing panic by the way she'd frozen like a deer in the headlights and Huey began whining and nudging at her hand.

If just going out in the city was that triggering for her, it made sense why she and Mila had moved. But Elena had been born and raised here, so something must have changed.

There was an obvious answer to that. The witch hunts.

For once, Kieran and his family hadn't been kept busy by shady business dealings and stolen goods the past few weeks, though Kieran honestly would have preferred that. Almost daily, he and his various family members were in meetings with government officials, other covens, and politicians to discuss the ever-increasing rise of conflict between humans and witches.

There had been a few retaliatory attacks by witches on humans, unfortunately on random humans who had no affiliation with anti-witch activities. There were no deaths from these attacks, but with magic, one could be much more creative than simply killing.

Kieran had traveled with his brother overnight to a foreign country in order to help break a nasty curse set on a human couple that was so horrible it gave him nightmares. The curse required an extreme amount of magical power to break—more than even a small handful of witches could provide. Declan and Kieran had been volunteered by their mother when the call for help went out, always willing to generate positive press for the family.

Humans fought back, of course, and so the cycle continued. A new bill was introduced in the Senate and struck down almost immediately by the overwhelmingly human majority of representatives. Things were bad, and it was clearly affecting Elena deeply.

The entire thing made Kieran feel sick. He wasn't sure what his father was planning, but there was clearly something in the works that he was keeping from his sons.

"He'll tell us when he's ready," Declan said when Kieran had expressed his concerns. "We just have to wait."

Kieran was sick of waiting, but what could he do?

Contemplating this while in line at a cheerful bakery was a huge downer, especially since it sucked all the joy out of the surprise he had arranged for Elena.

When she'd asked him to accompany her, he'd been embarrassingly excited. This was his chance to spend some actual quality time together, and he wasn't going to let the darkness invading their world ruin it.

When he got the text from Elena that she was wrapping up, he hurried back to the office building to pick her up.

Thankfully, the fear was no longer in her eyes and had been replaced by a flushed happiness as she walked across the lobby toward him, Huey trotting along beside her.

"Hey! Sorry that took so long."

"Don't worry about it." Kieran's eyes darted to a tote bag slung over Elena's shoulder, which she hadn't been carrying before. It looked heavy, with a pointed corner sticking out from the fabric that hinted at something book-shaped inside.

Kieran bit back his curiosity.

"So, I wanted to take you to one of my favorite spots in the city, if that's all right. It's not far." Kieran hoped she would say yes. If she said no, it would kind of ruin everything.

"Yea, okay." Elena smiled brightly, and Kieran's heart did a little backflip. "Lead the way."

This time, when they went outside, Kieran wrapped his arm around Elena's shoulder and tucked her close to him. It would make walking a little awkward, but he wanted to protect her and make sure she felt safe with him.

Some primal part of him preened when she leaned in and shot him a shy smile. From below, Huey gave Kieran a look that radiated displeasure, and he let out a little chuffing noise.

Elena ignored the dog, so Kieran did as well. They talked about the meeting while they walked. Elena's next book was about to be published, and he was ravenous for details. As expected, she was unwilling to give them, instead teasing him with little hints that gave nothing away.

They reached their next destination shortly, and Elena blinked up at the enormous skyscraper.

"Your favorite place in the city is the Nexus Building?"

"Trust me, there's way more than just offices here."

The Nexus Building was one of the older skyscrapers left in the city. It retained that old charm and artistic flair completely absent from modern architecture. They entered through the lobby, but instead of going to the main elevators, they walked to the main desk where Kieran informed one of the receptionists of his appointment. Elena watched with open curiosity as they were led to a separate elevator away from the bustle of the main lobby.

When they entered, and the doors slid shut behind them, Elena stared at their reflection in the mirrored walls. Kieran thought they looked rather good together, if he did say so himself. Elena's hair was a deep purple today, tied back in an elegant bun behind her head, her eyes glittering with excitement as she leaned closer to him.

When the doors open, Elena let out a small gasp. "What is this?"

"The Nexus Gardens," Kieran said proudly. "My family helped sponsor its inclusion when the building was first constructed, to act as a sort of sanctuary for nature spirits within the city. It's private and can only be reserved by appointment."

Elena took a few tentative steps, slowly turning to take it all in.

The entire garden was encased in a glass dome. Magically enchanted, it wasn't visible from the outside of the building. Inside, there were no gravel paths, only thick grass that weaved between the plant life growing wildly around them. There was everything from trees, flowers, and bushes to moss and mushrooms. The air was thick with moisture, though it wasn't unpleasant, and butterflies fluttered through the air all around them.

"Oh," Elena gasped as a tree rustled nearby, the ghostly apparition of a deer appearing then vanishing just as quickly. "Was that a spirit?"

"Yes," Kieran confirmed, placing a hand on her lower back. "You should introduce yourself."

Elena shook just a little as she got to her knees and bowed her head in the direction the deer had appeared. Huey lowered himself completely by her side.

"Hello," Elena said, her voice barely above a whisper. "It is a great honor to meet you. My name is Elena, and this is my familiar, Huey. We are so happy to be here, in your garden."

There was silence for a moment, then a breeze ruffled Elena and Huey's hair. Though it was accompanied by no noise, a distinct sense of approval settled over them all.

"I think they like you," Kieran teased, helping Elena rise.

"How old are they? Did they move in when the garden was built, or were they born here?"

Nature spirits, naturally, lived wherever nature did. Tied to the land, most of them were as ancient as the earth itself, but if new growth sprung up—such as this garden—it often produced a new spirit, if it lasted long enough.

"There is at least one ancient spirit that decided to stick around, though they don't engage with people ever," Kieran informed her. "The rest are young. As far as the researchers can tell, there are four total."

Moisture welled in Elena's eyes as they made their way deeper into the garden. "This is amazing. There aren't words."

"I wanted today to be special." Kieran summoned a picnic

blanket and spread it out on the ground. Gently, he guided a still-stunned Elena to sit down on it.

"Why?"

Kieran's heart raced as he summoned a small box. Elena watched as he opened it to reveal a cupcake decorated with large frosting marigolds.

"Happy Birthday, Elena."

Elena's jaw dropped. "How did you know?"

Kieran shrugged. "I did a background check on you for the coven, remember? I know it isn't a birthday you would normally celebrate, but still."

Elena was thirty-six today. Two years younger than himself. Due to their long lifespans, witches usually only celebrated every five years, so he knew Elena hadn't been expecting this. Her joy made Kieran feel more than just happy. For the first time in a long time, he felt alive. Content. Happy.

"Kieran." Elena shook her head and wiped at eyes that were glittering with moisture. "Thank you. This is so sweet." Before taking the cupcake, however, she grabbed her tote bag and handed it to him. "I got you something, too."

Kieran accepted and opened the bag. "Your book!" Kieran snatched it out and raked his eyes over the cover. *To Kill a King*, the conclusion of Elena's latest series that he'd been waiting for.

"I always get a handful of copies to give to friends and family. I wanted you to have one."

There was nothing Kieran could say that expressed how he was feeling. It was such a small thing, not even a huge effort on her part, but the fact that Elena thought of him was overwhelming.

No one thought of him for small gifts—for little signs

they were thinking of him. No one went out of their way to make him happy. The urge to express himself, to make her understand spurred something reckless in Kieran.

Unable to speak, instead Kieran leaned toward Elena. Her breath caught, but she didn't move away. Carefully, almost as if not to spook her, Kieran pressed a chaste kiss directly to her lips.

"Thank you," he whispered. "This means everything to me."

Elena's breath fanned across his face, and she bumped her forehead against his softly. "You're welcome."

Beside them, Huey let out a low growl.

Elena sighed and leaned back, glaring at the dog.

"Come on, that cupcake looks amazing!"

While she dug in, Kieran gave Huey a dark look, which the familiar returned.

Next time, the mutt would not be invited, he decided.

And there would most certainly be a next time.

* * *

The rest of their time in the garden passed by pleasantly. Elena devoured her cupcake, much to Kieran's amusement, but she would not be shamed. They talked about everything and nothing, simply allowing themselves to relax.

Elena admitted her resentments about Mila's family so readily accepting Ava, and Kieran sympathized by telling a humorous story about a fight he'd gotten into with his sister-in-law.

It was all so perfect.

He'd kissed her. He'd *kissed* her.

Nothing could bring Elena down.

Tragically, the universe loved to prove her wrong.

When Kieran brought her home, it was to find a man waiting outside the house.

A man who was both familiar and a stranger to her stood there, glaring at them.

"Dad?" Elena stood shocked in her driveway. She couldn't believe her eyes. It was years, actual years, since she'd seen her father in person.

William Everett was a tall, thin man. His long white hair was pulled back into a low ponytail, and his tan skin was wrinkled from many hours spent under the sun. His dark blue eyes were as cold as ice, and his facial expression grim. He did not look happy or excited to see his daughter at all.

"I was back in the country for the new exhibition featuring some of my research in the New Stirling City Museum, and I thought I would come by and say hello while I was in the area," he said flatly.

Elena didn't bother to hide her frown. Of course, he was here for something to do with his work.

William's eyes landed on Kieran. "I would like to speak to my daughter alone, if you don't mind."

Kieran regarded her father coolly. Gone was the sweet and gentle man she'd spent the day with. In his place was a cold and menacing stranger who looked like he'd be happy to obliterate William on the spot. Elena quickly tried to remember if she'd ever spoken of her father to Kieran, but she didn't think she had. Maybe their relationship was another thing he'd learned of while researching her.

"I'm sure you would," Kieran's voice sounded bored, which made it all the more terrifying. "But I think I'll stay."

"No, it's fine," Elena rushed to stand in front of him. "I'll call you later, okay?"

Kieran didn't budge, but when he glanced down at her, she gave him a pleading look.

"Very well. I'll see you soon."

Kieran squeezed her arm gently once before backing into a portal he summoned without even looking. Show off.

Elena let out a breath and turned back to her father. "Let's talk inside."

Kieran leaving didn't mean William was off the hook. Huey's hackles were raised, and he bared his fangs at William as they entered the house.

"You still have that mutt then?" William looked deeply unhappy as he regarded the dog.

"Of course, I do," Elena snapped, her temper flaring. It was always short when her father was around. After all the disappointments, all the pain he'd caused her over the years, it was instinct.

"Oh, you let him in, pity." Mila stood with her arms crossed at the entry to the hallway, glaring at William.

"Mila," William greeted, "how have you been?"

"Fine," she replied.

Elena's heart sank when she saw Ava poke her head out from around Mila.

"Hi, I'm Ava, Mila's girlfriend. Uh, nice to meet you?" She sounded unsure.

Elena shot a pained expression at her sister. "Would you and Ava give us a minute?"

Mila nodded and led Ava upstairs. When they heard an upstairs door close, William let out a breath.

"Right, well I will get straight to the point," he said, very business-like.

Elena crossed her arms over her chest, waiting.

"Word has reached me that you joined the Greenwood Coven. Is this true?" he demanded.

Elena tried to hide her surprise. How did he hear that? "Yes, it is."

William looked at her like she had grown another head. "Elena, what were you thinking? Why would you do such a thing?"

Elena's temper flared again. "I don't see how this is any of your business," she said sharply.

William sighed, pinching the bridge of his nose. "Look, I know I have no right to come here and tell you what to do, but I also thought, with the way your mother raised you, that you had enough sense not to join that coven, out of all the covens in the world!" His volume increased with every word, to the point where he was almost shouting.

"Mom wasn't right about everything, I've learned so much since joining. I can actually use my magic to defend myself now and heal others!" Elena, for some reason, felt a stab of desperation to make him understand.

"Well, we can both agree that when it came to your education, your mother let you down, and I never agreed on her stance that all covens were inherently bad, but Elena, the Andrastes control your coven," William told her, saying it like it was a revelation.

"I'm perfectly aware of that," Elena said coolly.

Her father glared at her. "Do you have any idea how dangerous that family is? How corrupt? Even in my field of work, they are known for their shady dealings and secret agendas. You can't trust them, not in business and certainly not as coven leaders." He raised a hand, seeing Elena was about to argue with him. "I understand you want to expand your magical skills, but you need to trust me when I say it is not worth what it will cost you in the long run."

It seemed William hadn't recognized Kieran as one of the witches he was now ranting about, which was a small blessing, but Elena was seeing red. She took a deep breath, pulling herself up to her full height. "So this is why you came here," she said quietly, her voice laced with venom. "I was almost murdered last year, and you couldn't be bothered to show your face, but now that I do something you don't like, you show up?"

William looked away from her, having the decency to look ashamed. "I'm very sorry about that," he muttered. "I was horrified when I heard what happened, but you must understand, I was in a precarious political situation with my dig. If I left the country to come see you, they wouldn't have let me back in."

That answer was not unexpected, but it still hurt less. There was never a moment in Elena's life where she hadn't known her father valued his job more than her.

"You know what, Dad, I don't give a shit about your work, I really don't," she spat. "I know you never wanted me, I know you don't like me, but you should have been there, and you weren't, just like when Mom died. I've asked you for so little over the years, the bare minimum, but you couldn't even meet that. I needed you last year. And *you weren't there.*"

William stared at her helplessly. "But I'm here now," he said, "and I want to protect you. I do love you, Elena, even if I don't always show it."

He sighed when Elena did not appear moved, and took a

step toward her, placing his hands on her shoulders. Elena tensed, glaring up at him even as she felt like her chest was crumbling.

"Just, think about what I said, and know that if you ever need to escape, you ever need a place to go, you can come find me, okay? I'll keep you safe."

Elena didn't know how to respond to that, so she looked at the wall past his shoulder, her eyes welling with tears. "I think you should go."

William dropped his arms, nodding. "All right," he said, and walked toward the door.

Stopping, he took one last look at his daughter. Elena refused to return his gaze, and he quickly exited without another word.

As soon as he was gone, Elena sank to the floor, wrapping her arms around Huey's neck. Huey licked her face comfortingly, and a few tears escaped her eyes.

"No," She wiped them away. "I will not cry over him. He doesn't deserve it."

Mila burst into the room a moment later and sank to her knees to wrap Elena in a hug. Ava was right behind her, and their warm embrace calmed Elena enough to stop crying.

"Sweetheart, what happened?" Ava smoothed her hand over Elena's hair.

"He didn't even remember my birthday." It was the only thing she could think to say. Perhaps it was foolish, but her father had taken this wonderful, precious day and ruined it.

Chapter 22

May began with rising temperatures and flowers blooming, signaling that summer was on its way. After her rather public meltdown during Kieran's apology, Elena avoided the coven as much as possible except for her lessons with Magnus. It wasn't just that she was embarrassed, but her feelings toward the coven members had changed after seeing how they'd treated Kieran.

Near the beginning of the month, Elena and Mila hosted a small party of friends to celebrate Elena's book making the country's top best-seller lists.

It wasn't exactly a wild party. For the most part, it was wine and games. During a competitive round of a card game called Yksi that left everyone angry and yelling at each other, Elena went to the kitchen to get more drinks for the group. Alex followed behind her.

"Did you hear about the big fundraiser ball happening in the city next month?" he asked.

"No, what fundraiser?" Elena asked, pulling cold cans of soda out of the fridge.

"It's being organized by the Coastal Coven to raise money for the Agatha Foundation."

Elena stumbled, nearly dropping the sodas, and quickly

put them on the counter. The Agatha Foundation had been founded last year by the brother of Agatha Martin, the first witch to die during the New Stirling City witch hunt. It raised money to help support causes that furthered not only social acceptance of witches, but also legal protections as well. Elena was intimately familiar with the foundation and its work, for obvious reasons. Not that Alex was aware of this.

"Oh, no, I didn't hear about it. Is it going to be a big deal?" Elena handed him a few cans.

"For sure. All the important covens will be there, along with the most fabulously wealthy families."

"Sounds like an event we will not be invited to," Elena remarked.

"You would think, but I heard a handful of coven members are going to be 'randomly' selected to receive invitations to make us lower-class witches feel better." Alex awkwardly made air quotes with his hands full of soda cans.

"Well, I doubt I would be on that list, or you," Elena said pointedly.

"That's very hurtful but also very true. Still, you never know!" Alex grinned. "I assume you're going on that museum trip though? I got the invite in the mail the other day."

"I don't really have a choice. Magnus is leading it and providing the tour. Apparently, one of his colleagues at the university had a large part in putting it together, so he's pretty excited. I was thinking of seeing if Tora can tag along."

"I'm sure it wouldn't be an issue," Alex told her, his eyes flashing to where Tora sat next to Mila. "Museums aren't my thing, but you seem nerdy enough to enjoy it!"

Elena rolled her eyes and they walked back to the group,

where Ava and Maggie were now setting up another game. Throughout the rest of the night, Elena's mind kept going back to the fundraiser. She wondered who was in charge of making the selections for the "random" invitations. Although, she supposed it didn't matter. Elena didn't think she would want to go or that she would be invited.

She was wrong.

The following week, Mila woke Elena up by dropping a very fancy envelope on her face.

"All I have ever done was love you!" Elena complained, sitting up and rubbing her eyes.

"Open!" Mila commanded, pointing to the letter.

Elena sighed and picked it up. There was no return address, but she had a sinking feeling where it came from. Ripping it open, Elena pulled out a card that was completely blank.

"I don't get it," Mila stared at the letter.

"It's a spell," Elena muttered, running her free hand over the card. The hidden words appeared, and Elena scanned it over.

"Well, shit," she said, flopping back into bed.

"Oh, give me that." Mila snatched the card up.

"Miss Elena Hall," she began to read, "You are formally invited to the Agatha Foundation fundraiser event in the White Peak hotel ballroom on June eighteenth. Your coven has covered the cost of your attendance, but please consider donating to this worthy cause. Your hosts, the honorable Coastal Coven, look forward to seeing you there. "

"Read the bottom," Elena moaned into her pillow

Mila looked down to see a handwritten note was added in.

Even though your past is not widely known, your presence would be an honor, Miss Hall. I hope you attend.

–Charles.

"That's the chairman of the board, right?" Mila asked.

"Yup, one of the few members of my coven that know the truth."

"Seems like he's laying it on thick," Mila noted.

Elena rolled over and stared at the ceiling hopelessly. It was easy to say she didn't want to go when she wasn't invited, but now the entire hypothetical was a reality, and it all seemed much more complicated. "I mean, it's an important cause, and it could be fun to stare at all the rich people, right?"

"Maybe," Mila conceded, "but if you aren't comfortable going, they can't force you to."

"I'll think about it."

"Okay, well let me know what you decide. If you want to go, we'll need to set up some time to find you a dress. Last time I checked, you didn't have anything fancy enough for this hanging out in your closet."

Elena spent about a week agonizing over her decision. Part of her felt it was her responsibility to go, to honor those that hadn't made it out that day, and to represent the survivors, even if no one there knew she was one. On the other hand, could she stand putting herself through this? The worst day of her life would be the main topic of conversation, and no doubt, the people there would have no idea what they were talking about. Could she stand it?

Finally, she decided to reach out to Tora.

"It's a tough one, babe," Tora said, through the phone. Elena put her on speaker while she sat in the grass under the tree in the front yard while Mila gardened. "Is there anyone else going that you know? That you trust? I think if you were going to be there without anyone you were close with, who could help you out if you were struggling, you shouldn't go."

"My mentor, Magnus, will be there," Elena said, "but no one else I know well."

"Does he know the whole story?" Tora asked.

"He does."

"Well, that's good then! And if shit goes sideways, you can always run away to my place. The venue isn't that far away from my apartment," Tora suggested. "Tell you what, why don't you come stay with me for the entire week? That museum exhibit thing you invited me to is the Sunday before this fundraiser, right? I can take off from work, and we can just spend the entire week together and help you get psyched up."

"That actually sounds really fun." Elena warmed up to the idea. "Let's do it."

* * *

The New Stirling City Museum was proud to present their newest exhibition on the co-development of humans and witches through time. Magnus had the pleasure of acting as the tour guide for his coven members during the special preview granted to local covens.

The tour was set to take place after general museum opening hours, and Elena and Tora were hanging out in the park outside the museum for a few hours, waiting for their turn to go in. They were sitting at a round picnic table in the shade of an enormous tree, hiding from the summer heat. After Elena mentioned to Tora that her father had been involved in curating this exhibit, they'd taken the opportunity to discuss his unexpected visit from a few weeks before.

"What is it like in his head," Tora mused, "that he thought it was okay to ignore you after your accident, but you join a new social club, and he arrives out of nowhere to boss you around. Like, how did he see that interaction ending?" As they were in public, they used terms like social club rather than saying coven.

"I don't know, I stopped trying to figure that man out years ago. I gave up on ever having a real relationship with him after he didn't show up to my high school graduation. You remember? I spent all that time writing the perfect invitation letter to try and get him to come."

"Yup, and then he sent a note back saying he was too busy. No congratulations, no gift. What an ass." Tora's face was grim as she spoke. "Some research project he couldn't get away from, right?"

Elena nodded.

"I guess him not being there last year affected me more than I thought," she admitted, then, spotting an approaching figure, raised her hand and waved. "Magnus, over here!" she called out.

Magnus smiled when he saw her and headed in their direction. He was wearing a sharp-looking suit, his hair pulled back in a low ponytail.

"Hello, Elena," he greeted brightly. "Beautiful day, isn't it?"

"The best," Elena grinned. "Magnus, this is my dear friend Tora Tanaka. Tora, this is Magnus Jelani, professor extraordinaire and my mentor."

Hellos were exchanged all around before Magnus turned to Elena.

"I think you're really going to enjoy this exhibit. I got an early look yesterday, and it is expertly done."

"Magnus, I don't think I've ever seen you this energized about anything." Elena laughed.

"Nothing makes me more excited than the pursuit of knowledge," he joked. "I think we could probably head in now."

The museum had just officially closed, and the three of them made their way inside, handing the security guards at the front their special tickets. Magnus led them past the various displays to a hall near the back. A museum representative was waiting for them, along with a few other people Elena recognized from their coven and a few others Magnus identified as members from other covens.

Magnus strode up to the representative to check their group in, while Elena and Tora hung back, chatting idly. Soon enough, more people began to show up, and the hall started to fill. While she was looking around, Tora nudged Elena sharply in the ribs.

"Ow!" Elena complained. "What?"

"Kieran Andraste just showed up. I didn't know he was going to be here!" she hissed.

Elena turned around, following Tora's gaze. Sure enough, Kieran was standing there, talking with Magnus, while the rest of the witches inched closer to him to hear what he was saying.

"I didn't either," Elena said, a little shocked. He hadn't said he was going to be here.

Kieran looked over in her direction and spotted her, his eyes widening. He excused himself from Magnus and quickly walked over to Elena, ignoring the dozens of eyes that followed him.

"Hello," he greeted, his gaze sweeping over Tora.

"Hey." Elena took in his appearance. There was a healthy flush to his skin and a brightness to his eyes she hadn't seen in a while. "I didn't realize you were going to be here today." The words came out like an accusation.

"Last minute decision," he said hastily. "I wasn't planning on coming, but Magnus called me up and made a very persuasive, and lengthy, argument for it."

Elena smiled at him, unable to stop herself. Tora elbowed her again, and Elena was shaken from her stupor.

"Oh, right, sorry." Elena turned to the others. "Kieran, this is my dear friend Tora. She lives here in the city."

Kieran smiled at Tora. "Nice to meet you." He shook hands while Elena did her best not to squirm.

Tora couldn't formulate words, and instead, just nodded. It was kind of funny watching Tora be so nervous, but it was making the situation awkward.

"Well, uh," Kieran said, shifting under Tora's wide-eyed stare, "I'll see you around, I guess, tonight."

Elena pursed her lips, trying not to laugh. "Why don't you walk with us? I'll protect you from your fans." She pointedly glanced at the group of witches staring at him.

Kieran's eyes briefly closed, and a pained expression crossed his features. "Yes, I would love that."

Life seem to have been restored to Tora, and she cleared her throat. "Let's get a spot near the front. I want to hear every detail your lovely mentor has to share with us." She dragged Elena to stand right near Magnus, and Kieran followed closely behind.

Kieran's body radiated heat from where he stood next to her, and Elena resisted the urge to grasp his hand. There were too many watching eyes who would be happy to blab their business as far as they could. What seemed so simple and natural to her and Kieran would be a full blown scandal to everyone else.

Magnus cleared his throat, and like a bunch of chicks gathering around a mother hen, all the coven members quickly scuttled to his side.

He beamed at them all. "Welcome, friends, to the opening of this truly wonderful exhibit," he began. "As you may know, the research on the co-development of humans and witches throughout history has greatly grown over the last few decades. This exhibit covers that research from the evolution of humanity, to the creation of witches by ancient nature spirits, through history, and to today. Now, math is usually my subject, but for this, I will make an exception! And to help us through the exhibit, we have with us a special guest, one of its top contributing researchers!"

For one horrifying moment, Elena thought she was about to see her father step up to Magnus's side, but was relieved when a woman she didn't recognize joined him instead.

"This is Dr. Jessica Wilder. She's a good friend of mine and was gracious enough to join us this evening."

Jessica Wilder smiled at the crowd, her eyes alight with anticipation.

Their group moved into the hall, and Elena listened with interest as Magnus and Dr. Wilder began to take them through the first few stops on the tour, detailing the evolution of humans up to the point of the magical intervention that had created witches.

"As far as we can tell, it took nearly two hundred thousand years after the first true humans evolved in the continent of

Auzlian for the emergence of witches to occur. Although it is impossible to verify the origin story of our people, science has shown that witches hold in our DNA magical markers that do not exist anywhere else in the physical world," Dr. Wilder explained. "Every culture has their own version of how witches came to be, but they all hold one common thread. They claim that nature spirits reached out to humanity, and for various reasons, gave select groups magical abilities that could be passed down to their children. In the next section, we will explore some of these origin myths from around the world."

The group began to move on, and as they reached the next display and Magnus began to speak, Elena leaned forward to examine an ornate pot shard depicting a human receiving the gift of magic from a spirit.

"Excuse me." Dr. Wilder appeared next to Elena, startling her. "But someone said your name was Elena Hall. You wouldn't happen to be William's daughter, would you?"

Elena forced herself not to scowl. "Yes, I am. You know him, I take it?"

"Oh, yes. We've worked together a long time. It's lovely to meet you, Elena. Your father has always spoken so highly of you."

He had? That made no sense based on every interaction she'd ever had with the man.

"It's nice to meet you, too."

Thankfully, Dr. Wilder went back to help with the tour, leaving Elena to stew. What exactly had her father told his colleagues about her? All these years, he'd never shown any interest in her career, so what exactly was he so proud of? The mystery made her skin crawl.

"You okay?" Kieran walked up next to her, his voice low.

"Yea, fine."

Kieran didn't look convinced but let it go.

"This section, we encourage you to explore on your own," Dr. Wilder announced as they entered a large, circular room. "Many of the exhibits are interactive, and in the center is our star attraction. An ancient pot, nearly five thousand years old. Yes, five thousand years!" she said excitedly, in response to some surprised faces. "It was crafted by magic, which is how it has survived this long, and still maintains a trace of the spell placed on it all those years ago. We are not sure of its purpose, but if you stand inside the dome we have constructed around it, some witches will still hear the singing voices that were imbued into the clay. These are the voices of our ancestors, long departed, but still alive to us here today. Enjoy!"

Most people immediately took off toward the pot to see if they could hear it singing, but Elena and her group decided to split off while everyone else crammed themselves into the tiny room at the center of the hall. Kieran wandered over to Magnus and started to chat with him, and Tora noticeably relaxed, Elena noticed.

Tora led her to a display of ancient witch's robes, gushing over the embroidery while Elena glanced at Kieran over her shoulder. Several witches were not even pretending to be looking at the exhibit, and instead, were trying to muscle their way into Kieran and Magnus's conversation. Elena looked away, annoyed.

After about twenty minutes, most of the witches abandoned the pot, disappointed they could not hear the singing that was supposed to emanate from it. The few who did stayed in the room, transfixed, but not so many that others were not able to fit.

Tora approached first, entering through the arch in the wall and gazing at the pot. The room was completely dark except for a single spotlight that shone on the pot, which was on a dais in the center. There was strong protective magic around it, strong enough that even a human would be able to detect it. Tora frowned at the pot, then stepped aside to let others in. Elena stood next to Tora as a few others wandered in behind them. They all waited in silence.

The pot was simple, with no paint and faint designs visible in the plain clay. It certainly didn't seem special.

Kieran entered, looking around. After spotting Elena, he moved next to her with a small smile. She returned it, her face barely visible in the dark, then returned her gaze to the pot. One of the other witches in the room was the first to hear it, letting out a gasp when the faint sound of singing voices hit their ears. Elena's heart fluttered in excitement, trying to focus extra hard so that she could experience it, too.

"I don't hear it," Tora whispered, frustrated.

Faintly, Elena heard something. It was like she was listening to music from another room, standing on the other side of the door with her ear pressed against it, straining to listen. As she stood there, frozen from head to toe, the sound grew louder, until it was the only thing she could hear in her head.

It was stunningly beautiful. The voices of men and women singing in an ancient language she couldn't understand were flowing and dancing through her mind. Although Elena didn't know the words, she knew there was joy in the song, and grief, and love. A tear escaped her eye, sliding down her cheek.

Kieran shifted uncomfortably. Turning her head to face him, Elena realized he couldn't hear the music. Without understanding why, Elena reached out and slipped her hand into his. Kieran sucked in a breath, staring so deeply at her, it was if she could see into his soul. What she saw there was swirling, and wild, and filled with pain. The song changed, the rhythm almost matching what Elena sensed writhing inside Kieran.

Dark, twisted, and constrained.

Elena desperately wanted to reach out and soothe it all away, but magic held her in its thrall.

"Your eyes are glowing," Kieran murmured, so quiet only Elena could hear him.

Elena couldn't speak, couldn't even move, barely register-ing what he said. All she knew was the music and the churning storm in the man next to her.

How could he live every day with this inside him?

But then again, how did Elena? If what the song brought out in Kieran was a wild tempest, what was inside Elena was a dense yet chaotic fog. But somehow, with the song weaving between them, it all seemed to meld and dance together—a peace Elena had only experienced with Kieran over the past year.

All through this, Kieran never looked away, their gazes locked on each other like nothing else existed.

They might have stayed there forever if Tora hadn't shaken them out of it. After allowing them some time to take it in, she pulled Elena, and by extension Kieran, out of the room. As soon as they were away from the pot and the music faded, Kieran hastily dropped Elena's hand, breaking whatever strange spell had fallen over them.

"That was amazing," Elena said breathlessly, wiping tears from her cheeks.

"Well, I'm glad you all got to experience it," Tora said glumly.

"Oh, Tora, I'm sorry." Elena tried to give Tora a comforting look.

"It's okay." Tora sighed dramatically. "I guess this is what I get for not spending time in nature. I mean, you're out living in the middle of a forest. I'm just too removed from the spirits."

"You could always move out to Alberdeen with me," Elena suggested teasingly.

Tora rolled her eyes. "No thanks. If the spirits want to talk, they know where I am."

They finished up the rest of the tour about an hour later and ended in an empty social room where refreshments were set up for the attendees to chat.

Elena was examining the cheese plate when Tora nudged her with her foot. "Kieran is staring at you," she muttered.

Elena looked around and spotted Kieran, who gave her a meaningful look. He turned and walked toward the exit, disappearing through it.

"What is up with you two?" Tora whispered.

"What do you mean?" Elena asked, plotting how to slip out of the room in her head.

"You think I didn't notice you two *holding hands* in that pottery room? Be honest, are you two dating?"

Elena gaped at Tora. "Holding hands? What are you talking about?"

Tora frowned. "Do you not remember?"

Elena shook her head. All she could remember from being inside the room was the music, her interaction with Kieran only a jumbled mixture of emotions and feelings.

"Hm." Tora was unconvinced.

"Look, there's nothing going on between us," Elena insisted, trying to ignore the incriminating blush rising up her cheeks.

"Uh-huh, so you aren't going to go follow him so you can have a private goodbye right now?" Tora asked skeptically.

Elena glared at her, but couldn't deny it. "I'll be right back," she promised, before walking briskly away.

She slipped through the same door and looked around in the dark hallway. Kieran stepped forward from the pillar he was leaning against while he waited.

"So, glad you came?" Elena asked.

Kieran smiled at her. "Very." He stopped in front of her. "Thank you so much, Elena, for sharing that magic in there with me. I wasn't able to hear the music at all until you intervened."

"I honestly don't remember that," Elena admitted with a frown. "Did I hold your hand?"

Kieran raised his eyebrows in surprise, and Elena's gut twisted with embarrassment.

"Yes, you did," he said, the corners of his mouth tugging upward. "That's strange you don't remember it, and that you were affected so strongly by the magic at all. From what I've read about this pot, everyone else only hears faint singing, but when I touched your skin it was like they were in the room with us."

Elena didn't know what to make of that and shrugged helplessly. "I don't know, maybe I'll ask Magnus about it." She refused to ask her father, even though he would be a much more knowledgeable source.

"Well, either way, thank you." Kieran's eyes were full of

sincerity. "That truly was very special."

Elena was glad for the poor lighting in the hallway as she was certain her face was burning scarlet at that moment. "Right, well," she stammered, "I guess I'll see you soon, at the fundraiser?"

"Possibly, my family hasn't decided yet which one of us is going to go. I didn't realize you received an invitation."

"Oh," Elena said, "I did. Random selection, I think."

"I see." Kieran pursed his lips. "Well, perhaps I'll see you there."

"Yea." Elena tilted her face up toward him. "If you do come, will you dance with me?"

Kieran's eyes warmed, and he leaned down. "If I'm there, you're the only one I'll want to dance with."

Elena's heart beat wildly as once again he pressed his lips to hers. It only lasted a moment before he adjusted and kissed the corner of her mouth, then her cheek.

"Kieran, you're driving me crazy," Elena whimpered, her hands grasping his arms to keep herself standing. "And you're terrible at this *friends* thing. Friends don't kiss like this."

Kieran chuckled, his warm breath fanning across her face. "Well maybe we aren't friends then."

Laughter from the reception broke them out of their haze. Now was not the time or place to talk about this.

With obvious regret, Kieran stepped back. "We'll see each other soon, all right?"

"Yes, soon."

"Goodbye." One more kiss planted on Elena's cheek before Kieran walked away.

She watched him leave, her heart aching. More than

anything, she wanted to follow him, to take comfort in his arms and try to rediscover what she'd experienced when the ancient spell bound them together.

But that would have to wait, and Elena returned to the reception with a fake smile plastered on her face.

Chapter 23

"One would think there would be a spell to make heels more comfortable," Elena murmured, shifting her weight as she stood arm in arm with Magnus.

"You could always make your feet completely lose feeling for the evening, but I don't recommend it," he chuckled.

It was the night of the fundraiser, and they were waiting in line to get into the ballroom. Elena had spent the entire week with Tora in the city. Things weren't exactly easy. The unease and fear of being back where the witch hunt had happened never left Elena alone, but she was tired of being kept from this place—from her home.

So she forced herself through it, employing all the coping strategies she knew. They went to the theater, a few of Elena's favorite restaurants, and saw a movie. No parks though, and no cafes.

It was easy to ignore the impending fundraiser when Tora was keeping her busy, but when Elena stepped into the stunning gown she was wearing for the night, it was time to face it all. She was going. The comfort of Magnus being at her side, and the promise of possibly seeing Kieran, gave her the strength to walk out the door and get to where they now stood.

The hallway of the grand hotel was packed with witches from around the country wearing their finest, all waiting to get in. Security seemed to be tight as agents from the High Witch's Council scanned each person as they entered and checked names against the guest list. Charles and a handful of board members stood in front of them in line, and a few other coven members were behind them.

Lydia, one of the board members Elena had met her first day in the mansion, turned around. "So glad you both could make it! Elena, you look absolutely stunning!"

"Thank you." Elena blushed.

"And, Magnus, so handsome as always," Lydia added, and Magnus nodded politely. He did look rather dapper in his dark green suit, towering over the crowd, his eyes scanning everyone watchfully.

They slowly made their way up to the front of the line, and as their group reached the security check, Charles moved forward to introduce them and help the agents move each person through. The scanning spell felt like a trickle of cold water down her spine, causing Elena to shudder, but she brushed it off as Magnus led her into the ballroom.

The ballroom was located on the top floor of the hotel, with glass walls looking out over the city and the mountains beyond. Throughout the room were glistening fountains, softly swaying flowers in extravagant crystal pots, and a live orchestra playing in the far corner. Tables with numbers were on one side of the room, and a marble dance floor with a presentation stage was on the other.

"Very tasteful," Magnus said, his deep voice vibrating.

Elena followed his line of sight, and her heart dropped into her stomach. Against the opposite side of the room stood a solid black wall that read *In Memorium*, and carved into the wall itself were the names of the fourteen witches who'd been killed.

"Oh," Elena said, suddenly feeling a little light-headed.

"Are you all right?" Magnus asked worriedly, holding onto her arm for support.

"I'm fine. I should probably just sit down for a minute."

"As you wish. Charles said we are at table number four." Magnus led her to the table and helped her into her chair. He looked at her, concerned. "Are you sure you're up for this, Elena?"

Elena took a deep breath. "Yeah, yeah. I don't know why that wall caught me off guard. I'll be fine," she assured him.

Magnus did not look convinced but didn't press her further. Taking a sip from the glass of ice water in front of her helped Elena recover from the shock, and for a moment she drank and focused on the stinging cold sliding over her tongue. It helped, and Elena was able to calm her breathing to normal levels.

They waited as the rest of the crowd filed in and took their seats. As soon as everyone was settled, the lights dimmed, and a spotlight appeared on the stage. A man walked up to speak.

"Friends and cherished guests," he began, his voice magically enhanced throughout the room, "my name is Arthur Cromwell, chairman of the Coastal Coven. I want to thank you all for being here tonight. We have come together to remember a tragic event that happened a year and a half ago, no more than a stone's throw away from this very building." He paused somberly, his gaze slipping over to the memorial wall. "We lost brothers and sisters on that terrible day. Sons and daughters, fathers and mothers, friends, co-workers, loved ones."

Tears welled in Elena's eyes, but she held them in, her throat tight. Even though no one was looking at her, Elena still felt like every eye in the room had turned her way—that everyone could heart her heart pounding and her grief written all over her face.

"The witch hunt of New Stirling City shook our community to the core and reminded us that we still have far to go in our quest for peace. Agatha Martin, for whom the foundation for today's fundraiser was named, was a unique and exuberant witch, full of life. I want to invite her brother, Frank, to speak."

Applause broke out as a second man joined Arthur Cromwell on stage. Elena recognized him instantly. Frank looked older than Elena remembered, his dark hair now peppered with gray and his frame thinner than it used to be.

Frank was a good man—kind and generous. Even though he hadn't known Elena and was grieving the loss of his sister, he'd visited Elena in the hospital every day after the attack and had food delivered to her apartment when she went home while she adjusted. He did the same for all the survivors—all the ones who accepted his help, that was.

Seeing Frank again was bringing back so many memories Elena had fought so hard to ignore.

"Thank you, Arthur," he began, his voice cracking just a little. "We are honored that this event has finally come together. My sister lived life to the fullest, and she lived her life for others. We hope that through your generous donations, we can make a difference, so what happened to her will never happen again…"

Frank's voice faded from Elena's mind as she focused all her mental capacity on the shining city behind him, trying to keep her emotions at bay. Unbidden, a memory floated to the surface.

"Sammi! Wait up!"

"Come on! We're going to miss it!" her friend called to her, laughing. They were children then, crawling through a crowd gathered on the side of the street to watch a parade. Sammi, her dark eyes filled with mischief, grabbed Elena by the hand and pulled her through the mass of strangers until they were right at the front.

"Wow!" Elena cried as the giant, colorful floats passed by.

"They're throwing candy!" Sammi yelled gleefully, holding her hands up. The two girls screamed with excitement as the candy rained down, the adults behind them laughing with delight at their antics.

"Look at how much I got!" Sammi beamed, holding up her fists filled with sweets.

"Me, too!" Elena held up hers as well, and the girls descended into giggles, leaning on each other as they turned back to watch the rest of the parade go by.

"Elena?"

Elena snapped out of it, and looked over to Magnus who was staring at her.

"What?"

"You're crying, my dear." Magnus handed her a napkin, and Elena quickly wiped her tears away. "They just said where you can buy raffle tickets and view the auction items up for bid. Dinner is about to be served, followed by dancing and socializing, then a special presentation of some sort, followed by the auction."

"Okay, sounds good." Elena tried to suppress a sniffle, turning to the table.

"You don't have to do this," Magnus whispered. "We can leave right now."

Part of Elena desperately wanted that, to flee this and the grief that was threatening to take over. But she couldn't. She'd made it this far, and her pride wouldn't let her admit defeat so soon.

"No, I'm fine." To prove the point, Elena engaged one of her fellow coven members in conversation about the decorations.

Elena expected the food to be delicious and was not disappointed, practically melting over the chocolate dessert that was served. As dinner progressed, the mood in the room lightened, and Elena started to relax. She took the opportunity to talk with her fellow coven members, most of whom she'd never spent much time with before.

She was talking to a man named Liam, who was a coven mentor like Magnus, about the intricacies of teaching theory when the orchestra began to play and people stood, some moving to the dance floor while others made their way to examine the auction items.

"Shall we take a look at what they have?" Liam asked excitedly.

"Even though neither of us could ever afford to bid on any of it," Elena pointed out.

"Doesn't hurt to look!"

Elena made her way to the back of the room with Liam, carefully maneuvering her gown through the tables and chairs.

"Elena?" someone asked.

She stopped to see who spoke, Liam carrying on without

her.

"Oh, hello!" she said awkwardly, vaguely recognizing the man she'd made out with at the singles party. "Kevin, right?"

"Kyle," the man corrected, looking unhappy that she'd gotten his name wrong.

"Right, sorry. Uh, how are you?"

"Very well, and you?" he asked.

"Fine, fine." Elena cast her mind out for something to say.

"You know, I'd hoped I would get your number at the party, but you disappeared on me," he said, half-jokingly and half-accusingly.

"Oh well..." Elena stammered. Before she was forced to give some lame excuse, she was saved by someone walking up behind her, someone whose presence made Kyle shrink away.

"Mr. Andraste!" Kyle said in surprise. "How nice to see you."

Elena didn't need to turn around to know who stood behind her. His body heat tickled her skin, and the aura of his magic washed over her like a comforting blanket.

"Do we know each other?" Kieran's deep voice said coolly.

"Uh no, no." Kyle blushed, embarrassed.

"Well then, if you don't mind, I must steal Miss Hall away for a moment. Coven business," he said curtly, gently taking Elena's arm and pulling her away before Kyle could respond.

Elena let him guide her but did not dare look up until they had walked several feet away. When she did, she found he was smirking, looking pleased with himself.

"I didn't need rescuing." She halfheartedly glared at him.

"No, of course not," he said, still smirking.

Elena glanced behind her to see that Kyle was gone, and

she stopped to face Kieran properly. He looked stunning, of course. He wore a black tuxedo that fit him perfectly, and his jet-black hair was slicked back, showing off his striking features.

"So, you decided to come after all." Elena couldn't keep the smile off her face.

"Yes, my brother and I volunteered." Kieran's eyes scanned over Elena's body, making her feel self-conscious again. "You look beautiful."

"Thanks," she responded, feeling warm. Not able to meet his eyes for fear of blushing and giggling like a schoolgirl, she looked around the room. "Well, you want to look at the auction items?"

Kieran nodded, and together, they walked toward the back of the room where a small crowd was gathered. There were large paintings, statues, rare magical objects, custom-made clothing from around the world and...

"Is that a signed copy of famed author Alys Sinclair's newest novel, *To Kill A King*?" Kieran asked, leaning in to examine the book.

"Maybe." Elena shrugged. "Charles asked me to donate it."

"Well, I know what I'm bidding on," Kieran teased.

Elena rolled her eyes. "You already have a signed copy," Elena reminded him. "And besides, you should really be bidding on that ceremonial robe. I mean, the craftsmanship! Where else are you going to find something as beautiful as that to conduct all your blood rituals in?"

Kieran grinned. "What do you want to bid on?" he asked her.

Elena snorted in a very undignified manner. "You know I

can't afford any of this, right?"

Kieran glanced at her out of the corner of his eye, becoming preoccupied with the painting displayed next to her book.

"If there was anything you really wanted, I could get it for you," he said casually.

Elena stared at him. "Don't be ridiculous," she said. "These things are going to go for thousands of dollars. I'm not going to just let you spend that kind of money on me."

Kieran turned to look at her. "Thousands of dollars is nothing to me, Elena," he said frankly. "Seriously, what do you want?"

Elena shook her head and looked around. "That necklace." She pointed to an emerald necklace nearby that, according to the sign, stored memories within its center.

"Then I'll get it for you," Kieran said.

Elena rolled her eyes. "Kieran, no. Be serious."

"I am being serious."

"Then seriously, I cannot accept something like that, so forget about it."

Kieran shrugged, then looked out toward the dance floor. "All right, but I do owe you a dance."

Elena looked up at him, his wide eyes looking hopefully into hers. Back at the museum, Elena had been teasing Kieran, but now that they were here with so people around, it felt different—more weighted. She should say no. There were a million reasons to say no, but fuck it all, she wanted to say yes.

"Okay," she agreed.

Kieran smiled brightly and took her by the hand, heading to the dance floor. Elena felt eyes watch them the entire way, and this time, Elena knew it wasn't her imagination. As the orchestra began playing a new song, they took their positions at the center of the floor.

"Kieran," Elena said, suddenly panicked.

"Yes?"

"I don't know how to do this dance."

"That's fine, just follow my lead."

He lifted her right hand up and placed her left on his shoulder. He put his free hand on her waist, then encouraged her to step backward. It was awkward at first, but Kieran was so confident in what he was doing, Elena felt herself relaxing into the dance and only stepped on his toes a few times. Unable to bring herself to meet his eye, she looked over his shoulder at the room as they spun around the dance floor.

"How have things been since you've been back in the city?" he asked in her ear, sending a tingle down her spine.

"Okay, for the most part," Elena answered.

"Are you happy you came tonight?"

"Very." It wasn't a lie now that he was there.

Kieran spun her around, and Elena gripped him tighter so she wouldn't trip. "I read an interesting article this morning," she mentioned.

"Oh?" Kieran's breath was hot against her skin, and Elena fought to remain focused.

"A witch from the Northern Mountains Coven was arrested for sending their familiar after an Andraste family familiar."

"Yes, I heard that."

Elena could hear the self-satisfaction in Kieran's tone.

"You didn't hunt him down yourself."

"I promised you I wouldn't, didn't I?"

He had, and he'd kept his word. Elena risked looking up at

him and was met by Kieran's intense gaze. She felt her throat clench, and she started to feel a little dizzy. His grip on her waist increased.

"Kieran I—"

"Mind if I cut in?" someone asked. They both turned to see Magnus standing there.

"Not at all." Kieran stepped back.

Elena watched him go before turning to Magnus, who seemed oblivious to the fact he had just interrupted something important.

"Did you see the illusion on the back wall?" he asked her, his deep voice rumbling. "A sophisticated piece of magic, and difficult to sustain, you should examine it and try to discern the spell."

Elena rolled her eyes. "Really? Homework at a party?"

Magnus kept rambling on, but Elena barely listened. Even as they danced, Elena was only focused on Kieran watching from the side of the room, his constant gaze setting Elena ablaze from the inside out.

* * *

Kieran watched from the wall where he snuck away to, his pulse racing. He'd known Elena would be there tonight, but somehow, she'd still caught him off guard. Her hair was braided beautifully into a bun on top of her head, with crystals covering the pure-white strands so that it looked like glittering, freshly fallen snow. She wore a dark blue and golden strapless gown that hugged her form at the top before sweeping away elegantly at the bottom. Her lips, which he could barely stop himself from staring at, were painted a deep red. She looked incredible. As she swept around the dance floor with Magnus, her dress flowed around her, showing off her curves.

Even as she smiled and talked with Magnus, Kieran couldn't help compare her demeanor to how she was at the museum. It wasn't until that night that Kieran realized it, but at all times, Elena was restrained somehow. There, with her old friend, however, she was completely free. She laughed easier, talked with more energy and animation, and was extremely physically affectionate toward her companion. Something about witnessing Elena like that made him ache with both delight and longing.

"Easy there, Kieran," a voice said in his ear.

Kieran did not turn to look at his brother, who had appeared at his shoulder. "I don't know what you mean," Kieran muttered.

"You got a sort of obsessive look on your face while watching that woman. It's creepy," Declan remarked.

"I'm not being a creep," Kieran snapped back. "She's my friend."

Declan snorted. "Sure, friend. Just keep it together," Declan told him, thumping him on the back.

Kieran sighed and looked away from Elena, following Declan into the crowd.

Kieran did his best not to fixate on Elena as the night went on, although, annoyingly, he seemed to always know where she was in the room. She finished her dance with Magnus then went back to the auction items, where she met up with the other coven members. She stayed back there and talked with people for a while before a woman asked her to dance, and she was whisked back out to the floor. Kieran avoided the dance floor again like the plague, though several people hinted they would like to dance with him.

After one rather persistent woman nearly backed him into a corner, Kieran hastily made his exit by claiming he needed to check in with his friend. He looked around the room desperately and spotted Elena. He walked straight toward her, away from the woman, but froze when he saw where she was.

Elena stood alone in front of the memorial wall, staring up at the names of the victims. She was holding her hands in front of her, and her gaze was unwavering. Something in her eyes stopped Kieran from approaching.

Pain and longing, misery and affection.

This quiet moment was personal—way too personal for Kieran to intrude on. There would be time to talk to Elena later. For now, he would give her space to reflect on whatever was on her mind.

* * *

Elena stared up at the name, *Saamira Khan*, eyes sparkling.

"You would have loved this," she whispered, "and all these rich men would have been throwing themselves at your feet."

Someone came up next to her, and Elena turned to see Frank Martin standing there. He offered her a small smile.

"It's been a while, Elena."

"It has." Elena smiled in return. Seeing him up close confirmed Elena's previous assessment that he looked older, and Elena wondered just how much all this had aged her as well. But seeing him—someone who understood better than anyone else what she was feeling—was comforting.

Frank turned to look up at his sister's name. "I wasn't sure I could do this," he admitted.

"Me either," Elena said. "But things seem to be going okay. No one has claimed they could have stopped the entire thing if they had been there yet."

Frank snorted. "Yet," he emphasized. "The night is still young."

People loved to imagine themselves as heroes, Elena had learned in the year since the witch hunt, but when it came down to it, very few actually had what it took. Elena didn't. When faced with such violent hatred, she'd frozen—her body betraying her and her magic abandoning her to the whims of the humans who'd attacked.

Even Sammi hadn't been able to fight back. At least, Elena thought that was what happened. Her memories from that day were so fragmented it was hard to know how Sammi spent her final moments.

Elena wasn't sure she would ever be able to forgive herself for failing to protect Sammi and herself, but she'd survived this long. She'd made it one whole year and a half. If she could make it through that, Elena was determined to keep going, for both of them.

Beside her, Frank pressed two fingers to his lips then to his sister's name before giving Elena another sad smile and walking away, leaving her alone.

Elena sighed, then pulled herself away from the wall and decided to look for Kieran. He'd vanished after their dance, and she wanted to talk to him again.

She didn't get the chance, however, as the spotlight turned on, directing everyone's attention to the stage. Arthur

Cromwell stood there once more.

"Hello, everyone! I hope you're enjoying yourselves. Before we move on to the auction and raffle drawing, we have a special presentation from one of our coven members, to remind us the reason we are all here tonight." He stepped away, and a large, clear image, like a movie theater, popped up on the glass behind the stage.

At first, the screen was black, but then confused shouting and yelling could be heard. White words appeared, stating the day and year of the witch hunt they were commemorating. Elena's heart began to beat faster, warning bells going off in her head. The confused yelling turned to screams of terror, and suddenly, the black screen changed into a shaky video that looked like someone had recorded on their phone. The person was in a crowd in a park in the city, as an angry mob holding guns and torches attacked those around them.

"Death to witches!" The mob was chanting, shooting their guns in the air. A hole formed in the mob and a group of people of around twenty were dragged forward, bound and gagged. As the crowd watched, horrified, the witch hunters moved down the line, shooting their victims in the back of the head, one by one. People screamed, many rushing forward to try and save the captives, but the mob fired into the crowd. The person holding the video made a run for it, shooting off a burst of fire bolt toward the witch hunters, creating a gap in the wall, and rushed forward to the captives.

The phone fell to the ground, but the video didn't stop. Instead, they had a clear view of the victims.

Bodies lay on the ground, and near the phone, a woman had broken out of her bonds. She was cradling a body in her arms and was covered in blood. The woman looked toward the camera, her white hair splattered with crimson, and Elena looked into her own, horrified eyes.

In the present, Elena collapsed to her knees, unable to breathe. All around her, people were gasping and yelling out in protest, but Elena couldn't hear them. She was choking, her entire body shaking uncontrollably.

"Have you no respect?" someone shouted.

"Turn this off now!" another person yelled.

People began to swarm toward the stage, magic sparks flying toward the screen in attempts to cover it up. Elena's vision blackened. All she could hear was the gunshot, followed by a *thud* next to her. All she could see was Saamira's lifeless body in her lap.

Everything was chaos, but Elena was trapped in her own mind. The voices of the crowd faded into a dull ringing noise in her head, and all she knew was the tang of blood in her nostrils and the crushing fear forcing her to the ground.

"Saamira" she gasped out, her voice strangled.

A pair of arms wrapped themselves around Elena and lifted her into the air. Elena's wild eyes looked to see who grabbed her. On instinct, she reached out in fear and grabbed their wrist, burning it with magic. The man didn't even react and simply held her tighter.

"I've got you, Elena, you're safe."

Elena knew that voice. Even in the midst of the panic attack that was wracking her body, she knew that voice. Kieran had her. Elena began to tremble uncontrollably in his arms, and she buried her face in his shoulder, unable to stop the sobs ripping from her throat. People watched as Kieran carried her away, but no one moved to stop him. Only Magnus dared approach, and the older man gave her a fierce look.

"Get her out of here, somewhere safe," Magnus said gruffly.

Around them, those who were not actively trying to stop the video were frozen, too stunned to react. Elena registered the video finally cutting out, and an angry voice booming throughout the hall.

"Whoever is responsible for this, show themselves, now!"

Kieran opened a portal and slipped through with Elena without looking back.

Chapter 24

The pair emerged in the quiet dark of Kieran's apartment. With its dozens of protective wards against intruders, it was the safest place Kieran could think of in his panic. He desperately tried to figure out what to do, never having been in a situation like this before. Heading for the living room, Kieran brought Elena to his couch and sat down, cradling her in his lap. She was still shaking violently, sobbing into his jacket between desperate gasps for air.

"It's okay, you're safe," he repeated, reaching for a blanket and wrapping it around her trembling frame. "I'm so sorry, Elena. I'm sorry."

Stroking her hair, Kieran could feel the crystals he was admiring earlier fall out between his fingers. She'd carried this for so long, and he'd never known. Why she'd moved away from New Stirling City after living there her whole life, her fear of being out in the open on the streets—it all made sense now.

Elena was there. Those humans had taken her, *hurt her*. She'd been seconds away from death and only made it out alive by pure luck. The video and Elena's empty eyes and blood-splattered skin were burned into his eyelids.

Kieran felt totally powerless as the horror of it all swept

over him. There was nothing he could do to protect Elena from this, no one for him to fight or drive away. There was nothing he could do to make this better. Nothing.

They stayed like that for a while, Elena in Kieran's arms. It seemed that some dam in Elena broke, and every feeling she suppressed, buried deep within herself, was flowing freely from her. It took a while, but eventually, Elena's choking sobs settled into soft sniffles, though she still shuddered with every breath. Cautiously, Kieran leaned back to peer into her face.

Elena's eyes were red and swollen, and her cheeks were stained with tears. The manic terror-filled look was gone, replaced by complete and devastating sorrow.

"Why?" she croaked.

Kieran shook his head. "I don't know why that happened, Elena. But I promise we are going to find who is responsible. I promise."

Elena shook her head. "Why did she have to die?" she asked.

Kieran's heart felt like it was breaking as he realized what she was saying. The woman she was clutching in her arms in the video, the name Elena was staring at on the wall. She'd lost someone she knew.

"I don't know," Kieran said. "She shouldn't have, none of them should have."

Elena rested her head against Kieran's shoulder and closed her eyes, utterly exhausted.

"Do you want me to take you home, Elena?" Kieran asked, wondering if bringing her to his apartment was presumptuous.

Elena barely reacted; her eyes still closed. "Can't. Mila's girlfriend is there," she mumbled.

"All right, that's fine, you can stay here if you want. Let's get you comfortable."

Carefully, Kieran slipped Elena's heels off her feet, and they fell to the floor. "I'm going to leave for just a second, but I'll be right back."

Elena nodded weakly, and Kieran reluctantly slipped from under her and left her curled up on the couch. He walked to his bedroom and began to tear it apart for anything he thought he could give her to sleep in. His arm was screaming in pain where she'd burned him in her panic, but he quickly healed it as he searched. Emerging a few minutes later, Kieran carried a large T-shirt, a pair of cotton shorts, and a washcloth soaked in warm water. He sat down next to Elena and gingerly lifted her up into a seated position.

"I'm going to clean your face a little," he told her before gently running the washcloth over her cheeks, her forehead, her nose, her lips, and her eyes. As he did, all the makeup came off perfectly with the magically enhanced water, leaving her skin fresh and clean. Once he was done, he tossed the washcloth away and cradled her face in his hands.

"Better?" he asked and Elena nodded. "Good. Here are some clothes you can change into." He offered her the shirt and the shorts.

Elena blinked, then looked down at them. "Oh," was all she said.

"I'll give you some privacy," Kieran said awkwardly, before standing up, and when she did not stop him, he walked into the kitchen to fill up a glass of water. He waited a few minutes, then poked his head through. The gown Elena had worn was tossed haphazardly on the side table next to the couch, and Elena sat, hunched over, wearing his clothes and staring at the wall. Kieran swallowed hard and walked in, handing her the glass.

"Thank you," Elena said, her voice hoarse. She sipped slowly, then turned away from him.

"Elena, I—" Kieran began, "I have no idea what to say. I'm so sorry this happened."

Elena did not respond for a moment, then she sighed. "It's not your fault, Kieran," she muttered, tapping her fingers against the glass. "Her name was Saamira."

"Did you know her?" Kieran asked cautiously

Elena nodded, then took a deep breath and looked up at the ceiling. "She was my best friend, my oldest friend. We knew each other our entire lives."

"I didn't know."

"I didn't want people to know." Elena's entire body was as rigid as a board, her grip on her glass tight. "I hated how people looked at me after, how you're looking at me now." Elena finally turned to gaze at him. "I survived, and she didn't. I'm not the one you should be pitying."

Kieran wanted to push back against that, to tell her that her suffering was deserving of compassion, but the words died in his throat. Arguing with her right now didn't seem to be the right thing to do.

"You don't have to talk about this if you don't want to, Elena. You don't owe me an explanation."

"No, I need to talk about this, right now." A note of determination appeared in Elena's broken voice, and Kieran immediately relented to it.

"Okay, then I'll listen." Kieran pushed the discarded blanket back up over Elena's legs. She looked down at his hands, then began to talk.

"We were going to our favorite coffee shop for lunch, just like we did every week. Saamira got a promotion at work, so we were celebrating. She was a businesswoman, smart and ambitious. She was one of those people who, when they spoke, people listened, and she never took shit from anyone." A pained smile flashed across Elena's face. "She had the most beautiful smile. She could stop traffic with her smile."

"She sounds wonderful," Kieran said.

Elena nodded. "The cafe we went to was really popular with witches," Elena plowed on. "It was owned by witches, most of the people who went there were witches. We were sitting down, chatting, when they attacked. The witch hunters. We didn't have time to react; they were already in the store, pretending to be customers, then next thing I knew, I was being grabbed and bound and dragged away. I saw Saamira, and she looked so scared." Her voice cracked, but she kept going. "I tried to fight them off, but they kept hitting me on the head, and I was too dazed. There were just so many of them. And then, it was all a blur until... until..." She couldn't continue, and Kieran reached over and grabbed her hand, holding it.

She gripped back tightly, her face contorting with the effort of not crying again. "I don't remember much after that, just her face. The next thing I knew, I was in the hospital, and Mila was lying next to me in my bed, holding me. We were in protective custody for a while after that, those of us who survived, though they let us out for the funerals..."

"So that is why you and your sister moved to Alberdeen," Kieran said.

Elena nodded. "I tried to stay, but it was too much. Every person I met, I thought was a threat, and Saamira—I saw her face everywhere. Mila found a witch therapist who helped me through the worst of it, but I realized I couldn't live in the city anymore, and Mila... she claimed she was wanting to start over in the country for a while anyway, but I know she only moved to look after me."

"I've been managing okay ever since we moved, but when I saw that video..." Elena's eyes widened with realization. "Oh, spirits, all those people, they saw me in it."

"Yes," Kieran said regretfully.

Elena pulled away from him, put her glass down on the side table, and placed her head in her hands. "I can't believe this happened," she moaned.

"What do you need, Elena, how can I help you?" he asked her desperately. How must she be feeling with her worst and most vulnerable moment displayed like that to strangers? Kieran was a little familiar with it. Back when he was younger his mistakes and mishaps always found their way to the front page of tabloids and all over the internet. It made him feel sick, humiliated, and used. For Elena, it must be ten times worse.

Her fingers grasped the skin of her face tightly for a moment before she released and sat up, looking at him with complete misery. "I don't know." Her eyes were swimming with tears again. "Just don't leave me alone?"

"Of course not."

Kieran swallowed, and Elena managed a small smile. She leaned over, wrapping her arms around him and placing her head against his chest. He held her back, resting his cheek on the top of her head, his breath tickling her hair.

His poor, sweet friend. No one deserved to have this happen to them, but especially Elena. Did he feel that way because she was good and kind and everything wonderful in the world, or because, deep down, Kieran felt like she was *his?*

When he noticed she was out, he carefully lifted her up and took her to the bedroom. Placing her in the bed, he tucked her in and smoothed her hair behind her ear. His fingertips lingered by her cheek, and he took a deep breath.

"I'll be right outside if you need me," he whispered, then turned and quickly left the room. He walked back to the living room and pulled out his phone and dialed Declan.

His brother picked up after one ring. "Hey, where are you?" Declan asked.

"At my place. Elena needed to get out of there. She's sleeping."

"All right, better stay put for now. Everyone's in an uproar. There's going to be serious fallout from this."

"There better be," Kieran snarled. "Did you find out who's responsible for showing that video yet?"

"The Coastal Coven is protecting themselves, but give it a day or two, and they'll cough some people up. Look," Delcan added, "everyone is asking after Elena. What should I tell them?"

Kieran thought for a moment. "Just tell them she's safe, and that she's going to be okay. And tell them not to tell anyone about what they saw in the video, out of respect for her."

"All right, and her sister? Should she be notified?"

"It's the middle of the night, let her sleep. There's nothing she could do for Elena now."

* * *

Elena woke the next morning in the softest sheets she had ever felt in her life, in a huge bed on pillows that were not familiar. Wait, where was she? Her eyes opened, and she looked around, utterly confused. She didn't recognize this room at all. Elena looked down at herself and saw she was wearing a man's T-shirt. That is when the memories of the previous night hit her, and she collapsed back into the bed, overwhelmed. Crossing her arms over her eyes, Elena tried to stop the flow of tears that started as she re-lived every terrible moment.

Who could have done this? Why would they do this? Were they deliberately trying to be cruel or were they that stupid?

Taking a deep breath, Elena lowered her arms and looked around the room. There was no sign of Kieran anywhere, and the clock on the nightstand read five in the morning. Elena carefully got out of the bed and walked over to the door, opening it slowly and looking out into a hall.

She wandered around the apartment for a few minutes, trying to find Kieran but quickly gave up. The place was huge. Very modern and bare; the entire place didn't really give off the vibes of being lived in.

It was likely Kieran was asleep in another bedroom, or gone out for a run, or whatever ghastly activity he engaged in at this hour.

Unsure what to do, Elena went back the way she came and slipped into the bathroom adjoining the room she awoke in. Facing the large mirror inside, Elena was startled by the person gazing back at her.

Her face was puffy and red, and there were huge dark circles under her eyes. Her hair was a wreck, half of it fallen out of the updo it was in the night before and completely tangled.

Most of the delicate crystals that Tora had so carefully applied were gone, while the rest clung to the rat's nest on top of her head for dear life. She felt grimy, like she was drenched in dry sweat, and in Kieran's clothes she looked like a teenage boy. Taking advantage of the large shower, Elena got in and allowed the hot water to wash away the previous day as she cleaned off.

What was going to happen now? How could she move forward from this? Word would spread through the coven soon enough, if it hadn't already. Elena didn't want their attention, their suffocating pity, or to be turned into their poster child martyr. Every day, she was fighting to regain her life back from the witch hunt, and staying anonymous allowed her to do that in peace. Now?

Not to mention the general public. Everyone knew that survivors of events like this were targeted by conspiracy theorists and people who just wanted to cause more trouble for the victims.

Perhaps she should take a vacation? Disappear into the mountains for a few months and hope, when she returned, this would all have blown over? The idea was tempting.

After getting out of the shower, Elena engaged in some light thievery so she could clean her face and teeth, hoping Kieran didn't mind. This brought her to her next dilemma, clothes.

Re-entering the bedroom, Elena realized she was saved from the humiliation of having to steal more clothes from Kieran as the bed was made, and there was a complete outfit folded neatly on top of it. She approached cautiously, and lifted up a shirt. It was a dark blue, silk, button-up, and designer on top of that. There was also a pair of dark denim pants. Looking down, Elena realized that her strapless bra from last night was tucked underneath the shirt. She picked it up and sniffed. It was cleaned. How embarrassing. Quickly getting dressed, Elena appraised her body. Everything fit perfectly.

Kieran was obviously awake and in the apartment, and she would have to go out there and face him. The idea made Elena's guts twist. He'd been so caring and sweet last night. She shouldn't feel ashamed of her breakdown, she told herself. Unfortunately, that didn't really help, and a storm of anxiety built in her stomach. Shaking her head, her hair magically dried.

"Okay, let's do this," she said to herself.

Taking a deep breath, she left the bedroom. In the hall, she could hear noises coming from the entryway she'd passed earlier that morning while looking around and headed there. She emerged into a large, sun-filled kitchen and dining room. An enormous island in the center of the kitchen and all the counters were made of white marble. Floor to ceiling windows covered one wall, and all the appliances were top of the line and much larger than Elena imagined Kieran actually needed.

The man in question was standing in front of the stove, dressed in jeans and a long sleeve shirt, his hair wet and slicked back while he cooked eggs. There must have been a second bathroom in this apartment, which wasn't surprising. Probably three more bedrooms and a pool as well hidden somewhere.

Kieran looked up when he sensed her standing there and smiled brightly. "Good morning," he greeted. "I hope you had a nice shower?"

"It was great." Elena shifted her weight uncomfortably. "Thanks for the clothes."

"You're welcome. Do they fit all right? Declan dropped them off earlier, and we weren't sure if they were the right size…" He trailed off, looking like he felt a little awkward himself.

"They fit great." Elena took a step forward. "Are those eggs?"

"Yes!" Kieran turned back to the stove and took the eggs off the heat. "Is scrambled okay? Perhaps with some toast?"

"Sounds perfect." Elena inched a little bit closer. Kieran didn't seem to notice, preparing two plates for both of them.

"What would you like to drink? Tea? Coffee?" he asked, pulling down a mug from a cabinet.

"Tea please, breakfast tea if you have it." Elena watched him move throughout the kitchen.

"Coming right up!" Kieran apparently had already prepared some hot water and poured it into Elena's mug along with the tea bag before handing it to her. She took it gratefully, the heat from the mug warming her hands. The toast popped up, and Kieran swiftly grabbed it, then placed it onto the plates with the eggs.

"Shall we?" he asked, gesturing toward the large dining table made of solid wood.

Elena nodded and followed him. Kieran placed the plates on the table, summoning some forks for them, and sat down in a chair across from Elena.

He waited until Elena took a bite before starting himself. They ate in silence, not meeting each other's eye. Elena looked through the window behind Kieran, out over the city, the sun rising behind the skyscrapers.

After Kieran finished his meal, he politely waited for Elena to be done before whisking their used plates away with a wave of his hand. Elena sat back, feeling a bit better with some food in her stomach, and held her mug to her chest.

"So..." she said.

"So," Kieran repeated.

"Kieran I—" She started, then looked away, letting out a shuddering breath.

"It's okay, Elena, we don't need to relive any of it if you don't want to," Kieran assured her.

Elena bit her lip and looked up to the top of the tall window, trying to control her emotions. "I just don't know how to thank you," she said, "for taking care of me... again." She mustered up the courage and looked back at him. "You've always been there for me when I needed someone, ever since we met."

"You don't need to thank me, Elena," Kieran muttered, a faint blush creeping up his neck. "I'm just glad I've been able to help."

Elena sipped her tea, wishing she could find the right words to express how she was feeling, but nothing came to mind.

"You said your brother was here?" she asked.

"Yes, and he had some news, if you want to hear it?"

"Please," Elena encouraged him.

Kieran took a deep breath, and leaned back, folding his arms over his chest. "After we left last night, things shut down pretty fast. People were outraged, most went home immediately, but the various coven leaders stayed to find out what happened. The Coastal Coven is being resistant for now, but Declan thinks that will change. The High Witch's Council has been informed of what happened. There will probably be an inquiry in the next few days."

Elena nodded. "Did anyone else... well..." She hesitated.

"Did anyone else freak out like me?"

Kieran's face fell. "No. As far as we can tell, you were the only actual survivor there, although Frank Martin was livid. He had to be pulled off the host and restrained."

"Poor Frank," Elena murmured more to herself. "He and his sister were so close. They lost their parents very young, and they were the only family each other had. I got to know him a little bit in the months after..." She trailed off.

"I spoke to Magnus," Kieran said hastily. "He said he reached out to your friend you were staying with. Tora, right? And let her know what happened. He also mentioned Mila wasn't expecting to see you 'till today?"

"That's right. She and Ava spent the week together at our house. I promised I would text her before I headed home though..." Elena looked around. "Do you have my phone?"

"Yes! I do. Declan was able to locate your purse, and he dropped that off, too. Let me grab it for you." Kieran stood and left the kitchen. He was back a few seconds later and handed Elena her bag.

"No missed messages; she must still be asleep," Elena muttered after pulling out her phone. She considered for a moment. "I'll just text her to say I'll be home in a bit. I don't want her to worry while Ava is around." Elena composed a quick text to Mila, as well as one to Tora. When she was done, she looked up at Kieran, who had a guilty look on his face.

"What is it?" she asked, shifting uncomfortably.

Kieran sighed, looking at the ceiling. "I was thinking about when we were in that garden and you told me about your anxiety attacks. It wasn't claustrophobia that made you have one before, was it? It was this."

"Yes," Elena breathed. "The crowd that day was... very

triggering. I should've known better than to go."

"It's not your fault." Kieran had a fierce look on his face. "This isn't fair," he ground out. "I shouldn't know this about you, any of it. I just happened to be nearby when these moments happened. I'm so sorry that I found out like this. You should have been able to tell me on your own terms, or not at all, if that's what you wanted."

Elena actually smiled a little at that. "You're in good company. Magnus and Maggie found out this way, too, and I had to tell Charles and Sarah Lorch in my entry interview. I've never willingly told anyone other than my therapist about what happened."

Kieran finally looked at her, sorrow on his face. "I know so much more about you than I've earned the right to."

Elena stood, and Kieran watched her warily as she approached where he leaned against the kitchen counter. She stopped a breath away, looking up into his face.

"You're right, it isn't fair that you found out like this. You're also right that I didn't want to tell you, and perhaps I never would have, but dwelling on what should have been doesn't help me right now."

Kieran clenched his jaw. "Of course, I'm sorry."

Elena snorted. "You're a mess, Kieran."

Kieran tensed, his expression guarded. "That's accurate," he breathed.

"But I see your mess, and I like you anyway."

"What do you mean?"

Elena searched his face, then plowed ahead. She was in that perfect state of emotional exhaustion where her filter was gone. All she wanted was to make Kieran understand how she felt about him because she was too tired to keep dragging this out.

"Look, we may not have been able to spend that much time together, but I know you, Kieran. I do," she insisted when he looked like he might object. "More than I have earned the right to. I know you hold yourself to an impossible standard and are very hard on yourself to the point of cruelty when you don't live up to it, and I think... I think you're constantly exhausted from trying to live up to those expectations and the expectations of your family and the coven. And everyone is always pawing at you all the time, treating you like an object to fight over and leer at, so you protect yourself by withdrawing, hiding from it all. You're so scared people will find out who you really are, scared of letting people close, but you shouldn't be, because I think you're incredible."

Kieran stared at her, frozen and unblinking.

"I'm sorry, that was really forward of me," Elena said, instantly regretting everything she'd said.

"No, no." Kieran swallowed, then shook his head like he was trying to clear her words from his thoughts.

Elena stepped closer, so that they were chest to chest. Slowly, nervously, she slid her arms forward and hugged him tightly. Kieran let out a shaky breath and held her back.

They stood in the embrace, supporting and holding each other tenderly. Elena felt herself relaxing into him, her anxieties slipping away as she was enveloped by his warmth. After a few moments, the tension slipped out of Kieran, and Elena could feel his breath on her hair, deep and even.

They reluctantly pulled apart, looking at each other while their arms were still intertwined. Elena offered a tentative smile, and Kieran responded with a look of pure determination.

"Come on," he said, his arms slipping down to take both of Elena's hands in his. "I want to show you something.

"What?" Elena asked, surprised.

"The truth."

Chapter 25

Kieran led Elena out of the kitchen and back to the living room, guiding her to the couch before turning his attention to the wall behind the television. Elena watched as he pressed his hand to it, and a small section of the wall melted away to reveal a safe. After entering the code, Kieran pulled something out before turning around to face her. Wordlessly, he turned to the couch and handed the object to Elena.

It was a photograph of a woman standing next to Anthony Andraste, who looked much younger than he did now, in front of a grand fireplace. Tall and young, she had a proud look about her, but what was most striking was her strong physical resemblance to Kieran. She had the same jet-black hair, the same bright green eyes, the same sharp features.

Elena looked up at Kieran, confused. "Who is this?"

"My birth mother," Kieran confessed.

Elena stared at him a moment, then back at the photo. "I don't understand."

Kieran sighed and sat down next to her, looking at the photo over her shoulder. "She is actually Anthony Andraste's only child from his first marriage. He's my grandfather. His first wife died young from cancer, and he raised my mother on his own. He got remarried to who you know as my mother and had Declan and then a few years after that, my actual mother got pregnant with me. She tried to hide the pregnancy and ended up dying giving birth to me alone in her apartment. Anthony sensed her passing and rushed to find her, but by the time he got there, she was gone, and it was just me, crying and alone."

Elena gasped, horrified. A witch dying in childbirth was practically unheard of, and the image of it all, baby Kieran lying next to his dead mother, was too much. Moisture filled Elena's eyes, but she fought to keep them in so Kieran could keep talking.

"What about your birth father?" Elena asked.

"It turned out he was a witch from rival coven that had been trying to usurp the Andraste family power for generations. He tried to claim me, but my father, Anthony, refused. It went to court, and the High Witch's Council sided with my father. He claimed my birth father was a drug addict, an abuser, a whole bunch of things to make sure the man could never come near me. I still don't know if any of it was true. I highly suspect he bribed the judge."

"Oh, Kieran, that's terrible." Elena didn't think her words even began to cover it. The fact that he was admitting all this to her also weighed heavily. The pain that Kieran seemed to wear like a cloak came into a little more focus, and a heaviness settled over her that he was sharing this with her at all.

Kieran took the picture from Elena gently and looked down at it.

"My father, Anthony, was deep in mourning, but he didn't want the truth out there for the scandal it would bring to the family name, so he faked the circumstances of her death. He said it was a potion experiment gone wrong, and to deal with me, well, he and his wife faked a pregnancy for her and told everyone I was their son. They legally adopted me and silenced anyone who knew the truth."

"So, when did you find out?" Elena asked him.

"When I was fifteen. The last member of my birth father's family died, and as the only living heir, I received what was left of their estate, which forced my parents to tell me the truth."

"Wow... does your brother know?"

"Yes, he found out when I did, but he's never treated me any differently for it. He remained my pain in the ass brother," Kieran joked, seemingly to lighten the mood a little, but Elena shook her head.

"But I don't understand. Why does he treat you so poorly if you're his beloved daughter's only child?"

Everything Elena had heard about Kieran and Anthony's relationship wasn't good. Maggie, in particular, always had a lot to say on the matter. Anthony always let Kieran take the fall, always had him doing the family's dirty work, always favored his oldest son.

Kieran looked at her, then leaned back, staring at the wall. "It took me a long time to figure that out. Of course, I had to acknowledge to myself that he *did* treat me differently than Declan in the first place, which wasn't easy. Anthony adored his daughter, and I think he blames me for her death. It doesn't help that I look so much like her. I suspect I'm a constant reminder of what he lost and how she betrayed him in the end."

It didn't make sense to Elena. Even when things were tense between her and her own mother, they never would have treated each other so badly. The thought of holding so much anger and resentment toward an innocent child—your own child—didn't compute in her brain.

"Why do you let him do that to you?" Elena asked, turning to face him fully. "Why do everything he tells you to? Like breaking into that coven leader's house? Isn't everything your family has enough for him?"

"For people like him, enough is never enough. There's always more to be gained if we're willing to take it," he said darkly, "but what choice do I have? They're my family; I can't turn my back on them. Without them, I'm nothing."

Elena looked at him hopelessly, then sighed, leaning over to cuddle up against his chest. It was the only thing she could think to do, the only comfort she could provide, being close to him. The Andraste family was all Kieran knew. How could he understand he deserved better if he'd never experience different?

Kieran wrapped his arm around her shoulder and snapped his fingers with his free hand. The picture of his mother flew back into the safe, which swung shut and vanished behind the wall again.

"What was her name?" Elena asked.

"Helena."

Elena inched closer and sat up so that she could look Kieran in the face. "Thank you for telling me this. I'm truly honored you trusted me with it."

"Now we're even," Kieran smiled, the expression somehow pained.

Elena leaned forward so that her forehead was resting against Kieran's, her eyes fluttering shut. She reached her right hand up and lightly placed it on the side of his face, stroking his cheek with her thumb. Kieran closed his eyes as well, placing his hand on her waist. Elena could feel the phantom touch of Kieran's lips on hers. She wanted him so badly, and he was only a centimeter away...

"Elena." Her name rolled off his tongue, and his lips brushed against her as he spoke.

Whatever he was going to say didn't it make it as Elena closed the gap and kissed him. A bone-deep relief spread through her body, like coming home after being somewhere else for a long time.

Before it could go any further, Elena's phone began to vibrate in her pocket. With a groan she pulled back and took it out.

"Tora is calling me," she mumbled, "probably freaking out."

Kieran nuzzled against her cheek. "You better answer then."

Tora was indeed freaking out. News from last night had already reached her from outside sources, which meant it was spreading beyond those in attendance of the fundraiser. The call ruined any desire Elena was feeling, and she hung up with her misery returned in full force.

"Do you want to go see her?" Kieran brushed a strand of hair behind her ear.

"No," Elena admitted, "but I should."

Kieran pressed a tender kiss to her cheek "All right, I'll grab your things for you."

For a moment, neither moved, but hiding where they felt safe wouldn't stop the outside world from turning. Elena needed to get home to tell Mila what happened before someone else did.

Without a word, they both stood and shuffled around to

gather Elena's belongings. When she was ready to go, they stood at Kieran's front door. Instead of exiting through the door, however, Kieran summoned a portal that would take Elena home.

"I can go with you, if you want." Kieran's face was full of concern.

It warmed Elena's heart that he wanted to stay with her, but she needed some time alone to process. "It's all right. I'll call you later?"

Kieran pursed his lips but nodded. With one last kiss on the cheek, Elena bid him farewell and walked through the portal.

One day, when they both were more clear headed, they would have to talk about their relationship, but for now, this was enough.

* * *

When she arrived, Mila wasn't home, and neither was Huey. Mila must have taken him out for a walk. A small twinge of amusement tugged at Elena as she trudged her way up to her bedroom. It was funny to her, after all this time, how close Huey and Mila had become. Especially since Mila had been so ambivalent about Huey in the past. Peeling off the fancy clothes Kieran had given her, Elena collapsed into bed, already asleep before her head even hit the pillow.

When she awoke later that afternoon, Huey was curled up next to her, and Elena could distantly hear Mila downstairs. Huey was beside himself when she woke up, licking her face and throwing himself over her body. Once she calmed him down, she got dressed in her favorite pair of sweatpants and a baggy shirt and went downstairs.

Telling Mila everything that happened was an extremely stressful process. She first explained the video, which led to Mila flying into a rage, and then the next day with Kieran, leaving out the part about Kieran's past. She told Mila everything, usually, but there was no way she would betray Kieran's confidence like that.

Mila seemed extremely uncomfortable with Elena's dilemma over facing a potential romantic relationship with Kieran and quickly changed the subject. She insisted Elena needed to go back to therapy and made her promise that she would do so. Elena knew Mila was right, knew she probably should have never stopped going in the first place, but her therapist was in the city, and transportation had been an issue. Now, she would just have to figure something out.

Over the next couple days, word spread quickly through the coven about what happened at the fundraiser and Elena's role in it. She only knew this, however, because Maggie told her. Apparently, a very strict command was given for all coven members to not attempt to contact Elena. Elena couldn't help but wonder if this mandate originated from Kieran, but she was extremely grateful, nonetheless.

Outside her chosen circle of friends, Elena didn't know the other coven members all that well and had no desire to discuss the worst thing that had ever happened to her with them.

Apart from Maggie, who already knew about Elena's in-volvement in the witch hunt, and therefore, felt the rule didn't apply to her, Alex also ignored the mandate and contacted her. He expressed his heartbreak on her behalf for the entire affair and assured her if she ever wanted to talk, he would be there. They both offered to come spend time with her, but she declined, citing that Ava was staying over at their house and had no idea what was going on.

Monday morning, she called her old therapist like she'd promised Mila she would and set up a time to meet with her later that week, which meant another trip into the city. She would have to ask Magnus to work long distance portals into the curriculum ASAP. Her therapist was not surprised to hear from her, as she had also heard about the fundraiser from her own coven, which made Elena feel even more dead inside. She wondered just how far the news had managed to spread.

That night, Elena was hanging out with Ava on the balcony while they waited for Mila to return with takeout as no one felt like cooking. Ava was regaling Elena with a thrilling story from her day, where she assisted in the birth of twin donkeys.

"I was honestly not sure I would be able to save both, twins in donkeys are so rare and usually don't make it, you know?" Ava was saying to an enraptured Elena. "The first one was in rough shape, and the second was stuck in the birth canal for so long."

"But they both made it, right? You know I hate stories with sad endings."

Ava laughed. "Yes, they both made it! It was just touch and go for a few minutes there." Ava paused, looking out over the trees. "It was weird though. When the first foal came out, it wasn't breathing, but I had to focus on the second, so the owner's neighbor jumped in, trying to revive it. I was so sure it was already dead, but then I looked back and it was sitting up, bright eyed! Made me wonder..."

"Made you wonder what?" Elena arched an eyebrow.

Ava shrugged. "Nothing, I just thought maybe the neighbor was a witch."

Elena's stomach plummeted, and she quickly said, "But a

witch can't bring back the dead. It's against the fourth rule of magic, everyone knows that."

"Yes, but if the foal was only almost dead, they could have brought it back with healing magic, right?"

"How should I know?" Elena shrugged in what she hoped was a convincing way. The fact that Ava was asking her about magic was uncomfortable. Did Ava suspect something?

Ava stared at her a moment, then smiled. "I guess. It was just odd. But either way, both foals are currently doing well at the hospital with their mom so I'm happy!"

Elena's phone, which was sitting on the table in front of her, lit up. Relieved for the distraction, Elena picked it up, and her heart started to beat faster when she saw it was from Kieran.

Hey, Elena, I hope you're doing okay. I wanted to give you an update on what is going on but can't slip away for a call. They found who was responsible for the video. There's a special meeting at the coven tomorrow to discuss it, but the board wanted to meet with you alone beforehand.

Elena stomach gave queasy lurch, and she quickly texted back, completely forgetting Ava was there.

Why? What's going on?

"El? Everything okay?" Ava's voice cut through Elena's growing panic, and she looked up.

"Uh, no," Elena admitted, her mind spinning. Why did the board want to talk to her alone? And why was their coven having a special meeting about the video?

"Whoa, you're getting really pale, are you feeling all right?" Ava leaned forward and put the back of her hand against Elena's forehead.

"I think I need to lay down for a minute," Elena muttered,

brushing Ava off and heading quickly for the door.

"Can I get you anything?" Ava called after her.

"No, I'll be fine." Elena didn't even look back and quickly headed inside to her bedroom. She collapsed on her bed, breathing hard, and read Kieran's newest text.

Jackie Hammond did it.

Elena stared, horror-struck at her phone. Jackie? She knew the woman didn't like her, but to do this?

She claims you weren't her target, that she didn't even know you would be there. Kieran sent next. *I don't know what to believe, but I'll be there when you meet with the board.*

Elena thought about Kieran's arms around her, his steady presence telling her everything was going to be okay. Even just imagining that made her heart stop racing.

A solid knock on the door jolted Elena out of her thoughts.

"Elena, can I come in?" Ava's voice sounded from the other side.

There was a grim determination to it that gave Elena pause. Taking a deep breath, she rose and opened the door. Ava looked her up and down before marching past Elena into the bedroom.

"Uh, it's a little messy," Elena said, kicking a stray bra under the bed with her foot.

"Look, I'm sorry for what I said out there. I was trying to get you to open up, and obviously it was a mistake."

Elena stared, not comprehending at all what Ava was talking about.

"What you said?" Elena asked, confused.

Ava tutted, crossing her arms over her chest defiantly. "About the witch reviving the donkey."

Elena's stomach plummeted, the overwhelming urge to flee

rising. "Why would that upset me?"

Ava's eyes narrowed. "Some people find witches to be a sensitive topic."

"Like who?" Elena asked as calmly as she could, already plotting her escape. She would use a spell to make Ava pass out, then gather her things and Huey and get to the mansion.

"Bigots," Ava responded, cutting through Elena's spiraling thoughts, "and witches in hiding. Which one are you?"

Elena blanched, her entire body shaking. Uncontrollable fear was taking over, and once again, she could barely think. Huey burst into the room, hackles raised, and placed himself between Ava and Elena. He let out a ferocious bark, laden with magical energy, which shoved Ava back with such force she fell over.

"Huey! Don't hurt her!" Elena cried, lunging forward to wrap her arms around Huey's neck and pull him back. His entire body was rumbling with growls, and Ava stared at them, wide eyed.

"I know you're a witch! I've always known!" Ava sputtered.

Both Elena and Huey froze. "What?" she demanded. "How could you have always known?"

Ava glanced at Huey, who still was baring his teeth at her, and pushed herself up to a sitting position.

"He's your familiar, right? I thought so ever since I watched him that one time. He's way too smart to be an ordinary dog. I mean, he watched TV with me, like actually watched it! And he could open doors on his own. It was *weird*." Ava was rambling now. "And your hair looks so perfect all the time! The color never fades, and it should be absolutely wrecked if you really were dying it that much, but it's super healthy! And you and Mila still look so *young*..."

"Okay, I get it," Elena snapped, her entire body still tense. "So, you're saying you knew this entire time, and you don't care?"

Ava let out a shuddering sigh. "No, of course I don't care. I'm a little hurt that you and Mila obviously thought I would! Otherwise, why wouldn't you just tell me?"

"What the fuck is going on here?" Mila's voice thundered from the bedroom door, and everyone jumped.

With Mila now present, what little fight there was completely went out of Elena's body, and she sagged to the floor. Huey immediately was crawling in her lap, aggressively nuzzling her with his fuzzy head and whining.

"I'm just scaring your sister half to death," Ava said with a pained smile. "The website I looked at for help on how to tell a witch in your life that you know they're a witch warned the accused can react badly, but I didn't take that seriously. Obviously a mistake."

Mila's mouth dropped open. "*The accused?*" Mila repeated.

Ava winced. "That came out badly. Look, I was just trying to gently let Elena know that she doesn't have to hide from me anymore. Neither of you do!"

Mila stared at her girlfriend crumpled on the floor, then glanced at her sister cowering by the bed. No one moved for a moment, then Mila reached out to Ava. Elena watched, barely breathing.

Ava gave Mila a relieved look and pulled herself up. Mila did not let go, however, and Elena spotted Mila's grip on Ava's hand tightening. With wide eyes, Ava looked up into Mila's face.

"Elena is a witch," Mila said, her voice darker than Elena had ever heard before. "I'm not. But that means little." Her eyes searched Ava's. "You know how much I love Elena, and you've questioned me for my protectiveness of her in the past. It must hurt that we've been keeping this secret from you, but..." Mila glanced at Elena, who gave her a shaky nod. "Elena has been targeted by witch hunters before. I nearly lost her, and I won't let it happen again. I won't be the reason she is put in danger."

Ava sniffled, tears filling her eyes. "I wouldn't ever," she said, gripping Mila's arm. "I would never betray either of you like that. I *love* you, Mila. Your family is my family. I clearly made a mess of this, but please don't believe that I did it because I wanted to hurt Elena. I was just trying to let her know that it was okay to tell me."

Guilt overwhelmed Elena. She could see Ava was being truthful, and now Mila looked at the woman she loved with suspicion, all because Elena couldn't keep her shit together for ten minutes.

"I'm fine, Mila," Elena said, getting to her feet with a great deal of effort. "She didn't upset me, well, at first, she didn't. We were just talking, and I got a text..." She trailed off. "Anyway, I freaked out, and Ava thought it was because of what she said. It was just a misunderstanding. Everything's fine."

Mila pursed her lips, then her entire body sagged. "I've wanted to tell you for so long," she said to Ava, "but I've been so afraid. I swore to myself I would never see El hurt again, and every time I considered telling you, I saw her laying there in that hospital bed."

"I understand, I understand." Ava hugged Mila to her, and they clutched each other while they silently cried.

Elena, feeling like she was intruding, tried to slip from

the room. Before she could, however, Ava reached out and snatched her arm, and she was pulled into the embrace.

Squeezed on all sides, Elena could barely breathe. And yet, as Huey shoved his head into the circle their legs made so he could feel included, something in Elena's chest that had been bound up tight and mangled for a long time, perhaps since the death of her mother, loosened and released. Breathing a little bit easier, Elena held her family close, feeling that now she was ready to face everything that lay ahead.

Chapter 26

Mila and Ava had a long talk to discuss everything Ava needed to know. It wasn't just the emotional things, like all the pieces of Mila's life she kept from Ava, but the rules of how this had to be. Ava could never tell anyone what she knew about Elena or any magical going-ons she witnessed. She might suspect that many of their friends were witches, but she couldn't ask which ones were magical without the sisters okay. And finally, for her own safety, there were still many things Ava could not know about. The existence of the Greenwood Coven and its members, for a start, and Elena's relationship with Kieran was another as even Mila wasn't fully in the know about that yet.

Ava accepted these conditions without question and even offered to engage in an oath ceremony if the sisters thought it was necessary. Elena pointed out that magical oaths with humans were illegal, and she didn't feel it was needed anyway. Despite her initial reaction, Elena trusted Ava.

Once Ava returned home, Elena filled Mila in on everything Kieran had told her about Jackie. She was furious and demanded to accompany Elena to face the board. It would be the first time Mila set foot in the mansion or traveled through a magical portal, for that matter. It was a relief to have her sister come with her, though a bit nerve wracking as well.

Elena knew it wasn't always easy for Mila being a human in a witch family, surrounded by witches in almost all areas of her life. There was an unspoken tension there, even with close friends. Instinctually, Elena wanted Mila to stay home, to protect her from any cruel comments or looks the witches of her coven might send Mila's way, but Elena honestly wasn't sure she could get through this day without her.

The coven-wide meeting began at five-thirty, and the board had asked Elena to arrive forty-five minutes before. So, at four-thirty Elena opened the portal. She walked through first, then held the door open for Mila, who took a deep breath and stepped across the threshold. Immediately on arriving, Mila stumbled, looking queasy. Elena caught her and held her up.

"Easy there," she said. "I told you going through the portal might be weird for you."

"Ugh, well, I believe you now." Mila steadied herself. After a few fortifying breaths, she looked a bit better, and her eyes narrowed on the garden around them.

"All flash, no substance," she muttered, leaning down to examine a flower. "Do they even care for their plants? Or do they just set a spell and leave them on their own?"

Elena laughed, taking Mila's hand. "Come on, this way."

She led Mila out of the garden and onto the grounds. Mila's face remained expressionless as she took in the sprawling lawn and expansive gardens beyond, her grip on Elena's hand tight. When they reached the front doors of the mansion, they opened automatically for them, revealing the empty great hall.

"Creepy statues," Mila commented.

"Some call them dignified."

"Who? Who says that?"

Elena chuckled but was cut off when a witch showed up and led them to a part of the mansion she'd never been to before and into a large office. Inside were all twelve board members, along with Kieran and a woman Elena recognized as his mother, Josephine Andraste. Elegant was the word Elena would use to describe the woman. Her gray hair was pulled up in a swooping bun, and she was dressed in fashionable, yet sophisticated, designer pieces. The most arresting thing about her, however, were her eyes. They regarded Elena with cold indifference that chilled her to her core.

Elena tensed at all the attention, but with an encouraging bump of the shoulder from Mila, she managed to move forward.

"Elena, thank you for coming." Josephine stepped up and took Elena by the hand. "And of course, Mila, very good of you to accompany your sister," Josephine added as an afterthought and without offering to shake Mila's hand as well.

Mila clenched her jaw tightly at the obvious slight. Behind his mother, Kieran was giving her a disapproving look.

"Ladies, welcome," Charles joined them. "We haven't had the pleasure of meeting," he said to Mila. "My name is Charles. I'm the chairman of the board and called this meeting today."

"Pleasure," Mila said tightly. "Elena has spoken very highly of you."

The sisters were guided to a small sofa facing the board, who all remained standing. Elena felt hot and cold all at the same time, her mind buzzing with a dull roaring noise as all eyes in the room turned on her.

"Perhaps we should all be seated?" Kieran suggested.

Elena saw a few board members throw very nasty looks in Kieran's direction, but Charles nodded, and chairs appeared from thin air for the others in the room.

"Elena, as you know we asked you here to discuss the terrible events that happened at the fundraiser," Charles began. Elena remained silent, so he continued. "I wanted to start by saying how awful we all feel on your behalf and how sorry we are that this was allowed to happen. I, myself, take personal responsibility, as I was the one who invited you in the first place. I am truly sorry."

Elena opened her mouth, closed it, swallowing hard, then opened it again. "Thank you," she managed to say.

A few board members gave her pitying looks. Anger cut through Elena's anxiety at that. She did not need or want their pity. Sitting up straighter, Elena forced a look of calm indifference on her face.

"As for what we wanted to discuss today..." Charles looked to Josephine, who nodded. "We wish to inform you that the investigation revealed Jackie Hammond was behind the video shown at the fundraiser."

The entire board watched Elena carefully for her reaction, but Elena merely shifted in her seat. "Is that so?" was all she said.

"Unfortunately, yes."

Charles glanced at Josephine again, and she shook her head a fraction of an inch.

"She claims to have worked alone, bribing staff at the fundraiser to play her video instead of the planned presentation. Miss Hammond also claims she did not intend to damage you, and that she didn't know you were at the party in the first place."

Elena looked over at Mila, and there was cold rage in Mila's eyes.

"Be that as it may, Miss Hammond faces very serious consequences, including formal charges from the High Witch's Council for disturbing the peace, bribery, and criminal mischief. Additionally, she has been expelled from the Greenwood Coven. You will never have to see her again," Charles said firmly.

Both sisters frowned.

"I won't?" Elena asked, confused that Charles seemed to confident of that.

"Definitely not," Lydia chimed in. "If you wish to seek a restraining order against Miss Hammond, or any other legal action against her, we will provide a coven-approved lawyer, Elena."

"But." Elena looked at Kieran now. "If she wasn't even trying to hurt me, why would I do that? What was she really after, if I wasn't her target? I don't understand."

Kieran's eyes darted to his mother, who had gone rigid.

"She claims that she did not intend to harm you. I, for one, do not believe her," Lydia said. "We believe legal protections on your behalf are warranted, Miss Hall."

"What does she claim to have been doing then?" Mila asked.

They were dodging Elena's question.

"Miss Hammond has become, I'm afraid to say, rather obsessed with her position in the coven," Charles said hastily. "Ever since the uh, unfortunate incident earlier this year"—his gaze cut to Kieran, who ignored him—"we believe she has been seeking revenge against you for the role you played in her loss of status."

"I didn't do anything to her." Elena's eyes narrowed. "They're the ones to blame for what happened." She gestured toward Kieran and his mother. "Shouldn't she have been going after them, if revenge was her goal?"

"People behave irrationally when they're angry," Charles said with a sigh, as if he was explaining something obvious to a child. "It's not hard to imagine she has displaced her anger onto you."

"I would like to hear it from Jackie myself."

What they were saying didn't make any sense. Elena didn't know Jackie well, but that woman was no fool. If it was revenge she was after, making Elena her target wouldn't accomplish anything. What was the board hiding?

A deadly quiet fell over the room, and it seemed no one was breathing. The tension was alarming, and for the first time since joining, Elena legitimately felt like she might be in danger. For whatever reason, they wanted to keep Elena away from Jackie, didn't want Elena to know what Jackie had to say. Just how far would they go to accomplish that?

"I'm afraid that is not possible." Charles sat back in his chair, his back rigid.

"And why is that?" Elena matched his posture, not backing down.

"Miss Hammond is currently in the custody of the High Witch's Council while they finish their investigation into this matter."

"And?"

Charles quickly glanced at Josephine for the third time, then back to Elena in a single blink. "And you cannot see her."

Elena's jaw clenched with frustration. Out of the corner of her eye, she could have sworn she saw Josephine give Charles a slight nod of approval.

"So, just to be clear, you're all deliberately refusing to tell me what Jackie says she was trying to do with that video, and you are refusing to let me speak with her, even though it is my right to do so."

Obnoxiously, tears threatened at the corner of Elena's eyes. They were lying to her, managing her, treating her like she was an idiot.

"We understand you're upset, Miss Hall." A man near the back stood up. "But you must understand this is for your own good and the good of the coven. You must put aside your own selfish desires and consider what is best for your fellow witches."

Mila's mouth dropped open, and Elena felt like she might actually be sick when Kieran stepped forward.

"That's enough, Florian," Kieran said loudly, walking closer to the sisters. "Elena is right. She deserves the chance to face Jackie herself and make up her own mind about her intentions."

Elena might have laughed at the stunned look on Josephine Andraste's face, and those of the council members across from them, if the situation wasn't so serious. The man, Florian, opened his mouth to speak again when Mila cut in.

"I thought this coven was supposed to be different," she drawled. "But perhaps our mother was right, El. Hidden agendas everywhere you look."

Several board members coughed at that, and Charles visibly paled.

"Now, now, this is just a misunderstanding," Charles said quickly. "We simply have Elena's best interest at heart. If she feels that strongly about speaking to Miss Hammond, of course we will not stand in the way."

Mila and Elena stared him down, and Florian actually had the audacity to scoff. Kieran sent a withering glare his way, and Florian silently slipped back to his seat.

"But as we said, she's currently in the custody of the High Witch's Council, and they will not allow you to see her. You'll have to wait until she is released, then you may do as you please," Charles concluded.

Elena pursed her lips but nodded, then made a show of looking at the watch on her wrist. "I believe you all have a meeting to get to," she said, her voice eerily calm. "I would hate to take up any more of your time."

Mila sneered at Charles as he adjusted his jacket.

"Yes, of course. If you need anything at all, Miss Hall, do not hesitate to reach out."

He quickly strode out of the room, the other board members trailing behind. Sarah Lorch, the woman who'd conducted her entry interview, actually grinned at Elena and gave her a discreet thumbs up as she passed.

"Mother," Kieran said, his voice tight.

Josephine offered Elena a fake-as-shit sympathetic look before she also left the room. Kieran hesitated at the door, giving Elena a meaningful glance, before disappearing as well.

* * *

"Holy shit." Elena collapsed against Mila's shoulder. "Holy fucking shit."

"I can't believe those assholes," Mila seethed, wrapping an arm around Elena's shoulders.

"I need to get out of here." Elena shot up, and Mila quickly rose as well.

"Let's go home." Mila took Elena's hand.

"No, not yet. I want to talk to Kieran. Let's go to a different room."

The sisters walked aimlessly through the mansion before opening a random door, revealing a small reading room with its curtains drawn.

"Dingy," Mila commented, going to the nearest window and throwing the curtains back to let in some light. When she turned back to Elena, she was pacing back and forth across the room, her teeth gritted and her hands balled into fists.

"Josephine Andraste is behind what just happened, I know it," she seethed. "Or the entire Andraste family in general. They ordered the board to try and keep me away from Jackie. Did you see how Charles kept looking to Josephine for approval?"

"Totally." Mila folded her arms over her chest. "So what do we do?"

Elena took a deep breath. "Nothing, there's nothing we can do."

"I wouldn't say that," Kieran's voice came from the door, causing both sisters to jump. Kieran smiled grimly at them. "I thought I sensed you two in here, but I wasn't sure. Mila, your aura is very confusing inside the mansion."

Mila strode forward angrily, ignoring his comment about her aura. "What the fuck was that Kieran, what's going on?" she demanded.

Kieran hastily shut the door and walked toward Elena. Elena looked up at him, her heart twisting. Despite what just happened, all she wanted to do was collapse into his arms.

"You're right, my family is trying to keep you from Jackie."

Kieran stopped a few feet away, glancing between the sisters. "Jackie showed that video because she wanted to sow dissent among the most powerful and influential members of our society. She wasn't trying to target you, Elena, she was attacking a system that she believes has allowed events like the witch hunt to happen."

"Seriously?" Elena gaped at him. That was not was she was expecting him to say.

Kieran grimaced. "Well, let's have Jackie explain it to you herself, shall we?"

"You can get Elena in to see her?" Mila stepped forward.

Kieran snorted. "It won't exactly be hard, considering she isn't actually being held by the Witch's Council."

"What?" Elena felt like her head was spinning.

"They lied about that, hoping you wouldn't investigate further. If you want to talk to Jackie, you can just call her up. I have her number. Take it." Kieran pulled a piece of paper out of his pocket and handed it to Elena, who grasped it with a shaking hand.

"Mom was right about covens," Mila said miserably. "I'm sorry, Elena, I'm sorry I pushed you into joining."

"I knew what I was getting into when I signed up," Elena assured her, "and I don't regret it, not yet anyway. But if they think I'm going to play their games, they're sorely mistaken. Once they figure out I won't go along with it, they can either kick me out or lay off. Either way, I'll have gotten what I wanted from this place by then."

Kieran rocked back on his heels, clearly uncomfortable. "My parents don't want the ideas Jackie has been spouting to spread. They think it could undermine their authority in the coven. They aren't willing to interfere beyond what they've already done, though. If they did, it would prove her right and only make things worse."

Elena nodded, letting out a breath, her mind still racing. Mila cleared her throat in the tense silence that fell over the three of them, and Elena looked at her sister.

"Can you give us a minute alone, please?"

Mila arched an eyebrow but nodded. "Don't do anything stupid," Mila said over her shoulder before leaving the room.

Kieran waited until she was gone before turning back to Elena. "If you want to end things between us, I understand." There was such resignation and defeat in his voice, like he'd already given up.

Like his family had once again taken away his happiness for their own petty reasons.

Enough, it was enough. Elena had not survived the worst witch hunt in over a century to have these rich, entitled, selfish assholes stop her from being with someone she cared about. She was not willing to sacrifice any shred of *her* happiness for them, even if that made her an idealistic fool. Now, all she needed to do was make Kieran see that, too.

"Aren't you tired of it, Kieran?" she asked, taking a step forward. "Aren't you tired of them controlling every aspect of your life? Forcing you to lie and hurt people and to hide behind closed doors when you do the right thing?"

Kieran went rigid and Elena wondered what he was thinking, if she was pushing him too far. Unable to meet her eye, Kieran was looking straight over the top of her head, a muscle in his jaw bulging as he clenched his teeth.

"What do you want from me?" he whispered

Elena cautiously stepped a little closer to him. "I want you to *try*, and I want to try with you. Your family is still your family, and it will be really hard if they set against us, but Kieran, I don't care. I want to try anyway, because I think this, whatever this is, could be worth it." Elena took a breath to steady herself, Kieran's eyes burning as they bored into hers. "I want you to stop doing what they want, and to do what you want, for once." Elena held his gaze, challenging him. "What do you want, Kieran?"

"You," he said without hesitation, "always you, from the very first moment."

Elena let out a breath, her heart pounding. "Then take me."

Whatever storm raging in Kieran's mind ended at her words, and he surged forward, placing his hands on either side of her face. They stared at each other wildly for a moment before Kieran leaned down and pressed his lips against hers. It was as if time froze and sped up at once, as months of longing and innocent touches narrowed in on that single moment. Elena felt her entire being surge, as if there was a wave about to break within her. Then the spell broke, and that wave crashed over them, sweeping their inhibitions away.

Elena wrapped her arms around Kieran's neck, deepening the kiss for the first time. She was on her toes now, and Kieran wrapped his arm around her back, holding her up, his other hand weaving into her hair. Elena's heart was pounding in her ears, and she moved her hands up the back of Kieran's neck and gripped his hair and pulled, causing him to groan in pleasure. They separated for a second, their eyes locking, then Elena captured his lips with hers again, her tongue slipping inside his mouth. Their bodies were pressed against each other fully, every inch of them on fire with desire.

Elena wasn't sure how long they were locked in each other's embrace, but Kieran was the first to break it, and he pulled back, smiling at her in a way she never saw before. No trace of grief, or anger, or pain of any kind. She returned it, trying to memorize his face in this moment.

A buzzing sound disrupted them, and Kieran's perfect smile instantly fell into a scowl as he gently lowered Elena down and pulled out his phone, his other arm still wrapped around her and keeping her body pressed against his.

Peering at the screen, Elena saw the words:

Where the fuck are you? Mom is about to lose it.

Kieran glared at the phone, then looked back to Elena regretfully.

"You have to go." It wasn't a question.

"Yes," Kieran said, that horrific wall of bitterness falling behind his eyes once more. "But this is not over."

Elena stroked her fingers over his cheeks, her thumb grazing his parted lips. He kissed her finger lightly in response, his eyes fluttering shut.

"I think this is worth it, too," he murmured against her skin.

The words made Elena pull his face to hers again, unable to stop herself, and Kieran laughed into the kiss, indulging her for a moment before fully pulling away and stepping back.

"I'll see you soon," he promised, then backed away, and with one final look, walked out the door.

Elena stood there, her heart racing, the ghost of his body still making her skin tingle. She took a deep breath, putting her face in her hands and let out a small scream of excitement, then quickly straightened and walked to the door. She didn't sense anyone in the hallway beyond it, and peeked her head out. There was no one there. Leaving the room, Elena began to walk briskly down the hall, hoping that she would not encounter anyone who wanted to speak with her.

Unfortunately, that was not in the stars, as the only exit was through the great hall. The meeting apparently had ended, and the hall was full of people who were lingering. Elena looked behind her for an escape. Maybe she could crawl out a window and get out that way? But she needed to find Mila before she left, and who knew where she went off to.

Elena slowly walked into the hall. Conversation stopped as she approached. Then, several people rushed up to her at once.

"Oh, Elena, I just want you to know that you have our full support! Whatever you need, we are here for you," a witch she'd never spoken to in her life said.

"You're so brave, showing up today, and after you've gone through so much," another gushed.

"Uh, thank you," Elena said, taking a step back, eyes wide.

"Now everyone, I'm sure Elena knows that the coven is here for her. Why don't we give her some space?" a deep voice cut through.

Elena felt instant relief as Magnus stepped between her and the witches.

"Oh, of course! Of course." They backed off immediately.

Magnus turned to Elena, a small smile on his face. "Need some help leaving?" he asked.

"Yes please," Elena said meekly. "But I need to find Mila. I'm not sure where she went."

"I believe I saw her going outside with Maggie. They can't have gotten far." He began to lead her away from the crowd, guarding her from sight with his massive frame. They reached the front doors and exited the mansion without anyone else trying to talk to Elena.

Almost immediately, she spotted Maggie's red head across the lawn. Squinting, she saw Mila squatting down, examining a row of flowers.

"Oh, good grief," Elena muttered.

As they approached, Elena could hear the two of them arguing.

"You're being ridiculous! It's just a flower! And now it's a flower that's even better!"

"It's a violation of nature is what it is," Mila shot back, standing up. "How would you like it if someone came along and tampered with your DNA because they thought you weren't pretty enough?"

"First of all, no one has ever looked at me and thought I wasn't pretty enough." Maggie threw her hair over her shoulder dramatically. "Second, it's a flower, not a person! It doesn't think or feel anything!"

Mila threw her hands up in exasperation.

"I leave you alone in one of the most famous coven headquarters in the country, and you go off to complain about the plants?" Elena said when they reached them.

Mila turned, her eyes narrowing. "You knew what would happen when you brought me here. Don't act surprised."

Elena rolled her eyes and turned back to her mentor. "Magnus, this is my very passionate-about-plants sister, Mila," she introduced.

Magnus offered his hand for Mila to shake, his eyes twinkling. "Honored to meet you, Mila. I've heard a great deal about you."

"Same here," Mila said, accepting the handshake, looking Magnus up and down.

"Well, I won't keep you. Elena, when would you like to

resume your lessons?"

"Next week?" Elena suggested. "Although I wanted to ask you about something. I know it wasn't on the schedule, but, well, to be blunt, I'm going to be needing to see my therapist for a bit, but she's in the city, and being able to long distance portal would make going to see her so much easier. We are going to do virtual sessions for now, but I would much prefer to talk to her in person, if I can. Do you think we could do that next?"

"Of course. It may take a while to nail down though. So, I don't want you to be disappointed if you don't pick it up right away."

"Thank you, Magnus."

"Until then." He nodded to her, then turned and walked away.

Mila watched him leave with interest. "El," she said when he was out of earshot, "you never mentioned that your mentor was so handsome, even for a man of his age."

"Can you not?" Elena groaned. "Also, you have a girlfriend. Keep it in your pants."

"Just because I'm taken doesn't mean I can't appreciate a silver fox when I see one," Mila countered.

Elena rolled her eyes, and Maggie cleared her throat.

"So, anything you would like to share with the class?" she asked suggestively. "Anything about a certain witch named Kieran?"

"Not at this time, no," Elena replied, looking away to try and hide her blush.

"Oh, my spirits." Maggie pointed accusingly at Elena's face. "What happened? Did he kiss you?"

"Shut up!" Elena hissed, looking around for anyone nearby.

"He did!" Maggie squealed. "I knew he was into you, I just knew it!"

Elena grabbed Mila's arm and began to drag her away.

"Don't think this conversation is over, young lady!" Maggie called after her, but let them leave without following.

Mila shot Elena a concerned look, but didn't say anything. They quickly made their way to the exit portal and went through it. As it closed in their driveway, Elena began to speak rapidly.

"Before you ask, yes, he did kiss me. And yes, I liked it, a lot. No, I don't fully know where we stand, but we are going to meet up later to figure—" Mila held up a hand to stop her, and Elena looked at her sister's face to see it had visibly grayed.

"I think I'm gonna be sick," Mila moaned.

"Oh, shit, sit down for a second." Elena guided Mila to the front step.

Mila sat down, and Elena summoned a cloth with cold water on it from the kitchen, pressing it to Mila's forehead.

"How do you witches get used to these stupid portals? This is terrible," Mila groaned.

"Our bodies are adapted to handle it. Just breathe; it'll pass in a second."

Mila took a deep breath of the cool night air, and Elena saw some color returning to her skin.

"So, you and Kieran are going to date?" Mila asked after a few moments.

"I think so."

"You've been holding out on me, haven't you?"

"Maybe, but I'll tell you everything, I promise."

Chapter 27

After another night of troubled sleep, Elena woke up horrifically early. Haunted by nightmares of gunshots and screaming, Elena wished she could blame her insomnia on just her nerves around her impending date with Kieran. They'd agreed via text to get together that Friday night, and Kieran promised he would arrange everything. However, his general vagueness about the entire thing was driving Elena crazy. There was also the matter of Jackie, whose phone number was sitting tucked away in Elena's nightstand. She hadn't yet worked up the nerve to call.

Sighing with resignation, Elena got up to look at her closet, feeling a totally bizarre and foreign need to exercise. Pulling out running clothes, which she owned for some reason, Elena trudged downstairs before trying to wake up Huey. Her familiar ignored her completely, and Elena quickly gave up before going out for a jog. It was a total disaster, and Elena barely made it half a mile before she stopped, her hands on her knees as she gasped for air. The return trip was more akin to a walk of shame than a run.

Limping up to the house, she found an envelope sitting on the stoop in front of the door with her name on it. Elena looked around, and seeing no one, leaned over to pick it up.

Eyeing it suspiciously, she tore open the envelope and opened the letter inside.

Beloved Sister,

"Oh good grief," Elena said out loud.

You have gotten up before 10 a.m.. This worries me. You also have gone out for a run. This worries me even more. I left you some breakfast on the counter. If you do not make it back and perish on your run because you are terrifyingly out of shape, you will be missed.

Love,

Your devoted sister.

Elena sighed and walked into the house. As promised, there was a breakfast sandwich waiting for her on the counter. She poked it and discovered it was still warm, so Mila couldn't have left that long ago. Sitting down and taking a huge bite, Elena glanced at the clock at the wall. Eight in the morning.

Horrible, unpleasant time of day. Elena finished her breakfast and vanished the plates away with a flourish, looking down at Huey who'd finally woken up and was moseying his way around the house.

"I could always text her," Elena reasoned out loud, and Huey paused, tilting his head. "I would sound much more intimidating over text, don't you think?"

Huey didn't seem to know what she was talking about and gave the closest thing to a shrug Elena ever witnessed from a dog. Rolling her eyes at him, Elena forced herself to go upstairs and retrieve Jackie's number from her nightstand. After spending an hour agonizing over the message she wanted to send, Elena decided on one she was happy enough with:

This is Elena. I don't think I need to explain to you why we need to talk. The board tried to stop me from reaching out, but I want to hear what you have to say about all this, face to face.

Elena re-read the message. It seemed authoritative enough, and also added the tempting bit of information about the board members that could potentially sway Jackie. Taking a deep breath, Elena hit send, her stomach plummeting as she did so.

Jackie did not respond for an entire day.

Elena was just about to text Kieran to confirm he'd given her the correct number the next morning after another failed attempt at a run when the notification came in.

Next Tuesday. 7 a.m. at the Roadside Diner in Spring Glenn.

Elena stared at the message. Elena knew of the diner, but had never been there before. At least it was close by and she could just drive there. But seven in the morning? That seemed cruel. It occurred to her, however, that Jackie likely chose the time and place because she believed it was a safe, neutral location for them to meet, but she still wanted a second opinion. Maybe even a third. She asked Kieran and Maggie, who both could not come up with a reason that the diner was a suspicious choice.

Despite this, Kieran was extremely distressed about the timing because he was busy that morning and could not go with her. Maggie, on the other hand, had no plans and was determined to come along.

"If what Kieran told you is the truth, and Jackie has gone political, then I don't want you facing her alone. She's not someone to be messed with."

With that set, Elena now forced herself to focus on the impending date with Kieran. As excited as she was to finally take this step, she was a little nervous.

It had been an embarrassingly long time since Elena went on a first date. Even before the witch hunt and her move to the country, she'd been in a bit of a dry spell and was very much out of practice.

The days dragged by, and the only relief Elena got was in her therapy sessions. Even though the virtual aspect was an adjustment to what she was used to, Elena was able to begin processing everything that happened at the fundraiser with her therapist, a woman she trusted implicitly. She knew one session wouldn't be enough to resolve all the trauma that was brought up, but it was a start. Her therapist was deeply concerned when Elena told her about the meeting with Jackie and urged her to proceed with caution.

"This could be a very triggering conversation for you, Elena. I want you to be prepared."

Ominous, but accurate.

Friday finally arrived, and a few hours before Kieran was scheduled to pick her up, Elena was agonizing in her bedroom.

"Why couldn't he tell me where we were going?" she asked Huey, who was sprawled out on her bed as she looked through her closet. "What do I dress for? A restaurant? A night at the theater? A moonlit stroll on the beach? Armed robbery?"

"He did say you two would be alone." Mila emerged into Elena's bedroom.

"Hey, didn't hear you get in."

"I would suggest…" Mila nudged Elena out of the way so she could access the closet. "Something casual but sexy, that way you are prepared for most scenarios, even armed robbery." Mila pulled out a blouse, considered it, then put it back. "If he's bringing you somewhere fancy, then that's on him for not warning you."

Elena watched Mila scrutinize her clothing.

"No, not that. It makes my butt look weird."

"Then why do you still own it?"

"I don't know, I might need it one day."

"Uh-huh, and one day, I'm going to go through this closet and get rid of half this stuff when you aren't around."

"You wouldn't dare."

* * *

Kieran was nervous, or excited. It was honestly hard to tell the difference at the moment. He did his best to ignore it, however, and tried to focus on the fact that for the first time in his life, he actually wanted to be with someone, and they wanted to be with him.

It shouldn't have taken nearly forty years for that to happen, but here he was. Now all he needed to do was go pick her up.

Getting past his family proved to be more of a challenge than he expected. Declan went to be with his wife, and his father was away on business. His mother, however, seemed to have a sense that he was hiding something from her and spent a good few hours that morning trying to convince the family to come together for dinner that night. Thankfully, Declan complained they'd been together that entire week and he needed some space. Of course, whatever Declan asked for he got, only this time it worked out in Kieran's favor.

Kieran spent all day after that preparing his surprise for Elena, and everything was ready just in time for him to go to her house. Checking his reflection in the mirror one last time, Kieran took a deep breath, opened a portal, and stepped through.

"He's here!" came a shout from inside the house, followed by a thudding noise from the second floor and a stream of curses.

That drew Kieran up short. He wasn't sure if he should find the sisters' behavior amusing or alarming. Walking up to the front door, he knocked, and Mila immediately swung it open.

"Hey, stranger," she greeted, "we meet again."

"Indeed. It has been a while since our usual meetings, but someone has stopped working at her shop, so she's never there when I come in anymore," Kieran said pointedly.

Mila scoffed. "Well, excuse me for being successful and wanting a personal life." She looked him up and down unabashedly. "You look very handsome today."

Kieran shifted, feeling a little self-conscious under her scrutiny. "Thanks, uh, is Elena coming?" he asked.

Mila looked behind her. "Good grief. Yeah, hang on. She was just there a second ago."

Mila shut the door in Kieran's face, leaving him standing there awkwardly. He heard some shuffling and Elena's voice yelling "I forgot my phone upstairs, would you chill out!" before the door opened again, this time with Elena standing on the other side.

"Hey, sorry about that," she said breathlessly, slamming the door shut behind her and stepping out. She was wearing a long black coat, and her hair fell loosely around her shoulders in an extremely attractive way that made Kieran want to run his fingers through the silky strands.

"No worries." He held out his hand to her. "Shall we?"

Elena took his hand without hesitation and followed him down the stairs. "So, you going to tell me where we're going?"

"You'll see in a moment," Kieran promised. He glanced

back at the house and saw Mila standing in the kitchen window. She made a "I'm watching you" signal with her hands before giving a cheery wave and disappearing. Kieran shook his head, and then, with his free hand, opened a portal.

They stepped through together and emerged on a grassy lawn on the edge of a large lake. Elena gasped, eyes widening. They were up in the mountains, distant peaks appearing as giant, jagged silhouettes in the distance. Mountain pines surrounded the far side of the lake, and all around them, the full moon reflected in the still water and bathed them in silver light. A million stars glimmered unobstructed in the sky. Elena was transfixed, and Kieran felt very pleased with himself as he watched her take it all in.

"It's so beautiful," Elena whispered, and she turned to look up at him. "Where are we, exactly?"

"At my cabin in the Auburn Mountains," Kieran explained.

"Cabin might be the wrong word," Elena said.

Kieran chuckled at the look on her face as she looked at his private home. "Shall we?"

Elena nodded, and they walked up to the house. When they reached the front door, Kieran pressed his hand against it. There was a shimmer of magic, then the door creaked open, allowing them to enter. They emerged into a completely open room with a beautiful kitchen at the far side and the rest taken up by a very comfortable and luxurious living space. To their left, the wall was completely glass, even though it appeared wooden from the outside. It opened onto a patio overlooking the lake.

"Very nice," Elena said appreciatively. "You said this was your place? Not a family property?"

"One hundred percent mine. My family doesn't even know

I have it," Kieran admitted.

Elena raised her eyebrows. "So this is kind of a big deal, you bringing me here?"

"Kind of." Kieran gave Elena a dazzling smile, which brought a blush to her cheeks. "Can I take your coat?"

Elena nodded, allowing him to slip it off her. Kieran hung it up in the coat closet and added his own. When he turned back to Elena, his eyes widened.

She was wearing a dark red dress that was cinched at her waist and flowed down to her mid-thigh. Light sleeves draped down her arms, and hanging down the plunging neckline of the dress was a simple silver necklace.

Stunning, she was stunning.

Elena was looking around the room but quickly caught him staring. "See something you like," she teased, although her blush deepened.

"You look beautiful."

The words came out much more passionately than Kieran intended, and Elena looked away for a moment before turning her eyes back to him. Her eyes raked over his body in a way that made the back of Kieran's spine tingle with anticipation. It seemed she liked what she saw as her eyes darkened. Kieran thought he looked pretty good, wearing dark pants and a gray button-up shirt. His sleeves were rolled up to his elbows in that way he knew people thought was attractive.

"So," Kieran broke the tense silence and cleared his throat. "I thought I could cook you dinner?"

"You can cook?"

"I'm decent." Kieran shrugged.

"Well, on that recommendation, how could I refuse?"

Kieran grinned, and he led her to the kitchen. "Care to sit?"

He gestured toward the stools on the other side of the large kitchen island.

"Would you mind if I helped? I could chop things or wash things..." Elena trailed off.

"Sure, if you want."

Kieran started pulling out ingredients from the fridge, and Elena watched him curiously.

"What are we having?"

"Herb crusted chicken over creamy tomato pasta."

"Sounds delicious."

Kieran separated out some tomatoes from the pile and handed them to her. "You can wash and cut these; I'll get the pasta started."

Elena took the tomatoes and brought them to the sink. "So, how is Briar doing these days?"

"Better, starting to go out on her own again. She'll be glad to hear you asked after her. I think she's been spending quite a lot of time with Huey actually."

"Really?" Elena returned to the counter where Kieran laid out a cutting board and knife for her. "I noticed he's been spending more time outdoors lately, but I hadn't seen her around."

Kieran pursed his lips, igniting the gas stove burner. "Bad news, if your familiar is keeping secrets," he said in a mock concerned tone.

Elena laughed. "I'm glad he's made a friend. He likes to pretend to be a big strong guard dog, but really, he's an ol' softy, who just wants to be loved."

"What a cliché," Kieran teased as Elena picked up the knife and began to chop the tomatoes.

Kieran prepared the seasoning for the chicken, and they fell into silence. A million things to say flashed through his mind, but he couldn't pick one. There had to be something—silence was a first date killer.

"So, how long have you owned this cabin?" Elena asked, thankfully not as tongue tied as him.

Kieran paused, thinking, a raw piece of chicken in his hand. "Ten years?" He placed the chicken on a plate and smothered it in sour cream. "It wasn't much when I bought the place. Really worn down, no electricity, no furniture. The ceiling was about to collapse."

"Wow, so a lot of work went into it?"

"I did most of it on my own, but the structural work I hired outside help for. Once that was done, I did all the painting and brought all the furniture, carpets, pretty much everything in here by myself."

"Really? You didn't have a friend who could help?"

Kieran dropped the chicken into the bowl of dried herbs, frowning. "No, not really."

"Oh."

Another awkward silence. Great, now Elena thought he was a weirdo with no friends. That was pretty much true, but still. This time, Kieran attempted to break the pause in conversation, throwing out a wild card.

"I saw something in the news recently about a discovery of an ancient witch's tomb in Caltina. The oldest ever found apparently, and the lead archeologist was a man named William Everett. That's your father, right? The man I met?"

"Yup, that's him." Elena openly grimaced. "These tomatoes good?"

Kieran looked over and nodded. "Perfect, you can pop them on that baking sheet, season with salt and pepper, then put them in the oven." The second piece of chicken ready to go, he went to the sink and turned it on using magic so he could wash his hands.

"It's interesting work your father does, have you ever been out to any of his digs?"

"Once, when I first started college. It was a brief visit, and he had only invited me to try to persuade me to follow in his footsteps, but once he realized I wasn't going to do that, he lost interest in me again," Elena explained, placing the seasoned tomatoes in the preheated oven.

"Ah, you two are not close then."

"Not in the slightest." Elena turned around to face Kieran, leaning against the counter. "He never wanted a kid, and my mom was content to raise me on her own. He paid child support up 'till the day I turned eighteen, and that was about all he contributed to my upbringing."

"Oh, I'm sorry to hear that," Kieran said, feeling guilty for bringing it up in the first place.

Elena shrugged, her eyes following his movements as he continued to prepare the food. "I used to resent him more for it, but in the little I have gotten to know him as an adult, I've been able to forgive him, mostly. His work is his life, and he just isn't capable of caring about much outside of that. He loves me in his own way, even though it wasn't what I needed growing up. It's not always easy, but I have tried to make my peace with it." The look on her face suggested a different story, but Kieran wasn't foolish enough to press it.

"Well, you had your mom, and Mila." Kieran considered for a moment, putting the pasta in the now boiling water. "I didn't think about it too much before now, but she's five years older than you. Your relationship when you were kids must have been very different."

Elena's lips twitched, and she handed him a wooden spoon to stir the pasta.

"She denies this now but she hated me when I was little, which I get. She was still getting over the loss of her father, and then her mother gave most of her attention to this screaming little baby. It was hard on her. Then one day, when I was like three, we were at the park and I was chasing a bug or something and tripped and fell into the pond. She dove in after me and pulled me out. I don't think I was in danger because the water was only like six inches deep since I was near the shore, but try explaining that to a toddler. After that, she was my hero, and she warmed up to me because I adored her so much."

"That's kind of adorable." Kieran grinned at the mental image of the two sisters as children. The pan on the stove was hot enough to add the chicken, so Kieran went to grab it. "When did you two actually become friends?"

"When I was fifteen. She came home for my birthday wearing all leather—she was in the middle of her punk rock phase—and snuck me out of the house to 'teach me how to live.' She took me out on her motorcycle to this concert for a band I'd never heard of and brought me right into the middle of the mosh pit. I ended up getting trampled and breaking my wrist. Our mom was so pissed, but it was one of the best nights of my life. After that, we were best friends."

Mila, the gardener and flower shop owner? That was quite the turn around.

"Wow, Mila a punk. I can't even imagine it, although I guess it explains the green hair."

"She calmed down in her early thirties," Elena explained,

watching Kieran place the chicken on a hot pan with a pair of tongs.

"So what was your wild phase? Did you also go punk, or was it something else?"

"Something else," Elena confirmed.

He raised an eyebrow at her. "Not going to tell me what it was?"

"Oh, I will, but I want you to guess first."

Kieran turned away from the stove and faced her fully, approaching and putting his hands on Elena's waist. Elena leaned into his touch, her own hands resting on his chest.

Staring into her eyes, Kieran forgot for a moment what he was meant to be doing.

"Flower child witch? You went full on daughter of the moon, lived in the woods on your own, growing herbs and not showering for weeks on end."

Elena laughed, and Kieran felt his heart quicken excitedly.

"Not even close." Her eyes sparkled with mirth. "I was a hardcore party girl. Out in the clubs 'till dawn, could drink men twice my size under the table, crazy dancing on tables, the whole thing."

Kieran blinked in surprise, then shook his head, smiling. "That is... very different from who you are now."

"A borderline shut-in that loves nothing more than sleeping?"

"You said it, not me."

Elena's grin faded, and she looked away over Kieran's shoulder. "Well, it didn't last long. I was on a pretty self-destructive path, trying to get back at my parents, according to my therapist, but then my mom got sick, and I realized I didn't want to spend whatever time with her we had left living like that, so I cleaned up my act. It was a little while after that I got my first book published."

"I never would have guessed." Kieran reluctantly turned back to the stove, trying very hard not to imagine Elena in her twenties in some club dancing in a sexy outfit.

Elena, oblivious to his mental struggle, stayed close and placed her hand on his lower back. "What about you? How did you spend your rebellious years?" she asked him, nudging him with her hip as she stirred the pasta.

Kieran grimaced, trying to think of a way not to answer. "You can't guess?" Kieran couldn't meet her eye.

Elena carefully placed the spoon down on the counter as she thought. "Oh!" Her face lit up, "I know this! It used to be in the tabloids all the time. You were uh, well…"

"A man-whore? Slut? Playboy? Sex addict?" Kieran suggested. Seeing people call him those things had never been easy, but he'd hardly been able to refute them. It was so much easier to forget the pain and anger that consumed him when he was beneath some stranger's thighs. But it never truly helped, and he only ended up making himself feel worse—not to mention bringing a bunch of public humiliation along with it.

"Those are the terms they used, yes," Elena said, shifting and not meeting his eye.

Kieran sighed. "I can't say there was some moment of clarity that snapped me out of it either. One day, I was thirty-one at the time, some of my father's goons pulled me out of my hotel room and took me to the family house. My father told me if I didn't start behaving like an adult, he would cut me off, and I would be on my own. Tough love I suppose."

"Hm." Elena pursed her lips. "I think this pasta is done."

While Kieran drained the pasta with magic, his stomach was doing backflips. She knew him, he told himself over and over again. She knew him, and she was here anyway. He shouldn't be embarrassed. Unfortunately, the internal pep talk didn't make him feel better. The affectionate smile on Elena's face when he turned back to her, however, did.

Chapter 28

The conversation turned a little lighter while they finished up dinner, Elena changing the subject to one of her favorite stories where Mila had tried to pierce her own lip when she was home from college on break.

"Obviously, I didn't know how to fix it, and she was bleeding everywhere. We were both freaking out, but we were too scared to call our mom, so we tried to make our way to the hospital," Elena said as they sat down at the small dining table in front of the kitchen. "Now, I was only fourteen at the time but hadn't hit my growth spurt yet, and Mila was as tall as she is now. So imagine a tiny little me and a freakishly tall Mila stumbling into an ER, me sobbing so hard the nurses couldn't understand, and Mila's mouth so swollen she couldn't talk."

Kieran shook his head, biting back laughter. "What did your mother do when she found out?"

"She was not pleased. Once she was able to bring Mila home from the hospital, she healed her up then let her have it. The funny thing was she was mostly angry because Mila didn't ask her to do the piercing! But after that, Mila majorly cooled on the idea, so it never ended up happening."

Kieran summoned two wine glasses and carefully placed them on the table, then summoned a chilled white wine.

Popping the cork with magic, he poured them both small glasses.

"One time when we were kids, I was thirteen and Declan was sixteen, he decided it would be fun to steal one of my father's cars for a joy ride. He'd just gotten his license and was feeling reckless."

"Oh, no." Elena's eyes widened.

"It didn't end as badly as you might think. Turned out, the car was manual, and he didn't know how to drive a stick. We barely made it to the end of the road and spent the entire time getting jerked around and stalling. My neck hurt for days after that. Luckily, Mom found us and not Father. She was pissed but kept it a secret. I don't think he ever found out," Kieran reminisced.

They spent the rest of dinner swapping crazy stories from their childhoods with their siblings. Elena noticed almost all of Kieran's stories started with his brother having a stupid idea and dragging Kieran along with him, while her own stories involved she and Mila bailing each other out of terrible situations the other got into.

"That was delicious," Elena said appreciatively, leaning back in her chair after clearing her plate.

Kieran, who'd already finished, gave her a pleased smile that made her melt. Talking with him like this was so easy and fun, Elena honestly couldn't imagine ever growing tired of it.

"Good, I'm glad you liked it." He lifted the bottle of wine. "Care for more?"

"Yes, please."

Kieran poured them both more wine and glanced up at her. "If you want, we could go out on the patio. I have a fire pit out there."

"That sounds perfect."

They stood, and Kieran vanished the plates away with a wave of his hand. Elena's heart started to race as they walked toward the glass door leading to the patio. This felt like the point where the mood would change. After one glass of wine, she wasn't drunk by any means, but sitting under a full moon next to a fireplace with a man you were insanely attracted to was its own kind of intoxicating. How far was she willing to go tonight? Why hadn't she thought about this before now?

Kieran, seemingly totally oblivious to her inner battle, opened the door and let her step out first before following and going up to the large stone fire pit to ignite it. It burst into life, sending dancing shadows all around them. There was a large comfy-looking couch facing the fire, and Elena sat down on it, placing her wine glass on a table nearby, her eyes on the moon.

"You really picked the perfect place."

"For my secret get away, or this date?" Kieran asked teasingly, putting his glass down next to Elena's.

"Both."

Kieran summoned a large blanket and handed it to Elena, who extended it out over the couch and her lap. She pulled the blanket back and patted the spot next to her invitingly.

"Care to join me?"

Kieran quickly sat down, pulling the blanket over him as well. He hesitated a moment, then wrapped his arm around her shoulders. Elena immediately scooted closer, slipping her shoes off and tucking her legs up underneath her pressing in against his chest. Face to face, Kieran's arm drifted down her back, and he began to draw light circles with his fingers on her arm. Elena's breath hitched in her throat, her mind glazing over from being so close to him.

"Can I ask you something?" Kieran, voice husky.

"Mm?" Elena's heart was pounding.

"Why did you stop coloring your hair?"

Elena leaned back and let out a small laugh.

"What?" Kieran asked, his smile uncertain.

"Nothing." Elena sighed, tucking herself into his neck. "I don't know. The reason I colored it before was to hide the fact that it was white, which is a pretty big give away for being a witch," she contemplated, "but when I joined the coven, I don't know, I guess I wasn't as afraid anymore. It just didn't feel necessary."

"It's good you feel safer with us, despite everything." Kieran began to rub his thumb up and down her arm gently.

That simple motion made heat spread through Elena's body, and she fought to focus on what he was saying.

"I do miss the color though, sometimes. Don't get me wrong, the white is stunning," he quickly added.

Elena smiled, shifting as she did.

"Did you have a favorite color?" she asked.

Kieran thought about it. "The lavender, I think. It really made your eyes stand out."

Was it possible for her to blush more than she already was? The amount of pleasure she got from such a simple compliment was almost embarrassing.

"Maybe I'll dabble with some color again, if I feel like it."

A lone howl broke the silence of the surrounding forest, making Elena jump. She sat up and looked around, her eyes wide. "There are wolves up here?" she asked nervously.

Kieran chuckled, his hand leaving her arm and trailing to

her back, playing with the tips of her hair. "Of course there are. Don't tell me you're afraid. What have you been learning with those lessons?" he teased.

Elena flopped back with a huff. "I'm not afraid," she defended herself. "But there's something about that sound, it just..." More howls filled the air, making the hair on her arms stand on end.

"I know what you mean." Kieran cast his eyes out into the darkness. "It triggers something, some ancient instinct that tells you that sound means you are about to be hunted."

"Exactly." Elena sighed, listening to the wolves sing to each other around them. After a few minutes, the wolves quieted, leaving the crackling of the fire as the only sound.

Elena shifted again, and it seemed Kieran had enough. He leaned forward and, gently brushing Elena's hair out of the way, placed a feather-light kiss on her neck. Elena breathed out in pleasure, tilting her head to give him better access. He started to kiss her more deeply, his left hand under the blanket sliding up her leg and resting on her thigh. Elena grabbed his hand with hers and lightly moaned, encouraging him. He nipped at her sensitive skin, causing her to tremble.

"Kieran," she breathed.

Kieran abandoned her neck and placed a hand on the back of her head, tilting her face to his and kissing her hard on the mouth. They kissed each other deeply, tongues sliding against each other and their hearts beating wildly.

Months of tension and longing exploded between them. Kieran reached forward and grasped her leg tightly, pulling her up so that she was straddling him. Elena gasped, wrapping her arms around his neck as his mouth slipped from hers and started to leave a trail of kisses down her neck. She moaned and gripped his hair as his mouth reached the center of her chest. His hot breath tickled her skin, making her tremble.

He was gripping both her thighs, and he looked up at her questioningly. In response, Elena leaned down and kissed him again, her tongue darting into his mouth. As she did, she released her grip on him and shimmied the top part of her dress off her shoulders. The fabric pooled at her waist, and the cool night air swept over her skin.

Kieran reached one hand up and placed it at her neck, pushing her back and breaking the kiss so he could gaze up at her. There was a look of awe on his face that stroked Elena's ego.

"You are so fucking beautiful," he murmured.

Elena laughed, throwing her head back, and Kieran swooped in, kissing her neck again. His hand moved to her back and began to tangle with the clasp of her bra. Within seconds, it was undone and fell from her shoulders. Elena pulled it off her and out of the way.

Taking control, Elena grabbed Kieran's head with one hand, weaving her fingers in his dark curls, and guided his mouth down. He responded enthusiastically, kissing and suckling one of her nipples, causing her to whimper his name and arch her back into him.

Once he was satisfied, he moved to her other breast, giving it the same treatment. An unbearable pressure pooled between Elena's legs, her thighs beginning to shake in anticipation.

Elena felt frustrated with how much clothing Kieran was still wearing and began to paw at the front of his shirt, trying to undo the buttons. Kieran pulled away from her, chuckling, and quickly pulled the shirt up over his head and tossed it away.

"Better, you greedy thing?" Kieran taunted.

Elena drank him in, her eyes raking over his lean, muscular form, her hands sliding down to his stomach. Her gaze lowered even further, and she noticed a very pronounced bulge in his pants. Smiling, she leaned forward and kissed him sweetly, softly, while one of her hands dipped into his pants and grasped him. He hissed at the contact, his hips bucking forward.

Elena nuzzled her nose with his own before kissing him again, more aggressively this time. She began to massage him, slowly at first, her range of motion limited by his pants. He grabbed her ass, moaning into their kiss.

Elena wanted him so badly and let out a desperate whine when Kieran reached down and grabbed her hand, pulling it away from him. Gripping her legs tightly again, he flipped her onto her back on the couch next to him in one swift motion, the blanket falling to the side, and Elena gasped in surprise. He sank down between her legs as they wrapped around his waist, their bare chests pressed against each other and his arms on either side of her, supporting the majority of his weight.

"Elena?" Kieran said questioningly.

"Kieran," Elena responded, giving him an adoring look.

"Do you want to do this?"

"Yes," Elena said firmly.

"Are you sure?"

"Super sure."

"Good."

Kieran kissed her on the lips and then slid himself down her body, kissing soft skin as he went until he reached her navel. He pulled her dress down, and she lifted herself up briefly so he could pull it all the way over her legs and toss it away. He slowly ran his hands up her thighs and settled on her hips, grasping her lace underwear with his fingertips. Within a few seconds, they, too, were discarded on the ground. Elena lay completely naked before him, the crackling fireplace sending shadows dancing over her skin, but she didn't feel shy at all.

She ran her leg up the side of his body teasingly while he took her all in. "Like what you see?"

"Yes," Kieran growled before grabbing her leg and kissing her ankle. The movement continued as he sucked and nuzzled his way up her calf, her thigh, and finally landing above the wetness between her legs. Smirking, Kieran dipped down and kissed her *there* lightly. Elena's entire body jolted, and she let out a small gasp.

Kieran slipped his tongue out and began to pleasure her enthusiastically, his hands wrapped around her thighs to keep her still. Elena's moans grew louder, and one hand darted forward to grip Kieran's hair while the other grasped the couch. Kieran took the nub between her legs into his mouth, swirling his tongue in a circular motion, eliciting a stream of breathy gasps and whines from her. Elena's hips jerked and bucked against him, but he held her down, continuing his attentions relentlessly.

"Kieran," she gasped, "I'm—"

Her peak hit her, and Elena arched her back, her eyes closed tightly, a long groan slipping from her lips. Kieran continued, drawing out her orgasm until she collapsed. Once it was fully over, he withdrew, wiping his face with the back of his hand, looking very pleased with himself. Trembling with every gulp of air, she looked up at him through half closed eyes.

"You all right?" he asked.

She nodded weakly. Kieran began to undo his pants, and Elena enjoyed watching him struggle with them for a few moments before he finally succeeded and ripped them off.

Before she could fully appreciate the sight of him naked, however, he was on top of her again, kissing her fiercely. She could taste the remnants of herself on his lips, which aroused her immensely, and her heart started to speed up again. She slipped her hand between their bodies and began to rub him again. Now freed from his pants, Elena was able to appreciate how big he was, and she felt herself growing even wetter at the thought of him being inside of her. She stroked the length of him, quickening her pace, and he groaned into her mouth.

Unable to wait any longer, she broke their kiss.

"Do the spell," she commanded.

"What?" Kieran asked, dazed

"The contraceptive spell!" she said urgently.

"Right," Kieran muttered, reaching a hand down between them. He muttered a few words, and Elena felt the tingling of magic pass through her, knowing Kieran was feeling the same. Kieran removed his hand and pushed inside her. Elena arched her back in response, her toes curling and letting out a little sigh. He paused for a moment, allowing her to get used to his size, and then began to move slowly. Elena felt jolts of pleasure roll over her as he ground his hips down and started to match his movements with her body.

"You feel," he gasped out, "so fucking good."

Elena smiled into his shoulder, holding on to him tightly. He began to speed up, grunting and moaning into her ear. Elena raked her fingers down his back, leaving angry red scratches in his skin, burying her face in his neck as her entire body clenched around him. Whimpers of pleasure spilled from her lips, her entire body tensing as Kieran's thrusts drove her to the edge again.

He came hard, groaning out Elena's name, and Elena followed right after, their cries of pleasure mingling together in the night air. He collapsed on top of her, his body shuddering, and Elena stroked his hair lovingly. After a few moments, he rolled off of her, wrapping his arms around her and pulling her close. She cuddled up to his chest, both of them still breathing hard.

They stayed silent, and within a few minutes, Elena started tracing her fingers over his body, down his side, to his hip, and back up again. Then, deciding cuddle time was over, she pushed him onto his back and crawled on top. He laughed, looking up at her with delight.

"Not tired out yet?"

"Oh, no, I am not even close to being done with you."

Chapter 29

The next morning, the sun crept over the mountain peaks, bathing the lake, trees, and cabin in a crystal golden light. The fire on the patio had gone out hours ago, and Elena and Kieran were still on the couch, a blanket wrapped around them.

Kieran was already awake, but he did not want to rouse the woman in his arms. Instead, he watched her sleep, stroking her hair, her chest rising and falling peacefully. She was unbearably beautiful to him in that moment, and Kieran couldn't look away despite the stunning scenery. Feelings of tenderness and affection he'd never felt before overwhelmed him, tethering him to her.

Kieran had been with a lot of people... a lot of people. But it never been like this with any of them, the sex never felt that good. Apparently, actually caring about the person you were sleeping with made a huge difference. Who knew?

Elena frowned in her sleep, shifting, and Kieran's attention immediately snapped back to her. She murmured something incoherent then rolled over to face away from him. He gently pulled her close so that her back was pressed against his chest, savoring the contact between them and taking a deep breath of her scent.

His heart was aching with how much he cared for her right

now, how much he wanted her, how much he never wanted to be with anyone but her again. It was overwhelming. It was amazing. It was somehow breaking his heart and filling it at the same time.

* * *

Elena woke to the sound of birds singing, and she groaned unhappily.

"Loud little shits," she muttered. Her pillow chuckled behind her, and her eyes snapped open. She remembered where she was, and who her pillow actually was. Her senses coming to her, Elena realized she was spooned up against Kieran's chest, his arm wrapped around her torso.

"Good morning to you, too," he murmured, kissing her cheek.

She scooched onto her back and smiled up at him. "Hi," she said, reaching up to brush a few strands of dark hair behind one of his ears.

He kissed her hand gently. "How are you feeling?" he asked.

Elena did a self-scan, moving her legs cautiously. She was met with a dull ache between and through her legs, causing her to wince. "A little sore," she said. "That was my first time in a while..."

Kieran frowned. "That won't do. A hot shower might help?"

"Mm..." Elena agreed, imagining the pleasant feeling of hot water running over her skin.

"The one problem is," Kieran said, looking up around them, "is that we are very warm here under our blanket, and it is warm inside the cabin, but between under the blanket and inside is quite cold."

373

"That is a problem." Elena shivered at the thought. "How do we fix that?"

Kieran considered the issue for a moment, then a wicked grin spread over his face. "This is going to feel very strange," he warned her, then opened a portal directly underneath them.

Elena yelped as they fell through and landed on a bed, presumably inside the cabin. She burst out laughing at the absurdity of it, and Kieran joined her, their limbs tangled together after the fall.

"I'll get the shower going," he said, pulling himself up.

Elena rolled over to watch him walk away, appreciating the view. He disappeared into what she assumed was the bathroom, and she could hear him turn the water on. Elena smiled to herself, then filled with a sudden giddiness, hid her face in the bed and did a little happy shimmy. She could not remember ever feeling this way before. She was happy, truly happy, for the first time in a very long time.

"It's ready," he called from the bathroom, and with tremendous effort, Elena pulled herself out of bed to join him.

The shower was a delight. The bathroom was the height of luxury with multiple shower heads spraying from different positions for a full cleaning experience. Not that they enjoyed them too much. As soon as they were naked and wet, Elena couldn't keep her hands off Kieran when led to him pressing her up against the shower wall and taking her while whispering sweet nothings in her ear.

After, Elena sprawled herself out on the living room couch, wearing one of Kieran's bath robes, watching him cook her breakfast while wearing just a pair of gray sweatpants.

That man, that stunningly beautiful man, was hers. So

many people wanted him, but he was hers. Was the world around them growing darker by the day? Yes. Was a part of Elena worried his family was going to force them apart if they found out about them? Also yes. But right now, she wasn't thinking about any of that, because Kieran was walking toward her, carrying a plate of pancakes and bacon, and it was the best thing she had ever seen.

When Kieran brought her home, they were greeted by a wildly unhappy Huey and an amused Mila.

"So, you have a good time defiling my sister last night?" Mila arched an eyebrow at Kieran, eyeing him.

"What the hell," Elena muttered.

"I did, yes." Kieran smirked in return.

Saying goodbye felt oddly painful, even though they would see each other again in a few days anyway. It almost felt like going to bed Sunday night after a nice weekend, knowing that you would be back at school in the morning.

When Kieran kissed her one last time, Elena held on just a little bit longer, trying to memorize his scent, the feel of his body pressed against hers—every part of her aching with a fear that she couldn't understand.

* * *

A frantic energy consumed Elena the rest of the weekend. Uncharacteristically, she always had to be moving—to be doing something in order to distract her mind. Kieran texted her throughout the day, and Mila was hanging around the house working on her garden, but something still felt off.

Was this anxiety around meeting with Jackie? Elena hated confrontation, and Jackie was not likely to pull her punches, but Elena wasn't sure that was it. Perhaps it was the letters and unexpected visitors showing up at the house randomly. It seemed the coven's order to leave her alone had only been effective for so long, and now, members were showing their "support." Mila immediately jumped in and screened the letters, removing those she deemed too patronizing or insincere. That turned out to be most of them. The few that did meet her approval, Elena read, but truthfully, they didn't make her feel better.

Her private life had been invaded, dissected, and put on display. Written down proof of that didn't help.

Then there were those who had the gall to show up to the house uninvited. They were witches Elena didn't know, and after interacting with them, she had no desire to change that. These concerned coven members were pushy and tone deaf, talking to her like she was a child or a scared animal while clearly trying to get more information about the witch hunt out of her.

After this happened three times, Mila started turning them away, using Huey to threaten them if they tried to ignore her.

Elena should have been celebrating her new relationship, basking in the glow of the wonderful night she'd spent with Kieran. Now, her world had shrunk even more.

When Elena's alarm went off Monday morning, she awoke completely alert. It was time to meet with Jackie. Her sleep had not been particularly restful, but the wild surge of adrenaline powered her through her morning routine. Mila was already waiting for her downstairs, unable to keep the concerned look off her face as she watched Elena nervously try to eat something.

"That will be Maggie." Mila turned to the kitchen window

at the headlights that were pulling into the driveway in the early morning light. Elena nodded and walked to the front door.

"I'll be fine," Elena said as Mila followed, and gave her sister a brief hug before snapping a leash on Huey's collar and leading him outside. Elena approached the car, and Alex opened the back door so Huey could jump in.

"Morning!" he said brightly, as Huey licked his face.

"Morning," Elena replied gruffly, getting into the front seat. In a spur of the moment decision the night before, Elena had texted Alex, asking if he would come, too, and he'd readily agreed. Elena honestly wondered sometimes how she ended up so lucky to have such supportive friends.

Maggie backed out of the driveway once Elena was buckled in, and the three witches sat in tense silence as they drove to the diner. Fog hung over the trees as the sun slowly crept up in the sky, bathing the surrounding woods and hills in golden light. Elena secretly loved the early morning but could never get herself into a sleep schedule that allowed her to see it. She wished the circumstances now were different, that she was off to a pleasant breakfast with her friends rather than what was actually happening.

But she had to have closure, or this entire incident would always be a thorn in the back of her mind, and confronting Jackie was the only way to get it. Plus, the idea that the board didn't want her to talk to Jackie intrigued her—what didn't they want her to know?

"So," Maggie said, ending the silence, "I was thinking I would go in with you, and Alex could keep watch outside? We don't want to seem too imposing, or else she might bolt."

"Right, sounds like a plan," Elena agreed.

"It's gonna be okay, we'll get through this together." Alex grasped Elena's shoulder from the back seat in support.

They pulled into the diner a few minutes later, and Elena took a deep breath before exiting the car. Looking around the parking lot, it seemed the diner was fairly busy that morning, and Elena wasn't sure if that was a good or bad thing. Huey nudged her hand with his snout, and she took his leash from Alex with a deep breath.

"Don't let her walk all over you," Alex said. "No matter what she thinks, you're way tougher than she is."

Elena nodded her head shakily, then turned to Maggie, who was standing at her side.

"Let's go."

They entered the diner and immediately spotted Jackie a corner booth. The hostess looked as if she might try to stop them as she eyed Huey, but Elena cleared her throat and looked pointedly at the "Dogs welcome!" sign in the window before strolling past her.

"Good morning, ladies." Jackie grinned as Maggie slid into the booth first, and Elena sat down next to her. Huey sat rigid at Elena's side, staring at Jackie.

Jackie glanced at him, her lips pursed. "You brought the entire crew, it seems."

"Just a precaution." Elena fought to keep her voice even as she stared at Jackie. The woman looked a little more unkempt than Elena remembered. Although she was dressed impeccably, Jackie's eyes had deep circles under them, she wore no makeup, and her hair was pulled back in a messy bun. Her eyes, however, simmered with unspoken power.

"I've cast a ward around this table so that we can speak freely." Jackie waved a hand around them.

"Mm." Maggie squinted into the air, as if she was examining the invisible ward. "You won't mind if I cast one of my own. Not that I don't trust you... Oh wait, I don't trust you at all."

Jackie's lip twitched. "Elena can't do it herself? What have you been doing with your lessons all these months?"

Elena scowled at her, and Huey let out a low, threatening growl.

"Watch your mouth," Maggie hissed, even as her hands began to twist in a pattern under the table.

Before tensions could erupt, however, a waitress walked over and plopped down three breakfast dishes in front of the women. Elena stared down at her pancakes and bacon, then looked up at Jackie questioningly.

"I didn't want to waste any time, and to get the humans out of our hair as quickly as possible," she explained.

Elena and Maggie shared a look.

"Fine then." Elena turned back to Jackie. "Let's not waste time. Before you explain anything, I want to say something to you first."

Jackie picked up a piece of her own bacon, taking a bite without breaking Elena's stare. "By all means, go ahead."

Anger flared to life in Elena's gut at Jackie's attitude, and it gave her the focus she needed to say what came out of her mouth next.

"You've never liked me. In fact, you went out of your way to make sure I knew you didn't like me from the moment we met." She paused, and when Jackie didn't dispute this, she pressed on. "I understand we've had our differences since I joined the coven, but I never thought your dislike of me went this far. The board claims you said you didn't mean to hurt me by showing that video, that I wasn't your target, and maybe you are about to say the same thing, but I don't understand."

Elena felt Maggie's hand gripping hers under the table, an anchor that gave Elena the courage to keep talking.

"I don't understand how you could see what was on that video and put it out there and think it wouldn't hurt me. You didn't know I would be at the fundraiser? Fine. But you knew there would be people there who knew me, people who would see my face and recognize me, and you showed it anyway. There was a damn good fucking reason why the council worked so hard to protect our identities. They wanted us to have a chance to start over, to move on with our lives in peace, and you took that away from me!"

Jackie seemed to be getting pale, her expression grim, but she still did not look away.

"That was the worst moment of my life. Do you understand that? My best friend was murdered in front of me, her blood was on me, her body in my arms. And you saw that and decided to broadcast it to a room of people who had absolutely no right to see it, no right to witness that moment. So whatever you're about to say, whatever explanation you are about to give, it better be a fucking good one, because right now, I want nothing more than to blast you through the window of this diner."

Huey growled at Jackie for emphasis, and she had the good sense to flinch. Elena's entire body was shaking, and she felt tears pricking at her eyes, but her rage held them back, her entire being narrowed in on the woman in front of her.

"Elena," Jackie began, then swallowed, finally looking away and down at her hands. "When that video was first given to me, when I watched it the first time, I wanted to destroy it. I was going to destroy it, but I... I changed my mind." Jackie picked up her fork and began to push her scrambled eggs around her plate. "It was the man who took the video who gave it to me. I was looking for any footage from the witch hunt for weeks, and he made me promise I would edit it to hide your face, but I knew I couldn't do that."

"Why fucking not?" Maggie demanded, and Jackie sighed.

"Because what I needed to do with that video was more important than the pain it would cause you. Because our world stands on the brink, being pulled toward chaos and destruction by those who are sworn to protect us, and someone needs to do something. I'm sorry, Elena, truly sorry, for what I did to you. But I would do it again, if I had to, because our people need to understand what's going on."

Elena gaped at her, and Maggie choked out, "What the hell are you talking about?"

"The truth," Jackie said bluntly. "The truth that the leaders of the magical world are not only actively profiting off the current rise in violence against our kind, they are encouraging it. That the most powerful witch families in the world, the coven leaders, are fanning the flames of hatred and ignorance on both sides, so that they can regain the type of power they once wielded in a world where humans and witches were constantly at war."

A stunned silence met Jackie's words.

"You are out of your mind," Elena said through gritted teeth. "You can't honestly believe that?"

"I understand why you're resistant to the idea." Jackie sat back, popping some eggs into her mouth. "Before what happened earlier this year, I wouldn't have believed it either. But then I had a very interesting conversation with Kieran

Andraste at a party where he was drunk out of his mind and full of so much self-hatred he could barely breathe. He told me about a deal going down between our coven and the Coastal Coven. It wasn't so much a deal as it was negotiations for an alliance, to share power and resources when the humans attack."

"With all the hate crimes going on, that isn't strange," Maggie pointed out.

But Jackie shook her head. "No, not *if* there was an attack, he specifically said *when*," Jackie said.

Elena felt a growing pit in her stomach, her grip on Maggie's hand so tight she was sure it was painful.

"Perhaps that isn't much on its own, but after the Andrastes threatened to expel me if I ever went near Kieran again, and made sure no one in the coven would even associate with me, I started to dig. They took everything from me, and I wanted to hurt them, but along the way, I started to realize what was going on was far bigger than just my own desire for revenge."

Jackie took a sip of her coffee, her eyes closed. When she opened them again, Elena recognized the emotion burning in her eyes: unbridled fury.

"Did you know that after the witch hunt that claimed your friend's life, new memberships in the large national covens increased over sixty percent?"

Elena nodded stiffly.

"As I'm sure you know, as I'm sure your mother taught you, when a witch joins a coven, they're giving up part of their life to that coven. Their power becomes the coven's power, and the coven, to a certain extent, has control over their lives. Over the last few decades, as relations between witches and humans have improved, more and more people have been leaving the old covens to live independently. The more equal our society became, the less powerful those old families running the covens were."

"That is a big accusation Jackie," Elena whispered, despite the wards protecting them. "You seriously believe the covens are all in some conspiracy to create a war between humans and witches?"

"A conspiracy? No." Jackie put her mug down. "I believe that they realized at some point that when bad things happened to witches, they gained some of the power they were losing. It probably started out as an accidental discovery, noticing that when a witch hunt happened, witches would flock to them. Then their actions became more and more deliberate in their quest to regain what they lost. The Andrastes for example? They used to be royalty in the magical world. Three generations ago, their word was law, and now they are barely more than celebrities. You think that doesn't eat away at Anthony Andraste day and night?"

"The Andrastes are one of the most influential families in the world, magical or human. You really think that isn't enough for them?" Maggie snapped.

Elena immediately remembered something Kieran had said to her the morning after the fundraiser. "For them, enough is never enough," Elena whispered.

Jackie nodded. "Whatever their original intentions, it escalated. And these families, including the Andrastes, have been actively pushing and pushing at the tensions between witches and humans. Interfering in attempts to bring the magical and non-magical communities together, encouraging witches to act out and break laws in ways to provoke and terrify humans, spreading rumors and lies about witches in the media."

Elena felt sick, and Huey let out a whine next to her. Maggie was shaking her head, but Jackie plowed on.

"They might not have directly been behind the witch hunt in New Stirling City, but these families, including the Andrastes, most certainly encouraged it into being. And they profited from it, I assure you. You are hardly the only new recruit to have joined our coven in the months after that attack.

"I showed that video at the fundraiser because they needed to see the truth of what they were doing. They needed to see the horror, the death, the pain of it for themselves, and to wake up those who were there, who aren't part of this mess, to the reality of what is going on. They needed to see your face, to see the worst moment of your life and know that they are the ones who did that to you." A humorless, wretched smile spread over Jackie's face. "And they did."

"What do you mean?" Elena asked, dreading the answer.

"I don't care if I got kicked out of the coven, I was basically out already anyway. I don't care that the Andrastes are watching me, and spirits know how many other families out there, because I got one of them on my side, and it was all because of that video. All thanks to you, Elena."

"Who?" Elena knew without Jackie having to say it, but she needed to hear it anyway.

Jackie's smile widened. "Why, Kieran, of course."

* * *

Far away, in the nation's capital, Congressman Garyn Parra opened the door to his home office, sighing and slipping off his coat. The day had barely begun, but he was already exhausted from the number of meetings he had to attend. He threw the coat onto a nearby chair and switched on the lights. As he did, he let out a yelp and jumped backward, his back hitting the wall painfully. Kieran Andraste was sitting behind his desk, watching him without emotion.

"What the hell are you doing here, Andraste?" the congressman gasped out.

"The workplace anti-discrimination law that is up for vote tomorrow, the one protecting witches from being fired for being a witch," Kieran began.

The congressman raised his eyebrows in surprise. "That's why you're here? You can save your breath, I'm voting to pass it."

"You misunderstand me," Kieran said calmly. "I want you to vote against it."

The congressman looked at him, stunned. "Why?" he asked, utterly confused. "Why do you want a law that protects your own people to fail?"

"We don't want it to fail, we just want it to be postponed for a few more months. We need the right amount of votes to not outright defeat it, just to send it back for debate a bit longer."

"No, I won't do it," the congressman said. "I will vote my conscience. I believe in this law."

"I see." Kieran rose to his feet.

The congressman could not stop the shudder of fear that tore through him.

"You want more money," Kieran said simply, and he waved his hand over the desk. A briefcase appeared on it, and the congressman leaned forward, suddenly interested, a hungry look in his eye.

"How does two million sound?" Kieran asked, his voice still dead.

"Oh," the congressman hesitated. "Well." He looked from the

briefcase to Kieran, and Kieran flipped it open, revealing neatly stacked bundles of cash.

"It's yours, in return for the no vote," Kieran said. "The next time the bill goes up for vote, you can, and should vote yes, but tomorrow, we need the no."

The congressman licked his lips, staring at the money nervously, then nodded. "Very well."

"Always a pleasure doing business with you, Congressman." He turned his back on the man, opened a portal, and stepped through it. Once he was gone, the congressman quickly approached the table and dug his hand into the briefcase, feeling the cold cash against his skin.

He let out a shaky breath, then quickly withdrew and snapped the briefcase shut. He walked it over to the secret safe hidden behind his bookshelf. After opening the safe, he carefully placed the briefcase inside, then closed it up again. It was not the first time he had taken a bribe from the Andraste family, and although it filled him with self-loathing, he knew it would not be the last.

* * *

"Sweet, darling Kieran," Jackie continued, "who has been doing his father's terrible work for years and was punished for it whenever he questioned why. Lovely Kieran, who suspected what was going on but was too afraid of his family, of his father, to stand up to them. My beautiful Kieran, who looked at that video, and perhaps for the first time in his life, really understood the consequences of what his family's actions were, the consequences of what *his* actions were."

Maggie was openly gaping at Jackie now, and Jackie looked back smugly.

"I thought he might actually hurt me when he showed up on my door last week. I'd never seen him so angry, but he gave me a chance to explain myself, and after I did, he was so quiet. I wasn't sure what he was thinking, but then, next thing I knew, he was putting up wards of his own design around my house, bought me a new secure phone, and promised to make sure you and I got the chance to meet without interference from the coven or his family."

"He didn't say you were wrong?" Elena's voice was wavering uncontrollably now.

"Nope, didn't argue a single point. So you see, Elena, whatever I did to you, whatever hurt I caused, it was worth it. It was worth it because I opened Kieran Andraste's eyes, and now, he can never go back to how things were before, how he was before. I couldn't have asked for a more useful ally."

"What exactly do you think he's going to do?" Elena's heart was pounding so hard she was sure the entire diner could hear it.

Jackie shrugged. "I'm not sure. He doesn't trust me enough to tell me his plans, but I think he might trust you." Jackie pulled out her wallet and placed some money on the table for the food. "I know this is all hard to believe, but you need to understand me when I say I am not done, not by a long shot." Grabbing her bag, Jackie stood, then paused, looking down at Elena. "You were right before, I don't like you, Elena. But I don't have to like you to want to fight for you, to fight to make sure what happened to you never happens to another witch ever again. So, you can forgive me, or you can hate me. I don't really care. But I am not going to stop. This is just the beginning."

Elena and Maggie watched her go, Huey placing his head in

Elena's lap. The witches turned to look at each other, both too stunned to speak. The world, and everything they thought they knew about it, had just changed.

* * *

Kieran emerged from the portal in his apartment in New Stirling City after meeting with the senator. As soon as it closed behind him, his entire body sagged. He felt utterly spent and filled with a deep and simmering rage. After taking a deep breath, Kieran headed for his bedroom. Stripping off his suit jacket, he dropped it on the floor, loosening his tie and removing it as he walked. He made it to the bedroom and headed straight for the bathroom, where he turned on the faucet and splashed cold water on his face.

The rage started to grow, infiltrating his stomach and making him feel sick. He wiped the water from his face with a washcloth and looked at his reflection in the mirror. The man who looked back at him was cold, angry, and dark; a man who'd just done evil. In a burst of fury, he lunged out and punched his reflection, shattering the glass and cutting his knuckles. Withdrawing his hand with a hiss, Kieran clutched it to his chest.

His reflection was gone, and as he looked down at the blood leaking from his hand, he felt the pain in his chest loosen, just a little. He knew what he had to do.

Kieran strode out of the bathroom and back into the bedroom, pulling off his shirt as he went so that he was bare chested. He walked to the bookshelf at the other side of the room and shoved the books aside, then reached to the back of the shelf and grasped the long antique knife that he kept there. Pulling it out, he looked at it gleam in the faint light that came in from the window. His father's family crest—his birth father's—stood out proudly on the hilt. Taking a deep breath, he strode over to the full-length mirror beside the bed and looked at his reflection.

Slowly, he pressed the blade of the knife to the skin above his rib on the left side. Then, taking a deep breath, he slid it across his flesh, applying pressure as he went. His skin split open, pain exploding, and blood dripped out, sliding down his body. He made an incision around six inches long, then stopped, withdrawing the knife, watching the blood leak from the wound for a moment, then he began again. He cut, and he cut, feeling more physical pain with each touch of the blade, but the anger and the self-loathing started to fade with every drop of blood. He became light-headed, but he kept cutting, following along every rib, until finally his torso was a tapestry of ghastly slashes.

"You deserve this," he snarled to himself through gritted teeth after the knife slipped and went deeper than he intended, sending jolts of pain up his spine.

It was punishment, it was release, it was a balm that soothed every uncontrollable ounce of hatred flowing through Kieran's veins.

Finally, after ten cuts, he stopped. Breathing hard, there were tears sliding out of his eyes and down his cheeks silently.

Kieran held the bloodied knife by his side, watching himself for a few minutes, before taking another deep breath, and waving his free hand over the cuts, healing them instantly. He wiped the blade on his pants, cleaning it, and carefully placed it back in its spot on the shelf. His torso was still covered in blood, but he left it. He would take a shower before going home to report to his father that all had gone well with the senator.

Then, he was going to do something he should have done a long time ago. Before, after this horrible ritual, he would go on as normal, go on like everything was fine. Not this time. This time, he would act.

Chapter 30

Approaching Elena's house, Kieran felt like he was walking into a chasm he might never escape. Despite his healing magic, his ribs still ached faintly with the memory of what he'd done, but that was not what was drowning him. This was the end for him and Elena when they'd only just begun. When he'd awoken that morning, he'd thought he knew how the day would go, thought there would be an uncomfortable conversation with Elena where they discussed how unhinged Jackie had become, and then they would move on, but now... now he was only here to say goodbye.

In truth, he hadn't believed a word of Jackie's conspiracy theory when he spoke to her, but recognized she believed it, and took steps to protect her until he could sort everything out. That was, he didn't believe it until this morning, when his father had told him exactly what he was supposed to do in his meeting with the congressman. They never went that far, never acted so blatantly against the interests of their own people. It was unforgivable, and still Kieran did it, knowing that Jackie was right about everything.

Reaching the door, Kieran took a deep breath and knocked. Silence met him, and after a few moments, he knocked again. There was a scratching noise on the other side, and the door slid open. Empty air greeted Kieran, and he looked down to see Huey standing there, looking up at him resentfully. They stared at each other for a moment before Huey snorted once and trotted away. Elena sat at the kitchen island, her head in her hands. Kieran's stomach dropped, and he carefully approached.

"Elena?" he asked, his voice gentle.

"Is it true?" Elena didn't move as she spoke. It wasn't a huge leap to realize what she was talking about. Jackie had told her everything.

"I know you have no reason to believe me, Elena, but truly I didn't know, I didn't realize."

Elena turned to face him, and Kieran saw her eyes were bloodshot.

"How could you not have known?"

Kieran walked toward her, but Huey let out a low growl, causing Kieran to stop dead in his tracks. He glanced at the dog nervously, swallowing. "I always thought all those things I did for my father were connected to our business. Or they were about personal grudges. It never seemed like they had anything to do with the magical world."

Elena pursed her lips, not looking convinced. "Then what changed your mind?"

"That meeting I had this morning, it was too obvious to ignore. My father ordered me to do something terrible, something that will hurt witches and cause mayhem."

"What did you do, Kieran?" Elena breathed.

"I can't tell you."

"Why not?" Elena demanded, jumping to her feet. "You can't just say you did something terrible to our people and expect me to be okay with that!"

"I'm not." Kieran felt like he might be sick. "But I can't tell you the details, Elena. If I do, I put you at risk. But I'm going to fix this, I promise."

Elena crossed her arms over her chest, Huey standing at her side with his fur puffed up to make himself look larger. If the situation wasn't so serious, and Huey's canines not so large, the image would have been comical.

"How?" she demanded.

"I'm going to take all the evidence from what happened this morning and turn myself in to the feds." It was the only thing he could do, really. Before Elena, perhaps Kieran might have been able to go public with everything he knew and had done and face the consequences alone. Now? If he did that, there was no telling what his father might do to Elena in order to punish Kieran and bring him to heel. Going to the government was the only way he could do the right thing and keep her safe.

Elena's arms dropped as she gaped at him. "You can't." Her voice cracked on the words.

"I have to," Kieran said as calmly as he could. "It's the only way to make things right, to make up for what I've done."

Elena began to shake her head, her shoulders trembling slightly. "If you do this, you're the only one who will face consequences. Your family will keep doing what they've been doing, and you'll rot behind bars the rest of your life."

"Maybe," Kieran admitted, "but I don't think so. There's a human federal agent who's been trying to get me to work with her for years. I've always refused, but if I go to her now, show her I'm willing to cooperate, then I can make a deal."

Elena's eyes snapped back to his. "And what if she's changed her mind. What if she refuses to make a deal?"

"Well, then, I go to jail, I suppose."

Elena let out a choked sob, and Kieran rushed forward, attempting to hold her, but she shoved him away angrily.

"So that's it then? You're going to bank your entire future on the hope that this agent will still want to work with you, that she's willing to give you a deal to betray your family, and I just have to live with whatever happens?" Elena gripped the stool she'd been sitting on for support, or maybe to throw it at him.

"What else can I do?" Kieran couldn't keep the desperation out of his voice. "If I don't make this right, if I don't do whatever I can to fix the damage I've done, I could never live with myself. I have to do this, even if that means we can't be together."

"Oh really?" Elena stormed forward until she was right in his face. "You made me fall for you, promised me a real shot at a relationship, and now you're taking it back! How is that fair?"

"It's not." Kieran clenched his fists at his side. "And I'm sorry, Elena, I'm so sorry for doing this to you. If I'd realized sooner, I never would have let things get this far between us, but..." He trailed off and hesitantly raised a hand to cup Elena's face. "Do you really think you could be with me, knowing what you know now about my family, and knowing I wasn't doing anything to stop it?"

Elena blinked, then her jaw tightened, and she looked pointedly at the ground.

"I'm not asking you to forgive me, Elena, or to wait for me if I end up in prison," Kieran continued. "I'm not that selfish or naive. The things I've done, they're unforgivable. Even if they do offer me a deal, I don't expect you to want to stay with me after this."

To Kieran's surprise, Elena snorted. "Is that what you think I want or is it what you want?" she asked dryly.

Kieran dropped his arm, taken aback. "Of course that isn't what I want."

"Are you sure? Because you just walked in already decided we were over, didn't you? You didn't even consider finding out what I thought first. You made that decision for me."

Kieran swallowed, his throat very dry. "That isn't what I meant to do."

"Sure."

Kieran felt a rush of anger at her dismissal. Did she really have no idea what she meant to him, what a huge deal being in a relationship was for him? How could she accuse him of wanting this, wanting any of it?

"Do you honestly believe that I want to leave you? That I *want* to let go of the only person in my life who makes me feel like I'm actually worth something?" Kieran was yelling, and he couldn't even remember the last time he'd ever yelled at anyone. When he realized what he was doing, what he'd said, he recoiled.

Elena watched him, her eyes wide. "I can't lose you," she whispered. "I only just got you."

Closing his eyes, Kieran leaned forward and rested his forehead against Elena's, breathing in deeply as he tried to reign in his emotions.

"Please don't do this," Elena begged.

Spirits, Kieran was losing his grip. This was hard enough as it was, and she was making it so much harder.

"It's too late, El. I already made the call." Kieran opened his eyes, pulling back slightly to look at Elena. "But if they do offer me the deal, and I can go free... you really want to stay with me?"

Elena bit her lip, her eyes still watering. "I don't know. I'm really fucking pissed at you."

Kieran's heart plummeted, but he'd known this would happen, known this was what *should* happen.

"If I work with the government, it will be dangerous. Being discovered could lead to worse things than prison. Would you be willing to risk that? Because I don't know that I am when it comes to you."

"Stop making choices for me." Elena glared up at him but didn't shove him away again.

"Okay, okay." Kieran raised his hands from her shoulders and cradled her face. "I'm sorry."

Elena closed her eyes, her brow scrunching as she thought.

"You don't have to decide now," Kieran offered. "I'm pretty confident they will offer me a deal. Then you can decide how you feel about all this."

"And if they arrest you instead?"

"Then this is goodbye."

Elena shuddered, and Kieran pulled her fully against him, where she sank into his embrace. He ran a hand soothingly up and down her back, needing her to stay focused.

"Listen," Kieran said as calmly as he could, even though his voice shook and cracked. "I need you to take care of Briar for me, okay? Give her a home where she'll be safe and loved, in case I don't come back."

"Stop," Elena groaned.

"Please, I don't trust my family with her, and she knows you, she knows Huey. Please, do this, for me."

Elena silently nodded, and Kieran felt a wave of relief.

"I regret so many things about my life, Elena," he said in

her ear, "but taking a chance with you will never be one of them, no matter how this ends."

Elena tilted her head back to stare into his eyes.

"You're such an asshole," she said, and Kieran choked back a laugh. Elena managed a pained smile, which vanished quickly and was replaced by a frown. "What if your family comes for Briar? What if they try to take her from me?"

"They can't. I'm binding her to you and Mila. The only way they could break that would be to kill her."

"I won't let that happen, I promise." Elena looked fiercely determined when she said this, and Kieran wondered how he was going to force himself to leave her, to let her go, knowing he might never hold her again.

He didn't think his family would go as far as to actually hurt Briar, but then again, he wasn't sure he knew them at all anymore. Brushing that horrifying thought aside, Kieran knew it was now or never. Dropping one of his hands, he summoned something and gently pulled away from Elena so she could see what it was. She blinked at the object, then looked up at him, stunned.

"The necklace from the fundraiser?"

Kieran nodded, holding it up higher. The emerald necklace caught in the light, sparkling between them. It was the necklace Elena had jokingly asked him to bid on for her. After everything went to hell, he'd tracked down the owners and bought it anyway, though he hoped to give it to her under better circumstances.

"It holds memories in its center." With shaking hands, he brushed Elena's hair away and secured the necklace around her neck. "It's empty, so you can put whatever you want in it."

Elena took a shuddering breath, then looked up at him, calculating. "I know what memory I want to add."

"What—" Kieran didn't get to finish his question before Elena grasped him by the back of the neck and hauled his mouth to hers, devouring him with her kiss. Fingers entwined in his hair, her grip was painful, and her tongue demanding in his mouth as she pressed her body against his.

"If this is goodbye," Elena said as they pulled a part for a moment, "I want to make sure we never forget it."

Huey made himself scarce as Elena dragged Kieran to the ground, him on top as she fell onto her back. Keiran could barely contain his surprise, even as lust pumped through his veins.

"Really, on the floor?" Kieran murmured into her lips, but Elena merely wrapped her legs around his waist in response and started to tear at his shirt.

There was nothing sweet or slow about this, nothing tender and loving. It was pain and ecstasy and rage twisting and writhing together as they clawed at each other. Kieran quickly disposed of Elena's clothes, until she only wore the necklace. He dragged his mouth down her body, leaving searing kisses down her breasts, her ribs, and settling between her legs where he began to suck and nip and lick her until she was screaming his name. He savored the taste of her, knowing he might never get to do this again.

Still shaking, Elena reached for him, and soon, she had him on his back as she sank down on his length, taking him inside her with a moan. They clung to each other as she rode him, hard, her fingers digging into his chest while he grasped her hips with a grip strong enough to bruise.

"I won't ever forgive you for this," Elena panted, and it

took Kieran a moment to hear her as her muscles gripped him tightly, making his head spin. "I won't ever forgive you for trying to leave me like this."

Kieran groaned, unable to speak.

"You made me believe we had a chance," Elena continued, grabbing his chin and forcing him to look at her face. "You made me believe we could have a future, then immediately tried to take it away."

"I'm sorry," Kieran gasped, pleasure building unbearably in him even as her words sliced him to his core.

"Selfish bastard," Elena groaned, and her hand slid to his neck, grasping him there, though not hard enough to restrict his breathing. She lay down over his chest, still grinding her hips into his, and kissed him hungrily.

Kieran spasmed, and he spilled into her with a desperate sound deep in the back of his throat. Elena kept kissing him through his release until he stopped moving, then collapsed on his chest.

They lay there, holding on to each other as the minutes ticked by. If Kieran knew a spell to stop time, to make this moment last as long as possible, he would have used it. But there was no such spell, and no matter how much they wished otherwise, they were out of time.

* * *

There was no turning back. Kieran stood in New Stirling City on the dark street corner, waiting for his fate to find him. Elena's touch still burned his skin, no matter how hard he tried to push her away. It was too late to change his mind. He had no right to change his mind. He needed to face this.

"Evening, Mr. Andraste," a voice said next to him.

Kieran, of course, had sensed Agent Donaldson's approach.

"You got the evidence I sent over?" Kieran asked, his voice tight.

"I did, yes." Donaldson paused. "After all this time, why now? Why are you turning yourself in now?"

"You know what I did this morning, isn't that explanation enough?"

"No."

Kieran supposed she was right to be suspicious, considering how many times he'd refused to help her investigations into his family in the past.

"Let's just say I had a change of heart."

Donaldson snorted, putting her hands on her hips. Kieran noticed, even in the dark, she was wearing that wretched gun. As if that would protect her from him.

"Does that change of heart happen to be named Elena Hall?"

Kieran's eyes flashed to hers, and she chuckled.

"Don't act so surprised. My department has been keeping a close eye on her ever since the witch hunt, and an even closer eye on you for much longer."

"Leave her out of this." Kieran's voice dropped to a threatening level.

Donaldson regarded him warily. "Elena Hall is an upstanding citizen with a squeaky-clean record. She has nothing to fear from us." She crossed her arms over her chest. "From your family, however, I wouldn't be so certain."

Kieran openly glared at her now. "What's that supposed to mean?"

"I mean, with you out of the picture, I worry about her safety. Everything you gave us Kieran, it's bad. You know that. You're going to jail for a very long time, probably longer than the rest of my life. With you gone, who will protect Miss Hall from your family seeking revenge after they realized you betrayed them for her?"

Kieran clenched his jaw as he stared at the agent. "They wouldn't dare move against her, it's too risky."

Donaldson shrugged. "Maybe, maybe not. Seems like an awfully big risk to me."

Kieran scowled at her, his mind churning. She was building up to asking him, he was sure of it. Now he had to just make sure to bait her the rest of the way.

"What are you getting at, Donaldson? I gave you all you needed; I'm coming in quietly. Are you trying to make me change my mind? It's a little late for that."

Donaldson smirked. "You can't play dumb with me; I know you're smarter than that."

Kieran titled his head, smiling sarcastically. "I don't know what you mean."

Donaldson snorted, rolling her eyes. "Walk with me, Kieran." She gestured down the empty street, and Kieran obeyed, stretching his senses out. There were at least four more agents hidden in the dark: two humans, two witch. Only four? He was slightly insulted.

"You know what I'm going to ask," Tessa said as they strolled down the street. "I've asked before."

"You want me to work for you," Kieran supplied.

"Of course, I do." They stopped, and Kieran spotted two of the agents approaching. "Look, I get in the past things were different. You knew what you were doing was fucked, but what happened today is next level. You feel guilty because you're hurting your people, and now that you got that sweet little woman on your arm, you can't live with it anymore."

"She's not a *sweet little woman*," Kieran grumbled, but she ignored him.

"Your father is on a power trip and out of control, and he's a danger to humans and witches alike. What you gave us today, it isn't enough to put him away. Sure, we could start building a case against him, but it *wouldn't be enough*. He's too smart, and his lawyers too good."

"You want me to get you more proof," Kieran muttered, clocking the final two agents flanking him. He was surrounded.

"Yes." Donaldson flashed her gun again, and Kieran wondered if she even realized she was doing it. "You can't live with what you've done? Fine. Do something about it, something that will actually make a difference. Help us take your family down and put an end to all of this. In exchange, you get to stay with your girl, and when this is all over, walk away with your freedom."

Kieran arched an eyebrow, pretending to look surprised while secretly feeling overwhelmingly relieved. "You're offering me immunity for all my crimes if I help you put my father and brother in prison?"

"Yes, but don't forget your mother."

Kieran's gut twisted. His mother, who he loved so dearly despite her flaws. But no, he made his choice already, just as she'd made hers.

"Of course not."

"Good. See, I told you he had a good head on his shoulders, just took a little longer than I'd hoped for him to come around," Donaldson said to one of the other agents as they all emerged from the dark.

"Let's get him to headquarters and explain the rules. You have a lot of work ahead of you, boy."

The agent who spoke grabbed his arm roughly, and Kieran closed his eyes as he was dragged into a portal, vanishing from the street.

It all went according to plan, but Kieran still felt like he was falling apart. Despite everything they'd done, everything they were planning to do, they were still his family, and he was betraying them. Kieran knew this was the only way to make things right, but now that it was done, he wasn't sure how he would forgive himself for turning on the people he loved.

When they emerged into the secure government office, Kieran barely registered the fact that there was no one around. Marched down another muted-yellow hallway, they deposited him in what was obviously an interrogation room. Black walls, a metal table, and two metal chairs. Kieran stared at his own reflection in the two-way mirror facing him. The dead-eyed look he saw on himself was chilling.

"Let's get started," Donaldson said, sitting down across from him. "Can someone get us some coffee? This is going to take a while."

"What are we doing?" Kieran asked.

"Starting from the beginning, you are going to tell me every illegal activity you know your family has engaged in. I want to know when, who, and what, and if you can prove it. Once you leave here, your main task is going to be getting that evidence as quickly as you can. If it's not enough, this is going to go on for much longer, and you'll have to keep working with us until it is."

Kieran was already exhausted. "Fine," he bit out. "When I was ten, my father had a secret familiar that he used to spy on our coven board members.”

"When you were ten?” Donaldson asked disbelievingly.

"Spirits. We are going to need food here, too. All right, keep going Kieran. Tell me about this familiar. Are they still alive?”

"Of course not. Familiars don't live *that* long...”

Chapter 31

The Hall household was in limbo, its residents adjusting as they struggled to move on while carrying the burden of knowledge they now possessed. Although not all bad, change was almost always exhausting. For example, having a giant raven living in the house was an unusual experience, but what was even stranger was the immediate bond that seemed to form between Mila and Briar.

Although Kieran bound her to both of them, Elena had never before witnessed a human and a familiar understand each other so clearly. Ava, thankfully, was more fascinated by Briar than anything and accepted their rather lame excuse that they were watching her for a friend. An animal lover, Ava followed Briar around trying to get her to agree to a physical exam even though the raven was extremely wary of the human. It didn't take long for Mila briar to come around, however, and soon they were the best of friends.

It was honestly a relief, as Elena was barely functioning as it was and wasn't sure she was in the right head space to take care of Kieran's familiar. Every day, she woke up and was immediately flooded with a range of emotions. She was angry, and bitter, and frustrated, and felt utterly betrayed, not just by the man she gave her heart to, but by those in her community who were meant to protect them. But most of all, she felt grief. Grief for those who'd suffered so needlessly for the sake of someone's else's greed, and grief for a future with Kieran that now seemed impossible.

Despite what he'd done, Elena missed him. For the first time since the witch hunt, Kieran had made Elena feel a sense of peace and security that had been violently taken away from her. How could she forget the gentleness with which he'd wiped away her tears, held her and took care of her when she was falling apart? Or how, despite everything he knew about her, he'd never treated her like she wasn't strong enough and valued the things about her that other people thought made her soft. Despite his flaws, Kieran had become her safe haven.

It all was agonizing and exhausting, the endless thoughts never gave Elena a moment's peace. Huey was staying very close to her, nudging her to eat and rest and flooding her with his own calming magic, which was the only thing that really kept her going. Mila, for her part, was pissed, though her focus was more on the Andraste family as a whole.

"You need to leave the coven," she told Elena. "You, Maggie, Alex, and whoever else you can convince. It isn't safe for you there anymore!"

"If I up and leave, that'll draw more attention to me than just keeping my head low," Elena said wearily. "Maggie and Alex agree. We need to be smart about this and come up with exit-strategies before we do anything. It's much harder for them, anyway. Maggie has been in this coven her entire life, and Alex's business, his livelihood, is totally under the coven control. They can't just walk away."

"We never should have moved here," Mila mourned. "This all was a huge mistake."

Elena couldn't agree or disagree, but she recognized Mila was taking this entire situation very personally, as she felt responsible for convincing Elena to join the coven in the first place. They both felt lost, angry, and scared.

A week after Kieran turned himself in, Elena was pouring herself a cup of tea in the kitchen, one eye on Briar and Huey, who were in the living room squawking and yipping at each other. For the most part, Briar was a model house guest, but there were some incidents of damaged furniture and broken glass before they were able to raven-proof the house.

The news was playing on the TV in the background, but there was no word of Kieran. Elena would have presumed his arrest would be global news, and if it wasn't, then perhaps the plan had worked, and the feds had decided to give him a deal. But if that was the case, where the hell was he? Why hadn't he come back to update her, to reclaim Briar?

As Elena's worries began to creep up on her again, Briar stopped conversing with Huey, her head turning to the front door, then started to flap her wings in excitement.

"Kieran!" she shouted in her deep voice.

Elena froze, her heart racing. A second later, the front door burst open, and Kieran strode through, a look of utter relief on his face. Elena dropped her mug. It shattered on the floor, and she ran forward without a second thought, launching herself into his arms.

"You're back!" she cried.

Keiran gripped her, breathing the scent of her hair as he held her close. Briar took to the air and began flapping around their heads, and they pulled apart so she could land on Kieran's arm.

"Hey, girl." He stroked her head affectionately, and Briar

made a happy rumbling noise from her chest.

"What the fuck is going on?" Mila emerged from her bedroom, looking extremely put out, but stopped when she saw Kieran.

"Holy shit," she said, then rushed forward, shoving Elena out of the way and gripping the front of his shirt. "Where the hell have you been?" Mila demanded. "You put my sister through all that shit, then disappear? Are you out of your mind?"

"Mila, let him explain!" Elena pried her sister's hands off.

Kieran stepped back, Briar hopping onto his shoulder. "Okay, give me a second to put up a ward. What I have to tell you can't leave this room."

The sisters exchanged a look while Kieran quickly put up some additional spells to protect them, at least three by Elena's count.

When he was done, he turned back to face her. "It went perfectly. I acted all prepared to fall on my own sword—"

"You were going to fall on your own sword," Elena reminded him.

Kieran looked at her bashfully. "Yes well, not important. Agent Donaldson gave me her best recruitment speech, and I reluctantly came around. Full immunity for enough intel to bring my father, mother, and brother to trial."

Mila and Elena gaped at him.

"And you agreed?" Elena squeaked. Anthony made sense, but Declan and their mother? Kieran clearly loved both of them dearly. He was going to turn on them... for her?

"Of course I did, that's what you wanted, isn't it?" Kieran asked, shifting his weight and looking at her with a sudden unease.

"But." Mila crossed her arms over her chest. "They're still your family, Kieran. Are you sure you can do this?"

Kieran went tense, but nodded. "I have to. If they're in on it too, it's the right thing to do."

"And what if you fail?" Elena pressed. "What if you can't give them enough to go after all three?"

Kieran shrugged. "Then I go to prison, hopefully with at least a reduced sentence, and they'll do the best they can with whatever I was able to get for them."

Elena's stomach dropped. She wanted to ask more questions, but Kieran was staring at her intensely, and a new kind of tension started to build in her.

"So, what happens now?" she asked.

"Now? I go home, and I go on like nothing happened, like I'm still my father's loyal son. Then, I'll feed whatever proof I can back to my handler."

"What if you get caught?" Mila asked. "Will they offer you protection, then?"

"Yes," Kieran assured her. "At least, to a point. If they think I got caught on purpose to betray them, then I'll be on my own."

Mila let out a breath, and Elena bit her lip.

"It's going to be all right, I know what I'm doing."

"For some reason that isn't comforting," Mila muttered.

"Mila, I'm touched. I had no idea you cared so much," Kieran teased.

Mila rolled her eyes, walking away from him to the kitchen. Briar leaped from Kieran's shoulder and followed Mila. She landed on the counter next to her and bumped her head against her arm affectionately. Kieran gave them both a bewildered look.

"You bonded Briar to Mila, too, remember?" Elena asked dryly. "The two have really hit it off."

Kieran pursed his lips then turned back to Elena, his eyes softening. "Could I talk to you, alone?"

Mila scoffed, running a hand down Briar's back. "You know she'll tell me everything you say once you're gone, right?"

"Doesn't mean you have to be there for the conversation," Keiran shot back.

"Come on." Elena gently took his arm, shooting her sister an exasperated look.

Mila gazed back, unrepentant, and Elena was struck by just how... witchy her sister looked standing there with Briar. Shaking her head, she led Keiran out of the room and up the stairs to the second floor. They were silent as they walked out onto the balcony. Elena wrapped her arms around herself as she looked out over the surrounding forest, taking a deep breath.

"Elena, I know the last time we saw each other, we said a lot of things..." Kieran began.

"Understatement, but go on," Elena replied, not facing him.

"I know you said you would never forgive me for how I handled things, and you were right to be angry. I was being stupid. I don't want to let you go. I want to stay with you, if you'll let me."

Elena let out the breath she was holding, turning to face him. "To clarify, you do or do not mean in a romantic way?"

"In whatever way you'll allow. I'm not foolish enough to assume you would take me back, and if we can only be friends, well then at least I can still protect you."

"Protect me from what, exactly?"

"Anything, everything," he offered lamely. "I don't know

how this is going to end, and what's going to happen along the way, but I think I know you well enough to say that you aren't going to let what you and Jackie talked about go. Am I right?"

Elena scowled at Jackie's name, irritation blooming in her. "Jackie is a hag, but no, I can't just forget everything she told me."

"Then let me help you, let me protect you in whatever way I can." Kieran held her gaze, and Elena reached out to him without thinking.

"Kieran, I haven't stopped thinking about you, missing you, since you left. I know it may be wrong after everything, but I don't want to give you up." She stepped forward and wrapped her arms around his neck, looking up at him. "I'm still pissed at you. I'm pissed you didn't realize what your family was doing all these years, I'm pissed you were going to push me away to deal with this mess by myself because you just *couldn't live with yourself*, but we can work through that. I want to work through that, because whatever is about to happen, I would much rather face it with you."

Kieran looked relieved and pressed his forehead to hers. "Whatever happens, if this works out or not, I promise I won't abandon you."

It was everything Elena wanted, and yet somehow not enough. Her father had abandoned her over and over since she was born. Her mother had died. Saamira had died. Elena had been left behind enough for a lifetime. Keiran's promise meant so much to her, but after everything she'd gone through, she hoped, perhaps foolishly, that love would be easy, that it wouldn't be another struggle she would have to overcome. But nothing was ever easy, and she'd known from the moment she had set eyes on Kieran that loving him would be a challenge.

This entire situation, however, was not anything she could have predicted. Elena thought she deserved easy, after all she'd endured. And yet... looking up into his eyes, she knew she would choose this all over again, choose him. He was worth the struggle.

"I won't abandon you either," she whispered, running a finger along his jaw while her other hand caressed the back of his neck.

Kieran's eyes welled with emotion, and he leaned forward, pressing a light kiss to her lips, cradling her face. "Whatever happens, you have changed my world, Elena Hall. I will always love you for that."

Unable to speak, the words stolen from her by Kieran's admission, Elena tucked her face into his neck, melting against his strong form. A bird sang in the tree behind them, a bush rustled in the forest below, and a warm breeze rushed over their skin. This was right, it felt right, like in each other's arms was where they were meant to be. An uncertain path lay at their feet, but they would walk it together and face that unknown with whatever strength they had left.

Acknowledgments

I want to say thank you first and foremost to my sister, Michelle. Without her this book would not exist. She has always been my first reader, first editor, and first fan. In January 2020, I started writing this book for her to keep us both entertained. Through every edit, every draft, she was there to give feedback and encouraged me when I wasn't sure what I was doing.

Of course I also want to thank my mother for always supporting me even when I was too nervous to let her read this book. Is anyone eager to let their mother read a romance they've written? But just like she has my entire life, she took it in stride and gave me the encouragement I needed.

Continuing the love fest, I want to thank all my friends who also provided their feedback and shoulders to cry on when I wanted to quit.

Which I wanted to do quite a lot.

Even right now I am freaking out about putting this story out in the world, but if you are reading this that means I did it and it's too late for me to turn back now.

Thank you for giving my book a chance, and I hope you enjoyed the experience.

About the Author

Kathryn is a writer from upstate New York who believes in the power of storytelling to illuminate the complexities of mental health. With a passion for accessible writing, she strives to create narratives that resonate with readers of all types. As someone with ADHD, Kathryn understands the importance of crafting stories that are not only engaging but also inclusive.

When she's not weaving tales of love, resilience, and magic, you can find her at home with her two beloved cats, Jane and Lizzie, named after the iconic characters from *Pride and Prejudice*. With each book, Kathryn aims to inspire and uplift, reminding readers that they are never alone in their struggles.

Join her on this journey as she explores the beauty and challenges of life through the lens of fantasy and romance.

You can connect with me on:

🌐 https://kathrynguild-author.squarespace.com

Subscribe to my newsletter:

✉ https://kathrynguild-author.squarespace.com/newsletter